Marcus Herniman works for the Civil Service in Jersey. *The Treason of Dortrean* is the second book in *The Arrandin Trilogy*.

Also by Marcus Herniman from Earthlight

The Siege of Arrandin

THE TREASON
OF DORTREAN

MARCUS
HERNIMAN

EARTHLIGHT

SIMON & SCHUSTER

London • New York • Sydney • Tokyo • Singapore • Toronto • Dublin

A VIACOM COMPANY

First published in Great Britain by Earthlight, 2001
An imprint of Simon & Schuster UK Ltd
A Viacom Company

1 3 5 7 9 8 6 4 2

Simon & Schuster UK Ltd
Africa House
64–78 Kingsway
London WC2B 6AH

Simon & Schuster Australia
Sydney

A CIP catalogue record for this book is available
from the British Library

ISBN 0-743-41513-2

Typeset by Palimpsest Book Production Limited,
Polmont, Stirlingshire
Printed and bound in Great Britain by
Omnia Books Ltd, Glasgow

MAPS

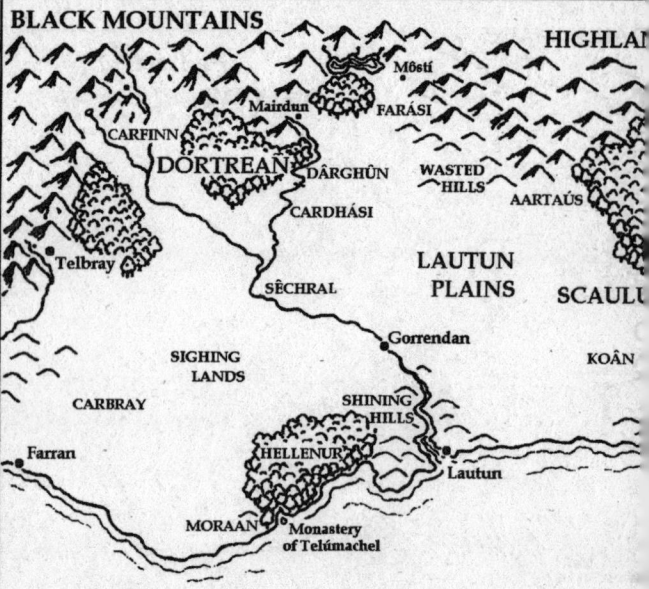

BLACK MOUNTAINS

HIGHLAN

Môstí

Mairdun   FARÁSI

CARFINN

DORTREAN   DÂRGHÛN

WASTED
HILLS   AARTAÚS

CARDHÁSI

Telbray

LAUTUN
PLAINS   SCAULU

SÊCHRAL

Gorrendan   KOÂN

SIGHING
LANDS

SHINING
HILLS

CARBRAY

Farran   HELLENUR

Lautun

MORAAN   Monastery
of Telúmachel

N

IGAERWA
the Wide Sea

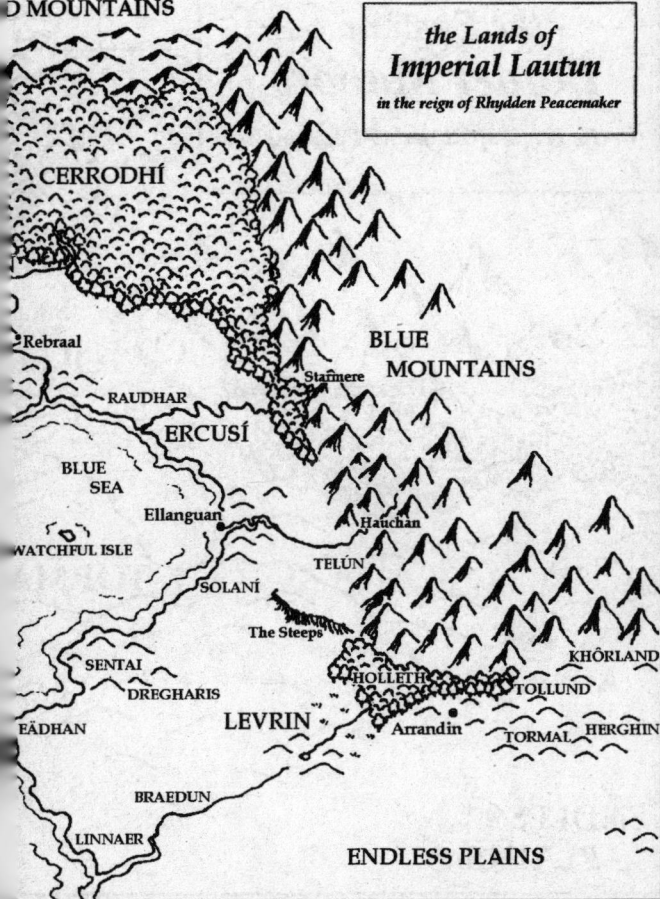

the Lands of
Imperial Lautun
in the reign of Rhydden Peacemaker

D MOUNTAINS

CERRODHÍ

BLUE
MOUNTAINS

Rebraal

RAUDHAR

ERCUSÍ

Starmere

BLUE
SEA

Ellanguan

Hauchan

WATCHFUL ISLE

TELÚN

SOLANÍ

The Steeps

KHÔRLAND

SENTAI

HOLLETH

DREGHARIS

TOLLUND

EÄDHAN

LEVRIN

Arrandin

TORMAL

HERGHIN

BRAEDUN

LINNAER

ENDLESS PLAINS

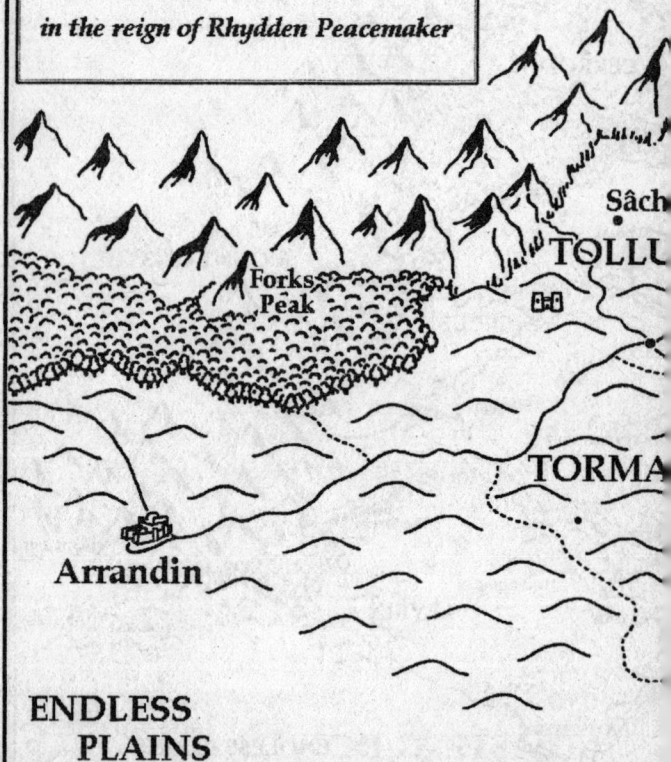

the Eastern
Border Manors

in the reign of Rhydden Peacemaker

0 1 2 3
Leagues

Sâch

TOLLU

Forks
Peak

TORMA

Arrandin

ENDLESS
PLAINS

fords

KHÔRLAND

Samsar

ND

ersí

HERGHIN

N

TWISTING DOWNS

Prologue

Corollin Dreams—

It is a treacherous feeling, the loss we suffer through war. The glory and hope of sacrifice, the honoured bravery of the fallen; the lament for the innocent; the regret, and the bitterness at so much waste and destruction. For those who count the cost, the cost that grows too high. The wise may strive ever to set war aside – the petty conflicts of ambition or greed, the clashes of faith or custom – but when the enemy comes upon their children with knives, they know that the time for wise words is past. Without war and battle, the world that we love would not have survived to give us birth.

In the siege of the city of Arrandin, in the year 1524 of Six Kingdoms Reckoning, the losses endured by defenders and Easterner attackers alike were heavy; so many magi and wizards, priests and knights, warriors and ordinary folk. The Lower City was overrun, and the dead lay piled like leaves along the streets between the burning buildings. The Chosen Priest Torriearn, foremost of the servants of the Sun within the Six Kingdoms, was brought down by the demons summoned against the city; and Herusen Dârghûn, Prime Councillor of All Magi, laid down his own life and honour to call upon Ilunâtor, the Father of All Dragons. And so the siege was raised, and the Easterners put to flight.

But war, like any gift from the gods, is a tool that reveals both the strength and the weakness of the wielder. In the first need to defend against the threat from the East, the Lords of the Six Kingdoms rallied together and victory was achieved. In the months that followed – and with the continuing threat from East and South – the flaws within their strength began to show; and the perilous wisdom of Herusen's sacrifice proved more far-reaching than even he himself might have guessed.

Yet on the threshold of summer in 1524, the Lords and Magi of the Six Kingdoms gathered within Arrandin knew only that the city had been saved; and that Herusen Dârghûn was but one among many who had given their lives in the city's defence – though perhaps his contribution had been more extraordinary than most. And the Easterner chieftains were but driven back toward the border manors, and peace had yet to be secured.

In the city port of Ellanguan, more than forty leagues to the northwest upon the coast of the Blue Sea, the Lord Steward Rinnekh had the remnant of the Souther fleet to deal with – the few broken warships limping toward his harbours in the wake of the sudden storms. The Emperor Rhydden and his armies were far away in Arrandin, and there was still no certain news of their success. The Souther Ambassador was held hostage in the Steward's own palace. With neither the wisdom nor the foresight of Herusen, Rinnekh drifted toward a bargain scarcely less momentous in the history of the Six Kingdoms.

'It's not a question of pity,' said Rinnekh. 'It's the practicality.'

The Souther Ambassador frowned, as if he did not understand. The five jewels of his high office danced on the furrowed waves of his forehead, tugging at the slender chain from which they hung.

'Three of your great warships are basking off the coast of Ellanguan,' said Rinnekh. He held up three fingers in the still air of the throne hall. 'Two more have been turned back from the Isle of Renza and are making their way here.'

The yellow jewels jumped on the Souther's arching brow. Rinnekh stifled a smile, secretly pleased that he had heard news which Ambassador T'Loi had not.

'I grant that these ships may be damaged,' he went on. 'But if I let them into my harbours, they could carry well over a

2

thousand of your Souther warriors straight into my city. I am not so stupid as to agree to that, when our two empires are at war.'

'There has been no formal declaration of war, my Lord Steward,' said T'Loi smoothly.

'Your ships were looting and burning along our coast only a few days ago,' Rinnekh countered. 'It's much the same thing.'

T'Loi spread his hands and bowed his head in apology. Rinnekh leaned back against the solid ebony of his Steward's throne.

It was not that he did not like T'Loi. In point of fact, he admired him. T'Loi had the olive-skinned, dark-haired beauty of his race, and the languid grace of the highborn of an ancient and elegant culture. Even in the sultry heat of the early afternoon, the Souther contrived to remain cool and unruffled in his perfumed robe of honeysuckle silk. Rinnekh himself had more the lean build of a runner than a dancer, with sallow skin and hair the colour of dusty walnut shells; and he was damp with sweat beneath his high collared tunic. He admired and envied T'Loi. But he was not inclined to trust him.

He glanced around the dim shadows of the hall – empty, save for one young attendant in the pale blue-green of the Ellanguan livery. For any other such audience, Rinnekh would have had at least a dozen people gathered round to advise him; merchants and household clerks, priests and scholars, visiting nobles and kinsmen. But those who might have been most useful to him now had all ridden away to war. Those who remained – though skilful in the running of the city, or even in the internal wrangles of the Lautun Empire – could not guide him in this present matter with T'Loi; or else he did not trust them to do so.

The Empress Consort, Grinnaer Sêchral of Lautun, was herself in Ellanguan with a small number of her household – another reason, Rinnekh remembered, not to let the Souther ships make harbour here. But Grinnaer was weak and fawning

3

as a lap dog, at a loss even when dealing with her own kinsmen among the Court Noble, let alone foreign envoys. In company with Grinnaer, and set to watch over her by the Emperor himself, was the inestimable Lady Karlena, Countess of Dortrean. Karlena, by contrast, was possessed of one of the most subtle political minds in the Empire, and would have known exactly how to handle T'Loi. She had already offered to advise Rinnekh on the subject earlier that morning. But Rinnekh did not trust Dortrean further than he could kick them with one leg tied, and especially not when the Emperor was away fighting a war against the Easterners. He had thought it safer to decline Karlena's offer.

For the rest who remained in Ellanguan – the priests and warriors of the guard, the merchants and some few of the Magi, and the thousands of ordinary citizens – Rinnekh had found similar objection. Either he could guess what they would say without the trouble of asking them; or else they were not wholly to be trusted, and would most likely be working with Karlena or the priests of the heathen Orders to further their own ends.

'The Lord Steward has me as hostage,' ventured T'Loi, breaking the silence. 'I should serve as guarantee that my countrymen will not attack your city.'

Rinnekh laughed. 'When your ships were attacking our coasts,' he said, 'your story then was that they were sent by others who stood higher in your God-King's favour, and that you were powerless to prevent them. Was that not so?'

T'Loi smiled, and gave a single nod of his head.

'All right then,' he said. 'Let me go free, and I shall go out and take command of the fleet. If they obey my order not to attack, then I shall signal for you to let me return. If I fail, you shall know not to let them in.'

Rinnekh had to allow that the offer was tempting. He was half minded to let T'Loi go, simply to be rid of the trouble of holding him captive, and then to refuse the Souther ships harbour regardless. But the Emperor Rhydden would not have approved. T'Loi was far too valuable a hostage to waste. And as one of Rhydden's trusted favourites, Rinnekh knew better than to incur his beloved Emperor's displeasure.

'Alas, Excellency, I can not spare a ship to ferry you out,' he said.

'My own vessel lies ready, my Lord,' T'Loi reminded him.

Rinnekh shook his head. The Ambassador's gilded and jewelled ship was a prize which the Emperor valued as highly as T'Loi himself. The Lord Steward would be doubly cursed if both were to escape his care.

The Souther Ambassador shrugged.

'If neither Ellanguan nor Renza will give them shelter,' he told Rinnekh, 'then my countrymen will be obliged to make a landing somewhere on your coast. They will take food and supplies by force, if needs must, to save their own lives. Yet I had hoped to avoid further conflict.'

'They could sail home again,' Rinnekh pointed out. 'It's not such a great dishonour, you know.'

'More storms are coming,' T'Loi demurred.

The prediction seemed likely. The city of Ellanguan lay under a dark pall of heavy cloud; and though the tall doors of the antechambers on the eastern side of the throne hall stood wide open, not a breath of wind came in from the courtyard garden beyond. If anything, it made worse the stifling heat in the hall. Rinnekh would have liked nothing better just then than to dismiss T'Loi from his presence, and to go and soak himself in a cool bath until the rain finally came. But imperial relations with the Southers were awkward enough, without adding further insult by such obvious disregard for the plight of their crippled fleet. Dortrean would not find it hard to turn that against him. For his own sake, as well as the Emperor's, Rinnekh supposed that he ought to make some pretence of caring about the Southers' fate.

He sat forward on his throne, his tunic clinging wet against his back, and leaned upon one carved armrest. The weight of his gold horsehead brooch shifted at the base of his throat.

5

The brooch. It was a gift from the Emperor Rhydden himself; and given that the golden horse was the symbol of the imperial House Lautun, it was an obvious token of Rhydden's personal favour. Whatever they might think of Rinnekh personally, the sight of that brooch alone was enough to persuade many to heed his words – perhaps even more so than the white steel circlet of the Lords Steward of Ellanguan which now weighed slick upon his brow. Rinnekh knew that the brooch had also an enchantment of power set within it, which might enable him to beguile lesser men to his will. Upon those who had mastered great strength of mind or will, such as the Magi or the more senior priests – or the Countess of Dortrean – that enchantment would have had but little effect; and indeed the Emperor had warned him that it might prove dangerous to try. Yet in all, the strength of Rinnekh's following among the merchants and craftsmen and lesser nobles of Ellanguan – and even among some of the more imperially minded magi and priests within the city – had come to be symbolised by this single golden jewel which had helped him to achieve it.

Whether the enchantment of his horsehead brooch might have worked upon the artful T'Loi, Rinnekh had decided not to put to the test. Instead he had chosen to fall back on his own instincts for guile and predatory cunning – instincts which, as the Emperor so often told him, could serve him just as well as any golden bauble. So now he leaned a little further forward on his throne, and fixed his bright gaze upon the Souther; and the focus of that gaze fell slightly short, so that T'Loi found himself drawn forward a step, as if to compensate.

'Sailors are used to weathering storms,' Rinnekh told him. 'I don't suppose this one will be anywhere near as bad as the last. For now, your ships can shelter on the far side of the estuary under the lee of the hills, without the need to go ashore. Perhaps after that, with suitable guarantees, we could spare them some food and supplies. Enough to see them safe home.'

T'Loi closed his eyes and bowed again, the silken folds of

his honeysuckle robe whispering together as if with the first rumour of approaching rain.

'I appreciate that your Emperor is still at war with the East,' he said, mollified, 'and that you must take thought to protect his back. Yet if Arrandin falls, and the Easterners come to the coast, the situation will have changed again. I can not promise, my Lord Steward, how long any good will between Lautun and the South may last.'

'The siege upon Arrandin has been raised,' Rinnekh smiled. The news was still not certain, and T'Loi would not have heard of it. There had been only a brief report from the magi of the College, a few hours before, for the Steward's ears alone. However irritating they might be, the Magi still had their uses. 'The Easterners are being pushed back toward the borders. So there is every reason, Excellency, to hope for lasting peace between ourselves and the God-King.'

The Souther Ambassador displayed suitable surprise – though he controlled it well, and the tethered jewels bobbed only a little on his elegant brow. After a moment he smiled in return. He moved to take a step back. But then he appeared to change his mind, or perhaps Rinnekh's gaze still drew him; and instead he drifted closer to the Steward's throne.

'Your Emperor Rhydden has no children at present,' T'Loi observed. 'Who shall succeed him?'

Rinnekh lurched at the sudden change of tack.

'None at present, Excellency,' he allowed. 'But His Highness has a new Empress, who it is hoped will bear him new heirs very soon. And of course the presence of the Empress Grinnaer here in Ellanguan is another reason why I may not risk letting your warships sail into my harbours.'

'Of course,' said T'Loi. 'But the Easterners are a fierce and vengeful people; and from what I have been led to believe, the strength of their army was several times that of Rhydden's own. Should your Emperor fall in this present conflict – though may your gods and mine forbid it – who then would succeed him?'

It occurred to Rinnekh that he had never seriously considered the possibility of Rhydden dying. Though he was aware of the Court's obsession with the need for an imperial heir, there was a vitality about Rhydden's personal presence – by rumour half divine, or half demonic – which seemed to be untouched by the normal human frailties of ageing and death, and so had rendered the question strangely irrelevant.

'His Highness has kinsmen among Vaulun,' he said, after several heartbeats; 'and maybe one of the Earls of the Houses Ancient has a claim. The Scholars of Blood Law are the ones who would determine such things. But I think your question a little impertinent, Excellency.'

It was a weak answer, and he cursed himself inwardly for saying it. The truth was that the Emperor's kinsmen among Vaulun were very much lesser cousins; and to Rinnekh's knowledge, none of the Lords of the Houses Noble had now any great strength of Lautun blood in their heritage. The rulers of Lautun had taken pains to avoid any substantial claim to their imperial throne being fostered among the rival Houses – which gave ground to the Court's demand for a recognised Lautun heir, and largely explained Rhydden's marriage to the tiresome Empress Grinnaer.

It occurred to Rinnekh also that his own fate hung upon Rhydden's continued survival. With his beloved Emperor gone, he might have few or no friends or allies in the struggle for power which would undoubtedly follow. Even if Rhydden died ten or fifteen years hence, leaving half a dozen healthy heirs behind him, Rinnekh would have no guarantee of favour from the next regime; and he would still have many powerful adversaries, especially among the heathen *Aeshta* Orders and the Houses Noble who sided with Dortrean.

'You must forgive me, my Lord Steward,' said T'Loi evenly. 'In time of war, alas, such questions will be raised. Should your Emperor's succession not be securely provided, the civil strife which would follow his passing would be a dreadful thing. This

8

I have learned from the turmoil which heralded the arrival of our present God-King.'

Rinnekh nodded faintly. He remembered that T'Loi himself had lost three children during the recent civil wars in the South; and his own favour with the new God-King was still uncertain.

'I have a great fondness for this small empire,' the Ambassador went on, 'and Ellanguan is a fair city. If you show compassion to our ships now, it may well be that we shall in turn be able to help you later. And if this war against the East should grow prolonged, the good will of my countrymen might well be of use to you and your Emperor.'

'Yes,' murmured Rinnekh.

It was in the hope of such an alliance that the Souther Ambassador had first been summoned here, a couple of weeks before. Rinnekh himself had suggested it, and the Emperor had seemed well pleased – especially since the coffers of the God-King were far more capable of funding a war than Rhydden's own. Even the promise of peace with the Southers at this stage would be an improvement on their recent raiding and their rumoured alliance with the East. And Rinnekh had to admit that the friendship of T'Loi might prove useful, if he should lose the Emperor's favour for whatever reason.

T'Loi had leaned closer to him, returning the focus of his gaze. Rinnekh could feel new rivulets of sweat running down his back, and trickling through the hair beneath his Steward's circlet. And then – whether stirred from memory or conjured by some trick of sight – he half imagined a second head, like a shadowed halo about T'Loi's dark hair. The hooded, faceless head of the Archmage Merrech, the Emperor's most trusted and loyal counsellor. And he remembered the words that the Archmage had spoken to him, on the eve of the Emperor's departure.

His Highness needs the Southers off his back, Merrech had hissed. *Promise them anything. Do you understand?*

Rinnekh thought that he understood quite well. Political

promises, like Ambassadors and Lords Steward, were altogether mortal. For the moment, Rinnekh and T'Loi needed one another; and for the moment, T'Loi was willing to bargain. They could worry about other details later.

'Your own succession, also, remains unprovided for,' said T'Loi, resting one hand upon Rinnekh's forearm; 'though you have the advantage of youth. Perhaps a highborn woman from among my own people could be found to suit you? Our Souther women are more biddable than those of your own lands or the Eastern Domains. She would bear you the sons you require, but not otherwise intrude upon your – enjoyment of life.'

Rinnekh remained motionless, still holding T'Loi's gaze with his own; accepting the touch on his arm like the dampness of his tunic, paying neither undue heed. His lure to the Souther had worked more swiftly than expected, so that it was almost at odds which of them was now the prey. T'Loi gave a half smile, his dark eyes twinkling with possibilities. Rinnekh blinked once, deliberately, and turned his head away.

'I shall send word to your ships that they may shelter off the far shore of the estuary,' he said aloud. 'We still have no guarantee that they – or the God-King – will agree to anything you propose. But I have no doubt that His Highness would welcome a surety of peace and good will from the South.'

T'Loi disengaged himself and stepped back.

'I hope, my Lord Steward, that my countrymen will welcome it too.'

Rinnekh nodded, without looking at him. 'We shall speak again later, Excellency.'

The Souther Ambassador bowed deeply, backing away down the throne hall, and went out. The young attendant began to approach, but Rinnekh signalled him to wait.

It was some time before he trusted his own legs well enough to stand.

I ARRANDIN

Chapter One

Kellarn thought he was drowning again.

The weight was gone from his legs, his body borne up by a numbing warmness. He was caught about the waist – tied, somehow – and the cord looped up and around his throat, pulling his head back, squeezing the life from him. The masks of the Dead drifted past in the darkening waters. The silver-fair face of his rescuer eluded him.

'Whoa now, Kellarn! Don't leave us,' said a voice.

The hold around his waist grew stronger, and the waters blurred and faded into mist. His head lolled heavy against a solid shoulder. A tanned and rather grubby face grinned down at him from beneath a mop of damp, dark golden curls.

'T . . . Takshar?' Kellarn managed thickly.

'Easy then, Sir,' said Takshar of Dregharis. 'It gets a bit much after a while, doesn't it?'

Kellarn tried to return the smile, by way of answer. He let his head rest against the warrior's shoulder, until the pounding quietened down behind his ears and the familiar smell of sweat filled his nostrils. But there were other smells there too – the bitter sting of smoke, and the sickly sweetness of blood and death. He tested his legs beneath him, and then pushed Takshar away.

'I'm all right now,' he said. 'Thank you.'

Takshar wiped his forehead with one sleeve and looked at Kellarn doubtfully. Kellarn avoided his gaze, drew a cautious breath, and braced himself to carry on.

Ahead of them the narrow street was still half choked with

the fallen dead. Though the sun had long since swung round into the west, the late afternoon warmth lingered heavy and oppressive beneath the pall of shadow from the high buildings. The dull echoes from others labouring nearby were broken only by the mournful buzzing of flies.

As far as Kellarn could tell, all of the bodies here were Easterners, clad in the sorry remnants of their colourful gear. Most of their serviceable arms and weaponry had been taken away earlier in the day – together with any warrior, friend or foe, who had still shown signs of life – by the able-bodied of the Arrandin guard and several hundred willing citizens; and no doubt some of that gear would have conveniently disappeared, being kept as trophies or to help pay for damages, and not been handed over to the city armouries. What remained was the long task of lifting the dead on to carts, to be carried out on to the plains for their final Rite of Burning.

'My Lord,' said Takshar. 'No one expects you to be here now.'

'Nor you,' said Kellarn shortly. He dragged his feet across the cobblestones to the next waiting corpse.

'And won't they be needing you, to prepare for the ride east?' tried Takshar again.

Kellarn ignored him. The body he had come to was that of an Easterner woman, her long hair plaited into half a dozen or more tangled braids. The left side of her face had been torn away, and the eye was gone from its socket. There was a dark flash of movement as a rat scuttled away from its chosen feast. Rats! Kellarn shuddered and swore.

Moving round to lift the body, his attention was caught by a wink of gold from beneath the collar of the woman's dark tunic. The sight triggered a warning note at the back of his mind. He signalled Takshar to wait, took a few seconds longer to master himself, and then carefully slid the tip of his own knife blade in beneath the collar to discover what was there.

As Kellarn had guessed, he discovered a small pendant or *talisman* on a leather thong about the woman's neck. It was

14

more likely of brass than of gold, and inlaid with pieces of a black stone to form the pattern of a lozenge within a square. He had not the skill to tell whether there were any charms or spells woven about it – though he thought that if there had been any particular danger of magic at work here, it would have been noted by those who had stripped the bodies earlier that day. Then again, with so many dead lying around, it was not impossible that even the sharp eyes of the priests and holy knights of the Braedun Order might have overlooked it. In either event, he thought it best to handle the pendant with wary caution.

A second note of warning came from the pattern on the pendant itself. It was an Easterner device, of course; yet it stirred something in Kellarn's memory, as though he had seen it once before. Not recently, perhaps; not in this latest battle for Arrandin. He would have to take care of it for now, and ask the priests – or High Councillor Rhysana – about it later, when he could find them.

Takshar was watching him, as mindful as Kellarn of the dangers of such unknown trinkets – especially when found upon the body of an Easterner warrior, with their strange gods and demonic patrons. At Kellarn's nodded signal he went and found a relatively clean strip of cloth from nearby; and then Kellarn wrapped the pendant in the cloth, cut the thong which held it about the woman's neck, and slipped the bundled object into the safety of his pocket. He found that he was sweating again by the time that he had finished.

They lifted the woman's body and carried her down to the piled wagon at the end of the street. Already it was nearly full again. A guardsman in the tawny gold livery of the Imperial Household was chatting to the wagon driver, and there were the sounds of some new commotion near at hand. They discovered that the main part of the Emperor's army had now reached the city, and that new troops were being deployed to help clear away the dead.

'That's us finished for now, then, my Lord,' said Takshar. 'Time to let others take over.'

'They will be as tired as we are, at the end of a long march,' Kellarn objected.

Takshar drew himself up to his full height, folded his arms, and grinned dangerously.

'Do I have to knock you out and carry you home, my Lord?' he asked.

'I'd like to see you try,' said Kellarn. 'But at least let me go to see our other folk first. I ought to put in an appearance.'

Kellarn had led a mounted war band of some two hundred horsemen to Arrandin, gathered from the lands further west toward the coast; and the last time that he had seen most of them had been earlier that morning, when they had helped drive the Easterners back through these streets and out of the city. Of those who had survived – and by the grace of the gods, it appeared that most of them had – he guessed that the larger part would be gathering in the great barrack piers which flanked the west gate of the Lower City, or with the wounded in the temples or the Guild Hall. Others would perhaps have teamed up with the religious Orders, or with the city guard.

But though he had been responsible for bringing them here, and as such still felt an obligation toward them, Kellarn's brief position of leadership had obviously changed. The city had its own war commanders – among them his own father, and of course The Arrand himself – and now the Emperor and his army had arrived, with its own structure of command. Kellarn's war band were not men and women of his father's earldom of Dortrean, but drawn from the retainers of other Houses – from Eädhan, Dregharis, Hershôr, Sentai, and a handful of priests and knights of the Braedun Order from their *commanderie* on the Galloppi river. Like Kellarn himself, they would no doubt soon be deployed more suitably by the senior commanders as the ride east was prepared. What Kellarn's own position might then be, he had yet to discover.

16

'I'm sure they would be glad to see you, Sir,' said Takshar. 'Especially since—'

Kellarn flicked him a warning glance. But as the son of a House Merchant Noble, Takshar was canny enough to leave the sentence unfinished with a member of the Imperial Household close by.

That was the other side of the coin, they both knew. On his ride hither, Kellarn had become all too aware of how willing his war band were to accept him, personally, as their leader – ranging from the gruff respect of the more seasoned warriors to the open adoration of some of the younger knights closer to his own age. Whether that was based upon his own personal merit or reputation, or simply because he was a son of Dortrean rather than of imperial Lautun, was difficult to tell. But the possibility remained that several of his band might be less inclined to join ranks in the Emperor's army unless Kellarn were with them, or at least urged them to do so. That was something which he would have to speak to his father about, when the Earl could get away from the Emperor.

What Takshar was also referring to was Kellarn's supposed conversation with the dragon – that same dragon who had turned the tide of the battle and put the Easterners to flight. Yet while it was true that Kellarn had stood before the dragon on the hillside, north of the city – and Takshar and a handful of others had been near enough at hand to witness it – there had been no exchange of words between them that he could remember. They had simply looked at one another for a while, and understood. Since then, Kellarn had blocked any attempts by Takshar to discuss the subject. But it seemed likely that the tale of it would be circulating within the city, increasing Kellarn's reputation in many eyes; and perhaps drawing unwanted attention from others, especially the Emperor and his commanders.

So all in all, Kellarn knew that Takshar was right – though perhaps for different reasons. He needed to see the folk of his war band safely settled in the city. But then he needed to let others take over, drawing attention away from himself, so that he could have time to think. It had been partly to avoid thinking – as well as to avoid the Emperor – that he had come back down from the Arrand palace to help clear the Lower City. But he knew that there were several things he must consider before, or if, he was to ride east the following day.

Takshar collected his pack, and together they set off for the more open spaces of the parks, on their way back toward the western barrack piers. Kellarn's own gear was all stowed safely in the Arrand palace, and he wore still the purple and grey livery of the city guard which he had borrowed earlier in the day from Lord Kierran, The Arrand's youngest son. Kierran himself had been wounded a few days before, and was not yet strong enough to have helped with the lifting and carrying of bodies, so he had stayed behind to attend to other matters – things which, he had told Kellarn, his own family were also less than eager for the Emperor to be asking questions about. Kellarn gathered that this had to do with some of The Arrand's kinsmen by marriage, who had been caught up in the treachery of one or other of the eastern border manors; and also the matter of the Easterner loremaster, Kata Aghaira, who was held in honourable confinement within the palace; and perhaps other things to do with the Magi.

As they came down a wider street to the bruised glory of the parks they heard the clatter of many hooves, and a group of horsemen came into view from behind a grey pillared building and rode at a leisurely pace toward them. Near the head of the group Kellarn recognised Lord Bradhor, The Arrand's eldest son, his face set and grim in the early evening shadows. To either side of him were guards in the purple and grey Arrand livery, and also in the golden livery of Lautun; and behind – Kellarn realised too late – came the Emperor Rhydden and the Earl of Dortrean, and several of the senior war commanders, making a tour of inspection through the Lower City.

'Bow down, quickly,' he hissed, grabbing hold of Takshar; and the two of them went down on one knee in the street, with heads bowed and right fists clenched to their chests in salute.

If Bradhor recognised them – which was not unlikely, given that he was Kellarn's brother by marriage, and both Kellarn and Takshar had been serving members of the Arrandin guard only a few years before – he was kind enough to make no mention of it, other than by a general nod of returned salute. But they did not escape attention for long. As the main body of horsemen drew level with them, the Emperor himself called a halt and bade them rise.

'Well, Dortrean, it seems that we have found your son,' he observed, with one of his most radiant smiles.

'Indeed, Sire,' said Erkal Dortrean. 'Kellarn puts his training in the guard to good use.'

'The Arrandin guard,' said Lord Drômagh of Sêchral, Knight Commander of Rhydden's Imperial Household Cavalry. 'By rights he should have come to us, you know.'

'You have my elder son, Solban,' returned the Earl. 'It would not have been fair to put Kellarn in his brother's shadow.'

Lord Drômagh snorted good-humouredly. The Emperor Rhydden laughed.

'Nevertheless, young Dortrean,' said Rhydden, 'we understand that our thanks are due to you for your timely arrival here in Arrandin this morning with fresh troops from Sentai. You have your Emperor's thanks.'

Kellarn looked up at him, clad all in white and gold astride his black Carfinn destrier, with his disturbingly bright eyes beneath a mane of ebon hair. He had an instinctive distrust of Rhydden Lautun, and little use for his thanks – though it might have been courting treason to say so. On the far side of the Emperor was the burly figure of Lord Drômagh, dark-eyed and beetle-browed, watching him intently. On the near left was his father, Erkal Dortrean, quiet-faced and confident, with only the faintest hint of warning to his son in his grey-blue eyes.

'His Highness is – most gracious,' Kellarn faltered, ducking

19

his head. 'I did only that which was my duty. I have no claim to such honour.'

'Nevertheless we grant it,' said the Emperor, glancing from Kellarn to Erkal as if trying to guess whether something had passed between them. 'We trust, Dortrean, that your son will ride east with our host tomorrow?'

'I dare say, Sire,' said Erkal, 'if any of our commanders will take him.'

'Well enough,' said Rhydden. 'Proceed.'

The horses of the imperial escort moved forward again, and Kellarn and Takshar bowed and saluted once more. Kellarn risked a brief glance at his father, and was rewarded with the barest nod of approval, so that the Emperor might not see. There were more open nods and salutes from some of the other horsemen at the rear of the group.

'Bugger,' said Kellarn, as they trudged on toward the muddied greens of the parks. 'The last thing I need is Rhydden taking an interest in me.'

'Your fault for being a hero,' said Takshar. 'We merchant nobles learned long ago not to draw such attention to ourselves.'

'He saw you standing with me,' said Kellarn. 'He'll know who you are before long.'

'Well at least that black Counsellor of his wasn't with him,' said Takshar. 'The old Archmage.'

Kellarn nodded. 'There is a High Council meeting, I think.'

Takshar stopped short, and looked at him strangely.

'Since when did Dortrean know so much about the Magi?' he wondered. 'I had thought that you were sworn enemies.'

'All the more reason to know more about them,' Kellarn returned. 'But no. Our distrust of the Council's neutrality is traditional, but that does not exactly make us enemies. Besides, with the death of their Prime Councillor this morning, it's common knowledge in the palace that the Magi would be holding an urgent assembly some time today. I doubt that *His Eminence* the Imperial Counsellor would want to miss it.'

Kellarn did not add that it had been the magi themselves who had told him of their planned assembly, during his visit to the palace earlier that day. Nor did he wish to broach the question that, from what he had gathered, his father and the Magi seemed to have worked closely together in the recent defence of Arrandin. Dortrean's distrust of the Council was, as he had just said, traditional. With the Emperor's dangerous attention focused on him just now, Kellarn did not want to risk giving anyone the impression that that relationship might have changed. He still had no certain idea of where he stood with the Magi himself.

'You don't think that the Emperor's Archmage will want to become the new head of the Council?' demanded Takshar.

'Oh, probably,' said Kellarn. 'But I can't imagine that the other magi would let him, not even with this war. Can you?'

The High Councillor the Lady Rhysana Telún of Carbray paused to regain her breath at the top of the steep hill rise, absently tugging the double sash of her dark grey robes back into place. Her husband rested one hand on her arm in anxious question. Rhysana shook her head gently beneath her deep-brimmed hood, and patted his hand with her own in reassurance. After a moment they moved on again together, toward the waiting pyre.

Behind them, the high squared towers of the Dârghûn manor house caught the last of the sunlight above the deepening shadows of the rolling grassland hills; and beyond, the hills sank down into the half-guessed purple twilight of the Lautun plains and merged into the early evening sky. Ahead of them, beyond the pyre, the eastern arm of the Black Mountains stretched the length of the horizon, its snow-capped ridges glowing lilac and rose, and draped with cloudy veils of copper and amethyst and gold. The western sky was already burning.

It was not so unlike the view from Arrandin, Rhysana thought, standing here on a hilltop between the mountains and the plains. Except that the Blue Mountains seen from

Arrandin were a little closer, loftier, and the plains came right to the city's feet; so that everything about Arrandin seemed larger, wilder and more exposed. The farmland hills of Dârghûn offered a more gentle, homely seat. There was no city here, no encircling host of enemies – no battlefield piled with fallen dead. Only a solitary pyre for a much loved lord, and a small family gathering to offer him this last, quiet service. For the man Herusen Dârghûn – sometime Head of his House, Principal of the College of Magi in Lautun and Prime Councillor of All Magi – the tranquillity and homeliness were altogether apt.

It had been Herusen's wish to have his Rite of Burning performed here, and Rogheïn had dutifully insisted on respecting that wish – the Lady Rogheïn Aartaús of Dârghûn, widow of Herusen's eldest son, who had for several years been chatelaine of the Dârghûn manor house and skilful manager of the estate while the old man pursued his many obligations elsewhere. Had Rogheïn had her own way, she would also have had every one of Herusen's children and grandchildren present for the rite, and a suitably lavish feast spread afterward. But with the demands of the war, there had been no time to delay the rite to gather them all together. Besides, Rhysana was not altogether sure that Herusen would have wished it. Concerning family gatherings, she remembered him saying on more than one occasion that he *enjoyed the company, but hated the fuss*.

Rogheïn was at the head of the solemn procession that had climbed its way from the manor house up over the hills – a slim-boned, rangy woman, with the wide brown eyes and nervous energy of a young mare. At her side was her son and Herusen's heir designate, the Lord Haldrin of Dârghûn. Haldrin was tall and dark, like most of the men of his family, and now well into his twenties, being only a few years younger than Rhysana herself; and he was but recently married to the Lady Camarra of Kelmaar, by report a journeyman mage of considerable promise. But Camarra was not here. Rhysana's husband, Torkhaal, had sought Haldrin out among the gathered hosts of the Emperor's army at Arrandin, and brought him straight here by magic. With them had come Herusen's second son, Gravhan, and his wife the Chosen Priestess Imarra of Môshári, who now walked side by side behind Rogheïn and Haldrin. Rhysana herself had been brought here from a High Council meeting by the Archmage Morvaan, who had been Herusen's closest friend and ally for as long as anyone could remember.

Few other kinsmen were present for the rite, most having been called or kept away by the war. Just in front of Rhysana was Aidhan of Dârghûn, the fair-haired son of one of Herusen's younger sons, who had developed a particular fondness for Torkhaal. Aidhan was now into his early teens, and as tall as Rhysana herself, and was soon to be sent to school with the Môshári. In front of him walked his younger cousin Morraï of Môshári, Gravhan and Imarra's second daughter, the budding image of her lovely mother; and with Morraï was her aunt Elissa, Herusen's only daughter.

Ahead of these, and offering support to the Archmage Morvaan, was Aidhan's mother the Lady Serinta of Dârghûn, a former votary of the little known contemplative Order of Aranara. Serinta was clad in a simple black hooded robe with a milk-white girdle at the waist, which Rhysana supposed to be part of the ritual attire of her former Order. During the few years that they had known one another, Serinta had never spoken of Aranara, nor made reference to any of its teachings; and so in spite of her tiredness and her grief, Rhysana found herself intrigued to wonder whether she might soon discover more about that most secret of all the *Aeshta* priesthoods.

Attending the small procession were a dozen or so of the manor household in their formal gold and brown livery, with the golden bear's paw of Dârghûn on their chests and burning torches of pinewood in their hands. Further down the slope, at a respectful distance, were lesser retainers and farming folk from the nearby manor lands, come to say their own last farewells.

It occurred to Rhysana that most of these people must have known Herusen all their lives, or at least for far longer than had she herself, or Torkhaal; and that they had a better right to be here. But then it was also true that in the few years that they had been together at the College of Magi in Lautun, Herusen had come to love Torkhaal as dearly as any son; and Rhysana – had she admitted it to herself – had been as a favourite niece, or as an adopted daughter. They had known more of Herusen's other life, the life of the Council and the College, than had anyone here, apart from Morvaan of course. And Rogheïn had always welcomed them here as family, then as now. That must, she thought, count for something.

They began to take up their positions on the hill top. Imarra stood at the eastern end of the pyre, nearest to Herusen's head, and behind her stood the Lady Serinta. Rogheïn and Haldrin flanked them on either side. Morvaan moved left to the southeast, while Gravhan and his sister and daughter moved right, and Aidhan stood just beyond in the north. Torkhaal and Rhysana, bringing up the rear, circled round to stand in the northwest, facing back the way that they had come; only now the pyre lay between them and the journey home. The torch bearers formed a wider circle around them all.

Rhysana dared at last to look at the silent body on the pyre. She had seen him before, of course, earlier that day, laid out on a cushioned settle in the Arrand palace as if merely sleeping. Now his body was set straight as a monument, his pale hands folded in symmetry across his chest, his long white beard and hair combed out in neat array and drifting only faintly on the failing breeze. His accustomed cloth of gold had been replaced by lighter robes of moon-white silk, though still washed with the memory of rose and gold in the glow from the sunset sky. The bundled brushwood and branches beneath him seemed to be laid out in an intricate, half guessed pattern of their own, and woven with the perfume of cedar and pine, and sweet incense.

Yet for all the sombre formality of his repose, there was not the sense of emptiness or loss that she had expected. The Herusen whom she knew was not there upon the pyre. It was as though he had laid aside that body, even as they had laid aside his golden robe. She doubted that he would return to it again, and yet she was still not sure. When she looked, she saw that a tiny bunch of blue meadow flowers was held almost whimsically between the fingers of his left hand; and his pale face, although deeply at rest, held somehow the promise of sudden merriment.

'You are sure that there is nothing more you could do for him?' Morvaan asked Imarra.

'Quite sure,' Imarra answered in her deep, gentle voice. 'His time among us in this life is now past, and he chose his end with wisdom. We can not draw him back. But in another life, in another time, we may hope to meet him again.'

Morvaan sighed, and then shrugged.

'Well, I thought it was worth asking,' he said.

Imarra smiled sadly. She looked at each of the assembled mourners in silence, and then lifted up her hands in prayer and began the funeral song of the Môshári. The Lady Serinta sang with her, her lighter voice sometimes in unison, and sometimes in harmony; and at the second line, Gravhan's deep baritone joined in.

> *Aetennôn aeshtrí suldhannon*
> *torghta telanna einnon*
> *engûlanôs drenn eïnarna.*

'*Receive now, oh gods, your servant, within the comfort of your wings, which enfold us throughout all ages.*'

The fiery disc of the setting sun was already half hidden behind the Mountains, now plumed with many clouds of smoke and flame. The Lord Morvaan of Braedun, Archmage of the Sun, lifted up his hands and conjured answering fire in the heart of the piled mound of Herusen's pyre. The rosy flames billowed up like the wings of the song, driving the onlookers back with the swift strength of their sudden light and heat. The three singers sang on.

Torkhaal let out a sob, and Rhysana felt her own throat tighten. She wanted to comfort him, but he was still closed in upon himself, unwilling to burden her with the weight of his own grief. There would be time enough afterward, she thought. She glanced to her left, where Aidhan stood quite still. The tears ran unchecked down his young face, glittering like crystals in the bright firelight – or like the iridescent flicker of the dragon's wings, she thought, even as she had glimpsed them in the dawn sky, high over Arrandin.

Morvaan's fire was burning swift and clear, hastening Herusen on his journey through the First Realm of the Dead. The Lady Serinta motioned for one of the torch bearers to come forward with the bowl of incense, from which each of the mourners might cast their own offering into the flames.

Rhysana turned her attention back to the pyre, too bright now almost to look upon. She closed her eyes, and gathered together all her best thoughts and memories of Herusen Dârghûn, sending them after him in loving blessing. His remarkable intellect and wisdom, from which she felt that she had barely begun to learn. His gentle diffidence in private debate, and his dreadful authority in the council chamber. His political shrewdness, and his indulgent affection for his family. His affection for Torkhaal and Rhysana herself, and for their own son Taillan. His incurable passion for milk rolls drenched in honey.

In all too short a time the family had finished their private offerings, and it was Torkhaal and Rhysana's turn to approach the pyre. She waited for Torkhaal to go first, and kept her gaze fixed on the swinging hem of his black robes as he strode across the scorched turf ahead of her.

She watched as he nodded to Imarra and Serinta, and scooped a handful of the grey incense from the proffered bowl. He turned toward the pyre, and lifted his head, and stood there for some while. Then slowly he began to extend his right arm, jerking and shaking with the effort. Imarra glanced at Rhysana in concern.

Not knowing whether it was the best thing to do or not, but knowing only that she needed to help him, Rhysana wrapped her left arm about Torkhaal's waist and stretched her right arm out along his, closing her fingers gently about his clenched fist, steadying, and then soothing.

For what seemed like several minutes – though in truth it was perhaps no more than a few heartbeats – he remained rigid in her arms. The heat from the flames seared painfully across her knuckles, and even beneath her hood Rhysana's eyes stung with the fire and the tears. But at length his shoulders relaxed, and his grip slackened. Gently she turned his hand palm upward, and prised open his fingers; and then together, with Rhysana's hand guiding, they scattered their incense on the flames, and offered Herusen their farewell blessing.

But even as they scattered their incense and the flames sparked green and gold, whether through her husband's reluctance or her own, Rhysana was not wholly convinced that Herusen had yet entered the Realms of the Dead. Not yet. In her mind's eye, the wings that enfolded him now were not those of the great lions of the Môshári, the angelic messengers of Earth. They were the wings of Ilunâtor, Father of All Dragons, bearing him upward in great joy to join the dance of the summer stars, and to behold the glory of All that Is; and only later, perhaps, as the night grew old, would the two of them turn back, to welcome the light of another dawn. But she kept this thought to herself.

In the meantime, Herusen's living kinsmen were regrouping for the descent back to the manor house, and Rhysana and Torkhaal were obliged to join them. Gravhan came over to give Torkhaal a brief, brotherly embrace; and after a moment's awkward hesitation, Aidhan did the same. As soon as the household torch bearers were ready, they all moved off down the hillside. Torkhaal and Rhysana came at the rear of the procession again, but this time hand in hand. Morvaan, Imarra and Serinta remained behind, to tend the fire and to allow the other folk of Dârghûn the chance to come and say their prayers and farewells.

It had not occurred to Rhysana until now to be anxious for her husband; and even now, there might be no great cause for concern. After all, the siege of Arrandin had been raised scarcely twelve hours since, and the news of Herusen's loss was hardly much older. They were weary from the struggles of the siege, and had had little enough rest that day; and barely no time at all to come to terms with grief and loss, before being confronted with this Rite of Burning.

For another thing, Torkhaal was a mage of Earth, and one with exceptional mental gifts. He seemed to experience everything more passionately and deeply than Rhysana herself, or at least more immediately. Being a mage of Air, she found it easier to separate her emotions into pigeon holes – though having said that, she allowed that two or three days after this war was finally over, she would probably be hit by the backlash of everything that had happened, and sink without trace beneath the emptied contents of all those pigeon holes.

And then there was the loss of Hrugaar. *Hrugaar!* Rhysana had not had the chance even to begin to grieve for him yet; or at least, she had not dared to begin to do so. As far as she knew, his body must still be at the Tollund manor house, east of Arrandin, unless Morvaan's daughter had made provision for him to be sent back to the city. If Herusen had been as a father to Torkhaal, then Hrugaar had been at least as close as a brother. In some ways, with their shared mental gifts, Hrugaar had been closer to Torkhaal than even Rhysana herself. To have lost both in one day was for Rhysana sorrow enough. For Torkhaal, it must be almost beyond enduring.

In their normal life – if one could call theirs a normal life – Rhysana would have been content to let her husband go his own way for a few days, respecting his right to personal privacy in dealing with his grief. But with the pressure of war still upon them, and the likelihood that they would soon be parted, she was not sure that she should wait. She was not sure that she wanted to.

Rhysana slowed her pace, and Torkhaal slowed with her, allowing the procession to draw away from them. At Rhysana's signal the torch bearers left them alone, and they came to a halt on the shadowed hillside. The first evening stars were winking into sight in the eastern sky.

She lifted back her hood, and looked up at him in the twilight, taking both his hands between her own.

'Let me in?' she pleaded gently.

Torkhaal looked down at her, his face twisted in a confusion of desire and despair. He slipped his hand around to lace his fingers between hers, but said nothing. The pale wood of their wedding rings clicked together.

'Look at it this way,' she said presently. 'It hurts *you* more, not sharing it. And it hurts *me* more to see you in pain, and to be shut out and so – so helpless. So why not make life easier for both of us?'

She was not entirely convinced by her own argument; but she did not want to mention the fact that now that the war was moving, it might call them away from one another. She tried to keep the tone light and gentle, even a little teasing. It seemed to draw some response. His lips twitched up into an awkward grin, for all that he tried to master it. After a moment he gave a long sigh, and stroked a stray silver-fair hair back into place above her ear.

'Are you sure?' he growled uncertainly.

'Not sure,' she said; 'but stubbornly determined.'

He lowered his face to kiss her on the mouth, and she held herself open and receptive to him. And presently she felt the warmth of his mental *presence* sweep up and around her like enfolding wings, drawing her close inside.

She knew that it was not the full sharing of minds that Hrugaar or Herusen could have offered him. But it was their own sharing. He could, of course, read everything about her like a book – though there were some private places, such as her work with the High Council, where Torkhaal knew better than to try to go – and she could share in that reading, drawing his attention to one thought or another, or to some treasured memory or imagining. In return, she had learned intuitively to read the swell of his moods and emotions, and could read any thought or image which he chose to send to her, or which he inadvertently let slip. For Rhysana, it was an intimacy which she had not experienced with any other human being – except, a very little, with Hrugaar. It occurred to her belatedly that perhaps she should have waited until they were in the privacy of their own chamber before she had attempted this.

The flood of sorrow and loss, and the vast emptiness beneath, she had expected; and also the shades of anger, of self-pity and despair, which blurred unbidden at the edge of thought. She knew her husband well enough to read them, even before he had turned and opened to her, and she had braced herself accordingly to share them, mingling them with similar emotions of her own. With the long discipline of a mage's training, she was able to weather it – as was Torkhaal himself, of course; though for him, as a mage of Earth, the emotional struggle was perhaps the harder.

What she had not quite anticipated was Torkhaal's now heightened passion for herself, his increased fear of losing her also. The loss of two close friends had lent a fresh urgency to his concern for her safety – a fierce protectiveness, so like the guardian winged lions of the Môshári that he loved. Even three years married to him, Rhysana still felt a little insufficient at times to cope with the strength of her husband's affection toward her.

You need not worry on that account, she reassured him mentally. *I have no intention of letting you lose me. And I don't intend to lose you, either.*

But the war—? His response was left open, spiralling off into a score of half guessed possibilities and calamities.

My work was in Arrandin, and the siege is over, she sent calmly. *I suppose that I shall return to the city for few more days.*

Rhysana considered briefly the latest High Council assembly, held earlier that afternoon, and decided that there was nothing in it which she could not really tell her husband. Nothing that he might not have guessed already.

There had been no election for a successor to Herusen at such an early stage. It had simply been agreed that High Councillor Sollonaal, as Prime Councillor of the Ellanguan Magi, was the natural and traditional choice to serve as a temporary successor, until such time as a formal election could be held. Sollonaal would oversee the running of the colleges, and the domestic matters within the Empire. The Archmage Morvaan and High Councillor Ferghaal of Braedun would continue to coordinate those magi who wished to offer their services in the war. In practical terms, very little had changed.

Since the college term was scheduled to resume in a couple of days' time, it had been agreed that the few students of the Arrandin College should be temporarily relocated to Ellanguan; and makeshift lecturing staffs for the three Colleges of Lautun, Ellanguan and Farran would be cobbled together from the depleted numbers of mage councillors still available. Dependent upon Arrandin's need for defence, Rhysana had agreed in principle to return to the Lautun College to resume her lecturing duties there.

Torkhaal could not disguise his relief that Rhysana had no intention to go riding east with the Emperor's army – though in truth he would not really have prevented her, if she had believed that it was necessary for her to do so; not even in her state of expectant motherhood. By the same token, he himself was now faced with the choice of returning to the College, or continuing to take an active part in the war. They both knew that he would find it hard to go back to lecturing while the threat from the Easterners remained.

When will the college staff be decided? he asked her.

There is a New Moon Assembly for all the Council, the day after tomorrow, she said. *But by that time, of course, several people*

will have ridden east with the Emperor, and be unable to attend.
Sollonaal will have to make the best of whatever he is left with.

There was a mischievous flicker behind her thought, and
Torkhaal marvelled how she had managed to turn him so
swiftly from grief, to plotting, to humour. True, the grief and
loss still remained; and the fear of parting was still ahead of
them. She had simply restored his sense of perspective.

We ought to be getting back to the manor, she reminded him,
before he embarked on any fresh declarations of affection.

Torkhaal chuckled, and kissed her once more, and let the
mental link between them fade to a barest whisper as they held
hands. She could tell that he was very tired.

As they prepared to move on, they noticed a slender
black-robed figure coming down the hillside toward them.
At first Rhysana thought that it must be the Lady Serinta;
but as the woman drew near she lifted back her hood to reveal
a cascade of soft golden curls, and eyes that gleamed bright as
silver in the twilight. The face was dimly familiar to both of
them, but neither Torkhaal nor Rhysana could remember from
where or when.

'Forgive me,' said the young woman. 'I am Ilumarin. We
have met before, in Dortrean.'

'Of course,' said Rhysana, nodding in courtesy. Ilumarin,
she remembered, was a Chosen Priestess of Haëstren, *Aeshta*
Lady of the Moon, and like Serinta had been trained by the
contemplative Order of Aranara. Other than that, she knew
only that Ilumarin was a friend of the Lords of Dortrean, and
of the Sun Temple.

'I had not realised,' Rhysana added after a moment, 'that
you knew Herusen.'

'I did not,' Ilumarin replied simply. 'But today he has cast a
diamond into the pool; and though the jewel itself lies hidden
in the waters, the ripples shall be seen and felt for many days
to come. For this reason I am come to honour him; though
I had not the honour, as you did, of knowing him in the
waking world.'

32

Rhysana felt Torkhaal's hand tighten about her own. There was a lilting, liquid quality to the priestess' voice, a curious mingling of sorrow, vision and excitement, which was strangely unsettling. The servants of Haëstren had a reputation for mystic vision, and for giving answers as enigmatic as those of the Fay. Torkhaal was warning her that they should proceed with caution. But Rhysana's own instincts told her that Ilumarin had already said as much as she was likely to say about Herusen on this occasion.

'What manner of ripples?' asked Torkhaal carefully.

Ilumarin smiled and shook her head. 'The surface of the pool was already troubled,' she said, as if answering a different question.

All three looked at one another in silence.

'You have heard about the Sun priest?' Rhysana ventured.

'Oh yes,' said Ilumarin softly, 'I know about Torriearn – and about our friend Hrugaar.'

Again there was that blend of sorrow and confident excitement within the priestess' voice, so that Rhysana was uncertain whether she wished to embrace Ilumarin or to slap her. She felt Torkhaal stirring restlessly at her side.

'We are sorry for your loss,' she said, keeping a tight hold of her husband's hand.

'When we travelled together, I think that Torriearn found me a little – well, *difficult* to live with,' said Ilumarin. 'But for his sake, I am sorry that he has been taken so soon from the present battle. He would like, I think, to have achieved much more.'

'And for all our sakes,' said Torkhaal, 'if his vision of the return of the ancient Enemy should prove true. He will be sorely missed.'

'Indeed so,' Ilumarin nodded. 'Yet the saving of Arrandin was a vital step, and Torriearn knew it. The pursuit of the Easterners is the next step – and even if you achieve it, there will be more difficult challenges to follow. We can only guess at the wisdom of the gods; whom they choose, and whom they take away. And so Torriearn is at rest, and Herusen is in joy; and still the dance goes on, and those who remain take up the measure.'

'And Hrugaar?' asked Rhysana.

'Of Hrugaar I may not speak,' said Ilumarin, shaking her golden head. 'Not yet. Perhaps another time, when you are ready.'

'Shall you be coming east, to join the Earl of Dortrean?' asked Torkhaal.

'I have been in Arrandin many days,' Ilumarin smiled. 'Farewell – until the next time.'

She made a half turn on the hillside, fading to a ghostly shape of starlight, and was gone. A faint echo of music lingered on the air where she had been standing, and then faded. Rhysana frowned.

'Why did you ask about Arrandin?' she wondered.

Torkhaal sighed, and slid his arm around her waist.

'She knows about Ru,' he answered; 'and she has foreseen things about the war, which perhaps she might want to tell Erkal, if she is a friend of Dortrean.'

'Or perhaps she wanted us to tell him?' said Rhysana.

Yet Ilumarin seemed to have told them nothing which they might not have guessed already – except for the fact that the priestess herself was here, and that she had also been in Arrandin. Rhysana wondered if that had been Ilumarin's only purpose in speaking with them. But she was too tired to think it about it now.

She slipped her arm around Torkhaal and hugged him; and then together they set off down the hillside toward the lights of the distant manor house.

It was fully dark by the time that Kellarn reached the Dortrean house in the Old City of Arrandin. He had left Takshar behind in the great barrack pier at the western end of the city, together with well over half the members of his weary war band. With Takshar's connections with the city guard – and permission to use Kellarn's own name to swing favours, if needed – he knew that they would be well looked after.

Kellarn had barely passed through the gate arch into the stable courtyard when he was intercepted by Marusâ, one of the older women of the household, with firm instructions for him to strip off his filthy gear and outer clothing before entering the house. They would all rest the better, she said, without the smell and stain of death about the place. She provided him with a large grey blanket to wrap around himself, and sandals for his bare feet; and when he was done, she bustled him inside with orders to go straight upstairs and bathe. All this Kellarn endured patiently, being in any event too tired to put up much of a fight. But he had the presence of mind to retrieve the Easterner pendant in its cloth bundle from his trouser pocket. Marusâ opened her mouth to protest, but then appeared to think the better of it. She simply shook her head, and blew out a motherly sigh of forbearance.

The great hall lay in comfortable silence as he padded through, lit only by the newly kindled fire at the far end. He passed the hanging tapestry of the Red Stag of Dortrean – a treasured gift from the Lords of Carfinn – and hauled his legs up the first of the stone stairs which led to the lamplit hallways of the upper floors.

In recent years this house had become home for Kellarn's sister Ellaïn, and her husband Jared and their children; though other members of the family often stayed here, and both Kellarn and his parents still had their own rooms set aside for them. But Ellaïn and Jared had been away when the war began, and for the duration of the siege, Erkal Dortrean had found it more convenient to stay as a guest in the Arrand palace itself. Only now, with the arrival of the Emperor and his commanders, had the Earl considered it prudent to withdraw to the relative safety of his own house – albeit no more than a stone's throw from The Arrand's doorstep.

Kellarn half pulled himself to the top of a second, narrower stair, to reach the landing outside his own rooms. His borrowed

35

sandals slapped against the stone, and his thigh muscles were protesting almost audibly. The panelled landing was as silent as the great hall, with just one lamp of patterned Arrandin glass atop the linen chest to his right. But he saw that a door stood open, across the hall and further down than his own, with a mingled glow of lamplight and firelight spilling out from the chamber beyond.

Even with the business of the war, Kellarn had not expected his father to have guests in the house that night; and especially not in the rooms which, as he remembered, belonged to Ellaïn's two boys. Kellarn doubted that his nephews would have returned – and Marusâ would certainly have mentioned it. So in spite of his tiredness, and his lack of suitable clothing, he hugged the blanket around himself and went to take a closer look.

He was met at the doorway by Kierran of Arrand – a little taller and older than Kellarn himself, and with the dark hair and lithe build of all The Arrand's sons. Kierran grinned in welcome, and stepped back to let him inside; and Kellarn discovered that the red canopied bed now held the small, sleeping form of Mage Councillor Dhûghaúr, whom he had last seen sleeping in Kierran's own apartments in the Arrand palace earlier that day. It was not hard to guess that Dhûghaúr's removal here had been prompted by the Emperor's arrival. It occurred to Kellarn to wonder who else might now be hidden in the Dortrean house.

'How is he?' he whispered.

'Oh, on the mend, I think,' Kierran said quietly. 'He was awake a little while ago. Not a sign of life from him in two days, and then suddenly he sits up, cheerful as the lark, and declares that he's famished. He was here by then, so Ellaïn's women brought him plenty of beef tea – though I think perhaps that he would have preferred more solid fare. He drank down the lot, and then went straight back to sleep again.' Kierran shook his head and chuckled.

'And that was it?' asked Kellarn.

'He did ask a few questions,' said Kierran. 'Magi always do. I just told him that the siege was ended, and the Emperor had arrived; and that the other magi were off at a Council meeting; and they would tell him the rest when they came back.'

'Nothing more?'

Even with Dhûghaúr asleep, Kellarn hesitated to mention the names of Herusen or Hrugaar, or what might have happened to them. With the Magi, there was no telling what they might or might not hear.

'That was enough to satisfy him, and let him sleep easy,' said Kierran. 'The rest can wait.'

He looked Kellarn up and down, and wrinkled his nose.

'You need a bath again,' he said. 'By rights you shouldn't be in here, until you've cleaned up.'

They went out across the landing and in to Kellarn's own rooms. The bed there had been freshly made up, and in spite of the warm season a small fire had been lit in welcome. Kellarn glanced around at the familiar chests and shelves and furnishings, and saw with relief that his sword and shield had been brought here from the Arrand palace and set carefully in one corner – probably, he thought, by Kierran himself. But Kierran did not allow him to linger. He pulled Kellarn through the low connecting door, and all but stood over him while he peeled off blanket and undergarments and lowered himself into the steaming pool of the sunken bath.

On most other occasions, Kellarn would have been quite glad of his friend's company and cheerful banter. But he had spent much of the day keeping busy, avoiding having to think of certain things, and he felt the need now to be by himself for a while. He told Kierran not to fuss, and to leave him in peace; and then at the other's crestfallen look, he relented a little and added that he might wait in the bedchamber until he was finished.

What Kellarn meant by *thinking* was, he supposed, rather different from the formal analysis which the Magi might use, or from the tactical planning favoured by his mother. For him it

37

was more a question of sitting quiet and still, and accepting the simple facts of the situation around him; and then, if necessary, relying on instinct to make his next move. He had never been able to plan very far ahead.

He still found himself overwhelmed by the sheer scale of the siege – the thousands of warriors, both living and slain, that had filled the Lower City – and the ruin and destruction left in its wake. Among so many dead, the loss of Herusen Dârghûn had no great personal significance to Kellarn, since they had had little enough to do with another; and although he knew that there would soon be a new Prime Councillor, and that the relationship between the Council and the Six Kingdoms might change under the direction of Herusen's successor, he knew too little about the Magi even to begin to guess what difference that might make. So he felt sorry for Rhysana and Torkhaal, and for the Archmage Morvaan, who he knew had loved Herusen dearly; and he realised that the loss of so powerful and wise a mage would be felt by all the Six Kingdoms, especially in this time of war. But that was the extent of it.

The loss of Hrugaar touched Kellarn more closely, of course, for they had enjoyed a merry friendship over the past few years, and his home had been a welcome refuge in Ellanguan. But like his meeting with the dragon, Kellarn found that he had simply to accept the fact that it had happened, without really being able to understand it. He could not weep for Hrugaar yet. And wherever he was, the ever inquisitive mage would no doubt be enjoying himself.

As for the question of what he should do next, Kellarn was in two minds. Up until a few weeks ago, he and his friend Corollin had been hunting for the scattered pieces of a strange artefact made to combat the ancient Enemy – the demon captain known as *Lo-Khuma* to the Easterners, and *Atallakûr* among the elvenfolk of the Fay; that same Enemy who the priests of the *Aeshta* Orders now feared was soon to return. But then had begun the cycle of events which had taken Kellarn to Lautun, and through slavery on a Souther warship to Arveil, and so here to the war in Arrandin; and Corollin, by report, was nearby at the Tollund manor. It seemed that he now had to choose again whether to take further part in the war, or to find Corollin and go back to search for the rest of the artefact.

Given the scale of the war, Kellarn supposed that he ought to ride east with the Emperor's armies. The threat of invasion was still more immediate and pressing than the likelihood of the Enemy's return. He disliked the idea of having to take orders again, having been his own master ever since he passed out of the Arrandin guard; and he knew the danger that others, less friendly, might even now be hunting for the same artefact pieces which he and Corollin sought. But the present need of the Six Kingdoms demanded no less. And when he thought about it, Kellarn realised that he had no idea what strategy the Emperor's commanders might even have planned. That was something he would have to ask his father.

The need to speak with Erkal stirred Kellarn into action. He scrubbed himself quickly, then climbed out of the bath and fetched clean towels from the deep marble shelf. He was still dripping when he went through into the bedchamber, with one red towel snugged tight around his waist, and rubbing vigorously at his hair with another.

Kierran had found him fresh clothes and set them to air before the fire, and was sitting on the edge of the bed looking thoughtful. A torn strip of blue cloth was spread out across his lap, with the square pendant of black and gold nestled in the middle.

'I should be careful of touching that,' Kellarn warned him. 'It came from one of the Easterners.'

Kierran looked up at him and smiled.

'I do have *some* notion of how to handle unknown treasures,' he said, wrapping the pendant up again. 'I presume you want to show this to Rhysana?'

'Hmm,' Kellarn answered from beneath the towel.

'Besides, how do you think I managed to bring your sword and shield here safely otherwise?' Kierran went on, standing up and coming over to him. 'Which reminds me, is there a story behind the sword? I don't remember seeing it before.'

Kellarn grunted. The subject of his sword, and the unknown prophecy that went with it, was not something that he wished to talk about just now.

'I'll tell you later,' he said. 'I need to speak with Father first.'

'I know,' Kierran grinned. 'His Grace asked me to bring you down when you were ready.'

Ten minutes later the two of them were welcomed into the Earl's small suite of rooms. Erkal himself was relaxing in a cushioned chair, his long legs stretched out toward the hearth. At his left elbow was a square side table, bearing a supper tray piled with fresh bread and cheeses and salted meats. Beneath the table was a leather box filled with several rolled documents. Seated across from him, and standing as they entered, was a younger man with golden fair hair, clad in black riding leathers and with a round buckle of silver and gold on his belt. Kellarn recognised him at once; but for Kierran's benefit, Erkal introduced the man as the Lord Priest Torren of the *Vashta* Order of Mairdun – a messenger from the redoubtable Abbot Commander Carstan Mairdun, Head of that Order.

'Father Torren brings other tidings from Ellanguan,' said Erkal, waving for the priest to be seated again. 'I think that you had better hear them.'

Kellarn nodded, heading straight for the supper tray. Since Erkal's invitation appeared to include them both, Kierran sat down on the low bench seat facing the fire.

'My news concerns one Brother Sarin,' said Torren, his voice deep and musical as a temple bell. 'I am not sure whether Lord Kellarn will have heard the tale?'

Kellarn shook his head in answer.

'Then in brief,' said Torren, 'Sarin is a votary of the *Vashta* goddess Serbramel. He claims to have been granted a vision that if the Emperor should quarrel with the Lord Steward

Rinnekh Ellanguan, then great calamity would follow; and he told the Emperor so much, publicly, on the harbour front of Ellanguan.'

'It hardly needs a vision to foresee that,' said Kellarn. 'I can't imagine how anyone could trust that little skunk.'

'The Emperor, or Rinnekh?' asked Torren. His expression remained unchanged, and it took Kellarn several moments to realise that the priest was joking.

'Anyway, the Emperor took Sarin away for further questioning,' Torren went on; 'and when pressure was at last brought upon him to release the poor man, he delivered Sarin into the keeping of my own Order, so that we might patch him up again before the priestesses of Serbramel saw him.'

'Why you?' asked Kellarn, sitting down beside Kierran.

'I believe that your Lady mother, the Countess, had a hand in that,' Torren smiled. 'But among other things, I think that it was a gambit on Rhydden's part. He was relying on our estrangement from the other *Vashta* Orders to delay Sarin's final release; and perhaps hoping to gain our better favour and support for the war, given that we are a military Order of some reputation.'

Kellarn nodded, too busy chewing to make comment. The reputation of the knights of Mairdun was well deserved. Yet he doubted that his mother would have supported their involvement simply to help the Emperor out of a tight spot. Of all the *Vashta* Orders, Mairdun was the most amenable to the Lords of Dortrean, and to the older *Aeshta* priesthoods. To strengthen Mairdun's influence with the Emperor might hopefully make Dortrean's own position more secure.

'Sarin showed few signs of physical hurt when he came to us,' said Torren. 'Surprisingly so, given the audacity with which he had confronted the Emperor and the Lord Steward in so public a place. But the damage to the inner man was far greater. He was witless and half raving; and his mind and will were in tatters, as though they had been ripped apart with great violence.'

41

'You mean that the Emperor's Truthsayers tore their answers from his mind by force?' gasped Kierran. His dark eyes were wide with horror.

'We think not,' said Torren. 'Of the few who have that gift, most – thank the gods – have the moral discipline and courage not to use it thus.'

'The Imperial Counsellor could have done it,' said Kellarn grimly.

'The Archmage?' said Torren. 'Possibly. But in this case, we think not. From what our priests and healers could tell, no human mind was responsible for the damage that they found.'

'That still doesn't rule out His Eminence,' Kellarn muttered.

'Believe me, my Lord,' said Torren firmly, 'he did not do it. At some stage – though whether before or after the Emperor's men took him, we can not say for certain – something altogether inhuman broke in to Sarin's mind and ravaged it. Not a vision or a messenger from the gods – or at least, not such as we know them – but a creature or *being* wholly malicious and evil.'

'You are speaking of possession?' demanded the Earl.

'Something like,' Torren nodded; 'only more destructive.'

'And how does your Abbot Commander interpret these tidings?' Erkal pursued.

Torren clasped his hands in front of his buckle, and looked straight at the Earl.

'Sarin is but a simple lay brother, from a *Vashta* Order,' he said. 'He has neither the knowledge nor training to journey to the spiritual Realms where such beings are found; nor to invoke their presence, even by ill chance. For such a horror to visit him, even in his dreams, would suggest that another, more powerful agency was at work, to draw the creature close to the borders of the waking world.'

'Might the presence of the Easterner armies here have caused that?' asked Erkal.

'Had he been but troubled in his dreams, perhaps,' said

42

Torren. 'But given the direct assault within Sarin's mind, I fear that is unlikely. It seems more probable that someone in Ellanguan had the power and knowledge to open a way between the Realms and call the creature in, and Brother Sarin was its victim.'

'But who would do so?' asked Kellarn; 'and why?'

'The *why* we may perhaps guess at,' said his father. 'If this happened before Sarin confronted the Emperor on the harbour front, then it might explain the source of Sarin's vision – though what purpose that false prophecy might achieve, whether to weaken the Empire or strengthen it, is still a mystery. If it happened after the Emperor took him, then it was perhaps intended as some cruel torment or punishment.'

'Or to prevent him from speaking further,' put in Torren. 'The servants of Serbramel have reason to believe that Sarin's vision did indeed come from the goddess herself.'

'Either way, it is an evil business,' said the Earl.

Torren nodded. 'As to who might have done it, my Lord Kellarn, well, the Council of Magi has proscribed such practices for centuries. Though of course there are some magi – and among them the Emperor's Archmage – who might attempt to use such forbidden arts in defiance of Council precepts.'

'Merrech would twist a rule, sooner than break it,' Erkal demurred. 'If he were responsible for Sarin's plight, I think that he would have masked his handiwork more subtly – unless he left him that way to mislead us.'

'The senior priests of the *Aeshta* Orders,' Torren continued, 'might have the knowledge and power to bring this thing from another Realm. But we do not believe them capable of such wanton malice; and indeed, such insight as we have gained from our own goddess tells against it.'

'Then how does your Abbot Commander read this riddle?' Erkal asked again.

Torren tapped his thumbs together.

'The simple answer,' he said carefully, 'is that an Easterner priest or wizard is at work in Ellanguan, while our attention is drawn toward the battle here in Arrandin. It is hardly surprising that the Easterners should send spies or agents ahead of their main host, and they are well versed in dealing with creatures from other Realms.'

'Then Ellanguan is in danger?' cried Kellarn.

'Of course,' said Erkal. 'As Father Torren says, it comes as no surprise; and the Emperor was prudent enough not to leave the city undefended. But what else is there, Father, if that was but the simple answer?'

'It is also possible,' the priest replied, 'that a Souther loremaster might be responsible, since the Southers have made their own assault upon the coast, in alliance with the Easterners.'

Kellarn shifted uncomfortably on his seat.

'And there are a few,' Torren went on, 'a very few, amongst the most senior *Vashta* priests, who might have achieved it.'

'So the threat could come from East or South, from the Magi or the *Vashta* priesthoods,' sighed Erkal. 'And if, as you seem to believe, Brother Sarin's vision was not the work of this unknown *being*, then we must assume that his mind was destroyed after he was taken prisoner, either to punish or to silence him.'

'Precisely,' said Torren. 'But there is one thing more. From the insight given to my Lord Abbot Carstan in his meditations, he believes that the person responsible for Sarin's plight is part of the imperial household – or at least, is known to the household and may pass freely among them.'

Erkal's face went very still. Kellarn and Kierran exchanged glances.

'No, my Lord,' said Torren, gazing straight at Kellarn. 'We can not rule out the possibility that the Emperor's Archmage is indirectly responsible. Though our elders think it unlikely, on this occasion.'

'You say that the Emperor released Sarin into your Order's keeping *before* he set out from Ellanguan?' demanded the Earl.

'He did, your Grace,' Torren nodded.

'Then it is possible that whoever summoned this creature to torment Brother Sarin might have come down with Rhydden's army to Arrandin?'

'Quite possible, your Grace,' said Torren gravely. 'Hence the urgency of my errand.'

Kellarn opened his mouth to speak, but found that he had nothing to say. For one thing, even his father and the priests of Mairdun seemed as puzzled as he was by this business of Brother Sarin. For another, the possibility that whoever was responsible – albeit indirectly – for Sarin's madness might now be here in Arrandin pressed in upon him, unaccountably, with a sense of increased personal danger. Though he knew well enough to be wary of the Emperor and his household, and indeed of the *Vashta* priesthoods and the Magi and of most of the Court Noble, this latest threat seemed wholly unknown, unguessable. It might, of course, have nothing to do with him. But it was here.

Father Torren was already standing and making ready to depart. They rose to bid him farewell.

'We are grateful, once again, to Mairdun,' said Erkal, bowing.

Torren bowed silently in answer, and flung his dark cloak about him. At Erkal's signal, Kierran led the priest away through the house to see him out. When the door had shut behind them, Kellarn sighed and returned to the supper tray.

'So what happens tomorrow?' he asked.

'The Emperor's army rides east,' replied his father, stretching his legs out again before the hearth. 'Beyond that, Collie-dog, the gods alone know.'

'And do we ride with them?'

'The gods, or the army?' drawled Erkal. 'Well both, I hope. At least, I shall go with them. The Emperor requires it. He needs someone out there who knows how to bargain with the Easterners.'

'But what is there to bargain over?' demanded Kellarn.

The Earl sighed, running his fingers absently along the edge of the supper tray.

'Even with the losses they suffered here in Arrandin,' he said, 'their strength of warriors must still number at least twice our own. Without your dragon around, it will be no easy battle.'

'He's not *my* dragon,' said Kellarn.

'Herusen's dragon.' Erkal frowned at the reminder. All The Arrand's commanders now knew that Herusen had been responsible for summoning the great dragon, in defiance of the strictest Council precepts. It had saved the day; but it had also served to rekindle old doubts about how far the Magi could be trusted.

'Nor Herusen's, really,' said Kellarn.

Erkal waved the matter aside. 'In our favour, perhaps,' he went on, 'is the fact that the greatest chieftain among the Easterners who led their armies here appears to have been the Mughuzhti, whom you slew at the gate; and his senior priest and several of the other leaders are also dead and gone. Thus it now falls to the lesser chiefs – or else their priests and wizards – to rally the different clans. It may be some time before those leaders will come to any agreement or alliance between them; and so we may find ourselves dealing with as many as half a dozen separate armies led by rival commanders – and perhaps some more amenable than others. It is in the hope that we may achieve peace with at least some of the clans that the Emperor requires me to ride east.'

Kellarn chewed thoughtfully on a hunk of cheese, and studied his father's face in the firelight.

'That also means we could end up fighting more than one battle,' he frowned. 'And if the clan leaders argue, they could head off in different directions. What have the Emperor's commanders planned?'

Erkal looked at him, and smiled wearily.

'You may well be the hero of the hour, my son,' he said, 'but that does not quite earn you the right to hear all of the Emperor's secret counsels.'

'But how else am I to decide what to do?' Kellarn objected.

'You could do as you're told, for once,' suggested Erkal.

Kellarn glared at him, but his father was only teasing. They both laughed.

'Well, I can tell you a little,' said the Earl. 'As you know, there are four border manors flanking the road east from Arrandin. Of the nearer two, Tollund is safely retaken by your friend Corollin. The Tormal manor house is now little better than a burned-out shell, and is too far south of the road to be of much practical use to the enemy. If any of the Easterners withdrew there, they would soon be cut off from the other clans, and from their supply lines to the east – and also from their road home.

'The farther two manors of Herghin and Khôrland are still in Easterner hands; and as you have guessed, their armies may retreat to either or both. Of the two, Khôrland is the more easily defended – backed up as it is against the cliffs, and that much closer to the Blue Mountain Fords and the road to the Domains. The Herghin manor house is in hill country, which raises problems of its own. If the Easterners dig themselves in down there, it could be a long while before we could chase them out. Were they to divide their hosts more or less evenly between the two, we have not the strength to dispatch either one without a prolonged fight – and, of course, the problem of having the other at our backs.

'So at present, Rhydden will send our armies east along the road as far as the village of Fersí, with a smaller force circling south to secure Tormal. By the time we gather at Fersí, the day after tomorrow, we should have clearer reports of what the Easterners are doing; and the commanders will plan their next moves accordingly.'

Kellarn sat down and closed his eyes, trying to picture in his mind the lie of the land and the positions of the border manors; drawing on his scant memories of maps of the region, and wide views glimpsed from a distance. He had never been to Herghin or Khôrland himself. His own travels with Corollin had taken him further south, through Tormal and Ferlund lands, and down into the shadow of the Low Mountains. He guessed that the reports his father spoke of would come from the Magi and priests, using their secret arts, rather than from any horsemen scouting ahead. And that in turn raised the question of how closely his father had worked with the Magi in the recent siege, and to what extent Dortrean's relationship with the Council had now changed – and what relationship the Magi might now have with all the Emperor's commanders, and not just Erkal and The Arrand.

The notion of scouting ahead, in its own turn, brought another idea into Kellarn's mind.

'The Easterners have few horses,' he said, 'and we have many. Could we not send a mounted troop to skirt round ahead of them, and take the Herghin manor before they can get there? That way we might be able to herd them all back toward Khôrland.'

'Your own war band, do you mean?' returned Erkal. A faint smile flickered across his lips. 'Well, it is true that we had considered sending a force of men to achieve what you suggest. The drawback is that the Easterners have a day's start ahead of us, and perhaps time enough to prepare ambush in the hills this side of Herghin, to prevent our reaching the manor. It is also quite possible that their armies will gather in the hills just east of Fersí village, and not withdraw to the border manors at all. In the light of that chance, the Emperor's commanders considered it unwise to divide our own army's strength for the attempt on Herghin – at least, not until the movements of the enemy are more clearly known.'

'But by then it would be too late,' Kellarn objected.

Erkal sighed and nodded. 'Herghin worries me, too. I had thought to ask the *Aeshta* Orders – the Môshári, and Braedun – whether they might get some knights down there quickly with their arcane powers. I should ask the magi too, when they return; though I hesitate to do so. They tried to defend

Herghin, back before the siege, and suffered dreadful losses through Selghan Herghin's treachery.'

'Yes, Rhysana told me.'

'And then they have suffered further losses, with the siege – as have we all,' said the Earl. 'But whichever way, Collie-dog, I think that you are right. It might be a good idea for you to go down there, if you are willing – though who may go with you is still an open question. Unless the dragon offered you any insight as to what you should do next?'

Kellarn ducked his head, aware of the keen scrutiny of his father's gaze. His silent meeting with the dragon was not something that he felt able to talk about just yet. Besides, it seemed more of a personal matter – a moment of greeting between friends, rather than a council of war.

'We really didn't talk about anything,' he said. 'I don't suppose he'd be that bothered about the way humans fight their battles.'

Even as the words escaped his lips, Kellarn had the feeling that this was not entirely true; that the Father of All Dragons had in fact more than a passing interest in the progress of this war, and in the role which Kellarn himself had to play. But it was true that he could not remember the dragon having offered him any advice on the matter.

Erkal frowned thoughtfully, and opened his mouth to speak; but then appeared to change his mind. And at that moment the door latch flicked open and Kierran of Arrand returned.

'So will the magi be back tonight?' asked Kellarn.

'Not until the morning,' said Erkal. 'Hopefully before we ride out – though if not, I shall have to stay behind here to speak with them before I go.'

'And how will you explain your absence to the Emperor?' Kellarn wondered.

'His Highness will not be riding east with the army,' replied the Earl. 'He will remain here in Arrandin. The official word is that the Easterners are already put to flight, and that he has full confidence in his commanders. But among other reasons, there is of course a certain practicality in the decision. Even an Emperor can be killed by a stray arrow, and Rhydden has left no heir behind him in Lautun.'

'I had also heard,' said Kierran, 'that His Imperial Highness is in a godless sulk, having arrived too late to win any glory in the raising of the siege.'

'Rhydden's mood has not been easy,' Erkal allowed. 'Still, even he ought to understand the need for his commanders to hear the latest reports that the Magi have to offer.'

'And to whom do we talk?' asked Kellarn. 'Rhysana?'

'Possibly,' said Erkal. 'I had in mind the Archmage the Lady Ellen of Raudhar. With Prime Councillor Herusen gone, it will fall to Ellen to hold ready the magical defences of Arrandin, should they be needed again. She should be told of these latest tidings from Mairdun. And Ellen is one of the few magi to have survived the treachery at Herghin manor.'

'Herghin?' said Kierran. 'Is something happening there?'

'We shall have to retake the manor at some stage,' said Erkal carefully.

'Preferably before the Easterner armies can get back there,' said Kellarn. 'We were hoping that the Magi or the *Aeshta* Orders might be able to help.'

'Then let me come with you,' said Kierran eagerly. 'I have my own score to settle with Herghin.'

'Your father The Arrand might have something to say on the matter,' warned Erkal; 'and the Healers, too. But nothing has been decided yet, Kierran; and I had rather you did not mention it outside of this house.'

Kierran rose and bowed. 'Of course, your Grace.'

'But if the Archmage Ellen can not be spared from the city,' said Kellarn, 'who else among the Magi knows Herghin well enough to get us inside the manor house?'

'Only two, that I know of,' said the Earl. 'One is Councillor Salbaar, who at the last report was helping to hold Fersí against the Easterner retreat. The other is Dhûghaúr of Moraan – who now sleeps upstairs, across the hallway from your own rooms. Dhûghaúr is kinsman to Herghin on his mother's side, I think.'

'Dhûghaúr,' echoed Kellarn doubtfully, glancing at Kierran. 'Will he be up to it in time?'

'With the Magi, who knows?' Kierran shrugged.

'For now, we should all get some sleep,' said the Earl; 'and then see what new counsel the dawn may bring. I, for one, am weary. This day has been very long.'

Chapter Two

Kellarn was asleep the moment his head reached the bolster. It seemed only a few minutes later that Kierran was shaking him awake again. The hearth was cold and dark; and through the open window, the first paleness of dawn was already stealing into the eastern sky.

They washed and dressed hurriedly, Kierran helping him on with his mailshirt and buckling his sword into place like a devoted squire. Kellarn still had no certain knowledge of whether he would ride out with the Emperor's army that morning; but with the closeness of war, and the danger hinted at by Father Torren of Mairdun the previous night, he felt more comfortable going armed again about the city. Kierran also wore a mailshirt beneath his Arrand livery.

'So what was the story behind this sword?' asked Kierran, standing up again. 'You still haven't told me.'

'It was a gift from my uncle of Sentai,' Kellarn told him. 'It's been in his treasury for years. There's not much else to tell.'

'Except that you killed the Mughuzhti with it.'

A memory of bright scarlet flame flashed behind Kellarn's eyes. He had struck the Mughuzhti once – and fire had leaped from the sword to devour the chieftain, and run triumphantly up and down the length of the blade.

'Yes,' he said aloud.

He left his star shield standing safely in the corner. But he picked up the bundled Easterner pendant, and stuffed it into his breeches pocket.

The soft glow of lamplight still welled from the chamber on

the far side of the landing, when they went out. Kellarn stopped to peer through the doorway. Mage Councillor Dhûghaúr still slept.

The lower floors of the Dortrean house bristled with activity. Kellarn singled out the knowledgeable Marusâ, and discovered by asking that his father had already gone on ahead to the Arrand palace, to attend the dawn rite in the temple shrine of Hýriel, *Aeshta* Lady of Fire. They might catch him – and the rite – if they hurried. Kellarn wondered if Erkal had slept at all.

The streets of the Old City were as busy as the house, with groups of warriors and horses making their way at varying speeds toward the North Gate. In the smoky torchlight they could make out several in the gold and brown of the imperial livery – or of other Lautun Houses, such as Scaulun and Vaulun – and in the grey and purple of the Arrandin guard. A much smaller number were in the blue of the Braedun Order, or the deep green of the Môshári, or the silver and grey of Kelmaar; and there was a scattering of other household liveries – both Noble and Merchant – and ordinary citizens loading carts and horses with supplies from their own diminished stores. Many waved or saluted, acknowledging either Kierran or Kellarn himself. But Kellarn did not slow his pace to speak with them. There was a tension on the air, a sense of excitement, and of something else which he did not quite recognise – except that he found his own pulse quickening in answer, lending a new urgency to his stride. Kierran's eyes were sparkling in the dim light.

'They have found a sense of purpose,' he told Kellarn quietly. 'It is a relief, after festering under siege for so many days.'

'Relief?' echoed Kellarn. 'For you, perhaps. I'll feel more relieved when the Easterners have gone altogether.'

'But then you'll have nobody left to fight,' Kierran laughed.

'I don't like killing people,' said Kellarn. 'There are enough other evil creatures in the world to keep me busy.'

'Well, the Easterners will provide a few of those, too,' said Kierran.

'From what we heard last night,' said Kellarn, 'so may someone else, nearer to home. Stay watchful, and stay close.'

Rhysana stepped back from the table and the vision faded from its swirling surface, dwindling to a random pattern of tiny coloured stars. She drew a deep breath, warding away the faint rush of vertigo as she turned her perceptions back to the waking world.

'Will they attempt a battle in the field, do you think?' she said aloud.

In her mind's eye she could still glimpse the vision of the Easterner hosts which the spell had shown to her, scattered like corn-cockle in a wide arc across the grassy hills to north and south of the road. It appeared that many of the fleeing warriors had begun to regroup under cover of night; and in the dawn light, at least one clan army and half a dozen other sizeable war bands were preparing to move. The gods alone knew how many smaller groups and lone survivors now lurked among the shadowed hills.

The Archmage Morvaan took another bite from his buttered muffin, and chewed the question over.

'It is hard to see what the Easterners might hope to gain from it, at this time,' he said.

'Honour in the face of defeat?' suggested Rhysana. 'And today is the dark of the moon, when the *Aeshta* Orders feared that the strength of the Easterner priests would be at its most dangerous.'

'Yes, not the most auspicious day for our armies to set out,' Morvaan sighed. 'But still, we know that many of their priests and wizards are now dead; and even if they could defeat our armies in the field, they have not the strength to come back and take Arrandin so soon. I think that the Easterners will attempt to fall back to a place more suited for defence. Whether the Emperor's commanders will seek to engage them in the field is, thankfully, not our decision.'

He grinned at her reassuringly from behind his beard, and popped the rest of the muffin into his mouth.

Rhysana managed a faint smile, in spite of herself, and moved away, stretching her legs in a gentle walk down the long gallery which had been set aside for the Council's use within the Arrand palace. By the time that she had returned to the city that morning, the dawn rites were over and the Emperor's meeting with the senior war leaders of the Six Kingdoms was already well under way. She supposed that they would soon be finished. Even had she been minded to go down there, Rhysana doubted that she would have been let inside. The Archmage Ellen had attended – so Morvaan had told her – as the senior mage now responsible for the defence of Arrandin; and High Councillor Ferghaal of Braedun, as representative of those magi who would ride east; and so had the Imperial Counsellor, the Archmage Merrech.

In his own way, Merrech posed a more personal threat to Rhysana than anything the Easterners might have to offer. She had found herself at odds with both him and the Emperor Rhydden, in their games of power and malice, on several occasions over the past few years; and although she had more or less made her peace with Rhydden, the ancient, hooded Archmage would forever remain an unknown quantity and her most dangerous adversary. Morvaan's main purpose in waiting to meet her, here in the long gallery, had been to warn her that the Emperor and his Archmage were to stay behind in Arrandin, and would not be riding to war.

The news had not improved Rhysana's morning. She had already had to say goodbye to Torkhaal, and he had gone away with Haldrin of Dârghûn, Herusen's heir, and Gravhan of Môshári, to join the armies outside the city as they prepared to ride east. Morvaan himself would soon be joining them, and so would Erkal Dortrean; and with Herusen now gone, Rhysana was beginning to feel somehow exposed and vulnerable, bereft of close allies. Part of her was minded to leave Arrandin at once, and to return to the Lautun College, or to the Telún manor house and her neglected son. Ellen could always send for her, at need. But that would not be entirely fair on Ellen;

and besides, it seemed to Rhysana to be a rather foolish thing to do. And her instincts told her that something else remained for her to do here, in the city.

'There is still a mist around the Tollund manor house,' she said, returning to the matter of her vision. 'It prevented me from seeing what was happening there.'

'Nothing can get in or out of Tollund, at present,' Morvaan nodded. 'The forest folk are still there. They will keep the Easterners away as long as it suits them, or they see the need. But that does not mean they will make us welcome. Hopefully our armies will have sense enough to leave them alone. In my experience, it does not do to meddle with them.'

'But your daughter is still with them?'

'Corollin? Oh yes,' said Morvaan, smiling fondly. 'But she is known to them, in a way that our imperial warriors are not. She will be safe enough.'

'And Ru?' Rhysana wondered.

'Still there, the last I heard,' Morvaan sighed.

Rhysana nodded. If no one had left Tollund since the forest folk had arrived, then it stood to reason that Hrugaar's body would still be there – unless Corollin had already contrived a funeral pyre for him. Somehow, Rhysana did not think that she had. The riddling words of the priestess Ilumarin of Aranara had sown a seed of doubt – or hope – in her mind. It would not be the first time that someone reported as dead had returned to the waking world, having sojourned with the forest folk or the Fay. And Hrugaar himself had the blood of the Fay in him. There had been something in Ilumarin's voice when she declined to speak of him, some excitement or mystic insight, which Rhysana could not quite grasp. She had thought it best not to mention it to Torkhaal, not just yet, for fear of raising in him a false hope. If a similar notion had occurred to him, he had likewise refrained from speaking of it.

The door from the outer landing was flung open, and a tall man strode in. Rhysana knew him at once for the Lord Bradhor – eldest of The Arrand's three sons, and of slightly broader build than his brothers. He was clad in mail beneath a surcoat of purple and silver, and his face was gathering thunder. She dropped him a courtesy, in spite of the intrusion, since this was his father's palace; but he hardly seemed to notice her. He made straight for the Archmage Morvaan.

Behind him the Archmage the Lady Ellen of Raudhar swept in to the gallery, the golden radiance of her magelight trailing in her wake; and behind her came two more armed men, one of them in the Arrand livery, and then the dark-haired beauty of the Chosen Priestess Imarra of Môshári.

'Where were you, my Lord?' Bradhor was saying.

'Not where you imagine that I was needed, it seems,' returned Morvaan mildly.

Imarra closed the door.

'The Emperor has relieved me of my command,' Bradhor burst out. 'He says that until the question of my late wife's treachery is settled, it would be unsuitable for me to lead the Arrand forces in the field.'

'Rhydden was not at his most tactful this morning,' the Archmage Ellen observed.

Rhysana could understand the conflict of angry disappointment and injury in Bradhor's face. Though there might be reason enough in the Emperor's decision, it would be a bitter insult to the pride of House Arrand to suspect them of treason after all their labours to withstand the Easterner siege.

'But no one will blame you for Arisâ's choices, my Lord,' she said.

'The Emperor will,' muttered the other Arrand warrior.

Rhysana glanced at him, and realised that he was Bradhor's younger brother, Kierran; and that the shorter, sandy-haired youth beside him was none other than Kellarn of Dortrean.

'Your own people know how bravely you have fought,' she finished lamely.

'Who has been appointed in your place, my Lord?' asked Morvaan.

'Boldrin of Levrin,' said Bradhor. 'But that is beside the point.'

'Boldrin is a good man,' said Morvaan, 'and well respected in the city. And your father knows and trusts him. It could have gone far worse.'

'But it is unthinkable that an Arrand should not ride out at the head of his own people,' Bradhor protested.

'It is unfortunate, certainly,' Morvaan sighed. 'Yet I doubt I could have prevented it, had I been there. How did your father take it?'

'Badly,' answered Bradhor. 'How else?'

It occurred to Rhysana that Bradhor's own sons might be glad enough to have their father at home, now that their mother had gone. But she was not sure that he would find it comforting to hear so. She hoped that The Arrand would not make himself ill over the matter, nor lose his temper with the Emperor.

'We had better go and see him,' said Morvaan.

He took Lord Bradhor by the arm, and ushered him out of the gallery. No one else moved to follow them.

'High Councillor,' said Ellen, when the door had closed again. 'These two young Lords have asked to speak with us.'

Rhysana looked at them, and smiled. Kierran seemed torn between the desire to follow his brother and his resolve to be here. Kellarn had more the look of a man plagued by an itch in a place that he could not reach to scratch.

'Is it safe to talk here?' Kellarn asked her.

Whether from her own preoccupation, or that of his family of Dortrean, the question put her in mind at once of the Archmage Merrech, and the very real possibility that he might attempt to eavesdrop on their conversation by magic.

'We may seal the chamber, by our arts, my Lord,' Ellen offered, ' to guard against intrusion. Or Holy Mother Imarra may do so, if you prefer.'

'But the use of power might in itself draw attention to us,' Rhysana objected.

'From His Eminence?' Ellen wondered.

Rhysana nodded cautiously. 'There is the antechamber,' she ventured, gesturing to her right.

'That is strictly for Council use,' Ellen demurred.

'Or for those who accompany us,' Rhysana countered. 'It is already warded, and he is unlikely to pass that way for a while. Otherwise we would have to leave the palace – which might again draw attention to us.'

Ellen frowned, but conceded the point. She led the way down the gallery, and through the door concealed in the panelling at the far end. Kellarn and Kierran went behind her, with Rhysana and Imarra following. Beyond lay a short passage in the thickness of the palace walls, ending in a screen of power that shimmered like a waterfall in Ellen's magical light.

'This is a warding archway,' Ellen explained, 'through which only magi of the Council may pass – or those who accompany them. My Lord?'

She took Kierran by the hand and drew him forward, and the two of them seemed to vanish from sight as they passed through the rippling surface. Kellarn gasped.

'You are safe enough, with us,' Rhysana told him gently. She rested her right hand on his shoulder and nudged him forward, and offered her left hand to Imarra for her to follow after.

Rhysana felt the familiar tingle of power brush over her temples and shoulders; and then they were through the open doorway beyond and into the brighter stillness of the formal antechamber.

The square chamber was loftier than the gallery in which they had been, and lined with the pale golden oak so favoured by the Magi of the last few centuries. The floor was a chequer-board of violet and grey tiles – the colours of House Arrand, to whom the surrounding palace belonged – and above and to their left as they entered, the morning light filtered in through the coloured panes of three high windows. Rhysana released her two charges, and headed straight for the nearest of the high-backed chairs beside a small side table. Though

60

she did not feel unwell, she felt the need to sit down for a while – especially if this interview with Kellarn of Dortrean was to take any great length of time. Everyone else remained standing.

'So what is it, Kellarn?' she asked, tugging the folds of her full-skirted blue gown into place, and then gesturing for him to draw nearer. Though Ellen had not said that his errand was specifically to Rhysana herself, she thought that she might present a less formidable prospect than either the Archmage or the priestess in their formal robes. And besides, she was better known to the rest of Kellarn's family.

Kellarn ducked his head, and loped toward her. Kierran followed, protectively close – though that action in itself told how little he understood of the dangers presented by the Magi. Had Rhysana been minded to use her arts against them, it would have made her job far easier to have them standing side by side, rather than a good distance apart. But of course, Rhysana intended no harm toward Kellarn; and perhaps Kierran had sensed that.

'There are a couple of things, my Lady,' said Kellarn awkwardly. 'The first is that there may be a new danger, from within the Emperor's household. Father thought you should know of it.' He related to her the news brought by Torren of Mairdun the previous night.

'And was there no mention of this at the commanders' meeting?' Rhysana demanded, once he had finished. She found that her sense of personal danger had returned – and now not just from the Emperor and his faceless Archmage, but from this new and unknown peril. She wondered whether this was part of what her intuition had told her, that there was still a need for her to be here in Arrandin.

'Of course not,' Ellen snorted. 'Not with Rhydden there.'

'But the Emperor himself might be in danger,' said Imarra.

'Unlikely, I think,' said Ellen. 'For one thing, His Eminence keeps far too close a watch on the imperial household for something like this to escape his attention. For another,

Rhydden himself seems to have taken a personal interest in the victim, this Brother Sarin. If there was aught in Sarin's plight that gave Rhydden cause to fear for his own safety, I think that we should have heard of it by now.'

'Perhaps he delivered Sarin to Mairdun in the hope that they might solve the riddle for him,' Imarra ventured, 'if his own priests could not explain what had happened.'

'Or perhaps he handed Sarin over to them in the belief that they would *not* uncover the truth of it,' Ellen countered. 'Or at least, not so readily as might the senior priests of the *Aeshta* Orders. That might be the case, if His Eminence knew of it.'

'Mairdun did not think that he was responsible, on this occasion,' Rhysana put in.

'It is a long ride from Ellanguan to Arrandin,' said Kierran. 'If this priest, or wizard, or whoever it is, was going to attack the Emperor, surely there would have been plenty of opportunities along the road?'

'Rhydden would have been surrounded by his guards at all times,' said Rhysana, shaking her head. 'Besides, no one really expected that the siege would be broken before the Emperor reached here. It might be that this unknown person was biding their time, waiting until a stroke against the Emperor could cause the greatest confusion among us. I think that we can not rule out the possibility that Rhydden himself may be in danger – even if, as the Archmage Ellen suggests, he has knowledge of what happened to Sarin, and yet does not consider himself to be at risk.'

Kellarn frowned, as if trying to follow the train of Rhysana's thought.

'Does that mean you think we should tell the Emperor, or not?' he asked.

Ellen sighed.

'It means,' said Rhysana, 'that we think Rhydden must already have some knowledge of this matter. If we tell him about it directly, then he will know that we know; and if he does not want us to know, that could make our position doubly dangerous. So it would seem wiser not to tell him.'

'Oh,' said Kellarn.

'But what it also means,' said Rhysana, 'is that we must keep careful watch on the doings of the Emperor's household; and bear in mind that Rhydden himself could be in as much danger as anyone else. And certainly we should inform The Arrand, and perhaps others in command of the defence of the city, as The Arrand may deem suitable.'

'I should like to consult with others of my Order,' said Imarra. 'It may be that we can gain some insight from the gods on this matter.'

'I note that Mairdun chose to inform Dortrean, rather than the Emperor,' said Ellen. 'That might suggest that their wariness of Rhydden's knowledge of this danger is similar to our own.'

'Mairdun have no great love for the Emperor, I think,' said Kellarn.

'No more than many of us,' said Rhysana. 'Yet we still serve him, do we not?'

Kellarn shrugged, and then nodded. No one spoke for several seconds.

'Then there is this,' he said. He drew out a bundle of blue cloth from his pocket, and unwrapped it carefully on the top of the small table.

'I found it on the body of one of the Easterner warriors,' Kellarn explained, 'down in the Lower City. It – reminded me of something. I think it might be important.'

Rhysana shifted round in her seat to study the black and gold pendant that he had brought. Ellen and Imarra also moved closer to see it. To Rhysana's eyes there was no dreadful significance in the geometrical symbol of the lozenge within the square; though she could sense that it had been crafted as a talisman of some kind, and that there was still the whispered energy of some simple spell or dedication laid

63

upon it. But Imarra drew breath sharply, and made a warding gesture against evil with her right hand.

'What is it?' Ellen asked her.

'The symbol of the ancient Enemy,' said Imarra softly. 'Even he whom the Easterners of old named Lo-Khuma, the Radiant.'

'Of course,' said Kellarn, clenching his fist. 'I knew I should have recognised it. But does that mean that his servants are responsible for the war?'

The three women looked at one another. Rhysana nodded for Imarra to answer.

'We had cause to believe that his influence was at work,' said the priestess carefully, 'and this pendant would seem to confirm that – though as yet I have heard of no others like it having been found. You are sure, my Lord Kellarn, that it came from one of the warriors?'

Kellarn closed his eyes, as if searching his memory, and then made a face.

'She seemed to be an ordinary warrior,' he said. 'As far as I could tell.'

Imarra nodded, and turned her green eyes to gaze fixedly at the pendant. Rhysana guessed that she was using her priestly arts to assess the nature of the energies within the spell; or perhaps one of the rare mental gifts possessed by those of Môshári blood, not unlike those used by Torkhaal and Hrugaar. After several moments the priestess stretched out her hand, and held it a few inches above the pendant's surface. Then she smiled and drew her hand away again.

'Well it seems to hold no great power or danger,' she told them. 'But I should like to take it with me, if I may. We might be able to discover a little about the person who wore it, and perhaps – other things. And then it should be unmade.'

Neither Rhysana nor Ellen had objection to this; and so Kellarn bowed and stepped back a pace, so that Imarra might wrap it up again and take it.

'Was there anything else, my Lord?' asked Ellen.

Kellarn shifted nervously from one foot to the other, and exchanged glances with Kierran.

'There is the problem of Herghin,' he said.

Ellen's handsome face went a shade paler, and she remained very still. Rhysana felt an answering chill in the hollow of her stomach. She was grateful to be sitting down. Of all the strokes of the war, the horror and failure of their attempt to save the Herghin manor had been one of the hardest for the Magi to bear.

'I'm sorry even to mention it,' said Kellarn awkwardly. 'But Father thinks that there is a real danger that the Easterners may split their armies between the Khôrland and Herghin manors; and we have not the strength to attack both.'

'The question was raised in the commanders' meeting,' said Ellen. 'It was suggested that a small troop of men ride south through Tormal lands and attempt to secure the manor house before the Easterners can reach there.'

'Yes,' said Kellarn. 'But time is short. And if they are ambushed in the hills along the way, the delay could prove our undoing.'

'So what are you suggesting, Kellarn?' asked Rhysana. She could already guess at his answer.

'I think that perhaps I should go to Herghin,' said Kellarn. 'Father agrees with me. I should be of more use there than with the main host of the army, anyway. And yes, I could simply take a small band of horsemen and ride ahead through the hills. But we were hoping that some of the Magi, or perhaps the *Aeshta* Orders, might be able to help us. Not just to get there more quickly, but to get us inside the manor house, to take it by surprise. And of course, we would probably need your help there anyway, if the Easterners have wizards or priests with them.'

Rhysana nodded cautiously. Though it was more or less the answer that she had expected, she still found herself at a loss to reply. Ellen offered no immediate help. Again, they both looked to Imarra to speak first.

'I dare say, my Lord,' said the priestess, 'that you will find many from the Greater Orders amongst the Emperor's army – whether Môshári, Braedun or Kelmaar – who would be willing to ride with you; and no doubt their senior leaders would release them, unless their conscience before the gods advised against it. Yet to use our gifts to speed your journey to Herghin, or to gain entry to the manor house, would only serve to increase your peril. For to do so, we should have to lead you through other Realms which border the waking world of human life; and it is from those same Realms that the Easterners draw their power, and summon creatures against us. So far from gaining you the advantage of surprise, we should but draw the enemy's attention toward you and make the battle more deadly. For sudden assault, the arts of the Magi might serve you better.'

Rhysana glanced at Ellen again. The Archmage shook her head, almost imperceptibly. Kellarn and Kierran stood between them, waiting.

'There are a few magi who ride out with the Emperor's army this morning,' Rhysana told them. 'Among them my husband Torkhaal, and the Archmage Morvaan. Some of them may be willing to go with you; and any mage councillor brought within sight of the Herghin manor house should be able to make the magical *leap* to carry a few warriors inside. But we can only carry a few warriors in a single *leap*, not an entire war band.'

'I only need a few,' Kellarn assured her.

'Yet that would still require you to risk the journey through the hills,' she reminded him. 'And although we could use our arts to grant you speed, and some measure of concealment from their sentries, that would be of little help if the Easterners have wizards at the Herghin manor – as seems likely. They would be on watch for just such a use of magical power, and would be forewarned against your arrival.'

'But couldn't you just take us straight there, from here, in your magical *leap*?' he asked.

'There lies the heart of the problem, Kellarn,' Rhysana sighed. 'To make a *leap* anywhere, a mage must have good knowledge of the place whither he or she is going – whether from a previous visit, or by having sufficient description to enable them to envisage it clearly in the mind's eye. And even then, the technique is not without its own perils. After our last attempt, I fear there are now very few among the Council who have enough knowledge of Herghin to take you there.'

Hrugaar would have taken them, she thought, had he been here. Councillor Dhûghaúr might have risked it – poor Dhûghaúr, whose plight she had all but forgotten with the business of the last several hours.

'I have been to Herghin,' said the Archmage Ellen. 'But with Prime Councillor Herusen gone, I regret that I am not free to take you there myself, my Lords. I must remain here for the defence of Arrandin – the more so, perhaps, in the light of this latest warning from Mairdun.'

'Could you take us there, and then come straight back?' asked Kierran.

'What, and cut off your means of retreat, my Lord?' Ellen replied. 'I should consider that most unwise. Besides, if any magi can be spared – or persuaded – to go with you at all, you will probably have need of their help against the magic of the Easterners. And probably the help of a few greater priests, too. I do not doubt your bravery my Lords, nor the sincerity of your intent. But this request should more properly be addressed to High Councillor Ferghaal or to the Archmage Morvaan, who are the senior magi working with the army commanders riding east.'

She stalked away across the chequered floor, her silken robes swishing loudly with the swiftness of her gait, and sat herself down upon another of the formal high-backed chairs.

Rhysana looked at the two young men with sympathy. Kierran had grown a little pale at Ellen's outburst, and Kellarn had the look of a rebellious puppy who did not quite understand what he might have been doing wrong. Neither of them, she thought, would have accused Ellen of being afraid. Yet perhaps they did not realise, as Rhysana did, that Ellen's irritation sprang more from a sense of personal frustration. The Archmage had been unable to save Herghin before, having been confounded by treachery. Nor was she free to return there now, to right that wrong; being obliged to remain here in Arrandin, and responsible for the magical defence of the city.

Considering the problem from Kellarn's point of view, however, Rhysana could understand Dortrean's reluctance to be seen openly soliciting help from the Magi and the *Aeshta* Orders in front of the Emperor's commanders. The Emperor Rhydden would undoubtedly be suspicious, even jealous, of such an alliance, given the traditional antipathy between Dortrean and the Council; and especially so close on the heels of Erkal's apparent truce with the Magi for the sake of the defence of Arrandin. It seemed that neither Erkal nor Ferghaal of Braedun had dared to suggest it during the course of the commanders' meeting. Instead, Kellarn had come here in secret; and Rhysana guessed that he wished his errand to Herghin to remain secret also.

'Rhysana,' Kellarn began.

'Yes,' she said, forestalling him. 'Now that your request is known to us, we shall see what help from the Council may be found.'

'Councillor Salbaar was one of those who escaped Herghin, I believe?' ventured Imarra.

'He was,' said Rhysana. 'But at the last report he was in Fersí village. Even if he were willing – and able – to go with Kellarn, it might take too long to find him. Morvaan might be able to reach him, I suppose.'

Had Herusen been here, she thought, he could have used his authority as Prime Councillor to summon Salbaar at once. But for now they had no Prime Councillor. And since Fersí was effectively in the middle of a battlefield, she was not sure that even Morvaan would risk the *leap* there to find Salbaar and bring him back.

'The Lady Lorellin Herghin of Arrand is still in the palace,' said Kierran. 'She must know the manor house better than anyone else. I am sure that she would be willing to help us regain Herghin, by telling the Magi what they need to know.'

'If it can help her slip the noose of treason,' said Ellen, 'I am sure that she will. But I doubt that the Lady Lorellin will be allowed to leave the palace. We shall have to catch the Archmage Morvaan before he goes, so that he can gather the information from her and relay it to whoever needs it. And I shall convey to him my own scant knowledge of the manor house, of course.' She sighed and stood up again.

'I shall send word to Gravhan at once,' Imarra offered. 'He should be with the other commanders of our Order by now, and Torkhaal is with him. Perhaps they can find some suitable people for this errand, before the armies set out.'

'There are few enough magi out there to choose from,' said Ellen. 'You are certain, my Lord Kellarn, that you do not wish to take your band of horsemen with you also, and ride south as the Emperor's commanders proposed?'

'Quite certain, thank you,' Kellarn answered. 'I have drawn rather too much attention to myself, of late. I should like to keep this errand as secret as possible.'

'There is also Councillor Dhûghaúr,' said Kierran, as they prepared to leave. 'He was awake last night.'

'Dhûghaúr is awake?' cried Rhysana. 'How is he?'

'What have you told him?' Ellen demanded.

'He was awake last night,' Kierran repeated. 'He was still sleeping this morning, when we left him. In the Dortrean house. And he knows only that the siege is ended. I thought that the rest was best left coming from you.'

'Thank you, Kierran,' said Rhysana. 'I shall go to him directly.'

'He may want to go to Herghin, if he hears of this,' warned Ellen; 'whether he has the strength to do so or not. I doubt the wisdom of telling him all, just yet, High Councillor.'

'Well, let us see how much he has recovered,' said Rhysana.

* * *

69

The Emperor Rhydden brushed the fumbling attendant aside and strode across the robing room.

'This business with Bradhor is a mess,' he said, studying his reflection in the tall mirror. 'The whole city is a mess.'

The young squire followed after him, endeavouring to arrange the heavy cloak correctly about the Emperor's shoulders. The cloak was black, but lined with cloth of gold, blending with the golden surcoat over his long mailshirt of black steel; and it was fastened with a golden brooch in the shape of a many-rayed star, a handspan across, set with a rose-cut yellow diamond. A short sword, more ceremonial than practical, hung poised at his hip on a white leather baldric.

'The siege has taken a heavy toll, Sire,' the Lord Priest Môrghran of Fâghsul reminded him.

'We are hardly ignorant of the fact,' Rhydden snapped.

'Perhaps His Highness should have the mail coif up, rather than cast back?' ventured the silken voice of the Archmage Merrech.

'The cost of this sudden war has proved strain enough on our imperial coffers,' Rhydden continued; 'and if the Southers do not stay off our backs, we are all like to be half starved by harvest time. That old fool The Arrand had better not expect his Emperor to pay for the repair of his city. The knights of Braedun can help him foot the bill – and the Council of Magi, perhaps. They were the ones who took charge of the defence of Arrandin.'

'Some small contribution might be wise, Sire,' said the Archmage, 'as a token of His Highness' largesse.'

Rhydden snorted.

'They did, after all, hold the city on His Highness' behalf.'

'And shall they be wanting medals and ribands next?' the Emperor demanded.

'The idea of some form of recognition has been mooted,' said Môrghran.

'And how are we expected to fund the casting of medals?' said Rhydden.

'You could always melt down the gold from that Souther ship held in the Ellanguan harbours,' said Môrghran helpfully.

'We could,' Rhydden smiled. 'But we had other plans in mind for that. No, we consider that a title of honour should be recognition enough. *Defender of Arrandin*, perhaps; to be conferred on all those who played a significant part in the city's defence. The title will mean more to them than any impressed coin.

'The coif stays down,' he added, as the young squire moved away. 'The troops will recognise us the more readily without it; and we are only going out to see them off, not to ride with them to war.'

'More's the pity,' sighed Môrghran.

'You question our judgement, Lord Priest?' asked Rhydden, with dangerous lightness.

'As a servant of Mighty Fraërigr, Lord of War, Sire,' Môrghran bowed, 'it should of course be my great joy to see my Lord and Emperor ride forth with his host to victory in battle. As matters now stand, I acknowledge His Highness' wisdom in remaining here, and letting the success of his commanders bring him glory.'

'Neatly dodged,' the Emperor nodded. 'Besides, Counsellor, we shall be hot enough beneath the weight of all this gear. The tightness of cap and coif would be as intolerable as it is unnecessary. Our crown, Zhiraún.'

The squire bowed, and hurried away across the tiled floor to where two older members of the household held ready the imperial jewel casket.

Rhydden picked up a fluted goblet of finest Arrandin glass from the marble shelf beside the mirror; twirled it lightly between his fingers, and then opened his hand to let it fall and shatter.

'For so much damage, at least, we shall make reparation to The Arrand,' he smiled. 'Now about this business with Bradhor. Shall we find him complicit with his wife in treason?'

71

'The man is a dullard, Sire,' said Môrghran. 'It is not hard to imagine that Arisâ would be drawn away to a liaison with a more colourful partner in Tollund's cousin. Nor that she should then pull the apron over her husband's eyes, to keep him ignorant of the deception.'

'But did his dullness cost us Tollund?' asked Rhydden. 'Or his negligence? Was Arisâ simply led astray by the treason of Garthran of Tollund, or did she actively encourage it? She was ever a headstrong woman.'

The squire Zhiraún came forward with Rhydden's crown – one of the older, less elaborate crowns from the treasuries of the imperial palace; a simple double circlet of yellow gold, set about with six round cabochon diamonds like pale circling moons. The Emperor received the circlet and placed it upon his own head; and then watched in the mirror while Zhiraún combed his mane of ebon hair into place over the folded mail coif with its soft leather lining.

'One might also wonder about Arisâ's brother, Lord Hardhen of Levrin,' said Môrghran.

'Hardhen is too timid,' returned the Emperor dismissively. 'Besides, Lord Brodhaur will vouch for him. Would you have us doubt the word of our own Commander in Chief?'

'Brodhaur is his kinsman,' Môrghran muttered, 'and apt to be soft hearted.'

'Lorellin, Herghin's daughter, is also married to one of House Arrand,' put in the Archmage. 'It would seem that the Arrands have an unfortunate gift for embracing treacherous bedfellows.'

'So it would appear, indeed,' said Rhydden. 'Though The Arrand himself may be loyal, we fear that his stewardship may have grown somewhat negligent. We must regain these border manors and learn the full tale of their betrayal before we can place our trust in House Arrand again. And that is another reason, my Lord Priest, why we choose to remain here in Arrandin, to hold the city secure.'

'Dortrean approaches, Sire,' the Archmage murmured.

Rhydden motioned Zhiraún away, and turned to face the tall panelled doors to the outer landing. Môrghran and Merrech bowed as the Earl came in.

'Erkal,' said the Emperor, his face lit by sudden radiance. 'Is the threat from the Easterners truly as great as our commanders fear, do you think?'

'Highness,' said Erkal, bowing low. 'Our strength of horse is good, and our knowledge of the land better. The commanders are right, I think, in that it will be no easy task to sweep the Easterners from the border manors. But with prudent caution, and good intelligence, I hope that we may achieve it without too great a loss of lives.'

'Though the loss of even one life is a grievous price to pay,' said Rhydden.

'Quite so, Sire,' returned the Earl, after slight hesitation. The Emperor, watching him closely, wondered whether some other answer had come first to Erkal's mind.

'The Magi have proved invaluable in the gathering of intelligence,' said Rhydden, signalling for Môrghran to bring his gloves; 'as indeed have the Orders Noble. And you have worked well with them, Dortrean, in securing the defence of this city.'

Erkal bowed his head in thanks.

'Their loyalty to the Six Kingdoms appears to have been proven,' Rhydden went on. 'Nevertheless, one might still question whether that loyalty extends to their Emperor.'

Erkal stiffened as he raised his head. Rhydden maintained a careful semblance of disinterest as he pulled on the first black leather glove.

'You are their Emperor, Sire,' said Erkal steadily. 'Though the Council of Magi may profess neutrality within the internal debates of his Highness' empire, they have shown their determination to defend against the threat from the East. For so much, at least, we must be grateful. The loyalty of the Orders Noble has been acknowledged for centuries; and even though his Highness embraces a faith other than their own, I have seen nothing in the recent conflict to call that loyalty into question.'

Rhydden raised one eyebrow, and reached for the second glove. It was much the answer he would have expected from Erkal Dortrean – grudgingly tolerant of the Magi, steadfast and benevolent toward the heathen Orders. And in the presence of the Archmage Merrech, Erkal would no doubt be doubly careful to control his private thoughts on the subject. There would be no easy way to trip him up, to trick him into unwitting revelation. Yet since his own arrival in Arrandin, Rhydden had the growing conviction that something in Dortrean's relationship with the Magi had changed; or that perhaps there was some alliance forming between the Council and the heathen Orders, of which Erkal himself knew and somehow approved. Though he knew that he could trust Erkal not to deliver any part of the Six Kingdoms into Easterner hands, it occurred to Rhydden that perhaps he should place an even closer watch on the activities of all the Dortrean family.

'Well, as you say,' he said aloud; 'for even so much, we must be grateful.'

He tugged his gloves into place, and slid a jewelled ring on to the outer finger of his left hand. Its single, pale blue gemstone glittered hard and bright against the soft black leather.

'And now,' said Rhydden, 'we must be off. It would not do to keep our armies waiting.'

While Ellen went to intercept the Archmage Morvaan, and Imarra sent word to Gravhan and the Môshári, Rhysana made her way to the Dortrean house to visit Mage Councillor Dhûghaúr. Kellarn and Kierran came with her as far as the stableyard entrance; but Kellarn was anxious to go down to the barrack piers at the western end of the Lower City, to check on the remaining members of his war band. There would doubtless be questions about their deployment; and there were a few whom Kellarn wished to keep in the city, in the hope

74

that they might go with him to Herghin. Kierran insisted on accompanying him.

Rhysana was not at all put out by being left on her own. For one thing, the Dortrean city house and its household servants were known well enough to her from her previous visits to Kellarn's sister Ellaïn. For another, she thought that she would find it easier to talk to Dhûghaúr – if and when he awoke – without other people around.

When she reached the bedchamber, her first impression was that Dhûghaúr was no longer there. The covers of the red canopied bed were thrown back, and upon the long linen chest at the foot of the bed was a wooden tray with what appeared to be the remains of a breakfast meal. Apart from the few chests and chairs, and the hanging mirror and tapestries, the chamber seemed comparatively empty to Rhysana's eyes. The usual paraphernalia and clutter of Ellaïn's two boys, Terrel and Korren, had been tidied away; or else they had taken it with them.

Rhysana was on the point of turning back to question the household girl who had brought her there, when she spied the bundled form of Dhûghaúr curled up in the deep window seat on the far side of the bed. The shutters had been opened and folded back into the recessed reveres, and Dhûghaúr was nestled close in against one panelled side, with his knees hugged up against his chest. He appeared to be gazing up through the latticed panes toward the western sky; though since his face was turned away from her, she could not tell whether his eyes were open. Rhysana quietly dismissed the household girl and closed the door behind her.

'Dhûghaúr?' she called out softly, as she approached him.

The little mage turned his head around toward her. His eyes were clear, and his face less pale than it had been of late. When he realised who his visitor was, he swung his feet down on to the floor and stood to bow in greeting. Rhysana darted forward around the bed, anxious that he might lose his balance and

75

fall. But he seemed quite strong and steady as she helped him sit down again.

'The servants told me about Herusen,' he said.

Rhysana nodded, and perched herself beside him on the cushioned window seat.

Dhûghaúr was wrapped in an ample dressing gown of creamy slub silk, quite different from his accustomed black robes, so that she found it a little difficult to judge how well he might have recovered. His dark hair was tousled, with several tufts sticking out at comical angles; and though his eyes were full of questions, they were clear and calm, with no trace of delirium or panic. Rhysana decided that he had very much the look of a child who had slept long and well, and was now ready to face the day's activity.

'It is good to have you awake again, Dhûghaúr,' she said. 'But should you be up and about, before the Healers have had the chance to see you?'

'I was feeling a little sick, lying there,' he told her. 'Though perhaps a large breakfast had something to do with that.'

He gave her a lop-sided grin, and she smiled in return.

'But what happened with Herusen?' he pressed. 'The woman who brought the breakfast tray told me that he was gone, but that was all that she told me. And how was the siege brought to an end? And if it has ended, why are there so many warriors and horsemen moving up and down the streets?'

Rhysana debated hurriedly in her mind, and decided that so much, at least, she might tell him.

'The last assault on the city was the worst,' she said. 'That was two nights ago now. You have slept for two days and three nights, more or less. In the final assault, the Easterners overran the Lower City; and the defenders were driven back into the barrack piers at the far end. Herusen went down there to help the defence – as did Torkhaal and Gravhan, and Morvaan and Ferghaal of Braedun, and others of the Council.

'With the dawn, yesterday morning, Kellarn of Dortrean arrived, bringing with him two hundred horsemen from the west. They rode in through Lôghur's Gate, and Kellarn himself slew the Mughuzhti, the great chieftain leading the Easterners. But still we were outnumbered.

'Then Herusen used his authority as Prime Councillor to summon a dragon – though it cost him his last strength to do so. The price of the summons was his own life, I think.'

'Herusen summoned a dragon?' gasped Dhûghaúr. 'But surely that is against all Council precepts?'

'Not just any dragon,' Rhysana told him. 'He called upon Ilunâtor, Father of All Dragons. I wish that you could have seen him.' She closed her eyes briefly, remembering the glory and splendour of the dragon's flight against the morning sky. 'Imarra said that it was more like calling upon a messenger of the gods, as would the priests of her Order, rather than the summoning spells of the Easterners. And Ellen seemed to think that the power of the Father of All Dragons is somehow linked to the power that is granted to the Prime Councillor of All Magi – though I have not had the chance to ask her about that.

'Yet however it came about, Dhûghaúr, it seems that Herusen laid down his life to bring the dragon; and when the dragon came, he drove the Easterners from the Lower City and put them to flight back east across the hills. And then the Emperor and his army reached Arrandin, a little later in the day; and even now they are preparing to ride east after the enemy, to drive them from the border manors and make an end of this war.'

Dhûghaúr nodded slowly. Rhysana guessed that for every answer she gave him, half a dozen more questions would spring into his mind.

'Is Torkhaal all right?' he asked her.

'Bless you, Dhûghaúr,' she smiled. 'Yes, he is quite well. And Imarra's Gravhan, too.'

'And Kata Aghaira, and The Arrand, and all the rest?'

'Quite safe,' she nodded. The remembered vision of the skirmish in the palace lobby flickered behind her eyes. 'Aghaira

77

was a little hurt, after you fell, but she was recovering well yesterday. I have not seen her this morning. You saved her life, you know.'

Dhûghaúr ducked his head.

'Lorellin was rescued,' Rhysana added. 'But her kinsman and the rest of the Easterners all perished.'

'That wizard with the spear,' said Dhûghaúr, 'was the one who attacked us at Herghin.'

'The wizard of the Morrinu,' she nodded. 'I know. He is gone now.'

Rhysana was still in two minds about broaching the subject of Kellarn's proposed attempt to regain the Herghin manor. The Archmage Ellen had advised against it; but then Dhûghaúr appeared to have recovered far more than perhaps any of them might have expected. She decided that it could wait a little longer.

Dhûghaúr turned his head away, as if looking around the room.

'Has there been any news from Hrugaar?' he asked. His voice was tight with apprehension and hope.

Rhysana reined in her own emotions, disciplining herself to remain calm. Almost from the moment that they had received word from Morvaan's daughter in Tollund, she had been anxious as to how they should break the news to Dhûghaúr when he awoke. It had been Dhûghaúr's first instinct to go to Tollund with Hrugaar, until they had persuaded him against it; and indeed, ever since Hrugaar had rescued him from the calamity at Herghin manor, Dhûghaúr seemed to have followed him around like a faithful puppy. The loss of Hrugaar – and the sense of guilt, that perhaps he might have saved him by going to Tollund – would not be easy for the little mage to bear.

Added to this was the growing ambivalence in Rhysana's own mind concerning the reported loss of Hrugaar, sparked by the words of the priestess Ilumarin. She did not wish to betray Dhûghaúr with a false hope; yet neither did she wish to plunge him into despair, if the truth might still prove otherwise. It did not help thàt she knew little of Dhûghaúr personally. Though she had worked closely with him in the past few weeks, he had but recently joined the Council; and she did not recall ever having come across him before, either through the Colleges or at Court. She could rely only on instinct to gauge what his reactions might be. And whatever the Archmage Ellen might think, Rhysana knew that they would need Dhûghaúr's help to regain the Herghin manor house.

'Tollund has been taken successfully,' she said aloud. 'Morvaan thinks that the forest folk must have helped in that. But they have woven a mist of power around the manor, to defend it from the Easterners; so at the moment, no further exchange of news with them is possible.'

'But Hrugaar is all right?' Dhûghaúr demanded, looking straight at her.

Rhysana returned his gaze steadily, though she felt the colour rising to her cheeks.

'No,' said Dhûghaúr quietly, before she found words to answer. He shook his head and stood up, moving away from her toward the bed. 'No.'

'The last news of him was not good,' she said gently. 'But there has been no more news from Tollund since yesterday morning, one way or the other.'

'But you fear the worst.'

'No,' said Rhysana, 'I do not fear it. In truth, Dhûghaúr, I know not what to believe just now. So much has been lost, and so much saved. I suppose that I am too stubborn to give up all hope.'

Dhûghaúr nodded, without turning round.

'Perhaps I am too stubborn, too,' he murmured. 'I can not believe that he is gone. Not in my heart.'

It occurred to Rhysana that her husband Torkhaal – having been far closer to Hrugaar than had either Dhûghaúr or herself – had made no such protestation. But she saw no merit in mentioning it; and at that moment a clamour of trumpets burst in upon her thoughts, echoing up from the city street below. She rose to her feet. Dhûghaúr wiped his eyes with the back of his hand, and hurried back to join her.

'What is it?' he asked.

'The Emperor, most probably,' Rhysana told him. 'Use no magic, just yet, in case His Eminence is with him.'

The two of them climbed up to kneel on the cushioned seat, pressing foreheads and noses to the latticed window panes like inquisitive children.

Far below they could make out a handful of figures in the grey and purple of the city guard, clearing a way through the street. Behind them came an honour escort of perhaps a score of Rhydden's imperial household guard, their uniforms a blur of fallow gold in the early morning shadows; and in the midst of the escort rode the Emperor himself, resplendent in sable and gold upon a great black warhorse. A radiance of pale golden light filled the air all around him – no doubt the work of the hooded archmage who rode like a shadow in his wake. As the echoing fanfare died away, the regular beat of a marching drum could be heard.

Behind the imperial escort came the stout figure of The Arrand, borne aloft on his grey litter chair by members of his own household; and behind The Arrand rode Erkal Dortrean and the War priest Môrghran of Fâghsul, and other senior commanders of the Six Kingdoms armies.

Rhysana drew back from the window and stood up again, shaking the folds of her blue skirt back into place. She tapped Dhûghaúr on the arm, signalling for him to withdraw also.

'I had rather not be seen looking out of Dortrean's window,' she explained. Dhûghaúr nodded.

'So the Emperor rides to war,' he said.

'Not unless he has changed his mind,' said Rhysana; 'though with Rhydden, I grant that that is not wholly improbable. But no, Dhûghaúr. The Emperor is to remain here in Arrandin. I suppose that they are only going out to bid the troops farewell.'

'And what are we to do?' he asked.

'Stay here, in Arrandin,' she replied. 'At least, Ellen and I must remain here for a few days, in case the magical defences are required again. And I should rather that Imarra take a look at you, before you make any decision about what you yourself shall do next. In fact, I think that we should get you back to the Môshári house fairly soon. It would not be wise for you to stay here, with Erkal out of the city.'

Dhûghaúr looked up at her in question.

'I seem to have a lot of catching up to do,' he sighed.

'A little,' she smiled. 'But there will be time enough for that later on.'

Chapter Three

As the day wore on, the plans for the retaking of the Herghin manor gradually came together. In response to Imarra's summons, Torkhaal and Gravhan left the gathered armies and slipped quietly back into the city. Down at the western barracks, Kellarn persuaded Takshar of Dregharis to remain with him in Arrandin; and also the Lady Haësella, holy knight of Braedun – though the other priests and knights of Braedun who had joined Kellarn on the ride from Sentai had now rejoined the rest of their Order.

Kellarn had also thought to ask the Lord Hollin of Logray to come with him to Herghin. But Hollin, being kinsman by marriage to the Lord Forval Sentai, had chosen to ride east with all those of Kellarn's war band who would follow him; and in Kellarn's absence, they would provide escort to the Earl of Dortrean. The greater part of the band – warriors of Sentai, Dregharis and the surrounding lands – were thus content to ride with him. Yet though Hollin was fit enough to sit astride a horse, his left ankle still bulged with a bandaged support. How fit he might be for battle remained to be seen.

The one person whom Kellarn would have most wanted at Herghin, but whom he could not have, was his friend Corollin; both because the two of them were so used to working with one another, and because the likely influence of Lo-Khuma behind the Easterner invasion had close bearing on their private quest for the ancient artefact. But there was still no way to send word to her at the Tollund manor house, and it seemed unlikely that she would return to the city in time.

The business of getting the Emperor's armies under way seemed to take a couple of hours, so Kellarn and Kierran were able to watch the latter part of it from the vantage of the Old City wall. The day was fine and clear, and the hillsides to the north of the city were bright with the many colours of the different liveries, and echoing with the songs of the priests and the shouts of the captains, and the cheers from the crowds of citizens who had turned out to wave them on their way. Yet though the mood was more easily festive than it had been earlier in the day, Kellarn still felt a vague sense of disquiet. From their high vantage he could also look back to the wreckage of the Lower City, where craftsmen and guards and ordinary citizens still laboured to patch up the breaches in the northern wall, now that the bodies of the dead had been cleared away; and as the hosts of the Six Kingdoms by turn marched or rode before their mounted Emperor, giving formal salute, there seemed to be a grim shadow across their faces in the morning light. They knew that no clean or easy battle lay waiting for them in the border hills.

Rhysana also watched the departure of the Emperor's armies; though somewhat later in the morning, and from the long gallery in the Arrand palace by the arts of the Archmage Morvaan's observation spell. Their number was scarcely one fourth the size of the Easterner clans that she had watched approach, not so very long ago; though their colours were no less splendid, and somehow more beautiful with the caparisoned horses and all the familiar liveries. Yet a different fear caught at her throat upon this occasion. These were her own countrymen, marching out to meet a danger which she herself had known and faced through all the long days of the siege – but they would be without the protection of the city walls, or the magical defences which Rhysana and her friends had awoken. As her eyes travelled down the length of the line, she saw the blue and silver livery of her brother's people of Telún, clustered behind the rippling silver-greys of the holy knights of the Kelmaar Order. She had quite forgotten that her brother would have come down with the Emperor's armies; and she felt a pang of guilt at not having gone down to see him, or his people, before they left. But she could hardly go chasing after them now.

Toward the rear of the line rode the red and gold figure of Erkal Dortrean, with the warriors of Sentai and Dregharis and some few of the other commanders. Morvaan himself was with them; and Rhysana half fancied that the Archmage turned and glanced at her, and smiled.

She watched as a smaller troop turned south off the road, some two leagues out from Arrandin, on their way to reclaim the Tormal manor. More than five score knights of the Mairdun Order rode that way, their sable livery glittering with silver and gold in the summer sunlight. The Lord Perdhan Tormal went with them, and his personal escort in the copper and purple of his colours; and half a dozen scarlet-clad knights of the Order of Hýriel. The rest of the Emperor's armies carried on, following the long road east.

Rhysana's main purpose in visiting the long gallery, however, was to try to discover more of the movements of the retreating Easterner clans. From what she could tell, the larger groups which she had observed earlier that morning all appeared to be taking a more northerly course, toward Khôrland rather than Herghin. But there was no guarantee that they would hold to that course; and the lands around were so littered with smaller bands of fleeing warriors, that any interpretation of their movements at this stage could be little more than guesswork.

She left the grey-robed Ranzhaar of Stanva to continue monitoring Morvaan's spell, with a reminder that His Eminence the Emperor's Archmage was somewhere about the palace. But so far Merrech had shown no inclination to visit this particular gallery – though he must surely have been aware of its existence. Rhysana could only suppose that he had methods of his own for gathering intelligence for the Emperor.

*   *   *

By the middle afternoon, the raiding party – as Kierran now called them – had begun to gather in Imarra's study within the Môshári house in the Old City of Arrandin. For practical purposes, given the imperial presence within the Arrand palace, this had been agreed upon as the starting point for the raid upon Herghin.

Kellarn was standing by the dark wood table before the empty fireplace, with Kierran at his right hand and Gravhan and Torkhaal upon his left. Together they had sketched out a rough plan of the rooms of the Herghin manor house, drawing on Dhûghaúr's memories from previous visits to his mother's kinsmen there. Dhûghaúr himself was seated at the end of the table, under Torkhaal's watchful eye. Imarra had agreed that the little mage was at least strong enough to advise them in the planning of the raid; though it cost him no small effort, especially with the remembered horror of his last sojourn at Herghin. Kellarn thought that his face was beginning to look pale and drawn again, set against the deep green of his borrowed Môshári tunic.

Standing at the far end of the table from Dhûghaúr were Takshar and Haësella; and seated beside them was the Lord Aerlan of Braedun, Chosen Priest of Telúmachel, *Aeshta* Lord of Air. Aerlan was by far the oldest person present, being well into his fifties and of comfortably ample girth beneath his cassock of deep sky-blue. He was here at Haësella's request; but Kellarn guessed that Aerlan had prevailed upon her to bring him, and that he had also the authority to forbid her taking part in the raid, if he deemed it unwise.

There was also another Lord of the Môshári present, whom Gravhan had introduced as the Mage Councillor Khôraillan. He was fully as tall as Gravhan, but with dark blond hair, and eyes as green as Imarra's; and he was perhaps in his late twenties, and so more of an age with Torkhaal and Rhysana. Khôraillan was seated on a carved faldstool desk at the other end of the room, and seemed to be far more interested in studying the roses and fruit trees of the cloistered garden beyond the tall window. Yet from the few brief questions or comments that he had tossed across to them in the past hour or more, it was clear that no detail of their conversation escaped him.

'I think I should be happier,' said Aerlan of Braedun, 'if we had a better idea of the private chambers of the Herghin family. If the Easterners have leaders of power within the manor, my guess is that that is where you will be most likely to find them.'

'We were hoping to speak with Lorellin Herghin of Arrand, Father,' said Gravhan. 'Unfortunately, the Lady Lorellin is under close guard in the Arrand palace; and the Emperor's men are taking a good deal of interest in her.'

'The Emperor questioned her earlier,' Kierran nodded. 'But it is still my father's palace, and the guards are loyal to him. We hope that it will be possible to reach her tonight. In fact, I think we should try to take her with us, as a guide.'

'Risky,' Kellarn frowned. 'We are too few to provide her with bodyguards.'

'And if Selghan Herghin and his son are both dead,' said Gravhan, 'Lorellin is the next heir, I think.'

'She is Herghin's daughter,' Kierran nodded; 'and that means she can defend herself quite capably. Give her a sword or bow in her hand, and she will acquit herself well.'

'But how shall we get her out, without the Emperor knowing?' asked Haësella.

'One might argue,' said Aerlan, 'that the Emperor *should* be informed of this – given that ultimately the welfare of his own armies is at stake, and the defence of his own empire.'

'His army commanders know,' said Kellarn. 'Or at least, my father does.'

'The Archmage Morvaan knows about it,' said Torkhaal; 'and so do High Councillor Ferghaal and the senior commanders of the Môshári. They will be kept informed of our progress, and will convey that information to the Emperor's commanders at the appropriate time.'

'And then the Emperor will hear of it anyway,' Aerlan returned. 'I accept that Dortrean may be reluctant to be seen working together with the Magi and the Orders in this way. But given his Highness' habitual distrust of us all, might he not be the less suspicious if we deal openly with him beforehand, rather than waiting to present him with tidings of a deed already done?'

There was an awkward silence. Kellarn wondered whether Aerlan had yet heard of Mairdun's news of possible treachery within the imperial household. Since neither Gravhan nor Torkhaal showed inclination to mention it now, he decided to take his cue from them. He realised, almost with surprise, that they were waiting for him to speak.

'Do you think that Rhydden now trusts either Braedun or the Magi the more,' he asked, 'because they defended Arrandin?'

Aerlan pursed his lips as he considered the question, and then spread his hands in a gesture of non-committal.

'Well, I doubt that telling him of this raid beforehand will bring us any new favour,' said Kellarn; 'and I don't want to give him the chance to command me not to go. But if you wish no part of this endeavour, Holy Father, you are free to bow out; and if you feel, in good conscience before the gods, that the Emperor himself should know of this, then you must of course do as you think best.'

Kellarn knew that he might risk much by letting Aerlan go. He could sense Kierran's muscles tensing beside him. Takshar was glancing wide-eyed from Kellarn to Aerlan and back. Haësella's fair face held a hint of secret rebellion.

Had Aerlan been simply a Lord of another House Noble, or one of the Magi, Kellarn's answer might have been different. Or at least, he would have offered him the chance to bow out, but might then have been obliged to detain him in the Môshári house until the raid upon Herghin was complete. He supposed that in giving the priest complete freedom to choose, he was giving the lords of the *Aeshtar* the chance to prevent him, if they would. He also guessed that the Môshári, and perhaps the

Magi, would not approve of laying constraints upon a Chosen Priest of the *Aeshtar*.

The grey oak door opened in the panelled wall behind Dhûghaúr, and Imarra and Rhysana came in bearing a tall jug of cordial and a piled dish of sugar biscuits. The seated Lords rose to their feet in courtesy; but Aerlan showed no sign of leaving.

'You were right about Arrandin, my Lord,' he told Kellarn, sitting himself down again. 'We are not fighting this war simply to win the Emperor's approval; and since His Highness has now entrusted the resolution of the war to his army commanders, I for one am content that at least some of those commanders are aware of your intent. But I should like to go with you, if I may. I think that you might have need of another priest.'

'We would be honoured, Father,' Kellarn nodded. 'Though it is up to the magi how many folk we can take with us.' He turned to Gravhan and Torkhaal for their approval.

'It would be wise,' put in Imarra, glancing up as she poured the cordial into green glass tumblers.

Dhûghaúr wriggled in his high-backed chair. 'But will there be any wizards left at Herghin?' he demanded. 'I mean, the Morrinu wizard was there. But he led the attack in the Arrand palace, with Selghan's son Scardhan of Herghin, and several other wizards and priests; and none of them survived, did they? Perhaps they left only warriors behind.'

'From our divinations,' said Aerlan, 'it would appear that at least one Easterner capable of wielding considerable power remains in the Herghin manor house. Possibly more. There is a shadow surrounding the place, like a veil, preventing us from seeing what else may be there.'

'This the Môshári have seen also,' said Imarra. 'And we have heard that Selghan Herghin has indeed passed into the Realms of the Dead. I am sorry, Dhûghaúr.'

'I tried to turn Morvaan's observation spell to search the hills around Herghin,' said Rhysana, helping herself to another sugar biscuit; 'but I could not find the manor house. The

Archmage Ellen promised to try this afternoon, since she has a clearer idea of what to look for. From what you are saying now, perhaps the Easterners have woven spells around the manor to keep it hidden from our sight. That is a skill of which we know them to be capable.'

'Can those spells prevent us from *leaping* into the manor house?' demanded Khôraillan of Môshári. Rhysana shrugged.

'It is possible,' she allowed. 'We shall not know until we try.'

'We?' growled Torkhaal.

'You, beloved husband,' Rhysana corrected herself. 'I suppose I must stay behind, and behave myself.' She wrinkled her nose at him, and took a bite from her sugar biscuit.

'But who else does this *we* include, my Lord?' asked the curly-haired Takshar.

Kellarn took a sip of the cordial before answering, thankful for the cool sharpness to help clear his head in the crowded room.

'Not counting the magi for the moment,' he began, 'you, myself and Kierran. Gravhan for the Môshári, and Father Aerlan and Haësella for Braedun. That makes six. I agree that we should try to take Lorellin of Herghin with us, if possible; but I should like to take at least one more good warrior.'

'What about Bradhor?' suggested Imarra.

Kierran shook his head. 'He will be more closely watched than Lorellin. Besides, surprise raids are not Bradhor's strong point.'

'And think of his poor children,' objected Rhysana, taking another biscuit. 'They have only just lost their mother. If something should happen to him—'

'Quite,' said Kierran. 'Thalden of Arrand, Lorellin's husband, might have been a better bet; but he has ridden east with Boldrin.'

'Well, one of our Môshári knights could be found,' said Gravhan; 'or perhaps someone suitable from Braedun.'

'Or Hardhen of Levrin, perhaps?' ventured Rhysana. 'He

is kinsman by marriage both to Arrand and the Môshári, is he not? And the shadow of Arisâ's treachery falls upon him also.'

'The aim is to regain Herghin safely, High Councillor,' Khôraillan reminded her; 'not to prove the innocence of those suspected of treason. I believe Hardhen to be a kind and gentle man, and not without skill at arms; yet I would question whether he is the most suitable person for the task before us.'

Kierran hummed his agreement. Kellarn looked to Imarra and Gravhan. He knew too little about Hardhen to make a decision on the matter. Imarra nodded to her husband, as if some hidden exchange had passed between them.

'No,' Gravhan said aloud. 'I think that Rhysana is right. Hardhen may not be the best warrior that we have, but he has been with us throughout the siege; and it was he, I think, who ran to help Lorellin, when her brother and the Easterners brought the battle right in to the Arrand palace. It seems fitting, somehow, that he should come with us to rescue the Herghin manor. At least, we should ask him.'

Kellarn looked around the study. Kierran shrugged. No one raised further objection.

'That brings the tally to eight, then,' said Kellarn. 'Can the magi take so many, High Councillor Rhysana?'

'Torkhaal and Khôraillan have offered to take you,' she said. 'They can learn whither to make the *leap* from Dhûghaúr's memories, or from the Archmage Ellen's. But a third mage will be needed, I think, if you are all to travel at the same time. There are a few remaining in the city, whom we could ask – Telghraan, perhaps, who is helping to repair the Lower City walls, or Ranzhaar of Stanva.'

'Why not me?' asked Dhûghaúr, his voice fading to a squeak with indignation.

'You know perfectly well why not,' returned Rhysana, in a very motherly tone. Kellarn began to grin, but quickly stifled it when she glared at him.

'I can do it,' said Dhûghaúr, finding his voice again. 'And I know the Herghin manor.'

Rhysana frowned, and turned to Imarra for support.

'Let us see how you are when you have rested, Dhûghaúr,' said the priestess gently. 'But I think that we should have another mage held in readiness, just in case you are not up to it.'

'And when do we leave?' asked Aerlan of Braedun.

'Tomorrow, at first light,' answered Imarra. 'By then the power of the Dark Moon will have passed, and the New Moon will be hastening toward her first rising.'

'But the Dark of the Moon is tonight,' said Haësella quietly. 'That does not bode well for our armies on the road.'

'Perhaps not,' said Imarra. 'But the strength of the Easterner priests was broken with the raising of the siege; and so we may hope, and pray, that no great harm will now befall us.'

Aerlan and Haësella went away soon after that, and Rhysana took Kierran to the Arrand palace. Kellarn went back to the Dortrean house to fetch the rest of his gear, since he would be staying the night with the Môshári in readiness for the early start.

The Môshári had prepared a guest chamber for Kellarn and Kierran close to where Rhysana and Torkhaal and the other magi slept, adjoining an upper gallery just above Imarra's study. The room looked down on to the same cloistered garden that could be seen from the study window, but from the western side; and its leaf-green hangings were broidered with flowers and fruits and animals and birds, all worked in threads of silver and gold, shimmering faintly with reflected light in the afternoon shadow.

As the sun marched down toward the hills in the west and the shadows in the garden deepened, Kellarn took his leave of his hosts and retired to his chamber. He opened the two casement windows wide to let in the garden scents and the gentle chatter of the birds; and then he stripped off his gear thankfully, and sat down cross-legged upon the bed in just his breeches, with his great sword in its scarlet sheath balanced across his knees. He looked at it for some time, stroking the soft leather and the smooth crimson jewel of its pommel, and wondering about the prophecy which – so his cousin Faëlla had told him – was written somewhere on the patterned blade. He was still contemplating whether to draw the sword and look for it again when there was a knock at the door, and Kierran came in to join him.

'Any luck?' asked Kellarn, shifting around to lay the sword down on the floor beside the bed.

'Hopefully,' Kierran nodded, looking rather tired. 'We shall find out when the time comes.'

He swept his dark hair back with both hands, and then wandered over toward the windows as he began to pull off his own gear.

'I don't care if the Easterners do come back tonight,' he announced. 'I am *not* sleeping in this stuff. Not in this heat.'

Kellarn lay on his stomach across the bed, resting his chin upon his folded arms. With Kierran's return the planned attack on Herghin seemed somehow closer, more real than when they had discussed it earlier. A coolness rippled through his stomach that had nothing to do with the quilted silk of the counterpane beneath.

'Did you ever feel,' he asked, 'that you were about to do something very stupid?'

'Oh, often,' laughed Kierran. 'It comes of being the youngest of three – just like you.'

'No, but seriously,' said Kellarn.

'No,' said Kierran. 'I think it very dangerous; and I think I am more scared than I would ever let on, even to myself. But it is too important to be stupid. And Rhysana and the Môshári would not be supporting us if it were, now would they?'

'I suppose so,' said Kellarn.

'Then try to get some rest,' Kierran told him.

Kellarn stuck his tongue out, but then obediently wriggled

round on the bed to lie flat on his back with his head on the bolster. Kierran moved around quietly, arranging his own clothes and Kellarn's in folded piles, and then laying out their mailshirts one on top of the other across the large linen chest, since there was no stand to hang them properly. Then he lay down on the other side of the bed.

But though the day had been long and he had had little rest the night before, Kellarn found it impossible to get to sleep. The sky was still bright outside; and there was the lingering heat and noise of the city, and the restlessness of waiting for battle. His mind was still running over the plans of the Herghin manor house, and the many unknown dangers that they might face there. It was not that he feared death – the painful moments of dying, perhaps, but not the peace which lay beyond. If anything, he feared the responsibility of leading others to their death; Kierran, Torkhaal, Takshar or little Dhûghaúr. He knew that he had faced it before, when he had brought his war band from the coast to beleaguered Arrandin. But then, perhaps, he had not realised the scale and horror of the war into which they were riding; nor had he yet walked in the streets of the Lower City among the piles of butchered dead. The blood price for the Herghin manor might be high.

He shifted and turned, and wriggled on the bed, until at last Kierran slapped his leg and told him to lie still. Kellarn slapped him back; and then they fell into a tickling match, which left them both overheated and breathless, but also more simply tired and relaxed. And then they fell asleep side by side, comfortable in their own company.

Kellarn woke once, at some time in the middle night. The air in the chamber had turned cold, and Kierran had pulled the edges of the quilted counterpane up over them, and wrapped his left arm over and around Kellarn, hugging him close. Kellarn found his face pressed hard in against Kierran's chest. Faint in the distance he thought he could hear the sound of thunder; though the pulse of a heartbeat sounding in his ears

– whether his own or Kierran's he could not tell – made it difficult to be certain. Their feet were tangled together, and his arms and neck felt cramped; but he was reluctant to wake Kierran to move him.

After several moments of increasing discomfort, he shyly slipped his right arm around Kierran's bare back, and shifted a little more on to his side. Kierran stirred and murmured in his sleep, and curled more fully but more gently around him. Kellarn smiled to himself in the darkness, and resigned himself to being held for the rest of the night. He kissed Kierran's chest where it brushed the edge of his lips, and then drifted back to sleep.

When he woke again the night had grown old, and Kierran was already gone. The summer stars shone bright in the heavens above the sleeping city, and a small lamp had been left burning low in the adjoining bath chamber. Kellarn blushed in the dim light, wondering what his friend had thought when he awoke with him in his arms. But then all the other thoughts of the war began to stir again in his head; so he crawled to the edge of the bed, still cocooned in the warm quilt, and turned his attention to the business of getting ready for battle.

By the time that Gravhan knocked on the door to see if he was stirring, Kellarn was already washed and dressed and sitting on the end of the bed again to pull on his boots. During the course of his ablutions, another complication to the coming mission had muscled its way in to his mind.

'Gravhan,' he asked, before the knight had the chance to slip away; 'assuming we take Herghin, will we have the strength to hold the manor house against another Easterner attack?'

Gravhan shook his head, and smiled.

'Once the manor house is secured, my Lord,' he replied, 'it will be easier to bring more warriors there if they are needed – either from Arrandin or from among the hosts of the *Aeshta* Orders with the Emperor's army. The difficult part is to gain the first foothold there, and to remove the enemies who now hold it against us. That is our task –

and more than enough for us to think about this morning.'

Gravhan smiled again, and Kellarn found himself smiling back at him. He was not wholly convinced by Gravhan's argument; but at least it seemed that the Môshári had taken thought about the matter.

'Food out here if you want it,' said the knight. He went away, leaving Kellarn alone.

Kellarn was not sure that he did want it. But once he had armed himself and buckled his great sword into place at his side, he thought that he might prefer the company instead of festering here by himself. He picked up the star shield of Heruvor, took a last glance around the room, and went out into the gallery.

Rhysana and Torkhaal were there before him – Rhysana looking calm and serene in her indigo high councillor's robes, Torkhaal clad in tunic and breeches of Môshári green, and cradling a black staff with familiar ease at his left side. Dhûghaúr was standing a little apart from them, in simple robes of dark green and black. He was holding a bowl of steaming porridge in one hand, and using the other hand to draw patterns in it with a silver spoon. He looked steady enough, and doggedly determined. Kellarn supposed that with his previous experience at Herghin, Dhûghaúr would have found this mission daunting even had he not been so recently unwell.

The magi greeted him warmly, though with few words spoken. Rhysana glided forward noiselessly and drew Kellarn along the lamplit gallery to a sideboard stacked with plenty of breakfast fare – soft rolls and pastries, dried fruits and cured meats and cheeses, a tall ewer filled with pungent hot tea, and an enormous covered dish of the creamy porridge that Dhûghaúr was eating. It struck Kellarn that there was far too much for just the magi and himself, even allowing for Rhysana's increased appetite. But then there was a clatter of arms at the far end of the gallery, and their other companions began to arrive.

Takshar came first, loping amiably across the boarded floor to pummel Kellarn in greeting. Behind him came Father Aerlan and Haësella with another knight of their Order – a taller, fairer version of Haësella, with bow and quiver slung across her back, and a mace of dull steel hanging ready at her belt. They introduced her as the Lady Tirilanna of Braedun, who had come down from Ellanguan with the Emperor's armies, and had yet to take active part in this war against the Easterners. With them also was Khôraillan of Môshári, dressed much the same as Torkhaal, but with a steel-shod staff of golden oak. There was no sign of Kierran, or any of his kinsmen from the Arrand palace.

Rhysana ladled porridge for Kellarn, decorating it with a threefold spiral pattern of acacia scented honey; and then she withdrew to allow the other warriors access to the sideboard. Kellarn looked at the bowl of porridge, and found that his appetite had returned after all; or perhaps the eagerness of his fellow warriors was catching.

Before long the Chosen Priestess Imarra came and summoned them to follow her. She led them down the stone stairs toward the study, but then turned aside and took them round through deserted hallways and into a temple shrine of the *Aeshta* Lords of Earth. The floor of the shrine was paved in squared flags of green and black marble, and the walls were filled with golden images of winged lions, leaping and circling and dancing in the dim candlelight against a timeless twilit meadow.

Kierran was there to meet them, and with him were Hardhen of Levrin and Lorellin Herghin of Arrand. The slender Lorellin was dressed in the borrowed arms of an Arrand guard, and her auburn hair was concealed beneath a light cap helm adorned with a silver circlet. Had she smiled, Kellarn might have thought her the more attractive; but her cold face was chiselled with determination, and the soft light of the temple shrine turned hard in her shadowed eyes.

Hardhen was also clad in the borrowed purple and grey of the Arrand guard, but his mailshirt and helm were of the finest crafted grey steel, which Kellarn guessed must be his own. His face was as sombre as Lorellin's, but more gentle; and indeed, he smiled and bowed to Kellarn with genuine warmth. Leaning upon his arm, and whispering in his ear as they entered, was a fair-haired young woman wrapped in a white cloak, whom Kellarn later discovered to be the Lady Lienna Môshári of Levrin, Hardhen's wife.

Standing farther back, upon the far side of the temple shrine, were Gravhan of Môshári and the Archmage Ellen. There was also a much older man beside them, with grizzled hair and grey mage councillor's robes. Kellarn remembered him to be Ranzhaar of Stanva – a mage of noble blood, with a reputation for severity and quick temper. He supposed that Ranzhaar was here in case he might be needed to stand in for Dhûghaúr. Fortunately, Dhûghaúr still seemed determined not to be left behind.

Gravhan came forward and called them together, and went over the proposed plan for the raid. Though Kellarn had right of precedence by Blood Noble, and though it had been more or less his idea in the first place, he was content to defer to the more experienced Môshári commander.

The plan itself was unchanged from what they had agreed upon the previous afternoon, and was almost frighteningly simple. The magi would take them straight to the tower where Dhûghaúr and his colleagues had suffered defeat. Once the tower was secured, they would attempt to strike directly at the Easterner leaders, whom they guessed would be in the Herghin family rooms in the southwest part of the manor house. When those leaders were safely removed from the game – and thus, hopefully, any recourse of the enemy to magic, or the summoning of terrible creatures from other Realms – they could worry about dealing with the remaining garrison. But as to what manner or strength of force they might encounter, neither the priests nor the magi could offer them further insight than they already had.

The Archmage Ellen told them that the Emperor's army

seemed to have suffered a few minor skirmish raids during the course of the night, but with no evidence of great use of power. The more sobering news was that the village of Fersí was now burning – though at least some of the villagers and men of Holleth appeared to have survived, and were labouring to fight the flames. There were no tidings of Mage Councillor Salbaar. Yet as far as Ellen and Imarra could determine, in their own separate fashions, the main remnants of the Easterner armies had now withdrawn to well over a league beyond Fersí, heading more north and east toward Khôrland.

The raiding party began to take up their places on the marble floor, preparing to depart. Kellarn wished that he had had the presence of mind to dash to the *garderobe* before coming downstairs, but it was too late to worry about that now. Rhysana and Lienna kissed their husbands goodbye, and then moved away with Ellen and Councillor Ranzhaar.

The three magi – Torkhaal, Khôraillan and Dhûghaúr – stood together in the centre of the temple floor, preparing to work their spell. Guided by Imarra, the others formed a circle around them, linking hands and facing outwards. Kellarn found himself flanked by Gravhan and Kierran, with Torkhaal's hand resting on his right shoulder. To Gravhan's left were Hardhen, Lorellin and Takshar; and to Kierran's right the Chosen Priest Aerlan stood between the two knights of Braedun, Tirilanna and Haësella.

Imarra stepped back from the circle and lifted her arms in prayer. A light of green and gold welled up around them as she called upon the blessings of the Lords of Earth; a light like a summer meadow, or the like the first new leaves of spring unfurling to greet the sun. Kellarn glanced at Imarra, but her gaze was turned above and beyond him, focused on her own mystic vision. And by some trick of the light – or some virtue of the priestess' blessing – he half fancied that the golden lions upon the walls stirred and turned their heads toward him.

The fair-haired Lienna had also raised her hands in prayer. Ellen and Ranzhaar stood composed, waiting. But Rhysana held her hands clasped before her; and though her face was calm and serene as ever, there was a tension in her poise as if she were preparing herself to go with them to Herghin.

'There is despair in the heart of hope,' recited Imarra, 'and hope in the heart of despair. Even in the waking world, let us walk in the will of the gods.'

Kellarn turned his attention back to her once more. Her face shone, and the ribands of her braided hair seemed to ripple with living flame.

It occurred to him in that moment that she had spoken no further of the pendant which he had found. But even as the thought came to him, the light was swallowed up in darkness, and the floor fell away beneath his feet; and the golden lions of the Môshári flew up and shrank to tiny balls of light, and passed like shooting stars above his head.

When Kellarn regained his balance a heartbeat later, Imarra and the temple were gone. Instead, he found himself in a plain vaulted chamber, with patterned tiles of red and yellow upon the floor; and Gravhan and Kierran held him on either side.

Erkal Dortrean flexed stiffened fingers within his gloves, and stared hard into the darkness. Above and behind him, the bright stars of the summer night shone clear beyond the tawny glow of campfires and drifting plumes of smoke. Ahead, toward the east, the lower margin of the heavens fell empty, swallowed into a broad span of lightless cloud. In the northeast, a dull smear of red above the shrouded hills warned of battle and flame. But though he could feel the stirring of dawn within his bones, no sight of it had yet reached the waking world.

Already half the camp was moving around him, with shadowed figures picking their way between the tents or moving quietly about the fires, and the grooms whispering as they began to walk the horses and get them ready for their long day. The latest attack had come barely half an hour since; and though it had been vain and short lived, like the other raids that night it had served its purpose. The Lautun armies were disturbed and little rested. They would be weary again long before the new day was done.

Erkal had discarded the thought of trying to sleep now. High Councillor Ferghaal of Braedun had told him the previous evening of the plans for the raid on the Herghin manor house – though how he had heard them, a day's march out from Arrandin, the Earl thought it best not to ask. There were many unfriendly ears among the gathered armies; and anything more than a passing greeting between commanders was also apt to be observed with interest by curious warriors, on the lookout for tidings of approaching battle. So now Erkal stood gazing into the darkness, tugging his cloak closer around him against the chill breeze from the mountains, and wondering into what dangers he might have urged his younger son.

'Soon,' said a gentle voice at his shoulder.

Erkal gave a start, and turned. The kindly face of Brodhaur Levrin, Commander in Chief of the Imperial Household Guard, smiled back at him in the ruddy firelight.

'The dawn will come soon,' said Brodhaur, wrapping his own purple and white cloak about him. 'But our greater trial will come later, I think. Perhaps the day after tomorrow – or today, now, as I should call it. By then we shall be bone weary.'

'It may come sooner,' said Erkal, pointing to the glow in the northeast. 'Does not Fersí lie that way?'

'Fersí offers them no great vantage for defence,' said Brodhaur. 'They will torch the village and keep moving.

'Still,' he went on; 'you, my friend, have had trials enough of late, without tagging along here looking for more.'

'Where the Emperor commands, I must go,' returned Erkal, his voice carefully neutral.

'This is me, Dortrean,' Brodhaur chuckled. 'Somehow I think that you would be here anyway, whether Rhydden asked it or no. The need of the Six Kingdoms, and all that.'

'Perhaps so,' Erkal allowed. 'Thrashing the Easterners' hides may win this present war. But given the size and power of the Domains, we have to sweeten them thereafter to make sure that they hold the peace. I am told I have some small gift for that sort of task.'

'Hence the Easterner woman you have with you,' said Brodhaur. 'I hear that she is a rare beauty.'

Erkal shook his head, smiling fondly.

'Now we are coming to it, my Lord,' he said. 'So this is the true reason for your visit, I guess? Well, Kata Aghaira is a rare woman, I grant you. But she is no camp follower to please a commander's fancy. She is a great loremaster, and a shrewd judge of men's minds. I need her as my interpreter. The coming battle may be messy, but I need to ensure that the end is cleanly done; and to that end, Aghaira's knowledge and skill in tongues will be invaluable.'

'And does your Lady wife know of this Easterner woman's skills with her tongue?' Brodhaur teased.

'My Countess knows everything,' sighed Erkal; 'as no doubt does your own.'

The Earl of Levrin dropped his gaze. He prodded the trampled turf with one booted foot.

'Your boy did well in Arrandin, I hear,' he said presently. 'I'm sorry he does not ride with us.'

'I asked him to stay behind,' said Erkal.

'Do you fear another attack on the city?' Brodhaur demanded.

Erkal shrugged beneath his cloak. 'From what I have learned of the Easterner wizards, it is not impossible.'

'But how likely?'

'A slender chance,' Erkal allowed. 'Perhaps I fear for my son's safety. What father does not?'

He smiled ruefully, all too aware of the irony of his words. Erkal did not like having to lie to Brodhaur – or at least, having to shuffle him off with half-truths. Though the Earl of Levrin was unquestionably loyal to Lautun, and had been obliged to side with the Emperor against Dortrean on a number of occasions, he and Erkal were of an age and had been good friends for many years. There were simply some questions upon which, by mutual consent, they had agreed to disagree.

As Commander in Chief of the Emperor's forces, Brodhaur had every right to be informed of the planned attempt upon Herghin; and yet – because the loyal Brodhaur would no doubt relay that information to his Emperor – Erkal was reluctant to tell him.

Brodhaur was studying him thoughtfully in the dim firelight.

'I know that Rhydden was a little jealous of your success in Arrandin, at first,' he told Erkal; 'both you and young Kellarn, of course. But His Highness is no fool. He knows that he can trust you, whatever your – differences.'

'I hope so,' said Erkal. 'Yet he trusts others more.'

'Now you sound jealous,' said Brodhaur.

'Not at all,' Erkal replied. 'Indeed, he trusts *you* the more, your Grace; and that gives us all hope in this war.'

Kellarn stepped forward, letting go of Kierran and Gravhan and turning as he reached for his sword. Apart from the twelve members of their small band, the vaulted chamber was empty. The apple-gold light of the Môshári had come with them – fainter now, but more focused around the long blade of Gravhan's drawn sword and the steel-shod staff of Councillor Khôraillan. The rumour of soft footfalls and shifting harness echoed disconcertingly around the close, shadowed walls, and there was the faint sting of incense on the heavy air. Yet as far as he could tell, there was no sound of the Easterners stirring in the manor house hard by.

At Gravhan's signal, Torkhaal and Lorellin moved to keep watch by a stout door in the middle of one wall, which would be the way into the main part of the house. Tirilanna of Braedun was already at the smaller doorway further round to the right, with her bow drawn and an arrow at aim up the narrow stairway beyond.

The other warriors and magi moved into position behind Tirilanna. The Chosen Priest Aerlan was treading a circling path in the middle of the tiled floor, spiralling slowly out toward the walls, and murmuring soft words beneath his breath all the while. A tiny silver censer was swinging from his hand, leaving slender curls of smoke drifting in his wake. Kellarn guessed that Aerlan must have brought the censer already lit from the Môshári shrine.

'It will bring help in the work we do,' Gravhan said softly in Kellarn's ear. 'And make the room a safe haven to fall back to.'

Kellarn nodded. He felt himself a little impatient and anxious at the delay; but then Braedun and the Môshári had been successful military Orders for several centuries, so he had to concede that they most likely knew their own business. He slipped his star shield into place on his left arm, and tested his grip on his great sword; and tried to breathe slowly to steady his beating heart.

It must have been less than a minute before Aerlan joined them – though in reality it felt much longer. There was still no sign that their presence in the manor had been discovered. Gravhan led the way up the narrow stair, his sword blade glittering in the darkness, with Kellarn close behind him. Tirilanna came next, her bow still ready in her hand; and then Dhûghaúr and Aerlan, Takshar and the rest.

The stair went up along the line of the tower wall, and then turned right at the top into the squared living chamber where so many of the Magi had been betrayed to their deaths. To Kellarn's relief, there were now no bodies to be seen; but all other signs of battle still remained. The long table and most of the carved chairs lay overturned, and the flagged stone floor was stained in many places with the dark shadows of spilt blood, and strewn with shattered glass and scattered flagons and platters, and the dried and mouldering refuse of the magi's long unfinished meal. The tall windows were sealed away behind closed wooden shutters and the air was stale and rank, with something of the reek of a muddy harbour at low tide beneath the summer sun.

Gravhan and Tirilanna moved quickly, picking their way with skilful ease between the glass and debris that could betray them with unwanted noise. Kellarn paused to check on Dhûghaúr as he came through. He could sense that the little mage was already bracing himself against the shock, and knew that it had taken no small amount of bravery for him to return here. If Dhûghaúr was relieved – as surely he must have been, Kellarn thought – that the butchered bodies of his colleagues were gone, there was no movement in his solemn face to show it. He moved past Kellarn and made his way more slowly across the floor, straying to the left, and looking here and there among the scattered tableware, as if searching for something.

Their other companions were hurrying through. Kellarn tapped the arm of Hardhen of Levrin, and signalled for him to keep an eye on Dhûghaúr. Then he moved swiftly to join Gravhan at the door to the next stair.

The second stair was like the first, and built directly above it. At the top it opened into a long study room, half the size of the square tower at this height, with windows to the west and north, and an open doorway into what Kellarn remembered, from their sketched drawings of the manor, to be a smaller bedchamber. There were no Easterners here, and the upper part of the tower seemed to have been left much as the fleeing magi had abandoned it. The charred stump of a half-burned log lay on a low mound of ash upon the hearth; and beside the far window stood a small gaming table, with the carved crystal pieces of a *sherunuresh* set poised in mid-stride across their chequered board, awaiting the next move in their unfinished game.

Tirilanna and Takshar checked the sleeping quarters, to make certain there were no hidden enemies lurking there. Kellarn leaned forward across the cushioned window seat and peered into the darkness outside, shielding the reflected light from Gravhan's sword with one hand. But the rest of the manor house lay behind him, to the south and east; and through the coloured glass it was all that he could do to make out the dark mass of the valley hills beyond, silent beneath a starless sky.

'I'd thought they would have a sentry posted up here,' he said quietly to Gravhan.

'The north tower reaches higher, I think,' the knight replied. 'Besides, they knew that the magi might return. If they had not the power to prevent our magi *leaping* here, then they could not make use of this tower in safety. Most likely they will have tried to seal it off from the rest of the house, to prevent us getting any further.'

'You expected the tower to be empty?' Kellarn frowned.

'I had *hoped* so,' Gravhan nodded. 'It means the enemy are less powerful than we might have feared – though no less dangerous, of course, in other ways. We must still be careful.'

They went downstairs again, to regroup in the vaulted chamber at the base of the empty tower. As Kellarn stepped on to the tiled floor, Torkhaal and Dhûghaúr appeared to be in the middle of a whispered conversation. Lorellin and Haësella were motioning for the others to keep well back from the door. The air seemed a little cooler and clearer down here, after the reek and debris of the room above – aided, perhaps, by some virtue of Aerlan's earlier blessing. The face of Dhûghaúr also appeared somehow clearer; less sombre, more alert as he focused on his exchange with Torkhaal.

As Gravhan came in to the chamber behind Kellarn, Torkhaal glanced up at the two of them and beckoned them over.

'I can not sense anyone beyond the door,' he told them quietly, his deep voice scarcely more than a purr within his chest; 'though there are people not far off – perhaps guards or servants, asleep in the great hall.'

'Many?' asked Gravhan.

Torkhaal ran one hand back through his ebon hair, and then shrugged. 'A dozen or more, perhaps. Our first problem is that the door is closed with a seal of power. The spell is simple enough; but there is enough energy there to kill or maim most of our company, and waken the whole manor.'

Kellarn and Gravhan exchanged glances.

'Can you remove the seal?' asked Kellarn. 'Safely, I mean.'

'With Dhûghaúr's help, I can try,' Torkhaal grinned.

'And if you fail?' asked Lorellin, her voice tightened to a whisper.

'Would you rather we returned to Arrandin, my Lady?' asked Torkhaal seriously.

Lorellin drew herself up even straighter, and gave a defiant shake of her head. Torkhaal looked back to Gravhan and Kellarn.

'There was also something else,' he told them. 'It is hard to tell for certain, but I think that there may have been another spell, on the floor of this chamber, not so long ago.

'Nothing that we have disturbed,' he added quickly, at Gravhan's questioning glance. 'It must have faded or been removed some days ago now. The traces are very faint. It may have been no more than a temporary measure, until the seal was placed on the door. But we must keep our eyes open for other such spells around the manor. It is fortunate, perhaps, that we did not try to come here before.'

Kellarn felt a coolness ripple up his spine – both from the sensuous warmth and confidence in Torkhaal's voice, and from the thought that the magical *leap* which had brought them here might have landed them right in the middle of a deadly seal of power. And that thought conjured another memory into his mind. He had come across such Easterner magic a few years before, when he and Corollin had dared to break in to a hidden shrine, in caves beneath the cliffs of the Blue Mountains. That shrine, they had later discovered, had belonged to followers of Lo-Khuma.

Torkhaal and Dhûghaúr were turning their attention to the door, to avoid any further delay. Gravhan placed one hand on Kellarn's arm, signalling for him to move back.

'Did a priest set the seal?' asked Kellarn hurriedly, reluctant to move away. It occurred to him that the Easterners might have made an unholy shrine within the Herghin manor; and they were scarcely past the Dark of the Moon.

'Perhaps,' Torkhaal answered, sounding distracted. 'I know too little of Easterner traditions. But whether wizard or priest, the principles should be much the same.'

Gravhan tugged more insistently at Kellarn's arm, and he gave in and moved back to give the two magi room to work. He supposed that even if there were a shrine here, they still had to try to take the manor; and with Aerlan and the magi and the holy knights, at least they had some chance of dealing with it.

As soon as Kellarn and Gravhan had drawn clear, Dhûghaúr pointed at the floor with two fingers of his right hand, and sketched an arcing line above the tiles. A wall of faint bronze light shimmered into view along the line, like a billowed sail, or a great squared shield twice the full span of a man's outstretched arms. The two magi stood beyond it, facing the door, each with a hand upon Torkhaal's black staff, which was planted upright between them. All other members of the company stood further back, watching through the shimmering wall as the magi went about their work.

Though Kellarn shared Dortrean's wariness of the Council of Magi, he watched more in admiration than in fear. The sense of imminent danger was still there, but somehow beguiled by the calm focus of Torkhaal's unhurried approach. To the Magi, he supposed, such self-discipline in the presence of such lethal power was the key to their survival in their art – much as a warrior called upon practised skill when confronted by a dangerous foe. And when, perhaps a minute later, the two magi turned to face them again, and Dhûghaúr removed his protective shield, the smile that flickered across Torkhaal's face was as much of satisfaction as of relief.

The rest of the company moved forward. Kellarn discovered that Kierran had reappeared at his left side, grinning in encouragement. Torkhaal bowed his dark head for a moment, as if listening, and then nodded for them to proceed. The chamber fell silent. The heavy door made no sound as Dhûghaúr teased it open.

Gravhan and Khôraillan were first through the doorway, carrying their faint Môshári light into the outer hall beyond. Kellarn and Kierran followed a moment later. As Torkhaal had told them, there were no enemy guards waiting here. The outer hall was in fact little more than a wide passage, with a grey stone stair at the far end leading up into the darkness of the old north tower. That way lay the guest apartments and the household quarters – and most likely a fair number of the enemy garrison. Near to the foot of the stair, and to the right of it as they came in, was a single door leading to what Dhûghaúr had called a small study chamber. Much closer at hand, and also to their right, was a taller set of doors with decorated panels, which would gain them entry to the great hall.

Kellarn and Kierran moved swiftly to the far side of the tall doors, their soft boots making little sound on the bare stone floor. Khôraillan and Gravhan went on to the far end of the hall, where it had been agreed that the mage would set a warding barrier across the stair, to prevent any guards coming down that way to attack them. As the rest of the company came out into the hall, Kellarn saw the pale glow already spreading from Khôraillan's staff into the air above the lowest stair like dewspun gossamer, or frosted crystal. The mage's voice as he murmured his spell was barely audible above the quiet movements of the others.

Aerlan and Torkhaal took up their places across the tall doorway from Kellarn, their faces set with concentration. Lorellin and Hardhen stood ready beside them. Dhûghaúr and Tirilanna positioned themselves beside Kierran; while Takshar and Haësella, at Kellarn's nodded signal, headed down to take the study door.

The glow above the stair faded from sight as Khôraillan finished his spell. Gravhan hastened back to join Kellarn. The knights of Braedun readied their bows, and the whole company fell silent, waiting. From somewhere beyond the doors, the sound of a guttural snore broke the stillness. Kellarn jumped, and nearly choked to hold back the unbidden laughter. Then he drew a cautious breath, and nodded his readiness to Gravhan; and they shouldered the tall doors open.

The great hall of the Herghin manor house was lit by the glow of a sinking fire, and the high windows running the length of the far wall were wholly dark. Yet even in the dim light, the hall was a riot of many colours. As in the Hall of Audience in the Arrand palace, the banners of several of the Houses Noble of the Six Kingdoms hung beneath the timbered rafters – though these were Houses of lesser lineage, perhaps. The upper parts of the walls were covered with painted scenes of battles or heroic stories; and the silvered oak panelling of the lower walls glowed tawny red in the firelight, patterned with many shadows. In the far corner to their right was a panelled door leading to the west wing and the Herghin family apartments; and above the door was the window opening of a small landing or gallery.

Across the middle of the hall stretched two long tables, still weighed down with the remains of a sizeable feast – furnished, no doubt, from Selghan Herghin's own cellars and storerooms. And on benches and chairs on either side, and even upon the rush-strewn floor, a dozen or more Easterner warriors stirred from the sprawling stupor of the night's excesses; and roused themselves – with various degrees of success – to see what the commotion was at the door.

The sons and daughters of the Six Kingdoms took full advantage of their surprise. Kellarn and Kierran skirted to the right, heading for the western door, knocking a couple of men cold with the pommels of their swords before the rest had scrambled to their feet. Gravhan grabbed two more by the scruff of the neck and slammed their heads together, putting them out of the fight. A third warrior scrabbled up from the floor behind him, knife in hand – but dropped like a stone when Dhûghaúr grabbed a stool and brought it down upon his head. Torkhaal stopped a red-headed woman in mid-stride with a hasty binding spell.

One scrawny Easterner, more wakeful than the rest, bounded like a ferret toward the principal doors at the eastern end of the hall. A single arrow from Tirilanna's bow brought him down. He fell with a shriek that cost them all hope of further surprise; but then already the level of noise within the hall was growing, as the remaining Easterners caught up weapons, furniture and even tableware to defend themselves, and the swift attack became more like a tavern brawl.

Yet for all the enemy's burgeoning defiance, the fight could not last long. Kellarn and Kierran cut down two that stood before them. Lorellin ran through another with her sword. Gravhan and Hardhen and their other companions brought down the rest. The hall fell briefly quiet again. And then from somewhere close at hand a single horn note sounded; and then a second, fainter note, which was not an echo.

Kellarn glanced up at the high gallery which ran the length of the northern wall, above the two great fireplaces and the doors through which they had entered. There was no sight nor sound of movement in the shadowed darkness there. He nodded to Gravhan and turned to lead the way to the western door. Kierran and Lorellin were just ahead of him.

He had not taken more than three steps toward the door before the sense of something *wrong* began to dawn upon him. Beneath the familiar smells of wood smoke and grease, of stale sweat and fresh blood and trampled rushes, there was a strange rottenness, a dampness of salt decay; and the back of his neck was prickling, as if with the nearness of an unseen foe.

He would have halted and called warning. But at that moment the door ahead of them burst open, and some half a dozen warriors rushed through. They were taller than the other Easterners and more powerfully built, and the braids of their fair hair were strung with beads that clicked and rattled together like dried bones. Some were bare-footed, and some bare-chested, and all carried heavy spears with heads of polished bronze. From their bearing and the number of braids in their hair, they were clearly warriors of high standing within their clan; and they drove forward to clash with the invaders as if they expected to give and take no mercy. A chill wind seemed to follow them, damp and salt with the memory of a distant sea.

Lorellin was knocked aside with one blow, her slender form no match for the greater strength and weight of the Easterner brute before her. Kierran hewed the arm of the man who had struck her, but then found himself defending against a furious onslaught. Hardhen of Levrin gave a great shout as he leaped forward to their aid.

Kellarn clove through the shaft of the first spear that reached him, and the blade of his great sword kindled with sudden flame. That flame was the last thing the astonished Easterner saw, as the blade turned and ran him through. The warrior behind sprang around to Kellarn's left, hurling his spear across the hall. An answering shriek warned Kellarn that the spear had found its mark; but he had not the chance to turn and see who had been hit.

The wind was growing stronger, and the sense of other danger increasing. Above the clash of spear and sword, Kellarn could hear the voice of Aerlan – a rumbling chant, swelling with building power. In counterpoint, the gentler voice of Dhûghaúr rippled with sudden song. There was a flare of bronze power like sheet lightning to his right, knocking the warriors back and leaving Kellarn briefly dazzled. Hardhen fairly hauled Lorellin to her feet and dragged her clear of the fray. Kierran stumbled closer to Kellarn's side.

As their vision cleared, the figure of a woman appeared in the western doorway, barely half a dozen strides from where Kellarn stood. Her naked arms were raised up above her head; and there was a dim light from somewhere behind her, so that the dull green of her simple shift revealed the shadow of the body within. There was a whispered glimmer of many jewels about her neck, and upon her hands. But her long hair drifted like matted weed on the cool air, and there was something about her broad nose and upturned face that was horribly familiar. And then a storm wind buffeted through the hall, and the full force of their danger was upon them.

Kellarn and Kierran fought to remain standing. The floor seemed to pitch and roll beneath their feet. There was a clattering from the laden tables, and from the high gallery behind. Aerlan's song foundered in a sudden cry.

The colours of the hall blurred and faded, and the fallen Easterners stirred and began to rise. Kellarn pushed himself toward the woman, his feet dragging as if through thick waters, the floor rushes drifting and swirling about his knees like foam on an unseen tide. Kierran laboured heavily beside him. But the dead warriors surged up around them, clutching and biting at legs and arms and waists, hindering their movement further; and then other shapes began to surface, faces and bodies not seen in the hall before, though vivid in memory to Kellarn's eyes – bloated faces of Souther slaves and shipmen, their tanned skins blurred with the purple of tattoos, their dark eyes wide and unseeing; and they stank. Row upon row they rose up all around him, faster than he could knock them down; and he knew them for the people he had left behind in the storm at sea, and the woman was that same Easterner who had held them spellbound with her wild dance as the Souther warship went down beneath the waves.

The whole hall was filled with the storm, and the dark tide of seething bodies. The red glow of the fire was gone. Kellarn's sword burned bright as a torch in his hand, searing through the Dead with much hissing and smoke; and the star shield of Heruvor showered white sparks at every touch of the Dead upon it. There were flares of blue and gold from somewhere behind, and gouts of green fire rained down all around.

The woman left the doorway and walked slowly toward him, passing untroubled among the heaving crowd. A light like the dying moon bled from her pale face and upraised hands. A flare of deep green power skittered on the air around her, and failed. She paused for a moment, tilted her head a little further

113

back, and moved on again. Kellarn and Kierran prepared to engage her.

The Chosen Priest Aerlan gave a great shout, and the storm wind ceased abruptly. The woman recoiled as if struck, and the light faded from her face. The crowded bodies of the Dead stood motionless, waiting. Kellarn seized the moment and barged forward toward her. Kierran followed hard at his heels.

But the moment was passing. A bowstring hummed in the stillness, and an arrow bounced off Kellarn's shield. More arrows flew down, and there was movement on the shadowed gallery overhead.

The woman gave a shrieking laugh, and the Dead began to stir again. Kellarn reached her and swung down his great sword. She dodged him, quick as thought, and grabbed hold of his wrist. A spasm of ice flashed through his sword hand, and then was gone. She snatched away her own hand in shock, and her face flashed brighter in fury.

Another volley of arrows rained down into the hall. Kierran sank beneath a wave of grappling hands. Gravhan waded toward him, with Torkhaal and Dhûghaúr following in a burst of green and gold power.

Kellarn raised his sword again, preparing to strike. The Easterner woman had stepped back, her eyes gazing straight through him as her hands danced into another spell.

Whether through instinct or growing habit, or through the building power of the spell, or by some prompting of the sword itself, Kellarn found his eyes drawn to the flickering blade. Beneath the running flames, the inlaid patterns and six squared runes shone bright as molten gold; and looking at it now, he perceived at last where the words of the sword's prophecy could be read. His cousin Faëlla had been right, all along.

The insight took only a moment, and then he was back in the fight. The woman was still weaving her spell with her hands, her pale face mocking him. Gravhan had almost reached him.

There came a flare of light at the far end of the hall, up on the high gallery. Three archers were standing there, clad in the purple and grey of the Herghin livery. Lorellin cried out – calling a name, perhaps, though Kellarn did not catch it. Two of the men loosed their bows, aiming down into the fray. The third paused, and then turned his aim aside. The bow sang, and the arrow flew the length of the hall and buried itself deep into the Easterner woman's throat.

Then the archer toppled forward over the balustrade, and fell down among the Dead; and left behind him on the gallery was a hooded figure, like a forgotten shadow in the returning darkness.

Chapter Four

The Easterner woman staggered, but did not fall. Her pale hands groped at the shaft in her throat, and her eyes rolled white and bulging. Kellarn brought down his blade with all his strength, and severed her head in a fountain of flaming blood.

Gravhan and the magi reached him. The Dead all around were burning.

There was light and commotion up on the gallery, as more warriors streamed in from the far end. The hooded shadow had attached itself to another archer, with a flicker of drawn steel between them. The shorter, stockier shape of a dwarf in a scarlet cloak came bounding behind, a black-bladed axe swinging above his head as he ran. A tawny figure, almost more lion than man, sprang up on to the balustrade, and then leaped down with a roar among the swirling Dead.

Uncertain whence this help had come – if help indeed it was – Kellarn turned and hewed at the blistering corpses in the place where Kierran had fallen. Gravhan and the magi laboured beside him; though the number of their foes was now greatly lessened, and the tide of bodies receding.

Then the great doors at the eastern end of the hall swung wide and a silver light flooded in. A young woman came through, clad in simple leather garb and holding a white staff before her. At her side came a taller, silver-haired figure, who could only be one of the elvenfolk of the Fay. His tunic and cloak were of deep, shimmering grey, and there was a glitter as of many jewels about his head and arms. A staff of mother-of-pearl was in his right hand; and a light like the full midwinter moon upon clean snow seemed to enfold him and flow out from him, blessing all that it touched. Tirilanna gave a shout of joy and thanksgiving. And for the first time in all the battle, the Souther Dead opened their silent mouths and screamed.

The woman and the fay strode in to the hall; and wherever the silver light came, the Dead fell back and dissolved, fading into the falling rushes. Kierran came up for air, thrashing and roaring. Kellarn dragged him clear and crouched down beside him.

The last of the Dead had fallen, and the battle overhead seemed to have come to an end. The tawny, lion-like man stood up, more simply human now. The great sword in his hand shone with an apple-green light, like the light of the Môshári. Barely half of Kellarn's company remained standing.

The young woman came on toward him, ahead of the fay, and he saw that she was Corollin. More people were streaming in through the far doors; and then bobbing up the hall at speed came the silver-fair head and merry grin of Mage Councillor Hrugaar.

'Ru!' cried Torkhaal, springing toward him in joy; and Dhûghaúr echoed his cry quietly, his face shining.

'Hello you,' said Corollin, kneeling down beside Kellarn and Kierran. 'I thought that I might find you here.'

'I still can't work out,' said Kellarn, 'how you come to be here at all.'

Hrugaar laughed.

They had taken Kierran out into the manor yard, away from the reek of the hall, and were sitting on the stone steps before the small dovecote door to tend him. The dawn sky glowered red in the east, staining the heavy clouds overhead, and the air was cool. There were lights in many places behind the high windows, as Gravhan and Lorellin saw to the clearing of the manor house, and the last of the rebels of Herghin were being rounded up. The fay and his strange companions were still inside, helping; as were the men of Ferlund who had come with them, and those of Kellarn's own company who were able. Only Torkhaal had come out into the yard, unwilling to let Hrugaar stray out of arm's reach; and Corollin had followed soon after. Dhûghaúr had come with them for part of the way, but had then seemed to change his mind and gone back to join Gravhan.

'We have the moon fay Tinûkenil to thank for that,' said Corollin, looking up from her work of cleaning Kierran's wounds. 'His skills of healing are greater than mine, and the power of the Moon is strong within him. It was he who called Hrugaar back.'

'Yes, I have met Tinû and his friends before,' said Kellarn; 'some time ago now, though. Father knows them. When I first saw Tinû, I thought he was Heruvor. They are so alike.'

'They are close kin,' Hrugaar nodded. 'But Tinûkenil has violet eyes.'

'And he is far more serious, somehow,' said Corollin. 'Older, perhaps.'

'No, he is younger than Heruvor,' grinned Hrugaar. 'In fact very young, as the Fay would reckon it. But he has spent much time with his human friends. Give him a couple of hundred years, and he may grow out of it.'

'But we had thought you were dead, Ru,' said Torkhaal. 'Is that what you mean, about being called back?'

'I saw not the Realms of the Dead,' said Hrugaar – almost, Kellarn thought, as though he were disappointed. 'My body was dying, but the life of the Fay sustained me. I was *elsewhere*, I suppose. It was Tinû who healed the work of Arisâ's poison; and he who found me and brought me back. And then we journeyed through the Realm of the Moon, and he brought us here to join his friends.'

'But how did he know you were at the Tollund manor?' demanded Kellarn. 'Or that we would be here at Herghin?'

Hrugaar shrugged. 'He said that the servants of Haëstren told him.'

Kellarn felt that he would have liked a clearer answer than that; and Torkhaal also looked as if he had further questions upon the matter. But they were prevented by a disturbance on the far side of the yard, as the moon fay and several other people came out through a covered porch.

'Well that's the Herghin scum dealt with,' said the lion-like man. 'What next?'

Kellarn remembered him to be Gwydion, a borderlander from the earldom of Vansa on the western edge of the Six Kingdoms; plain spoken and high handed, but by report an excellent warrior. He had put away his glowing sword, and walking beside the jewelled beauty of the moon fay he looked almost ordinary in his green and brown garb.

At Tinûkenil's left hand was the shadowed figure whom Kellarn had glimpsed up on the balcony of the hall; but her hood was now thrown back to reveal a head of long brown hair, and an unremarkable face. Kellarn knew that he should recall her name, but for the moment it eluded him. Beside her strode the *noghr* in his scarlet cloak and splendid mailshirt, still weighing his black-bladed axe with dour purpose.

'Not all the Herghin men were treacherous,' said the moon fay. Kellarn was unsure whether the look on his fair face expressed irritation or mild forbearance. 'We ought not to offend the Lady of this manor, perhaps?'

'Why not?' said Gwydion.

'For Gwydion, that was quite tactful,' put in the dwarf. 'But I dare say the Lady – wherever she is – will treat him with honour, as her guest; and wait till he leaves before she has him shot down.'

The woman in shadow-grey said nothing. The four of them came on across the yard, while other people – Gravhan and Lorellin among them – emerged behind. The moon fay bowed low before Kellarn.

'You have a new sword, since last we met,' he said.

'Yes,' said Kellarn awkwardly. He could not stand in greeting, since he was still supporting Kierran while Corollin finished her work. But Hrugaar and Torkhaal rose and bowed.

'It might be best if all of you were to have your wounds cleaned and healed,' said Tinûkenil. 'The touch of the Dead is not clean. We are willing to offer our help in this, such as it is, if you so wish.'

Gwydion nodded his shaggy head in support.

'Thank you,' said Kellarn.

'I seem to be in good hands already,' said Kierran.

The moon fay smiled down at him kindly. Then Gravhan arrived to discuss the business of the morning.

'We shall speak later, perhaps,' Tinûkenil told Kellarn.

Gravhan's tidings were both good and bad. Of Selghan Herghin's original household, some thirty-eight had survived. They were now held under guard by the tall Ferlund men who had come here with Tinûkenil's companions. No Easterner remained alive within the manor house; and there was no sign of a shrine having been made by them, nor any of their magic remaining.

Of Kellarn's own company, Takshar of Dregharis now lay dead, impaled by a bronze-headed Easterner spear; and the Chosen Priest Aerlan had been gathered to the gods, for all the efforts of Haësella and Tirilanna to save him. Councillor Khôraillan was torn and bloodied in a dozen different places, and Hardhen of Levrin had been put out of the fight by an angry cut above his right eyebrow; but both were still on their feet.

Kellarn was grieved at the news of Takshar's death, though there was little that he could have done to prevent it. He felt somehow responsible, since Takshar, in particular, had come here at his own request. Aerlan he had known less well; but at least it seemed that the priest had lasted long enough to hear that the tide of the battle had turned in their favour.

It was agreed that the men of Ferlund would stay to hold the manor, under the Lady Lorellin's command; and Tirilanna

121

would remain with them also. The men and women of the Herghin household would have to make answer to Lorellin later that morning – and perhaps to The Arrand, afterward. Those whom she felt she could trust would be given the chance to prove their loyalty in the manor's repair and defence.

Khôraillan was to return to Arrandin, taking the bodies of Takshar and Aerlan; and he would make report of their success to The Arrand, who in turn would be obliged to inform the Emperor. With him Dhûghaúr would go, taking Kierran to Imarra and the Môshári Healers, and arranging for further defenders for the Herghin manor house should that prove needful. All the rest were to ride north to join the Emperor's armies, hoping to deal with whatever Easterner sentries they found lurking in the border hills, while avoiding any larger conflicts with the enemy clans.

Kierran protested loudly that he had no need to return home, nor were his hurts so great that he could not stay in the saddle. But Corollin overruled him, saying that he was in no fit state yet to fight with the Easterners, and would only be a hindrance to them along the way. Kellarn had reluctantly to agree with her.

Though Dhûghaúr was clearly pleased to see Hrugaar, and had suffered little hurt in the battle, he seemed to have no desire to ride north with the rest. He said that his own gifts were best suited to helping Rhysana in Arrandin, or in bolstering the defence of Herghin; and that besides, he had still not wholly recovered his own strength. Kellarn, watching him, wondered whether Dhûghaúr might not have changed his mind, had Hrugaar asked him to do so. But Hrugaar did not ask him; and neither Torkhaal nor Khôraillan saw fit to suggest it.

Rhysana was in the long gallery in the Arrand palace when the imperial summons came. From the moment that Dhûghaúr and Kierran had returned to the Môshári house, she had known that it would come; and so she and Ellen had made their *leap* here to the Magi's chambers, both to avail themselves of Morvaan's observation spell to try to see the Herghin manor house, and to hold themselves in readiness for the Emperor. Thus the welcome news of their success – made doubly joyful by the tidings of Hrugaar's safe return and the unexpected help from Ferlund – was undershadowed by the anticipation of Rhydden's response.

'You do not have to come down,' Ellen had told her, 'if you do not feel up to it. Technically, I am the senior mage answerable for the Council in the city. And Rhydden is already wary of your friendship with Dortrean.'

'He will be mindful of that whether I am present or not,' Rhysana had replied. 'Besides, I have more experience of dealing with Rhydden than do you; and I do not think it wise for either of us to go before him alone.'

But when the summons came, it was in the person of the Archmage Merrech himself; and whether by the Emperor's bidding or through His Eminence's own device, both Ellen and Rhysana were called by name.

The new day was barely an hour old, and the garden courtyard outside still lay deep in shadow, fragrant with the heavy dew. They followed the ancient Archmage in silence through the lamplit corridors of the palace, and down past guarded doors into the subdued splendour of The Arrand's Hall of Audience.

The carved throne on the far dais, with its sweeping wings of amethyst and quartz, stood empty. On a smaller chair before the throne sat the Emperor Rhydden, surrounded by an aureole of golden light which made dim the pale sky beyond the high clerestory windows, and cast the hanging banners of the Houses Noble into deeper shadow. The Emperor was clad once again in sable and gold, with his heavy cloak of cloth of gold cast back across his chair; and his face shone bright as a beacon in the magical light. For lesser nobles or more ordinary folk, the splendour of the sight alone would have been sufficient to command awe and obedience. For the enlightened Rhysana and Ellen, the effect of the glamorous facade was something closer to irritation.

The Arrand was seated on a cushioned chair on the right of the dais, with the Lady Minnaíra fussing quietly beside him. To the left, at the foot of the dais steps and with his back to them as they approached, was Mage Councillor Khôraillan, now clad in fresh robes of Môshári green. A handful of Rhydden's liveried guards and The Arrand's household were stationed elsewhere around the hall; and there was also a broad-shouldered man whom Rhysana recognised as one of The Arrand's guard commanders, and Sister Serengaïa, a priestess from the Temple of Serbramel in the Lower City. Lord Bradhor was not there.

The Arrand struggled to his feet as Rhysana and Ellen entered, in spite of his wife's habitual reproach. His kindly face was flushed and heavy with the exertion, and Rhysana thought that he looked less well than she had seen him in a long time. The Emperor also rose; but even this slight courtesy seemed contrived to enhance the grace and benevolence of his own appearance.

They came to a halt a few paces from the dais steps, Ellen slightly ahead and to Rhysana's left, and bowed deeply in their formal robes. The Archmage Merrech continued up on to the dais, circling in silence to take up his accustomed position behind the Emperor's chair. The Emperor gestured for The Arrand to sit down again, and for Ellen and Rhysana to rise.

'We understand,' said Rhydden, 'that once again the Council of Magi deserves our thanks for their contribution to this present war; upon this occasion for the safe recovery of our lesser manor of Herghin.'

His tone and manner were faultlessly gracious; and his beatific smile suggested that there was scarcely any news, in all the Six Kingdoms or beyond, that might have pleased him better.

'The Council remains neutral, Highness,' Ellen replied, 'and had no part in this endeavour. We are content, however, that the efforts of some few magi from among our number should have proved of service in the defence of His Highness' lands.'

If Rhydden felt any irritation at her reminder of the debatable distinction between the Council of Magi as a body and its individual members, he did not show it.

'We also understand,' he said, 'that the Lady Lorellin Herghin of Arrand and the Lord Hardhen of Levrin have acquitted themselves well, and reaffirmed their loyalty to us through this endeavour – even if they were removed from the care of ourself and of our host The Arrand without our prior knowledge.'

The censure was there, but uncommonly mild, and without the usual danger of lightness in the imperial tone. Had he been speaking directly to Rhysana at that moment, she felt that he might almost have tricked some stumbling apology or defence from her lips. But Rhydden's gaze was upon Ellen; and Ellen calmly held her peace, waiting for him to continue.

'We trust, of course, that due preparation has been made against any return strike,' said the Emperor, 'whether against Herghin, or our armies in the field, or against this city. Although in the last case, it is to be hoped that we might have the pleasure of seeing for ourself the redoubtable power of the city's magical defences in action.'

'The defence of Herghin is in hand,' Ellen replied, 'as no doubt His Highness has been informed. The armies and the city are already well prepared for Easterner attack – though it is to be hoped that Arrandin herself has seen the last of this war.'

Rhydden's nostrils flared a little wider, signalling that the Archmage Ellen trod dangerous ground in presuming to lecture him upon the state of his own troops; but his manner did not falter. Indeed, Rhysana thought, he seemed to be going out of his way to remain as pleasant as possible. That in itself was another sign of danger.

'Well enough,' said the Emperor. 'We should be grateful if you could convey our thanks where appropriate. For now, we shall not keep you further from your work.'

He nodded in gracious dismissal. Ellen and Rhysana bowed, and backed away with due courtesy down the length of the hall. Rhysana more than half expected some parting shot or veiled threat to follow them as they left. But the Emperor sat down again, and they reached the doors with no further word being spoken.

'Well that went better than I had hoped,' said Ellen quietly, once they had drawn clear of the guarded antechamber and were making their way up the marble stair of the high pillared hall beyond.

'Perhaps,' said Rhysana, keeping a weather eye open in case they might be overheard. 'A little too well for my liking.'

Though her presence had been specifically requested, she was all too aware of how little attention had been paid to her by either the Emperor or his hooded Archmage; and in its own way, she found that more unsettling than Rhydden's apparent good humour. Yet it was not a subject which she wished to discuss while they were still within the palace.

'Perhaps war has made you cynical, High Councillor,' said Ellen. The dry edge to her deep, handsome voice hinted that she shared Rhysana's misgivings.

They had barely reached the top of the stair when a blur of gold came streaking across the landing toward them, and a young squire in the imperial livery skidded to a halt scant inches from Rhysana's breast. Both women put out their hands instinctively, as much to steady him as to ward off a feared attack. They had a brief glimpse of his upturned face – of eyes wide with fright, and eyelids reddened and swollen from many tears – and then he turned and eluded their grasp, and fled away again at great speed. Rhysana doubted that he could be much older than fourteen.

'Should we call him back?' she asked Ellen anxiously, uncertain whether she was more startled by the sudden shock or by the boy's evident distress.

'Better not,' said Ellen. 'Rhydden may think that we have interfered enough for one morning, without our meddling with his own household.'

'But will he be all right?' asked Rhysana. The unspoken

thought hung between them that Rhydden's household now harboured a more deadly peril than usual, which had already claimed the hapless Brother Sarin as its victim.

'We must hope so,' said Ellen, after a moment; 'and we have other ways of finding out. But we were so well received just now, it may be simply that someone else has suffered His Highness' displeasure in our stead.'

Kellarn stretched the stiffness from his legs, and shifted the star shield of Heruvor more comfortably across his back. The cloud cover overhead had broken and scattered, and the summer sun beat down on the open hillside. The day was turning sultry and hot.

Amid the weathered outcrop of stone just above him, Tinûkenil and Hrugaar crouched half hidden as they searched the lands ahead to the north with their long sight. Corollin stood at the foot of the rocks, her head bowed as if listening. Gwydion, meanwhile, was searching the ground nearby, together with the woman in shadow-grey – Skaramak, as Kellarn now remembered she was called – and one of the three Ferlund men who still rode with them. They thought it likely that the Easterners had had sentries posted here not so long ago; though whoever had been here had made themselves scarce by now. Gravhan and the rest of the company had stayed back with the horses, a stone's throw away down the slope beside the gurgling stream.

Whether through their own success early that morning, or at some call from the invading armies, they could not be certain; but it seemed that the Easterners had withdrawn from the Herghin hills. The land lay quiet, with few noises carried on the sluggish breeze. Yet the signs of the enemy's recent presence were everywhere.

The first legacy of the Easterner troops had confronted them even as they rode out through the gates of the Herghin manor house – on borrowed horses of sturdy stock, taken from the manor stables and from among those that Gwydion and the men of Ferlund had brought with them. On the woodland slopes on the far side of the valley, facing them as they rode out, the bodies of Selghan Herghin and more than a score of his household had been discovered in the morning light, hanging like blighted fruit from the green branches, all torn and ravaged by feasting carrion birds – a grim reminder of the price of betrayal. The task of lifting them down and preparing them for their proper Rite of Burning had been left to the surviving members of the household, under the stern eyes of Lorellin and Tirilanna and the warriors of Ferlund.

Then as they rode north and west through the jumbled hills, similar scenes had unfolded before them – farming settlements and outlying cots and barns all looted and burned out; long-haired cattle slaughtered in the yard, or roughly butchered on the open slopes; and the splayed or roasted bodies of the men and women who had paid the final price for their Lord's fateful treaty with the Easterner clans.

Yet the worst part of that morning's ride, to Kellarn's mind, was not the images of death and burning, but rather their few brief meetings with those borderlanders who had survived. If not altogether hostile, the folk of Herghin were resentful and accusing, refusing any help or kindness offered by himself or his companions. It was as though they held the men of the Six Kingdoms as much to blame for their present plight as the Easterners who had betrayed them. In the end, Gravhan and Gwydion had decided between themselves to steer clear of these settlements as much as possible, since there was little hope even of gathering news from any of them.

Gwydion had ridden at the front with Gravhan and Kellarn throughout the morning, being a skilled guide and tracker as well as a superb warrior; and there was a welcome comfort in his easy confidence and practicality. Skaramak had stayed mostly at the rear, keeping her own counsel or speaking softly with the *noghr* who rode beside her. Haësella and Hardhen and the three men of Ferlund rode in the middle of the company, together with Torkhaal and Hrugaar. The moon fay Tinûkenil

128

divided his time between Hrugaar and Skaramak, maintaining a quiet diffidence except when called upon, as now, to look ahead. Corollin had stayed at Kellarn's left hand, taking in everything around her in her own silent vigil.

Yet though they mingled and worked well together, Kellarn noticed that Tinûkenil and his companions kept a subtle distance in most of their dealings with the rest; and perhaps in particular toward himself and Corollin. This was in part, he guessed, a deference born of respect, or even shyness. Yet there was something else – a reserved aloofness, akin to the self-contained privacy of the Magi – which lent the impression that an unseen threshold lay between himself and them, which might prove perilous to cross. It was a feeling that he found both unsettling and strangely exciting.

Their one encounter with Easterners on their journey had proved brief and to little purpose. They had overtaken a handful of warriors on foot, who had fought fiercely and then attempted to flee. Only one of their number had suffered himself to be taken alive; and it seemed that he had no understanding of the Six Kingdoms tongue, and had in any event refused to speak at all when questioned. So the Easterner had been bound and gagged and thrown like baggage across Tinûkenil's saddle, and given into Skaramak's care; in the hope that he might be persuaded to talk later in the day, once they had joined up with the Emperor's armies. The moon fay himself had gone on foot thereafter, keeping easy pace beside the riders.

Kellarn looked up as Tinûkenil and Hrugaar crept back across the rocks and dropped lightly to the grass below.

'So what's happening?' he asked.

The moon fay came over, while Hrugaar slipped away to relay the news to the other riders.

'The Easterners are gathering again, not far to the north,' Tinûkenil told him. 'The nearest are less than two leagues off. There are perhaps a couple of thousand warriors there, and their banners are blue and silver and green. There are more, a league or so further to the northwest, up toward the road; but they have different banners, mostly of black and red and gold. There is greater danger with them, I think – some power or magic is at work among them, though it is of a kind unknown to me, and its purpose uncertain. There are other warriors, still fleeing, away to the northeast. But these nearer at hand seem to be creeping back west; preparing some ambush, perhaps, for your Emperor's armies.'

'And where are the Emperor's armies?' asked Corollin.

'That way lies the village of Fersí,' said the fay, pointing almost due west to where a few slender strands of smoke trailed up into the sky. 'That would be a journey of some two hours, at the pace we have been travelling. The Emperor's armies are further west along the road, but they could reach the village shortly before us – a little after noon, perhaps. I suppose that we shall try to join them there, before the enemy can attack.'

Hrugaar and the rest were already beginning to gather again further down the slope. Tinûkenil turned to go down.

'Just a moment,' said Kellarn hurriedly. 'There's something else I'd like to ask you.'

The fay turned back, his silver hair flashing in the sunlight and shadowed with amethyst and ultramarine.

'Yes?' he said.

'You – you mentioned my sword, before,' Kellarn faltered. 'I should like you to take a look at it.'

He had the feeling that he might be pressing dangerously close to the curious threshold of privacy surrounding the fay and his companions. Yet it seemed suddenly important to Kellarn that he should know more about the prophecy of the sword before he drew it again in battle. Tinûkenil wrinkled his nose, almost as if in amusement, and then nodded. He appeared quite unruffled.

'Show me,' he said.

With pounding heart, Kellarn drew the sword from its scarlet sheath. The white steel of the long blade flickered dazzlingly bright in the late morning sun; but the interwoven lines of yellow gold along its length stood out quite clearly, punctuated with the heads of hawks and serpents and hounds, with stretching haunches and paws and fine feathered wings. Corollin moved closer to him, craning her neck to see.

The moon fay did not touch the sword. But as he leaned forward to look, he seemed to grow even taller; and a silver-grey shadow sprang up around them, dimming the morning light, so that the pattern of the blade shone brighter still. He held his staff of mother-of-pearl in his left hand, and Kellarn saw now that many runes of silver were inlaid across its polished surface, up and down the full length of the shaft. The air around them grew cooler, and tense with the whisper of hidden power.

'The six runes in the squares,' said Tinûkenil, 'there close to the hilt, are the virtues of power within the blade. This is a holy blade, dedicated to Hýriel, Lady of Fire; and it was made, I guess, in the early days of your Six Kingdoms, or perhaps in the wars of the Bright Alliance that came before. Torriearn, Chosen Priest of the Sun, would have liked to see it.'

'I am sorry about him,' said Kellarn.

'Oh, I think he is in good company now,' said the fay. There was a wry, half smile in his fair face, as if at some private joke; but Kellarn thought it best not to ask him about it just then.

'There is also other writing along the blade,' he told the fay. 'But it is made by the spaces between the patterns, do you see?'

'I see,' Tinûkenil nodded.

There was a silence of several heartbeats.

'But can you tell me what it says?' Kellarn demanded.

'Not very well,' the fay confessed. 'It is written in one of your older human tongues, of which I have but passing knowledge. The scholars of the Magi could probably tell you better than can I. But then perhaps you knew that already, before asking me?'

'Yes,' said Kellarn awkwardly. 'What does it say?'

'Here is written,' said Tinûkenil, 'in the tongue of the West of the Middle Lands of old, as I understand it, *You shall burn the illness that blights the land, you shall rule in glory from the highest seat.'*

'And what does that mean?' asked Corollin.

Tinûkenil shrugged. 'To me, it sounds like something from the *Lay of the Courtship of the Sun and Moon*, or perhaps from the mystical *Ascendancies of Hýriel*; and there, I think, it would refer to Torollen, Lord of the Sun – which might be thought curious in a blade so clearly belonging to Hýriel. But Torollen is the son of Hýriel; and in the days when this blade was forged, the worship of Fire and the Sun was closer, more blended than it became in later years. Wield it well, Kellarn.'

The silver shadow faded, and Tinûkenil seemed to dwindle again beneath the protective veil of his grey cloak – though still he stood several inches taller than Kellarn and Corollin. Kellarn sheathed his sword, and the moon fay gestured for them to join him in the return journey down the slope.

'So how did you really come to be at Tollund?' Kellarn asked as they set off.

'The Moon has many servants,' said Tinûkenil, 'and it is given to them to see and hear many things. We were returning from a journey far to the south when word reached us of the troubles here in Arrandin; and the messengers of the goddess whom I serve told me that my gifts were needed at the Tollund manor, if I would go. So while my friends brought help north from Ferlund, I went on ahead to Tollund; and managed – by the grace of the goddess – to rescue Hrugaar. And then Hrugaar and' – he hesitated – 'your friend, the Lady Corollin, asked to come with me to join my friends in the assault on Herghin. Thus by chance, as it might seem, we are all met together. Yet the messengers of the goddess had told me that we might hope for help from others in the attempt on the Herghin manor. Hrugaar guessed that the Magi might play their part in that; and the Lady Corollin thought that perhaps you yourself would also be there.'

'And why did you think that?' Kellarn asked her.

'Call it intuition,' said Corollin. 'But Tinû, shall you risk riding openly with us when we join the Emperor's armies?'

'I shall keep my hood up and my head down,' said the fay lightly, 'and do my best not to be noticed. I remember once, soon after I came to these lands, I ran into an imperial War priest upon the road. I think that he mistook me for an errant demon, and tried to drive me away – not that he had much hope of success, of course.'

'That will be even more likely a mistake for people to make, just now,' said Kellarn, 'with the Easterner priests so close at hand.'

'I know,' said Tinûkenil, growing serious again. 'But the demons summoned by the Easterners are in truth one of the main reasons for our coming here.'

They had reached the edge of the gathered company. Kellarn saw Hrugaar's head go up like a hound's at Tinûkenil's last comment, and the mage turned and came over to join them. Torkhaal and Gravhan were close behind.

'You have heard,' the moon fay went on, 'that the demon captain from the days of the Bright Alliance now seeks to return to the waking world – though it is best not to name him, perhaps, with the enemy so near at hand.'

'Yes,' said Corollin and Kellarn together.

'We have good cause to believe,' said Tinûkenil, 'that there are followers and servants of his among the Easterner clans who have come here; and that some may draw upon his power within this war.'

'One of the dead warriors found in the city wore a talisman with his symbol,' said Kellarn. 'I found it – the day before yesterday, I think.' So much had happened since that time, it took him a few moments to work it out.

'The Môshári have feared this for many days,' said Gravhan; 'and during the last assault of the siege – on the night before Lord Kellarn reached Arrandin – there were demons with heads like horses' skulls summoned against us. They were powerful among the servants of the ancient Enemy, so our stories tell; and it was those demons that brought about the downfall of Torriearn, Chosen Priest of the Sun.'

'What happened to the priests that summoned them?' demanded Gwydion.

'The Archmage Ellen destroyed them,' Torkhaal answered. 'There was a great priest, with a golden head-dress, and a circle of servants or lesser priests around him. All perished.'

'Good,' said Gwydion.

'Did you find out any more about the talisman?' Kellarn asked Gravhan.

'Nothing more than we had guessed already,' the knight answered. 'It has been melted now.'

'Then there was Drengriis,' said Hrugaar.

'Drengriis?' Gwydion echoed.

'Mage Councillor Drengriis of Româdhrí,' Hrugaar explained. 'When we found him at the Tollund manor house he was controlled, perhaps even possessed, by a demon of some kind. But Corollin saved him.'

'He was possessed,' Corollin nodded. 'Yet not, I think, by the Enemy himself.'

Gwydion and Tinûkenil exchanged glances.

'You'd have known if it was,' said Gwydion.

Corollin looked at them both; and then frowned, as if puzzled.

'Yes,' said Tinûkenil; 'and it has been revealed to me by the servants of the goddess that we may learn more of the answer to this riddle when the Easterner armies are held at bay. And so we have come here, a little out of our way, to see what we can learn.'

'I doubt that the Emperor would be pleased, to hear the safety of his empire taken so lightly,' said Gravhan.

Tinûkenil answered with a graceful shrug.

'I suppose,' said Skaramak, 'that we could always pay a visit to His Imperial Highness, and ask him his opinion.'

The New Moon Assembly of the Council of Magi sat in the

latter part of the morning, faced with the task of providing for the continued running of the Colleges the following day, after the mid-term break. For once, Rhysana had decided that she would not attend.

For one thing, she knew that had she gone to the assembly she would almost certainly have found herself persuaded to return to part-time lecturing duties at the Lautun College, whilst holding herself ready to return to Arrandin at a moment's notice to assist the Archmage Ellen in the raising of the city's magical defences. Rhysana considered such an arrangement to be far from advisable. For another, their conversation with the Emperor had left her increasingly unsettled – not only because of the apparent genuineness of his attempts to be pleasant over the affair of Herghin, but because he had raised the question of a possible avenging strike against their armies in the field, or against Arrandin itself. With her husband out somewhere close to the enemy hosts, and with the lack of magi remaining within the city, Rhysana felt even less inclined to leave her post to listen to her fellow lecturers bickering over timetable shuffles and the increased demands on their precious time. And then there was this unknown danger within the imperial household, and the threat of betrayal even inside the city walls.

She might have asked Dhûghaúr to go in her place – though he himself had no experience of lecturing, nor of college administration. But Dhûghaúr was tired from the assault on Herghin, and still occupied with the Môshári; and besides, she felt that she would rather have him here, since he was the only other mage in the city – apart from Ellen and herself – who had experience of working with the magical defences. Khôraillan of Môshári would have been her second choice; but he was also weary and wounded, and it seemed unlikely that the Healers would release him so soon from their care.

The Archmage Ellen was no more inclined than Rhysana to attend the assembly that morning. Ranzhaar of Stanva had declared his intention to go, being a lecturer of the Arrandin College; but neither Ellen nor Rhysana felt that they could trust him to bring them an unbiased report of the proceedings, and it was more than likely that the squabbling of the other councillors would put him entirely out of temper.

In the end, Rhysana lighted upon Mage Councillor Telghraan to act as her eyes and ears at the New Moon Assembly. Telghraan was more or less her own age, and an *Aeshta* mage of Earth; and though he had been on the Council for less than a year, this was now his second term as an honorary lecturer at the Ellanguan College – a position which both Ellen and Hrugaar had held at some point in their career. He had proved invaluable in the defence and repair of Arrandin's Lower City; and apart from all of this, he was available, and would in any event be at the assembly. With High Councillor Sollonaal as Principal of the Ellanguan College, even war with the East would not be held sufficient excuse for Telghraan's absence.

With the New Moon Assembly thus provided for – and with the wide-eyed Telghraan under strict instruction to report back to her as soon as possible – Rhysana had taken herself off to the Temple of Telúmachel in the west of the Old City; both to pay her final respects to the Chosen Priest Aerlan, and to avail herself of the chance for quiet meditation and prayer.

The Braedun Order – from which the Temple Guard of Telúmachel in Arrandin were drawn – had skilful healers; though none quite so gifted as those of their fellow Orders of Môshári and Kelmaar. The strength of Braedun lay in knowledge and learning, and in the mastery of many crafts. So when Rhysana reached the cloistered garden of the temple precincts she was quite prepared for the sight of all the wounded people – both members of the Order and other warriors and citizens – resting on stools or pallets in the green shade to take the morning air. Now that the siege was ended, there seemed to be more people here than ever.

She was less prepared, however, for the reaction to her own arrival. The whispered rumour of her approach echoed like beating wings beneath the branches, and faces and limbs stirred and turned in curiosity. It was true, she supposed, that

136

the deep indigo of her formal high councillor's robes, together with her distinctive silver-fair hair, must proclaim instantly who she was; and that her own role in the defence of the city was surely known in the temple precincts. Yet she found it flattering and a little startling to be the focus of quite so much unexpected attention.

As a daughter of Blood Noble, Rhysana knew by instinct that she could not ignore these people or pass them by with a simple smile. Though as a mage and a temple visitor she had every right to retreat behind her claim to personal privacy, the faces before her needed something more. If they admired her, they also feared her; and the Council was not so secure that it could hold the trust of others lightly in hand.

So though it cost her no little effort, she ran the gauntlet of the crowded garden; smiling and nodding, or taking hold of outstretched hands, or stroking tired brows. Rhysana had never felt wholly comfortable with simple pleasantries; and there were only so many variations that she could think of for, *but you risked so much more than did I*, or, *the Lord of Air be with you*. But somehow she managed it. And when at last, more than half an hour later, she reached the pillared lobby before the temple doors, she found that she was less weary than she had expected. Though she might hardly have changed the face of the Council in so short a time, and though some few of the men and women had shown an awe of her approaching terror, yet many had greeted her with genuine warmth and kindness – so that Rhysana found herself moved to genuine affection in return.

Still, it was with some sense of relief that she passed through the guarded doors into the peaceful coolness of the temple beyond. The temple itself was a high-domed chamber of white marble, eight sided, with a patterned floor of blue and grey flagstones; and the inside of the great dome was lined with rich blue jasper and bordered with silver. Beneath the rim of the dome ran a full circle of window arches, open to the clear summer sky and the winds from the mountains and the plains; and below ran a second circle of arches, giving on to a narrow gallery walkway, where singers and musicians would be gathered on high festival days. But the gallery was empty that morning.

In the centre of the floor, as was the custom in *Aeshta* temples, stood the altar – a half cube of white marble, four feet high and eight feet square; and its four corners were carved into the likeness of winged horses emerging from the stone. Legend had it that this altar had been raised above the tomb of Furghollan, father of Ferrughôr, first King of the First Kingdom. But burial under stone had never been a custom among the human kindreds of the Six Kingdoms, even in their earliest days; and Rhysana thought it more likely that the legend pointed to a subtler mystery, which perhaps even the Lords of Braedun themselves had long since forgotten.

On the nearer side of the altar as she entered, upon a painted wooden bier, lay the body of the Chosen Priest Aerlan of Braedun. He had been washed and clothed anew in formal robes of midnight blue edged with silver, and the jewelled silver circlet of his office rested upon his breast above his folded hands. On either side of the bier knelt two armed knights of the Temple Guard, their heads bowed in silent vigil. A fragrant incense of cedar and myrtle drifted on the air.

Rhysana guessed that Aerlan's Rite of Burning would not be held in Arrandin. As a senior priest of his Order, he would doubtless be carried back to the high terraces of the ancient monastery isle of Telúmachel, west along the coast beyond the imperial city of Lautun. But his final parting there would be a private ceremony; so he lay here now in the open temple in Arrandin, for other folk to come and say their farewells.

There were perhaps a dozen other visitors gathered in the temple, standing in prayer or talking quietly together. Rhysana recognised one or two of them by sight, though not well enough to call them by name; and besides, she had not come here for company. She went to look once more on Aerlan's face, and to commend him into the care of the gods; and then she went out again, gliding through the crowded garden with just a few brief smiles and nods, and seeking refuge in the smaller garden beyond, where lay the alcove shrines to the other Lords of the *Aeshtar*.

As she had hoped, the smaller garden was deserted at this late hour of the morning – unless one counted the birds fluttering from branch to branch, or perched up on the eaves of the surrounding buildings. On her last visit here, with Boldrin of Levrin, she recalled that there had been some of the tiny white birds of Dortrean in the ancient ash tree in the middle of the garden. But there were none here now; and Boldrin had ridden away to the east with Erkal Dortrean and the Emperor's armies.

Rhysana sat herself down on the curved white bench beside the central pool, in the shade of the tall ash, and composed herself to calm. The temple chamber had been too occupied with the presence of Aerlan's body, and the movements of other people, for her to be wholly comfortable. Here she could relax, and be more keenly aware of the closeness of the gods – not only in the shadowed alcoves of their encircling shrines, but thrilling on the heavy sunlit air, and in the gentle stirring of the leaves and the comical dances of the birds, and in the murmur of the wellspring waters of the pool before her feet.

She had much to bring before the gods that morning, and much for which to be thankful. The whole business of the safe recovery of Herghin, and the efforts and sacrifice of those who had made it possible, and the continuing efforts of those who still gave themselves to the safe conclusion of this war. The problems with the Emperor Rhydden and his household, and the difficulties faced by the Council and the Colleges. And then there was the great joy of Hrugaar's return, and how much it would mean to Torkhaal, as well as to herself.

Rhysana had heard of Tinûkenil and his friends before, both from Hrugaar – who had met them on occasion – and from other sources. But as she gave thanks for their timely intervention, it occurred to her that there had once been a

Moon mage among them, named Dakhmaal. Dakhmaal had earned his mage councillor's seat the previous year, though she could not recall him attending more than one assembly since then. Yet Dhûghaúr had made no mention of his presence at Herghin, and she wondered what had become of him. Herusen, as Prime Councillor, would have known – or at least, would have been able to call upon him, were he still in the waking world. But Herusen was not here.

She must have missed the noon bell, caught up in her own meditations. She simply came to a point where her thoughts led her back to the waking world of the temple garden; and as her eyes travelled down the path toward the outer doorway, she saw that Mage Councillor Telghraan was approaching.

Telghraan, she thought with gentle humour, might be a likely messenger of the gods, if only because he was so unlikely. He had dark brown hair and brown eyes, and a nose slightly too broad and flat to be considered truly handsome. He was of scrawny build, so that his plain green robes seemed to have grown tired waiting for him to grow into them; and his cautious deference as he approached lent him something of the air of a rogue, or of a wayward youth. When she rose to greet him, he jumped like a startled deer. Rhysana smiled and beckoned him forward, and they sat down together on the bench.

With her experience of the Colleges and the Council, Rhysana had already guessed at most of Telghraan's news. From the four Colleges, only two of the Principals and one of the Bursars had attended the assembly – the rest being either dead or committed elsewhere with the war. Of the remaining lecturers, only fifteen were readily available to resume the work of the current term; barely half the number that they had had only a few weeks before, when the mid-term break began. Again, the rest of those lecturers were now either slain or caught up with the work of the war against the Easterners.

Unlike the religious Orders or the Houses Noble, the Council of Magi could not command its members to perform appointed roles. At most, had they deemed it necessary, the

High Council might have called upon such magi as Rhysana and Torkhaal and requested that they set aside their efforts in the war and return to their lecturing posts, for the sake of the Colleges. But since Sollonaal was only acting as Prime Councillor, he had not the gift – as Herusen had done – to be able to contact all those magi at will. So at present, such a solution was in any event impracticable.

The assembly had thus agreed that the activity of the Arrandin College should be suspended for the present, and that the students of that College – most of whom had survived unharmed – should be divided between the other three Colleges to continue their studies. High Councillor Iorlaas, the most senior mage of Serbramel within the Empire, was to join the depleted staff of the Ellanguan College; and the usually reclusive Trialmaster Ekraan had offered to help out at Rhysana's own College in Lautun. Some three or four of the Itinerant Magi – mostly from among the younger members of the Council – had also agreed to take on temporary lecturing roles.

High Councillor Sollonaal had expressed his regret that Rhysana and Ellen had felt unable to attend the assembly, though he had added that he appreciated the awkwardness of their position. Rhysana had hardly expected Sollonaal to take kindly to her absence; nor had she held out much hope that he would pass up the opportunity to make some snide observation at her own expense. Yet she knew – as Sollonaal himself had pointed out to the assembly – that this makeshift arrangement for the Colleges could not endure beyond the few remaining weeks of the present term. By the time that the new moon waxed to the full, they would have to choose a new Prime Councillor, and make more permanent provision for the tuition of their students. But hopefully by then the war with the Easterners would have been brought to an end, and they would be free again to concentrate their efforts on the welfare of College and Council.

There had been a small amount of news from elsewhere in

the Empire. Armies from the western part of the Six Kingdoms had gathered around Lautun and Farran, and there had been some movement between the two cities along the coast. But there had been no evidence of further attack by Souther ships; and indeed, the Lord Steward of Ellanguan appeared to have persuaded the Souther Ambassador to call for peace – though whether the Countess of Dortrean had had a hand in that persuasion had been a point of contention in the assembly chamber.

Another point upon which there had been heated debate – as Rhysana had expected – was Herusen's summoning of the Father of All Dragons. Though someone had pointed out that it was subtly different from the summoning spells used by the Easterner Wizards, and more importantly had saved Arrandin, the whole question had left the assembled councillors unsettled. Sollonaal and the *Vashta* magi had not been slow to point that it was a dangerous precedent for a Prime Councillor to have set, especially one so respected as Herusen had been. Rhysana's own efforts with the defence matrix were left largely unmentioned, though it seemed that they were as much feared as approved by those magi who had been present.

What Rhysana had not anticipated – though in hindsight she told herself that she should have done so – was Sollonaal's personal address to the New Moon Assembly. As Telghraan recounted it to her, Sollonaal had urged those councillors present to reconsider the future role of the Council in the light of recent events. Though in the days of their Golden Age, he had said, the Council of Magi had provided a stabilising central force amid the internal conflicts of the Six Kingdoms, the political situation had long since changed. The Emperor of Lautun now provided a single, central focus; and given the present Emperor's need for support against foreign invaders, and especially with his own succession far from secure, it might seem prudent for the Council to set aside their neutrality in favour of the Emperor – though still, of course, upon their own terms. Sollonaal had cited the disastrous attempt to defend Herghin, at the beginning of the war, as just one example of the dangers of letting individual magi act independently when the safety of the Empire, and indeed the wellbeing of the Council itself, was at stake. Three of the magi murdered at Herghin had been lecturers from his own College in Ellanguan. Herusen's summoning of the dragon was another case in point.

'And what did the assembly say to this?' she asked Telghraan.

'There was the usual outcry,' he answered. 'But given the context of a war against outsiders, I suppose he did have a point.'

'Oh yes,' said Rhysana; 'a point that has been raised by many others over the centuries, and which is no more valid now than then.' She wondered privately whether she should have gone to the assembly after all.

The sun had not long passed his noon height when Kellarn's company rode down from the hills into the wider valley basin of the village of Fersí. The village itself straddled the course of one of the summer rivers, fed by the melting snows of the Blue Mountains a couple of leagues to the north. It was not the only place where the white-foamed waters could be forded, but it was more suitable than most for heavy wagons; and so the line of the border road crossed the river at that point – as did the line of the Emperor's armies, having arrived just a short time before. From what Kellarn could recall, the river flowed on south through Tormal lands, to lose itself in marshy ground somewhere among the Twisting Downs. The main reach of the Footstool Hills of Arrandin now stretched to their west and south; while to the northeast of the valley basin the folded hills spread wider into more open rolling grassland – though still pocked with many sudden dips and hollows, where the enemy lay hidden.

As they rode across the level ground along the eastern river shore, Kellarn shaded his eyes to see the village up ahead. A few of the low stone cottages were still smouldering, and most of the wooden structures around the village edge – the barns and cattle pens and smaller outhouses – were blackened ruins. Yet without the river nearby, and the recent rain, the damage might have been far worse. The larger part of the Emperor's armies were still on the western side of the ford; but already several score of warriors seemed to be at work within the village, clearing and salvaging and tending the survivors. More were gathering further east along the road, keeping a forward guard. Kellarn guessed that they had been warned of the ambush waiting ahead.

All along the shore there were the signs of the enemy's passing, the river banks trampled and churned to mud in many places, and strewn with abandoned gear and ruined bodies. The horse beneath him grew restless with the scent of recent battle.

'His Grace the Earl of Dortrean is there,' called Tinûkenil from behind him. 'By the largest building on the western shore.'

'That would be the inn,' said Kellarn, looking that way. The Fersí inn was famous in Arrandin as a meeting place for travellers and merchants on the border road, though Kellarn had never ridden out here to visit it for himself. It was still more than half a mile away, and he could only guess at his father's scarlet shape amid all the other horsemen in their brightly coloured liveries.

'The Archmage Morvaan is with him,' came Hrugaar's voice. 'He has seen us, I think.'

'There are also many knights in the Mairdun livery, on the near shore,' said Tinûkenil.

'Mairdun were to have ridden south,' said Gravhan doubtfully, 'to retake Tormal.'

'Perhaps they rode north afterward, as we did,' said Kellarn.

As they drew nearer, he could make out for himself the black surcoats bordered with silver and gold which were the livery of the Hyrsenites of Mairdun. There were several of them moving around in the nearer parts of the village. Two errand riders in the brown and gold of one of the Lautun houses broke away from the sentry guard further to the east and came riding toward Kellarn's company, but the knights of Mairdun waved the riders back again. They also waved to Kellarn's company, signalling for them to veer more to the left, down toward the shore.

The Abbot Commander Carstan Mairdun himself came out from among the buildings to greet them. He was dressed as any other knight of his Order in mailshirt and surcoat over breeches of black leather and sturdy riding boots, though he carried no weapon with him. His kindly face was streaked with grime and ash and blood, and his pale fair hair was tousled and ruffled like a windblown haystack. But there was no mistaking his quiet confidence and purpose.

Gwydion and Gravhan were already dismounting. Tinûkenil slipped forward past the other riders, now cloaked and hooded in deep grey to hide his silvery beauty. Kellarn reined in and dismounted more slowly. He did not know the Abbot Commander well – though he knew that his parents held Carstan in high regard, and it seemed that most of the other people present were very pleased to see him. Corollin matched her pace to Kellarn's, as if more concerned about her horse's comfort at that moment. However amenable the Hyrsenites might be toward Dortrean, the awkward fact remained that they were a *Vashta* Order of the House of War.

'Well, Tormal and Herghin are safe,' said Carstan, nodding to them in general greeting, and sketching more formal bows toward Gravhan and Kellarn. 'But more trouble lies just ahead.'

'Yes, we know,' said Gwydion.

'You will forgive my asking so soon,' Carstan went on, 'but I wonder if I might prevail upon you? Tinû and Hrugaar, especially. There are folk burned or wounded here who need our help. We have begun to gather them.' He gestured back toward the middle part of the village.

'I shall come,' said Tinûkenil.

145

'The other Orders will be here soon,' Gravhan reminded them.

'Indeed they will,' Carstan nodded. 'But they will have their work cut out for them later in the day, and the army commanders will not want to tarry here long.'

'Is Mage Councillor Salbaar here?' asked Torkhaal. 'Dark hair, blue robes.'

Carstan looked at him steadily.

'I am sorry,' he said. 'He perished in the fires. A friend of his survived – Rinnir, the men of Holleth name him, though he does not speak. His face and hands are very badly burned. He tried to rescue your Salbaar from the flames.'

'Rinnir?' cried Hrugaar. 'But he was a musician, and a singer of songs. Will he be all right?'

'That is for the gods to grant,' said Carstan; 'and for us to help, as we may. Tinû?'

He turned and led the way toward a ravaged stableyard, gesturing for the moon fay to join him. Gwydion and the two magi followed behind. Corollin handed the reins of her borrowed horse to Kellarn, and hurried after them.

'Lord Kellarn,' said Gravhan. 'Perhaps we had better go to find your father?'

'I suppose so,' Kellarn sighed, suddenly tired again. 'But it looks as if they know all our news already.'

Chapter Five

Kellarn remembered little of the battle that afternoon, except for the sight of hundreds of Easterners streaming down the hill slopes toward him in the sunlight, and the bewildering assault of colours and noises and smells in the sweltering heat.

Having climbed up beyond the Fersí valley, the border road ran north for a stretch of some two miles before turning east again; and it was there that the enemy had chosen to make their ambush. Given the time of day they had not, of course, chosen well. More than half of their number were to the east of the road, and thus had the westering sun full in their eyes as they launched their attack. Those to the north and west of the road, at the far end of the straight run, had slightly better vantage; but they had failed to take into account that they were out-scouted and so easily out-manoeuvred by the large numbers of mounted knights in the Emperor's armies. Had Rhydden's armies been wholly on foot, and kept wholly to the road, the Easterners might have fared a little better.

It was clear almost from the start that the enemy were at a disadvantage. Though the men of the Six Kingdoms were tired from their long marching and the heat of the day, their morale was high and few of them had yet seen battle in this war. The Easterners, on the other hand, had endured the long conflict of the siege and the strains of the general rout thereafter; and though they had been rallied to stand and fight, they were poorly fed and poorly provided for, and there was a desperation in their moves that made them both more dangerous and more carelessly vulnerable.

The Easterners had made little use of magical power on this occasion, with only a few wizards or priests scattered among them. Most of these were to the north, as Tinûkenil had warned, and the priests and knights of the *Vashta* Orders had acquitted themselves well against them. There had been lightning and fire, and the smoking reek of charred bodies; but there had been no summoning of creatures from other Realms.

Kellarn himself had been farther to the south, toward the rear of the long file of the Emperor's armies, together with his father of Dortrean and the remnant of the war band who had ridden with him from Sentai. Boldrin of Levrin and the troops sent by The Arrand were just ahead of them on the road. They had taken the battle up on to the hill slopes, skirting round to the southern flank of the oncoming hordes. Beyond the blue and silver banners of the Easterners, Kellarn had glimpsed their chieftain – a woman clad in plated armour enamelled and painted to resemble fish scales, whom he discovered to be the Sholerghti – lashing her warriors forward into the sun, over the mangled bodies of their fallen brethren. But the Sholerghti withdrew behind an armed escort, and he had not the chance to come near her. There were also, the Arrand knights told him, many warriors among her following who appeared to be of the Zhaughrai clan – the Zhaughrai himself having been slain several days ago during one of the earlier assaults of the siege.

The Easterners to the north, with their banners of red and black and gold, Kellarn later learned to be warriors of the Korzhai and the Andrakhai – both lesser clans under the sway of the Mughuzhti. The chieftain of the Korzhai was believed to have been slain during the raising of the siege of Arrandin, soon after the death of his overlord the Mughuzhti; but the Andrakhai was still very much alive, with his scarlet armour and huge dragon-crested helm. Like the Sholerghti, he drove his warriors before him. By report, he had left the field unscathed – though the hillsides he left behind him were stained red and black as his banners, and stank like a slaughterhouse in the late afternoon heat. There seemed to be no warriors of the greater clan of the Mughuzhti among his rallied forces.

Outnumbered and outflanked, the Easterners had not held their attack for long. When perhaps a sixth of their number had been cut down, they sounded the retreat with braying horns and shrieking cries. Lord Drômagh, Knight Commander of the Imperial Household Guard, gave the order to hold off any pursuit. Though the mounted knights of the Lautun armies might easily have overtaken the fleeing enemy, Drômagh said that he thought it unwise to divide their own forces without due need, and that their present victory was enough.

The Andrakhai and the Sholerghti thus withdrew with some three thousand warriors, and with some semblance of order, heading east and north beyond the road toward the Khôrland vale. From what scant information could be gleaned from captive enemies and from the maimed and dying – and from the arts of their own priests and magi – it seemed likely that thither most of the scattered enemy forces were now hastening. But this was no more than Kellarn and his father had already expected.

The Lautun armies made their camp up beyond the eastward bend of the road, and set about the weary business of tending the wounded and the dead. Lord Brodhaur, Commander in Chief of the Emperor's armies, was one of those who had been caught by arrowfire in the ambush; and though his hurt was not great, it was agreed among the other commanders that he should remain behind to oversee the safe return of the wounded to Fersí the following day, and to hold secure the road west back to Arrandin. The main host of the armies – still almost five thousand strong – would continue east to Khôrland without him.

Kellarn could sense that his father was less than pleased at the loss of Brodhaur Levrin from their company, in spite of genuine concern for his health and wellbeing. Among the

149

imperial war leaders Brodhaur was perhaps the most amenable to Dortrean, particularly when it came to defending Erkal's actions before the Emperor; and if Erkal was required to make peace with the Easterner chieftains, he would far rather have had Brodhaur at his side than his second in command, Lord Drômagh. Though an excellent warrior and commander, Drômagh had not Lord Brodhaur's tact and subtlety for negotiation; nor did he wholly trust Dortrean. But Erkal could only make open argument for Brodhaur's riding east on the grounds of his military skill and senior rank. And since there were many commanders there with skill to rival Brodhaur's own, and since in truth Lord Drômagh was a far more spirited leader of men upon the field, Erkal had to concede that his argument held too little weight to carry the vote.

As the sunlight faded in the west, and the first stars winked down through the haze of the evening sky, Kellarn lay moodily on his stomach beside the camp fire, watching while Haësella fussed over the dressings on Hollin of Logray's swollen ankle. Corollin sat beside him, staring at patterns in the leaping flames. His father and Boldrin of Levrin were talking quietly nearby. The grey and purple of the Arrand pavilion stood protectively behind them, the colours still rich and vibrant in the deepening twilight.

Corollin had many questions about his adventures in the past few weeks, and Kellarn had questions of his own. But there was nowhere really private to talk in the midst of an army camp; and besides, his mind kept leaping forward to the Khôrland vale, and the challenges of the battle that must surely await them there. He could not imagine that the Easterners would make an easy peace, and the Lautun armies would be hard put to hold the vale under siege for many days; and if – as Tinûkenil believed – they were to discover more of Lo-Khuma there, the prospect of what that knowledge might be was also far from comfortable.

In Ellanguan, the Lady Karlena of Dortrean had her own

misgivings about what lay in store for the Emperor's armies in the Khôrland vale. Even before the news had reached her of the safe recovery of the Herghin and Tormal manors, she had guessed that the Easterners would dig themselves in beneath the cliffs at Khôrland for their last defence. Karlena held out little more hope than her younger son that peace could be achieved without further conflict and dark magic; and tied to the Empress' household, here on the coast, there seemed to be no practical help that she could offer.

Even in Ellanguan she found herself hindered, if not altogether thwarted, at almost every turn. Though some few of the Court Noble had stayed in the city, most had ridden away with the Emperor or returned home to their own manors to make provision for the needs of the war. She was every day with the Empress Grinnaer, and still in residence within the guest apartments of the Steward's palace; and yet even that was not the advantage which it might have been, only a few years before. Grinnaer's small household was wary of Karlena, and less well informed than it should have been of the turns of the war; and the new Empress had neither the skill nor training as yet to provide her own means of gathering news. The household of the Lord Steward Rinnekh was better informed; but given the lack of trust between Rinnekh and herself, Karlena could not presume too much on the loyalty of his servants. She had also perceived that her every move was now being watched.

Having been brought here so precipitously by Rhysana at the start of the war, she had none of her own people with her and precious little of her familiar paraphernalia, which gave rise to the added complications of many small, everyday practicalities. Most pressing of these had been the simple lack of suitable changes of clothing, given the summer heat and the amount of time that she had to spend with Grinnaer. Though in the city port of Ellanguan, at the time of the Summer Fair, there had been no shortage of fine cloth and excellent tailors and seamstresses ready to oblige – and though none dared question that the credit of Dortrean was good, even in time of war –

she had found the distraction more frustrating than enjoyable. Elmirra, Countess of Ercusí, had thoughtfully loaned her the services of one of the senior women of her own household, the long suffering Lisella. But since the Ercusí were habitually at odds with Rinnekh's kinsmen of Solaní, poor Lisella had no easy time of it. Elmirra had also invited Karlena to make use of the Ercusí city house, near by in the Nobles' Quarter – an offer which she had reluctantly declined, since it would have deprived her of the simple excuse to gain access to the Steward's palace whenever she wished. Nevertheless, she felt very much the guest who had outstayed her welcome.

Her progress with Grinnaer had been similarly frustrating. Where the former Empress, Lissaïn, had been more or less of an age with Karlena, Grinnaer was fully young enough to be her own daughter; so that Karlena found herself received as something of a relic from a previous generation. The new Empress treated the Countess with respect and no small amount of awe, but seemed unable to grasp the relevance of Karlena's experience to her own position.

What could be said at once in Grinnaer's favour was that, like her younger brother Goshaún, she did not appear to be possessed of the predatory, often violent nature of most of her Sêchral kinsmen. Karlena guessed that they must have inherited this kinder disposition from the Serra and Hershôr blood of their late mother's line. Grinnaer was timid, both craving affection and support and yet fearful of it, in the manner of an inbred puppy. She had also a wilful and rebellious streak, though it was hidden deep enough to require several goblets of wine to dredge it to the surface. Grinnaer showed a greater fondness for the winejar, and for her brother, than Karlena thought altogether wise in a young Empress Consort. But then again, these two were perhaps the only true sources of comfort now left to her.

When it came to training Grinnaer to fulfil her imperial role, Karlena had her work cut out for her. Though the daughter of a Greater House Noble, and not insensible of noble courtesy, the new Empress had been poorly educated in the arts of diplomacy and rulership. She was, Karlena reflected sadly, a creature of the fashionable imperial houses, who seemed to be breeding their daughters as decorative objects intended chiefly for making marriage alliances and bearing children. By long custom, the Empress was not permitted to play *sherunuresh* with anyone, save the Emperor himself. But Karlena discovered that even attempting to discuss the basic principles of the game with Grinnaer – a time-honoured manner of training in all arts political, philosophical or mystic – or asking her to comment on games played between Karlena and Goshaún, was to little avail. Grinnaer simply had not Karlena's instinct or passion for abstract principles, nor her intuition for the workings of the human mind and heart. Karlena had swiftly come to the conclusion that the girl would learn best by the long road of experience and guided observation; and had thus settled herself to the more practical work of winning Grinnaer's confidence, and keeping her company, and regaling her with amusing stories of life at the Court illuminated by her own insight and experience.

The first real sign of breakthrough had come late that afternoon, as they prepared to go down to the Steward's palace. The Lord Steward Rinnekh had commanded a feast; both to celebrate the relief of Arrandin two days before and the continuing success of the Emperor's armies, and also the promise of peace which he himself had secured from the Souther Ambassador T'Loi. Karlena – who knew more of the Souther empire's internal conflicts than did the upstart Rinnekh – thought that promise of peace to be tenuous, and likely to be short lived; and it struck her as tempting the gods to celebrate Arrandin's safety so soon. Nevertheless, this was the first formal invitation that the Empress had received from the palace since the Emperor's departure, more than a week before, and the rare opportunity was not to be missed. Though Grinnaer was Rinnekh's first cousin on his mother's side, the two of them did not get on well together; and he had too obviously been trying to keep both the Empress and Karlena out of his sight as much as possible.

They had been in one of the smaller, circular tower rooms of the Emperor's city house, which looked out over the bright green of the trees in the western park of the Nobles' Quarter. Grinnaer had chosen to put on a full-skirted gown of russet silk – a colour which flattered her well – and her dark chestnut hair was swept up into soft billows with pins of amber and gold. A faceted topaz the size of a Souther *abrecock* hung just below the hollow of her pale throat. Her women had advised her against donning any other jewels. Karlena herself had put on a new high-collared gown of deep mulberry linen, which complemented the beauty of her piled copper hair. She might have borrowed jewels from the Empress' collection, or even from the vaults of the Steward's palace; but she would not have felt comfortable with such decoration while her menfolk were still at war, nor did she wish to appear beholden to either Ellanguan or Lautun.

The household women had gone away again with the paraphernalia of the Empress' dressing chamber, and only Goshaún remained with them, leaning against the wall beside the doorway in the fallow gold of his imperial livery. Grinnaer was moving back and forth before the tall standing mirror that had been brought for her, practising the slow walk and balanced poise which Karlena had been trying to teach her. Karlena was keeping one eye on Grinnaer, while watching the antics of two collared doves in the chestnut branches outside. The salt breeze from the sea fluttered at the open window.

'Karlena,' said Grinnaer, looking back over her shoulder. 'If I wanted to make trouble for Rinnekh, how much trouble could I really cause?'

Goshaún chuckled, idly scuffing the toe of one booted foot against the polished floor. Karlena turned her attention wholly back to the Empress, at once startled and intrigued. She decided that a frank answer was probably the safest course.

'A little,' she told Grinnaer. 'Not much. This is Rinnekh's

own city, and the Emperor is far away. Rhydden loves him, and Rinnekh knows it; and he can use that to great advantage. Rhydden married you for heirs, not for any great affection. That is a reflection of the needs of the Empire, and no fault on your own part; yet it puts you at a disadvantage in this case. Were your Uncle Drômagh to support you, I suppose that you might have a chance of influencing Rhydden against him.'

'But you can handle Rinnekh,' Grinnaer countered.

'Is that what I do?' Karlena laughed. 'Well, if *handling* means avoiding causing trouble with him, then yes, that is what I try to do. But any untutored fool can cause trouble, Serenity. The greater skill is to learn how not to be caught.'

Grinnaer considered that answer for a moment, and then a slow smile of understanding spread across her face. And then the conversation turned to other things, and they went down to process through the parks of the Nobles' Quarter beneath the Empress' golden canopy, and so joined the swelling crowd in the Steward's palace for Rinnekh's feast.

A gilded and cushioned chair had been set ready for the Empress at the mid-point of one of the side tables; and above and behind it was a large hanging tapestry that Karlena did not remember having seen before, with many storied images of battles and feasting which she guessed to be drawn from tales of the *Vashtar*. At the head of the long feast hall were two heavier carved chairs, intended for Rinnekh and the Souther Ambassador T'Loi.

There were a dozen or more of the Lords and Ladies of the Court Noble present, and several of the rich and powerful merchants from the city; a handful of priests and elders from the *Vashta* temples, others whom Karlena took to be senior Guildmasters of Ellanguan, and a small group of musicians from the Harperschool. There were no representatives from the Kelmaar Order or the *Aeshta* temples, as there would have been in old Gradhellan's day. High Councillor Sollonaal was there with two of his fellow magi; but those two, like Sollonaal, wore hooded turquoise robes – the colour of the

Lords Steward of Ellanguan – and Karlena did not recognise them. There were also several more Southers than she had expected among T'Loi's following, not simple attendants or slaves but men of moderate rank or station. Karlena guessed that they came from the storm-battered warships which had been permitted safe harbour in Ellanguan, under the terms of the new peace agreement.

While Karlena did not consider Rinnekh quite so foolish as to betray his Empress, it struck her that both she and Grinnaer were vulnerable here. Apart from Goshaún, they had with them only the five armed guards of the Empress' honour escort; and glancing around the feast hall, there were far too few whom she thought capable of standing up to Rinnekh in his own palace – or to T'Loi, if he had Rinnekh behind him.

Her gaze lighted on the fair hair and rose-pink gown of the Lady Melissa of Vanbruch. Melissa was more or less of an age with Karlena's own children, the only daughter of the Lord Farad Vanbruch and heir designate to the considerable wealth and power of his estate. Farad was a merchant of the highest grade in his own right, as well as Head of a Greater House Noble; and like all merchant nobles, Vanbruch were – of necessity – past masters at charting a safe course through the shifting tides of alliance and loyalties among the rulers of the Six Kingdoms. Whatever Melissa might think of Rhydden or Rinnekh personally, she could ill afford to stand idly by and watch the Empress, or Karlena herself, come to any harm. And besides, Melissa had always been rather fond of Karlena's children, and Kellarn in particular; and she also had an escort of four strong guards in the black and copper livery of her House.

But before Karlena could speak with Melissa, and even before she had seen the Empress settled comfortably upon her cushioned chair, the Steward and the Ambassador came over to hover behind her.

'T'Loi,' she said pleasantly, bowing in greeting. 'I am glad to see that you are well.'

'And I to see you, my Countess,' T'Loi replied. He favoured her with a deep, sweeping bow, a swirl of sky-blue robes borne upon a wave of sweet perfume, with a half turn to include the Empress. Rinnekh gave a leering grin, and favoured both women with a mocking half bow.

'Now that the unfortunate misunderstanding between us is past,' the Ambassador went on, 'permit me to present this belated festival gift, in thanks for your long kindness to my countrymen in visits to your Emperor's Court.'

A white-robed attendant was instantly at his side, bearing a silken cushion with the proffered gift – a ruby the size of a pigeon's egg, set in a brooch of Souther gold in the shape of an eight-rayed star. T'Loi picked up the brooch and held it out to her.

Karlena smiled. While it was true that in recent years she had found him most agreeable, as a person, to work with, she was irritated with T'Loi for testing her in this way before so many witnesses. She had no wish to offend him by refusing the gift; nor could she risk, by accepting it, the implication that there was any special friendship or alliance between Dortrean and his master the God-King, or that she had played any part in this latest agreement between Rinnekh and T'Loi. And every eye in the feast hall now seemed to be turned upon her.

'His Excellency is most gracious,' she said, with another bow. 'Yet it would be unseemly for me to accept such a gift in my husband's absence; and he and I are but servants of the Emperor, to whom all such displays of gratitude should rightly be addressed. Still, Excellency, such generosity may not be refused; and I am sure that Her Serene Highness the Empress Consort will receive this jewel on the Emperor's behalf, and hold it in safe keeping against his return.'

T'Loi's dark eyes glittered with amusement, and he gave her a half-nod, conceding the point. He returned the brooch to its silken cushion, and it was carried forward to Grinnaer. The Empress glanced nervously toward Karlena, and then signalled for Goshaún to take it.

'This gift I shall receive, Excellency,' said Grinnaer, her voice a little too loud and shrill with the effort, 'until my Lord and Emperor returns.'

T'Loi bowed elegantly, the five jewels of his office dipping and bobbing on his forehead.

'I can not promise,' Grinnaer went on, 'that His Highness will accept it – unless it be to help pay for the damage you have caused along the coast. Indeed, I wonder whether he would be at all pleased to learn that five of your warships are now sitting in the harbours here.'

Karlena was as surprised as any by this unexpected show of spirit. To her certain knowledge, the Empress had been permitted no more than one small goblet of wine before they had left the imperial city house.

'On the contrary,' said Rinnekh mockingly, 'His Highness is well aware that the ships are here, and has of course given his approval to the promise of peace between us. I regret that *Her Serenity* has not been informed of this.'

Grinnaer looked discomfited.

'Still,' he added, 'you will be happy to hear that the Emperor has already dispatched another of his own ships from Lautun, with a certain number of his own household guard, to sail hither to Ellanguan. This is simply to ensure that the business of refitting the Souther ships may be conducted peacefully and amicably – though no doubt their presence will be of comfort to our citizens and to yourself.'

'More like he wants to be certain that he doesn't lose the city,' returned Grinnaer.

The comment was certainly to the point, Karlena thought. There could be few in the feast hall, except perhaps among the Souther shipmen, who had not heard of Sarin's warning of strife between Rhydden and Rinnekh, down on the harbour front. Rinnekh's face reddened, and a dampness of sweat appeared upon his brow.

'Rhydden has my love and loyalty,' he said viciously. 'He only married you because he needed an heir. If you can't produce the goods, Grinnaer, there are plenty more daughters of Blood Noble to take your place.'

'Or is it that you would rather be his heir yourself, Rin?' put in Goshaún. 'Though there is no chance of that, of course. Anyway, how do you presume to know that Her Serene Highness is not already with child?'

Rinnekh's face went even redder. His mouth opened and shut, but no sound came out, giving him the appearance of an exotic goldfish.

'Lord Steward,' said Karlena, calmly taking control; 'if these cordial greetings are ended, perhaps we could take our places for the feast? Your guests await you.'

She nodded to T'Loi, and signalled for the musicians to begin. T'Loi favoured her with a half bow, then took Rinnekh by the arm and fairly marched him away toward the upper end of the hall. Watching them go, Karlena observed a familiarity between them that she had not noticed before; so that she wondered how far each might have sold himself to achieve this present peace.

Then Karlena set the thought aside, and looked around in search of Melissa of Vanbruch. She feared that this trouble stirred by Grinnaer and Goshaún had made their position more dangerous.

The night turned clear and cold among the hills, and the dawn came up in fire, staining the sheer cliffs of the mountains to crimson and violet. The Emperor's armies made an early start. The first reports came in that the ambushing armies had moved a few miles further on under cover of darkness. The clansmen of the Korzhai had now dropped down on to the road, fleeing eastward with great speed. The remaining warriors, under the leadership of the Sholerghti and the Andrakhai, still seemed to be heading for the Khôrland vale.

Kellarn and Erkal rode near the head of the Emperor's armies, in the company of the Lords Drômagh of Sêchral and

Boldrin of Levrin. The golden horsemen of the Imperial Household Cavalry were before them, and the much smaller band of The Arrand's forces immediately behind. The Easterner loremaster, Kata Aghaira, rode openly between Erkal and Drômagh for this last stretch of their journey, attempting to answer their questions in her rich, mellow voice.

By noon they had reached the far edge of the Tollund lands, where the road ran north again; and ahead of them, little more than two leagues distant, loomed the nearest mountain spur which marked the beginning of the Khôrland vale. The manor house itself, so Kellarn was told, stood at the inner end of the vale, some two leagues again beyond; but they would have to leave the road to reach it. To their south and east the land stretched wide and flat, basking beneath the shimmering haze of the midday heat. Though many wild things lived and grew there, it was unfriendly to humankind. The men of the border manors seldom journeyed that way.

As they came down from among the hills, Kellarn could see the fleeing warriors of the Korzhai clan far ahead to the east along the road – no more than a smear of black and red, like crushed beetles on the tawny ground. The far-flung village of Samsar, most eastern of all the settlements of the Six Kingdoms, lay nestled amid a smaller spur of mountain foothills just a few miles further again along the road; and from Samsar it was less than seven leagues to the fords of the great Blue Mountain River, and the end of the Middle Lands.

'More Easterners have left the village, perhaps an hour since,' said Hrugaar. 'The fair-haired giant, the Raunazhrai, is with them. They are leaving these lands and heading home again.'

'So the Raunazhrai is gone,' said Aghaira, nodding to herself. 'This is a sadness. He has a good heart. Our talk will go less well without him.'

'How do you know that, Hrugaar?' Kellarn asked.

'A mage sees many things,' said Hrugaar mischievously; 'even though the hills hide them.'

Lord Drômagh growled, either at Aghaira's words or at the strange arts of the Magi – or possibly at both.

Hrugaar and Torkhaal had ridden close by for most of the morning, as if drawn by the lure of Aghaira's presence. The Archmage Morvaan and other magi had all kept their distance, a good way further back down the long line of the marching armies. Of the others who had ridden with Kellarn from Herghin, he knew that Gwydion and Gravhan were now with the knights of the Môshári; as was Odhragh, the red-cloaked *noghr*, who by report had slain more than a dozen Easterners with his black-bladed axe during the ambush east of Fersí. Haësella and Hardhen and the Ferlund men rode with Kellarn's war band from Sentai, just to the rear of The Arrand's forces. Corollin stayed close to Kellarn – though whether for his protection or her own, neither of them seemed quite certain. He had not seen Tinûkenil again, nor the grey-cloaked Skaramak, since they had parted company the previous day.

As the afternoon wore on they left the border road and climbed up into the mountain shadow. The vale of Khôrland was shaped like a wide half moon some ten miles across, or a sea bay ringed by the towering cliffs of the Knees of the Blue Mountains and filled with rolling farmland slopes like huge sea swells; and the shadow from the west spread further across the vale before them as they rode, as though left behind by an ebbing tide of sunlight.

At last they reached the crest of a trampled slope, within two miles of the manor house gates; and there the commanders of the Six Kingdoms armies called a halt, and set about the ordering of their camps within sight of the cornered enemy.

The Khôrland manor house was built right against the cliffs, or partly into them, and fashioned of the same blue-grey mountain stone; so that from a distance it might have passed for no more than a rocky spur at the head of a broad green rise, at some height above the rest of the vale. But now the walls and towers were hung with many banners of different

161

colours, and in a wide half circle around the foot of the rise several thousand enemy warriors were arrayed in readiness.

'Will they attack us tonight?' asked Lord Drômagh.

'Perhaps yes, if they think that your warriors are tired,' said Kata Aghaira. 'In the siege they attacked at night. Or perhaps no, if they think that they are stronger where they are. You are the war commander. What would you do?'

'You're the Easterner,' Drômagh scowled. 'You understand these devils.'

Aghaira shrugged. Her face looked very tired.

'They are not devils, my Lord,' she said. 'Though what they may call forth is another matter. There is magic at work up there, I think.'

'Yes,' said Hrugaar. 'They shield the manor from us, concealing what lies within. But that is all, as yet.'

'If we talk to them,' said Erkal, 'will they grant us peace until morning?'

'There is no loss of honour in the asking,' Aghaira nodded. 'If they have the honour to keep their word, they will do so.'

'Then I suppose that we should try,' said Erkal. 'Let a small escort be prepared. And Torkhaal – Councillor – would you please ensure that all the Orders and Magi are aware that there is power at work in the manor; but impress upon them that I expect no one to provoke the Easterners by meddling at this stage. Is that understood?'

'I shall urge them not to intervene, your Grace,' Torkhaal answered, bowing.

'Tell them,' Erkal insisted. 'You saw what the Easterners summoned against Arrandin. You know the greater danger.'

Torkhaal exchanged glances with Hrugaar, then bowed again and hurried away. Lord Drômagh sighed loudly, and spat upon the ground.

There were many who wished to ride with the escort, but Erkal would permit only a few. He said there was no point in wasting all their best men, should the cornered Easterners prove treacherous. So with Erkal rode Lord Drômagh, as the senior commander of the Emperor's armies, and Boldrin of Levrin as both The Arrand's envoy and a representative of the *Aeshta* Orders. The Lord Priest Môrghran of Fâghsul joined them on behalf of the *Vashta* Orders. The Archmage Morvaan came at Erkal's request, to serve as Truthsayer; and Aghaira was there as Interpreter. Drômagh chose two knights of the Imperial Household Cavalry to guard the rear flank on either side. All others were refused.

'But what about me?' demanded Kellarn. Though he knew that there were risks in drawing too much attention to himself in the eyes of the Emperor's men, he felt that it was important for him to go. Apart from any other reason or instinct, he knew that if his father were about to ride out toward several thousand Easterners, he wanted to be there to defend him.

'There is no need for us both to go,' Erkal told him.

'But how am I to learn to deal with the Easterners peacefully,' Kellarn protested, 'if all I ever get to do is fight them?'

It was not the argument he had expected to use; but when he thought about it, he realised that it was as honest a reason as any other that he might have given.

'Your son is right,' said Kata Aghaira. 'He slew the Mughuzhti. The clans fear him as a great warrior. If he comes with us, he will be better than two hundred knights. It is good.'

Kellarn groaned inwardly. That was just the kind of comment that he did not want the imperial guards to overhear. But whether from his own argument or Aghaira's support, Erkal gave in, and another horse was ordered.

It was a strange ride across the empty ground between the two opposing armies. Fully two-thirds of the vale was now deep in mountain shadow, and a cool wind blew down into their faces. But the summer sky overhead was still bright with the late afternoon; and away to their right, on the eastern side of the vale, the massive bluffs of the cliffs stood out clear in the sunlight, the pale blue stone whispering with flecks of sapphire and amethyst and glittering falls. High up above the cliffs, the summer haze turned to mist, and trailing banners of white cloud veiled the distant snowy peaks; and darker specks in the middle heaven told where the carrion birds were gathering.

Erkal Dortrean rode at the fore, his deep red cloak spreading back over the matching caparison of his great warhorse, his head crowned again with the borrowed helm of coral and gold from The Arrand's treasury with the stooping eagle upon its brow. At the Earl's side rode Kata Aghaira, bolt upright in the saddle of her smaller riding horse, the long braids of her honey-gold hair bouncing rhythmically against the back of her strawberry-pink gown. Behind these two, and immediately to Kellarn's left, rode Boldrin of Levrin, clad in the blue and white surcoat of a holy knight of the Temple Guard of Telúmachel over burnished mail. Boldrin's deep blue eyes shone brighter than ever in his tanned, handsome face; and the air around him seemed vibrant with confidence and strength. The others of their company were beyond or behind him, and Kellarn did not turn his head to look at them.

They drew further away from the safety of the Six Kingdoms armies, and the strength and number of the Easterner clans seemed to swell and multiply ahead of them as they approached, stretching ever further to left and right in their long, bristling arc. To the left were the red and gold banners of the Mughuzhti, and the red and black of the Andrakhai and the Vengru; and to the right the blue and green and silver of the Hrudhli clan, and the Zhaughrai and the Sholerghti. But unlike the household forces of the Lords of the Court Noble, the Easterner warriors themselves held to no formal colours or liveries; and so the gathered crowds were a riot of endless different hues and varied gear, beyond pattern and bewildering for the eye to follow.

The retreating chieftains, or those who had held the manor in their absence, had not been idle. Everywhere about the sloping rise there were burrowed trenches and mounded banks of earth hedged with spears, and duckboards and fire pits and open latrines, and covered shelters and strange engines of war, all carved and butchered from the ravaged manor lands. From closer to, the manor house itself seemed cast into deeper shadow, crouched spider-like between the rise and the vast wall of the cliffs towering above. Its many windows were closed and dark; but beacon fires now burned atop two of the outer towers, and there were flickers of furtive movement down by the guarded gates.

The displaced Lord Zhertan Khôrland, Kellarn knew, had ridden with the Emperor's armies; but the commanders had advised against his presence at this parley. This was no sight for a raw-passioned borderlander to see, on an errand to sue for peace.

Erkal signalled a halt, a scant furlong from the nearest edge of the enemy armies; and there they sat in the saddle, and waited. A decent bowman of the Six Kingdoms, Kellarn thought, could have picked them off one by one at such a distance. Yet though they could see the enemy watching them, no attack came.

'Is this getting us anywhere, Dortrean?' growled Drômagh, after several long minutes had dragged by.

'They will come,' said Erkal calmly. 'We lose honour only if we turn back.'

'Something is rattling them, anyway,' said the Archmage Morvaan. 'Over there, to the left.'

Kellarn looked, but he could not see what Morvaan meant because his father and Lord Drômagh were blocking his view. A cold rivulet of sweat ran down his back, and he shifted his seat uncomfortably.

'Do we lose honour if we eat while we're waiting?' Morvaan asked.

'I should prefer that you did not, my Lord,' Erkal answered.

There was a ripple of disturbance along the ranks of the enemy, and the shrill wail of a single horn echoed against the cliffs. Kellarn's horse stamped and shied sideways beneath him, tugging impatiently at the reins with her heavy head. His own heart was pounding as he steadied her. A low roar of many voices rolled down on the breeze, with a scattered beating of drums. A cluster of five horsemen broke out from the forward

165

line and came cantering across the open ground toward them. Aghaira named each in turn.

First came the Vengru – a solid brute of a man, very powerfully built, astride a stolen bay warhorse as large as Erkal's. His long mailshirt was of red steel like burnished copper, divided into broad panels over thighs and saddle, and the hilt and pommel of a great sword stood up above his shoulder from a sheath across his back. His heavy face was paler than was usual among the Easterner clans, with dark eyes, and a mane of black hair tethered into many braids and threaded with beads of jewelled gold and ivory. His cloak was of black fur, like a bearskin; and the heavy clasp at his shoulder bore a squared device of black and gold.

To the Vengru's right rode the Sholerghti in her fish-scale armour, also on a horse of Six Kingdoms stock, and with a bow of grey wood slung across her back. To his left was the Andrakhai, tallest of the three, and made taller still by the high dragon crest of his great bronze helm. Like the Sholerghti he wore armour wrought of many hardened leather plates, but enamelled with red and gold; and he bore two short swords, hanging in black sheaths on either side. His face – or what Kellarn could see of it beneath the patterned cheek guards of his helm – seemed younger and more tanned than those of his fellow chieftains; and he was mounted on a lighter horse, with only a green blanket for a saddle, as though the others had chosen before him. There was a gentler note in Aghaira's voice, either of fondness or respect, when she came to speak of him.

The two riders who came behind were mounted on much smaller, stocky horses, which had undoubtedly been brought here from the Easterner Domains. Neither of these two men was a chieftain. The shorter was clad in heavy black robes – slightly too large for him, Kellarn thought – which were embroidered all over with silver thread in a maze of spiralling patterns around tiny mirrors or coins. His face was hidden behind a smooth mask of polished silver, and his hood drawn

166

up and well forward. Aghaira thought him to be a priest of the Keeper of Secrets; but that title meant little to Kellarn.

The fifth rider was garbed in shirt and breeches of violet, sewn with many beads of jet or ebony. He was auburn haired, lean, and probably somewhere in his late twenties; and there was an air of self-satisfaction about him, a smugness, which was distinctly off-putting. Kata Aghaira did not know his name, but believed him to be a Wizard of Might. A slender staff of black and gold was slung across his back.

The Vengru drew rein sharply, coming to a halt a few lengths away. The other Easterners did the same. The two companies faced one another in silence. The Vengru stared at Erkal, and Erkal stared back. The Sholerghti and the wizard seemed to watch everything with studied disinterest. The Andrakhai glanced around between his opponents, before letting his gaze rest on Kellarn; and Kellarn found himself staring back at the shadowed eyes beneath the great dragon helm. Then the Vengru started speaking – his voice softer and more sibilant than Kellarn had expected, and yet somehow familiar – and the Andrakhai turned his head away to look at him.

'This chieftain says,' explained Kata Aghaira, when the Vengru paused, 'that you must be either very great fools or very brave warriors, to leave the safety of your city and come here to seek your deaths.'

'Tell the Vengru,' said Erkal, 'that even if he could defeat our armies – which I think unlikely – the city is still well defended; and he will recall that even with more than three times his present strength, and greater chieftains, the city could not be overcome. Other chiefs and warriors are already on their journey home. He would be wise to sue for peace now, so that he may leave these lands alive.'

The Vengru bared his teeth as Aghaira relayed the Earl's answer, in what Kellarn guessed to be a smile. Then he replied in the same soft voice.

'He says,' said Aghaira, 'that you have not the strength to lay siege to this place for long; and that there are many

167

other clans and other warriors who will come down from the Domains.'

'We also have other armies,' said Erkal; 'and Arrandin still stands, and is but the first of many cities, all strongly defended. These chieftains should consider well before committing themselves to a long and difficult war with little hope of success. Will they agree to hold peace until dawn, and perhaps take thought about their answer?'

Aghaira repeated his words to the Easterners. The Vengru's smile shifted into a more obvious sneer. The Sholerghti twined the mane of her great warhorse about her fingers with a bored indifference. The chieftain's answer was brief.

'The Vengru does not see the wisdom of peace,' Aghaira sighed. 'He declares that his answer will not change with the dawn. He gives no guarantee for this night.'

'Then the Vengru is the greater fool,' said Lord Drômagh. 'Their own warriors are tired, and many of them have just fled here from their latest defeat. A battle tonight would be a pointless waste of strength on both sides. They could put up a better fight if they waited till morning.'

The Easterners' contempt turned to jeering laughter as this speech was relayed to them. The Vengru leaned forward in the saddle to make answer, his voice deeper and more guttural than before. Kellarn could not see Aghaira's face, since she had her back to him; but he could sense a subtle change in her own voice and bearing as she explained what the Vengru had said.

'They will stay or go as they please,' said Aghaira. 'Even in numbers of warriors, their strength would count greater than yours. But their strength does not lie in mere mortal men alone. There are no city walls here for you to hide behind; and you have not the great shields of power to save you.'

'Our Magi could still bring those cliffs down on their heads, and bury the lot of them,' returned Drômagh.

'Or the dragon could come back,' said Kellarn.

He did not know what had prompted him to say it; and

168

the moment that the words were past his lips, his heart leaped pounding into his throat as though chasing to snatch them back again. The Vengru glared at him, signing to Aghaira that it was Kellarn's words, not Drômagh's, that he wished to understand. The head of the Andrakhai also turned toward him.

Kellarn was breathless with fright – not from any fear of the chieftains or the Easterner armies, or whatever dark powers they might summon against him; but from his own presumption of tempting the gods, or of daring to lay claim to any influence with the Father of All Dragons.

Neither his father nor Lord Drômagh turned to look at him, concealing their surprise well. Kellarn glanced at Boldrin beside him. Boldrin smiled back; and looking up into those blue eyes, Kellarn found sudden hope and understanding. The eyes of the gods were upon him – and not just in the person of this holy knight. Their presence was alive in the valley, the cliffs, the birds, the sky, even on the shadowed air all around him; watching, confident and undismayed. His fright melted toward wonder. He felt that he was but two steps away from laughing.

But there were still the Easterners to contend with. The Andrakhai had moved his horse to one side, and the wizard had ridden forward to speak. He used the everyday language of the Six Kingdoms, so that there was no need for Aghaira to interpret for him.

'Do you still know so little of this war?' he mocked. 'Has the great loremaster Aghaira not told you?'

Aghaira did not look at him. She held herself serene as if there were no one else but her in all the vale.

'It has been foretold,' said the wizard, 'that the Beautiful One, the great Lord of the Lords of Might, will soon return to rule in glory in these Middle Lands. We come to make ready a place for him, and to worship him when he comes.'

'He tried to return last year, and failed,' said Erkal. 'Or so I have heard.'

Kellarn had heard the same rumour. The Easterner's lip curled into a half smile. It was difficult to tell whether this was news to him or not.

'Your Sun priest is dead,' the wizard sneered. 'We saw him fall, before lesser lords of Might. But there is none who can stand against the Master when he comes in glory. And he will come. He will rise in the very heart of your petty empire. Your strength will crumble, from the centre to the rim.'

'Then why not wait until then?' said Drômagh; 'and save yourself the bother of a war?' From the tone of his voice, he clearly set little store by this wizard's tale.

'We come to make ready a place,' the man said again, as though repeating a lesson to a backward child. 'And of course, the servants who have shown themselves loyal will earn the greater reward.'

'But there is more to it than that,' said Boldrin. 'The evil master you serve can not enter the waking world unless a way is opened for him from here – from within the waking world. You want your people here so they can call him in.'

'The Beautiful One has many servants,' said the wizard. 'It could be one of *your* people, not ours.'

'People are mortal,' said Môrghran of Fâghsul. 'If we kill them first, they can't do it.'

'Kill as many of your own clansmen as you like,' the wizard laughed, 'if you think that will make you safe. It will save us the bother.'

'But it was our people who defeated him,' said Kellarn, 'and banished him from the waking world long ago. Our forefathers – our own blood and kin. That is why you fear us, isn't it?'

For the first time, the languid arrogance of the wizard appeared shaken. He drew himself up to his full height in the saddle, and shot a glance of pure venom in Kellarn's direction. But then the Vengru lashed him with a word of command, and the wizard turned away to confer with the three chieftains. Aghaira explained to Erkal that he was simply translating the conversation for the chieftains' benefit.

It was perhaps a full minute or more before the wizard was sent back to rejoin the masked priest and the Vengru spoke again. The shadows in the Khôrland vale were deepening.

'He says that if we are to speak of clan and kin,' said Aghaira, 'there is another errand that has brought him here. There was a kinswoman of his clan who fled to these lands with stolen treasure of great price. His priests tell him that she is dead. The Vengru comes to reclaim the treasure she took.'

'If this was such an important errand,' said Erkal, 'why did he not speak of it sooner?'

'And if every grievance in the long history of the Domains and the Empire is to be raised now,' put in Drômagh, 'we could be sitting here for months.'

'Yet the Vengru has named only one,' said Erkal. 'If we can help him to redress this wrong with justice – and without further battle – then he could withdraw his troops with no loss of honour. Indeed, he may wish to consider that this errand is now all the reason he has to stay. What is this tale, Kata Aghaira?'

The Vengru wished to have all this exchange repeated to him before he would answer. There were muttered curses from the Easterners, presumably at Erkal's suggestion that they should withdraw without battle. The Vengru raised a heavy fist to silence them, and then spoke rapidly and at some length. Aghaira nodded her honey-gold head as she listened.

'I remember this story now,' she told Erkal. 'The woman was a priestess of some power and influence in his clan. She was his close kin – though he disowns her, and will not suffer her name to be spoken. There were great quarrels between them; and last winter she fled west into the mountains, taking with her a great treasure – an *heirloom* you would call it, yes – of the chiefs of the Vengru clan. The priests of the Keeper of Secrets say that she reached your kingdoms before she died, and her body was torn apart by birds; but the treasure was taken by your own people. By the law of his clan, the Vengru claims that her life was forfeit; and that thus her death may be seen as the justice

171

of the Keeper gods whom she once served. He claims no blood feud with you over that. But he will have back the treasure that is his own.'

As Aghaira recounted the tale, Kellarn had the uncomfortable feeling that he already knew the rest of the story. The remembered image came unbidden to his mind of an Easterner woman lying dead amid the winter snows in the ruined city of Hauchan, with the great eagles of the Blue Mountains tearing her body apart. She had been pale skinned and raven haired, like the Vengru himself, though of much smaller stature; and her clothes had been snow white, until the work of the eagles had dyed them to the same colour as her scarlet cloak.

'I have no memory of her,' said Erkal, turning to Drômagh for confirmation. The Knight Commander shook his head. 'What is this heirloom?'

'A necklace of many dozens of red jewels, linked with yellow gold,' Aghaira told him. 'The Vengru says they are rubies, but that may not be so. The wealth of his clan has never come close to what their greed could wish for.'

'But apart from any value in coin,' said the Earl, 'would it have spells of power upon it, or within it? Or some significance, perhaps, to the matter of which the wizard spoke?'

'I think not,' said Aghaira. 'Such necklaces were great bridal gifts, in an older age of our own history; and those few that now remain are held as important symbols of rank and authority among the clans. The loss of this treasure brings dishonour upon the Vengru. But I have not heard that it was an artefact of power. Still, you can test it before you agree to hand it over, no?'

'If we knew where to find it,' said Erkal.

'I – I think I know,' stammered Kellarn.

Lord Drômagh swore. For the first time since the parley had begun, Erkal turned in the saddle to look back at his son.

'Do you, now?' he said.

Kellarn's sense of guilt, or at least of embarrassment, had been growing steadily over the past few minutes. He and his friends had come across the Easterner woman in the depths of winter, in the ruined temple of the ancient city of Hauchan – though what they had been doing there at all was another story, which he had no intention of explaining now. The woman had sent demonic creatures against them, horrors of scale and horn and bone; and even when overpowered and taken prisoner, she had fought them with guile and deceitful magics. Kellarn himself had been blinded for a time, and Corollin all but slain, by the priestess' treacherous arts. In the end it had been Kôril, their Fay companion, together with the mountain eagles, who had brought about the woman's demise. Among her few belongings had been a necklace of many rubies, even as Aghaira had described it.

Kellarn was not sorry that the evil priestess was dead. Yet it had never occurred to him that she was carrying stolen clan treasures, or that a war might come of it. They had simply handed her belongings to the priests in the nearby Monastery of Maësta, on the northern cliffs of the Hauchan valley. Only now, in the presence of his father and her aggrieved kinsman, did he wonder whether perhaps he should have done something more about it.

Erkal, however, showed no sign of irritation, or that he thought his son might have done anything amiss. Beneath the stooping eagle of his helm, his face was a blend of approval and relief, and almost of boyish amusement.

'Where?' he prompted.

'The priests of the Kelmaar Order have it in their safe keeping,' Kellarn told him. 'Or at least they did, not so long ago.'

It occurred to him that the priests might well have broken the necklace down and sold the precious stones to help pay for the war; but he put that thought hurriedly out of his mind.

'If Kelmaar have it, Your Grace,' said Morvaan, 'then we can no doubt retrieve it in a matter of hours.'

'Splendid,' the Earl nodded. 'Kata Aghaira, please inform the Vengru that we believe that the necklace may be found, and that we will restore it to him here at dawn – on condition that he and the other chieftains then take their armies and go home, and leave us in peace.'

'And remind them that horse thieving is a serious crime in this Empire,' added Drômagh, 'and that we expect to see those horses they are sitting on left behind.'

Aghaira bowed her head in acknowledgement, and then relayed the messages. The Easterners apparently thought little of the offer. But again the Vengru held them to silence while he spoke.

'He says that the horses are trophies of war,' said Aghaira. 'But bring them the necklace and they will consider leaving. For now, they will make no attack before dawn, unless your armies challenge them.'

'The Vengru shows wisdom and honour,' said Erkal, bowing to the Easterners. The Vengru gave a jerking nod of his head in answer. Then Erkal nudged his horse forward and to the right, and led the way back toward the Emperor's armies.

'Well, you got your peace for tonight, Dortrean,' said Drômagh, when they were well out of earshot of the enemy. 'If the Vengru will hold to it.'

'If he can hold the others to it, more like,' said Môrghran of Fâghsul. 'Especially that stoat of a wizard.'

'The Vengru is chief of a greater clan,' said Aghaira. 'The other two will be swayed by him in this. If the wizard defies him, the Vengru will kill him.'

'Is there something different about the Andrakhai?' Kellarn asked her. 'From the other two, I mean.'

'I knew his father well for many years,' Aghaira smiled, 'so I have watched him grow from just a little baby into a tall warrior. But the Andrakhai has more reason than the other two to hurry home. With the deaths of the Mughuzhti and the Korzhai, he has the chance to increase his own power and following greatly among their peoples. He may even try to replace the Mughuzhti as a greater clan chief.'

'And would that be a good thing?' Kellarn wondered.

'For the Domains, perhaps yes,' she nodded. 'I have been too little at Kara Ko-Daighru of late to know how the winds blow with the High Clan Chief.'

'Whether we can buy lasting peace without a fight is another matter,' said Drômagh. 'It was damned lucky about that necklace.'

'We do not have it yet,' said Erkal; 'and we still have to establish that the necklace is the right one. Aghaira has told us that several such jewels were once made.'

'But will the Vengru take it and go?' asked Drômagh.

'I think that he might,' said the Earl. 'Returning home with a clan heirloom will be no dishonour to him; and he can not hope to survive here for very long. Even if he has brought in supplies to the manor house over the past few weeks, he can not feed an army that size for many days. They can not eat rock and stone. And our strength of cavalry will put him at a great disadvantage in the field, should he choose to move.'

'We still do not know what strength of wizards and priests they have in there,' said Morvaan. 'They are using their arts to shield that from us. Then there is also the question of other clan armies coming to join them – though I think the Vengru did not tell the whole truth there. Perhaps it was wishful thinking on his part, that help might arrive soon. We shall look in to that, your Grace.'

'I should be grateful,' nodded Erkal. 'But may I stress again to the Magi that the Easterners should not be provoked in any way before dawn.'

'I shall speak with them, your Grace,' Morvaan nodded.

Later that evening, Kellarn again lay on his stomach by the small fire before the Arrand pavilion. The clouds were creeping down from the mountain heights against the darkening sky, and an air of uneasy watchfulness filled the camp. His father had gone away with Lord Drômagh for a meeting with the other army commanders. Kellarn and Corollin were holding a smaller meeting of their own.

175

The moon fay Tinûkenil was sitting cross-legged upon the ground on the other side of the fire. He was now clad wholly in deep grey beneath his hooded cloak, so only his fair face and violet eyes could be seen clearly in the dim light. Skaramak and the *noghr*, Odhragh, were to his left, and Gwydion to his right with Mage Councillor Torkhaal. Hrugaar had been dispatched to fetch the Vengru necklace, since he was a mage of Water and the monastery in the Hauchan valley was known to him; and since the priests of the Kelmaar Order with the Emperor's armies had confirmed that the necklace was still there. The priests themselves had offered to fetch it; but it was thought safer for Hrugaar to make the magical *leap* there than for the *Aeshta* priests to make the journey by opening a way into another Realm, with the Easterners so close at hand.

'It seems strange,' said Tinûkenil, 'if they came here because of the demon, that they should go away again for a handful of jewels.'

They had all watched the parley from a distance, and had been gathered waiting when Kellarn returned, to discover what had been said. Kellarn's brief account of the conversation with the Easterners seemed only to have raised more questions in their minds.

'They lost many of their great priests and wizards in the siege of Arrandin,' said Torkhaal; 'and their army is now too small to challenge the whole of the Six Kingdoms.'

'And taking the necklace means that they can withdraw with some kind of honour,' said Kellarn. He was not sure whether his mention of the Father of All Dragons had been another factor in persuading the Easterners to go; but the subject of the dragon was still rather personal, and he did not want to speak of him just now.

'Yet it will not prevent them from returning again, with greater strength,' said the moon fay.

'Father was hoping for a more lasting promise of peace,' agreed Kellarn. 'But perhaps that has to come from the High Clan Chief, rather than the Vengru. I'm not sure.'

'The real danger is not the war,' said Corollin, 'but the servants of the demon. They could return at any time – with or without an army behind them.'

'We could kill them all,' Gwydion offered.

'That wizard, certainly,' said Skaramak; 'and any other priests or servants of the demon that are still here.'

There was an awkward silence. Kellarn plucked strays bits of grass and breadcrumbs from the blanket beneath him, and tossed them into the fire.

'You say that you found the woman and the necklace in Hauchan,' said Tinûkenil. 'Was that when you slew the green wyrm?'

Kellarn ducked his head in embarrassment.

'No,' he said. 'It was only a few months ago.'

'One might say that it was fortunate you went there when you did,' observed Odhragh.

Kellarn shrugged, not looking at them.

'A sun dog of Torollen warned us there was danger there,' said Corollin; 'so we went. We did not know then, of course, either who the woman was, or that anything else would come of it.'

'Such is the way of the dances of the gods,' Tinûkenil nodded. 'A single step forms part of many patterns.'

'So have you learned anything more yet about – about the demon?' asked Kellarn. 'You said that we might, when the Easterners were held at bay.'

With the gathering clouds and darkness, it was all too easy to believe that they might discover more about the powers of Lo-Khuma and his servants, in a most unpleasant way, should the Easterners fail to keep to the truce agreed by the Vengru. Kellarn hoped fervently that the Lords of the *Aeshtar* might offer further insight without such a trial.

'A little,' said Tinûkenil. 'We now know that the Easterners expect him to appear somewhere within the Middle Lands, and that they believe he will come soon. We already knew that he had followers and priests among them; and the wizard at the parley was clearly one of his servants. The Vengru also bears his symbol upon his cloak clasp.'

'Yes,' said Kellarn. Though he had not come close enough to the chieftain to see for himself, he could well imagine that the black and gold of the clasp had formed the familiar pattern of the lozenge within the square.

'Yet apart from that,' said the fay, 'I have not sensed anything of his power, or of his servants' power, at work within the valley.'

'They could be shielding themselves from us,' said Torkhaal.

'They could,' said Tinûkenil. 'Or perhaps there are none of his priests left here now – which might explain why the Vengru was willing to bargain and go home.'

'He has not gone yet,' said the *noghr*. 'It could still come to a fight in the morning.'

Chapter Six

Kellarn's waking dream was that he stood in a world of mists. Before him were two figures, each radiant with their own light. Upon the left was a moon fay – either Tinûkenil or Heruvor, he was not sure which. To the right was Corollin, in the strawberry robes she had worn as a student of the mystical lore of Zedron, sewn with a row of glittering crystal beads. Behind them stood a group of some half a dozen people in tunics of different colours – human by appearance, though perhaps not so by nature. And above and behind them, filling the misty air, was the huge, half-glimpsed head of Ilunâtor, Father of All Dragons.

'He is not a tame dragon,' the moon fay chided him, 'to come at your call.'

'His friendship is perilous for mortal men,' said another voice.

Kellarn wanted to protest, but found that he had no words for his defence. He looked to Corollin for help; but Corollin was not there. In her place stood a woman – like the woman of the Vengru, and yet not so. She was clad all in scarlet, with braided hair like tethered serpents. Her eyes were black and empty, and blood dripped from her long tresses into a necklace of many droplets across shoulders and breast. She stretched out one long arm toward him – no more than white bone, hung about with rags of shredded flesh – and a mist of blindness filled his eyes; and then many hands were all around him, unseen, clutching and tearing with fiery claws.

His throat laboured in spasm as he tried to cry out. He knew that the dragon would come at his call. He knew that he himself would perish, along with his enemies, if the dragon should attack. His voice failed him.

And then the dragon came, and the coolness of his breath was all around him; and the pain and terror melted into peace, and the glittering rainbow hues of another world. And then the vision faded, and he looked up into the familiar face of Corollin, shadowed in her own light against the purple hangings of the Arrand pavilion.

'Hrugaar has returned,' she whispered. 'It is time to move.'

Kellarn growled, and snuggled himself deeper beneath the blankets. Even inside the tent the valley air was chill and damp. His eyelids began to flutter closed again.

'Now,' warned Corollin, prodding him firmly through the bedclothes.

She would not leave him in peace; and besides, he was not sure that he wanted to go back to sleep, to more dreams. He wriggled and sat up, and reached for the pack that had served as a pillow. Satisfied, Corollin slipped out past the hanging curtain into the main part of the pavilion, leaving the dim light of her magic behind for him to dress by.

When he went out to join her a few minutes later, he found that several other people were there before him. His father and Lord Boldrin were seated on folding chairs, fully dressed and awake, so that Kellarn wondered whether they had slept at all. Corollin and Hrugaar stood facing them, with their backs to the outer doorway; and at Erkal's left hand stood one of the dwarvenfolk of the *noghru*. The dwarf was unusually tall for one of his kind, so that his head was almost on a level with that of the seated Earl; and with his surcoat and cloak of fiery red he might have passed for a retainer of Dortrean. But Kellarn did not remember seeing him before; and the formal bow with which the *noghr* greeted him as he entered was more elaborate than would be expected from a member of the family household. Kellarn nodded in return, and hurried over to Corollin's side.

As soon as he had joined them, Hrugaar produced a bundle

of pale blue silk from the satchel on his shoulder and unwrapped it with graceful care. He held out the Vengru necklace for them all to see.

'A ransom for a chieftain indeed,' said the *noghr*, breaking the silence with his gruff voice.

The clustered rubies glowed softly with the reflected light of the hanging lamp overhead, yet still dark against the watery silk that covered Hrugaar's hands. Kellarn frowned and looked away. They reminded him too strongly of so many droplets of fresh blood. But the sight of the necklace had also stirred a different memory in his mind.

'There was another one like this,' he said. 'At Herghin, I think. A green one.'

The clearer memory was of an Easterner woman aboard a Souther warship – golden haired and broad-nosed, with a necklace of many gems glittering like rain-washed leaves in the bright sunlight. By unknown arts she had reappeared at the manor house of Herghin; and Kellarn thought that he remembered seeing the jewel again during the shadowed battle there.

'There was,' said Hrugaar. 'The Lady Lorellin gave it to Khôraillan, to be handed to the Emperor in tribute; as a sign of good faith, after the treachery of her kinsmen.'

'Did she, now?' said Erkal.

'And will it be let go, as a spoil of war?' wondered Boldrin. 'Or are we to expect another army to come marching down, wanting it back?'

The *noghr* snorted. His hand strayed to his belt, as if to rest on a weapon that was not there.

'The loss of this necklace was not the cause of the present war,' Erkal reminded him; 'though by the grace of the gods, the Vengru may agree to let it be the means of ending it. If the Easterners wish to reclaim the other necklace, there are other ways of asking. Lorellin has simply acted as she thought best, for the welfare of her own house. But are we certain, Councillor Hrugaar, that this Vengru necklace is no artefact of power that could prove deadly in the Easterners' hands?'

'There is no enchantment upon it, your Grace,' Hrugaar assured him; 'nor no power stored within. Nor was there any power that we could find upon the necklace taken at Herghin. But the priests of Kelmaar have washed and cleansed these jewels, and laid upon them the simplest of their own blessing – which may not please the Easterners overmuch, though it should do them no great harm.'

The corner of Boldrin's mouth twitched toward a smile. The *noghr* stroked the plaits of his long beard, and chuckled quietly.

'Well enough,' said the Earl.

The necklace was put away again, and they held their own dawn rites to honour the Lords of the *Aeshtar* in the privacy of the Arrand pavilion – though the dawn was still more than an hour off, so that it had more the feel of a waiting vigil. Kellarn discovered then that the *noghr* was a priest of Hýriel, of great standing among his own people in the distant Highland Mountains, and a fellow of the Temple of Fire in Arrandin; and that he was called Dharagh. The *noghr* kindled holy fire in a small bowl of gold and red coral; which he had brought with him for the purpose, and set it upon one of the folding chairs while they all stood round; and as he chanted the prayers to Hýriel in a furl of rich, rolling notes, it seemed to Kellarn's eyes that the flames flowed down from the bowl and spread out across the carpeted floor, and then ran dancing up the silken panels and sloping roof of the tent to the topmost ridge; so that he stood in a shrine wrought of living fire, or in the furnace of the gods where the dwarvensmiths of legend had fashioned their greatest works of craft. And yet the heat of the flames was gentle, and suffered no harm to anything it touched.

Dharagh prayed for strength of heart and arm, and for deliverance – for both Middle Lands and Eastern Domains alike – from the scourge of evil demons from other Realms. Kellarn silently added his own prayer that the Easterners would go away soon, either with or without a fight; and that at least his father and friends might survive the day, even if he himself did not. When it came to asking for his own life to be spared, in all honesty before the gods he could think of no fit enough reason for it.

The rite ended, and the flaming shrine flowed back into Dharagh's bowl and was gone. They were armed and dressed and riding out before the last summer stars had faded from the western sky, and the coming dawn was no more than a grey blur of cloud above the darkness of the mountain cliffs to their east. Not just the small envoy of Erkal's parley rode out that morning, but the greater part of all the assembled armies of the Six Kingdoms – ready either to escort the Easterners safely under guard to the edge of their lands, or else to do battle should the Vengru not hold to the terms of peace.

The sky grew paler as the armies spread out up the Khôrland vale, and the clouds in the east were thrown into deeper reliefs of light and shadow, brushed with the first ruddy glow of Torollen's fire. The dark hollows of the valley were lit with many torches, and filled with the tramp of booted feet and heavy hooves, and the clatter of gear and human voices calling; and the snorting and blowing of horses, and the smells of sweat and hide and newly churned earth all sharp on the cool air.

They stopped a short distance from where the parley had taken place the previous evening, just beyond bow range from the arcing line of the enemy clans. Erkal rode on a little way ahead, with Boldrin of Levrin and Môrghran of Fâghsul, the Archmage Morvaan and Kata Aghaira. Kellarn was told to remain behind, and for once his father would brook no argument. And then the mountain clouds kindled to sudden fire, and a horn call echoed from the cliffs ahead, and the Easterner chieftains came down.

The Vengru came first, his solid figure glowing in the light of more than a dozen torches borne by an armed escort upon either side. Behind him came the great dragon helm of the Andrakhai, swaying to left and right as if weighing the strength of the armies arrayed against them. And beside the Andrakhai

183

rode the faceless priest, his mirrored mask like a window into a dying furnace beneath the shadow of his hood. The Sholerghti and the wizard were not with them.

Kellarn sat watching, his borrowed mount stirring restless beneath him. He had ridden with his father as far as he was allowed, and was still closest of all the Six Kingdoms warriors to Erkal's small escort. To his right was Corollin, on a skewbald riding horse of much lighter stock; and before her, clinging tight to the saddle pommel with his right fist, sat the dwarven priest Dharagh. The *noghr* had no greater liking for sitting on horseback than had most of his kindred, but he had been determined not to be left behind. He was clad in fine mail beneath his surcoat and cloak; and a sturdy battle-axe was now thrust beneath his belt, the patterned smithcraft of its steel blade flickering in warning in the torchlight.

To Kellarn's left were Hrugaar and Torkhaal, watching carefully as the Vengru rode nearer. Behind him were Haësella of Braedun and Hollin of Logray, and the remnant of his own war band from Sentai; and behind them again were The Arrand's own forces, led for the moment by the Lord Thalden of Arrand, husband of Lorellin of Herghin.

Further back, and stretching round on either side, were the other armies of the Six Kingdoms, their many torches giving the impression of two vast spreading wings in the gloom. To the left were the forces of Kelmaar and Môshári, and to the right were Braedun and the golden ranks of the Imperial Household Cavalry; and then behind them stood the household troops and levied armies of the Lords of the Court Noble – Levrin and Galsin, Ercusí and Vaulun, Telún, Solaní, Eädhan and many more.

Where Tinûkenil and his companions might have gone, Kellarn did not know; unless they were with Gravhan and the Môshári. He could not see them in the crowded shadows. The *Aeshta* Orders were to the fore, he knew, since they were the best able to counter the powers of the Easterner wizards and priests – apart from the fact that they had some of the best trained warriors in all the Six Kingdoms, outside of the Imperial Household Guard. They were also, Kellarn realised, the most expendable of the Emperor's troops as casualties of war – from the Emperor's point of view, at least – now that this war with the East had been reduced to more manageable proportion. And so also, perhaps, were Kellarn and Erkal themselves.

The thought startled him by the suddenness, more than the content. After all, the rivalry between Dortrean and Lautun, and the declining favour of the *Aeshta* Orders, had been part of his life since before even his earliest memories. But why it should occur to him now, when his thoughts had been focused on the danger from the Easterners, he could not fathom. He wondered whether he was going to develop his mother's habit of thinking several moves ahead of the game; or whether the idea had been suggested to him from outside – by Corollin, perhaps, or one of the magi.

'The manor house is still shielded from my sight,' said Hrugaar. 'I can see no other signs of power at work elsewhere. But where is the Sholerghti?'

'And where is the wizard?' said Torkhaal. 'I should rather have him where I can see him. What mischief are they plotting?'

'Aghaira said that the Vengru might kill the wizard, if he tried to defy him,' Kellarn remembered.

'Don't raise your hopes too high, young Lord,' said Dharagh. 'Keep your eyes skinned for the first sign of attack.'

'I am,' said Kellarn.

But the feared attack did not come. Erkal Dortrean and the Vengru met together, and the Archmage Morvaan brought out the necklace and held it up; and there was a brief exchange of words between them. Then Morvaan packed the jewel away again in its silken wrapping, and a few more words were spoken.

At that point two of the Vengru's guards rode forward toward Erkal's party. But the stocky Easterner horses shied and reared, and their riders were thrown. The dragon helm of the Andrakhai jerked up. The crowded air of the Khôrland vale grew tight as a bowstring.

'What is it?' Kellarn demanded, preparing to ride.

'Aghaira, I think,' said Hrugaar. 'There is some private dispute, between her and the Easterners. But see, it is ending.'

Even as he spoke, Erkal took the bundled necklace from Morvaan's hand and carried it to the Vengru. The great chieftain bowed in the saddle as he received it; then unwrapped the jewel again and held it aloft for the Easterner armies to see. Erkal turned and raised both hands to the Six Kingdoms armies, in the agreed signal that peace had been achieved.

A great roar of noise rolled down across the vale from the Easterner armies, a clamour of shouts and drums and braying horns and the clashing of weapons against shields. The Six Kingdoms armies began to cheer, raggedly at first, but gaining strength and confidence as the truth of their deliverance sank in.

In that moment, Kellarn's world slowed almost to a halt; so that he felt that he stood upon the brink, waiting for the enemy to surge forward and attack. Waiting to see his father cut down from behind by the Vengru's men, undefended and unwitting. Waiting for the fiery triumph of the dawn to fall apart into a chaos of blood and death.

But the moment passed. The Vengru and his father turned toward one another again and bowed, and the Andrakhai bowed also. And then the chieftains rode away with their guards, and Erkal and Aghaira were riding back toward Kellarn, with Boldrin and Morvaan and Môrghran following.

Kellarn found himself swaying in the saddle, suddenly dizzy for lack of air. Hrugaar's arm was there at once, supporting him.

'I'm – all right,' he managed. 'Relieved, I guess.'

It was only partly true; and from the faint frown on Hrugaar's fair face, it seemed that the mage was not deceived. But Kellarn smiled and sat up again, and they let the matter pass. More pressing was the need to hear what had been said at the parley; and Erkal and Aghaira were already riding up to join them.

'The Vengru simply agreed to the terms suggested last night,' Erkal told them, in answer to their questions. 'He will take the money and run. Or to put it more politely, he will withdraw with all that remains of their armies, with no great loss of honour.'

'And live to fight another day?' wondered the *noghr*.

'May that day be far off,' the Earl returned. 'But I am reliably informed that there are no other clan armies marching down from the East to join him, as he had hoped. And with the loss of the Mughuzhti and the other chieftains, he may be hard put to find new allies for a while.'

'But what of the Sholerghti and the wizard?' demanded Hrugaar and Torkhaal.

'They were not there,' said Erkal. 'I thought it might be impolite to ask about them.'

'And is that it?' asked Kellarn.

His father was all smiles and confidence, but Kellarn knew him too well to be taken in. Perhaps Erkal, like himself, was made uneasy by the ease of their success. Or perhaps it was because they both knew that the greater danger which threatened the Middle Lands could not be turned aside so simply.

'It is still a long road from here to the Blue Mountain Fords,' Erkal allowed. 'But I think that the Vengru will hold true to his word, and go away without risking another battle.'

'Why did the horses throw their riders?' asked Hrugaar.

'Ah, that was my fault,' said Kata Aghaira. 'I confess. The Vengru – may he rot on his own gibbet – wished to take me hostage. I would not suffer myself to be seized by his guards like any common criminal.'

'You had us a little worried for a moment,' said Kellarn.

He might have added that she presumed a great deal, to risk the lives of several thousand warriors in battle over a personal squabble with the Vengru. But he did not like to say so, since Aghaira had gone a good deal out of her way to

187

help his father in this war. Besides, he could not really blame her for not wanting to be the Vengru's prisoner.

Aghaira looked up at him with wry humour.

'That is how the game of honour is played, my Lord,' she told him. 'But it was not possible to lose. The Vengru knows that he has need of me, to make his peace with the High Clan Chieftain in Kara Ko-Daighru. I gave my word that I shall go with him, when the time comes – if he keeps his side of the bargain with your father.'

'But first we must arrange for the safe escort of his armies to our border,' said Erkal. 'We have a long day ahead of us.'

The withdrawal of the Easterner armies took far longer than Kellarn had expected. Not all the warriors on either side were well pleased with the agreed peace; and as the sultry heat of the day increased, so mischief spread and tempers flared, and the commanders had hard work holding discipline. Then the Easterners had also great store of provisions and gear laid up in Khôrland, which they needed to take with them for the long journey home; and the border village of Samsar was still in enemy hands – though most of the warriors and wagons that had been there had now fled home, following the Raunazhrai – so that the treaty had to be explained to them, and confirmed by their own people, before they would agree to move. There were brief skirmishes in the hills around the village, which further tested the patience of both sides.

Some few of the Khôrland folk had survived as prisoners and slaves, either in the manor house or at Samsar. The Easterners counted them as spoils of war, and it was only after the intervention of the Andrakhai himself that there seemed to be any real hope of securing their release. Erkal in turn had sent word back to Fersí and Arrandin, requesting the release of those few Easterner prisoners taken by the Six Kingdoms armies; and that those fit enough to travel should be brought east under guard so that they could return home.

By the end of the day the last of the Easterners had been

moved out of the Khôrland vale, and they made their camp in the hills north of Samsar. The Sholerghti was seen among them, with her arm in a sling, and a face like a woman chewing sea salt. If any priests or wizards were with them, they kept their presence well hidden.

The Môshári had been the first to brave the Khôrland manor house once the Easterners had left, with the magi and the troops of the Kelmaar Order to support them. But though the shielding spells of the wizards still clung about the walls like the reek of burning fat, there was nobody left within. The magi and the Môshári then began the much longer task of cleansing the manor house and making it safe again; clearing not just the physical debris of the enemy's occupation, but the lingering presence of their spells and charms; and searching also for hidden traps or cunning magics that might have been left behind in malice. The disgruntled Lord Zhertan Khôrland was obliged to delay his homecoming by another night, and pitched his tent further down the valley.

The following morning, being the twelfth day of the month of Röstren and the fourth of the new moon, the Easterner armies with their wagons and beasts began the long, slow march up the road to the fords of the Blue Mountain River. The Emperor's armies provided a mounted escort along the way, under the command of Ferghaal of Braedun and Boldrin of Levrin; but the greater part of their own troops remained behind to continue the work of clearing the border lands and restoring some sense of order, and to take thought for their future defence.

Kellarn rode behind the Easterners for the first half of the day, more for Lord Boldrin's company than from any great fear of immediate danger. Corollin had gone away with the magi to continue the work in the Khôrland manor house, and his father was busy with Lord Drômagh and the imperial commanders; and Kellarn had had his fill of clean-up duties whilst in the Lower City of Arrandin.

By the early afternoon they had emerged from the hills and

were nearing the last northward run of the road toward the fords. To their left, the ground rose steeply into the foothills surrounding the southeastern spur of the Blue Mountains. To their right, the land sprawled in an endless expanse of scrubland plains, broken here and there by the paler grey of rocky knolls, or the darker greens of junipers and clustered trees, and the half-glimpsed specks of grazing herd beasts. The sky deepened to stormy purple on the eastern horizon, and the hazy air shimmered with rainbowed hints of distant rain. To the northeast, Kellarn thought that he could make out the line of the river as it flowed away on its long journey toward the Stormrider Sea; but ahead, closer in to the mountains, the river and the fords were still hidden from sight by the folds of the land.

It was clear that no more than the first vanguard of the Easterner armies would be across the river before the end of the day, and that it might take the best part of the following day for the rest of their warriors and gear to make safe passage to the farther shore; and though Kellarn knew that the sight of him riding with the armed escort might be an added reminder to the marching Easterners to keep moving, he began to doubt the usefulness of his own presence here. There was still an outside chance that the Vengru might prove treacherous, but it seemed highly unlikely at this late stage in the game. Kellarn had the growing feeling that he should be getting back to his father and friends; and that there were other dangers now facing the Six Kingdoms – the Southers, the trouble within the Emperor's household, and the prophecy of Lo-Khuma's return – against which he should be starting to act.

Boldrin must have sensed his unrest, even if he did not seem to share it. So when they paused to ease their horses in the middle afternoon, he caught Kellarn in the gaze of his deep blue eyes, and suggested that he might like to ride back to Samsar before nightfall; and Kellarn – neither minded nor wholly able to refuse those eyes – gave in.

'No doubt I shall see you again soon,' he said.

'Not soon, I think,' Boldrin smiled. 'We have much work here still, and you have your own calling. But there will always be a welcome for Dortrean in Arrandin. As long as I have life and breath, there will be a welcome.'

They hesitated for a moment, and then hugged one another farewell – mailshirts and weapons and all – and Boldrin kissed Kellarn on the forehead with the kiss of a holy knight. And then they mounted up again; and Boldrin went on with the Easterners, and Kellarn turned back and rode after the westering sun.

He spent the night in the Arrand pavilion, just to the north of Samsar. Corollin and the Môshári had come down to the camp, weary after their long day. Though the work of clearing the manor house had not been pleasant, they had found no certain traces of the power or influence of Lo-Khuma at work there; and the Lord Zhertan Khôrland had now taken up residence again. Erkal Dortrean intended to ride west the following day, to report back to the Emperor in Arrandin, since his own role in the conclusion of the war with the Easterners was now complete. Kellarn and Corollin decided to ride with him.

The next morning brought more farewells. Tinûkenil and his companions came to the Arrand pavilion, to take their leave of the Lords of Dortrean before turning south again toward Ferlund. The moon fay was still cloaked and hooded in sombre grey; but his face was radiant in the dawn light, and Gwydion's shaggy mane of hair seemed kindled to auburn fire.

'So did you learn anything more?' Kellarn asked them.

'No more than we had guessed already,' said Tinûkenil. 'The demon has many followers. Soon he will try to return to the Middle Lands.'

'But how soon?' asked Corollin. Tinûkenil laughed.

'Humans and Fay reckon time a little differently,' he reminded her. 'Yet soon, even by your human terms, I think.'

'I had half expected to see you chasing after the Easterners,' said Hrugaar, arriving with Torkhaal at that moment.

Gwydion grinned. Tinûkenil tilted his head with an air of diffidence.

'South and east lies our way, Hrugaar,' he said; 'to the havens of my people – and perhaps beyond.'

'We could pop in on the Easterners afterward,' offered Skaramak brightly.

'Have you any message for the Lord and Lady of Valemur?' Tinûkenil asked Kellarn.

Kellarn felt the colour rise to his cheeks. It was true that he and Corollin had visited the havens of Valemur the previous autumn, when the first part of their search for the strange artefact to combat Lo-Khuma had led them down to the wild coast of the Stormrider Sea; and that they had fought in the defence of that ancient citadel against a host of evil creatures that came down from the Low Mountains. But though they had found favour with the elvenfolk of Valemur, Kellarn had the sense to know that that had been more through the presence of their fay companion Kôril than through any great merit of his own. And besides, he was embarrassed by the reminder of his own deeds, even among friends. He did not want to be thought more exceptional than he really was.

'No, not really,' he stammered. 'Thank you.'

'Other than our best greeting,' added Corollin.

The moon fay bowed, and his friends bowed with him; and then they went away, smiling and laughing. Even with Hrugaar standing beside him, it seemed to Kellarn that the morning fell suddenly dull and ordinary when they had gone.

Then Kata Aghaira came to say goodbye, leading a gentle bay riding horse which Erkal had arranged to be given to her in gift. The Earl was most apologetic that many of Aghaira's belongings had been left behind in Arrandin, but she seemed not to mind.

'The Arrand will look after them for me, yes, if they are found,' she said. 'Then I can claim them when I come again.'

'Shall you come back then, my Lady?' asked Hrugaar.

'Of course,' Aghaira laughed. 'And some of you magi are to

come with me to Kara Ko-Daighru, one day – we agreed, yes? But not yet. Not for some moons, I think. I must go first myself to the High Clan Chieftain, and see what is happening there.'

They walked with her down through the busy camp to the border road east of Samsar.

'Are you quite sure that you shall be all right?' asked Torkhaal doubtfully. 'With the Vengru, I mean.'

'Yes yes,' she said.

At a prodded signal from his father, Kellarn made a stirrup with his hands to help her mount. Aghaira swung herself easily into the saddle, and smiled down at him.

'Can you really make peace between the Vengru and the High Clan Chief?' he asked her.

'Perhaps,' she said. 'Perhaps not. The Vengru has no better hope than me. But the High Clan Chief will listen to my tale of what has happened here, and then decide.'

'And what will you tell him?' Erkal wondered.

Aghaira tossed back her honey-gold braids and held her head proud. 'Of great magics and evil demons,' she answered. 'Of dreadful battles, and the Lifeblood Oath; and a young hero with a sword, and even a dragon. The High Clan Chief will like to hear about the dragon. He may be less pleased to hear about the deeds of the other chieftains. It will go hard with the Vengru, I think.'

'And Lo-Khuma?' asked Kellarn quietly.

Kata Aghaira frowned, and made a warding gesture against evil with her right hand.

'Name him not,' she warned, her voice deepening. 'But indeed yes, Kellarn. I shall speak of it, if I deem it wise. The worship of the demon is a sickness, spreading among the clans of the Domains. I do not know if that sickness has reached Kara Ko-Daighru. So I must be gone.

'Honour grows where honour belongs,' she said, addressing them all. 'We honour the Living, and we honour the Dead; and the Wheels of the Worlds grind on. Or, as you would say, the dances of the gods move on, yes?'

She lifted her right hand to the base of her throat, and bowed her head in farewell. They all bowed in return.

'Yes,' said Aghaira. 'This has all been most interesting.'

She nudged her horse forward, and rode away toward the sun. They stood and watched her go. At about a stone's throw distance she wheeled around and raised her right hand in farewell. Erkal waved back.

The air behind her swirled suddenly into life, like a swarm of fireflies or a thousand newborn stars. Aghaira turned and rode straight into it, and vanished; and the stars rolled in upon themselves and winked out.

'What was that?' cried Kellarn.

'Her own power,' said Hrugaar. 'Aghaira opened a door between Realms and rode through – as simply as that.'

There was a note of wonder and respect in his voice. Erkal rubbed his chin. Kellarn felt a chill prickling all over, and shivered.

'But – she could have left at any time, then,' he said.

'So it would seem,' Hrugaar nodded.

'Then why did she stay?'

'Why did any of us stay?' said Erkal. 'To achieve peace.'

'Or to glean a new story,' said Torkhaal.

They turned back toward the camp in silence.

'Speaking of stories,' said Hrugaar presently, 'Zhertan Khôrland has heard the tale of the Vengru necklace. Or rather he has misheard it, I think. He seems to believe that the taking of the necklace caused the war; and that since Dortrean took the necklace, Dortrean should help pay for the damage to his manor lands.'

'And what did you say to him?' demanded Erkal, before Kellarn had a chance to protest.

'I am mage of the Council,' said Hrugaar. 'I did not presume to meddle in a matter between two Houses Noble.'

Erkal said nothing. Kellarn saw the familiar tightening about his father's jaw.

'Yet I did speak of it to Gravhan,' Hrugaar allowed; 'and he reminded the Lord Khôrland that there were far greater matters behind the war; and that since the defence of the whole Empire was at stake, it would perhaps be more fitting to approach the Emperor for help.'

There was a bubbling mischief in the mage's voice, and Erkal's expression softened again, almost twitching toward a smile.

'The Emperor may be none too pleased,' he said. 'I suppose that I had better warn him.'

'We are returning to Arrandin ourselves, your Grace,' said Torkhaal; 'by magic. We can take you with us – all three of you – if you so wish.'

'Thank you Torkhaal, but no,' said the Earl. 'Though I am grateful beyond words for all that you magi have done in these past weeks, and no offence is intended. But I need to see Lord Brodhaur and gather reports from his men on the way back. It is best that I ride along the road.'

'I had rather ride, too, thank you,' said Kellarn.

He had in truth more than half a mind to go with the magi, to see how Kierran was faring. But the Emperor was also in Arrandin, and Kellarn did not want to see Rhydden without his father there. Or else some other instinct told against it.

Torkhaal nodded, as if he understood. 'I doubt that we shall stay long in Arrandin,' he said. 'But perhaps our paths shall cross again soon.'

'Perhaps,' said Kellarn.

When Torkhaal and Hrugaar returned to the Môshári house in Arrandin, Rhysana was there waiting for them. She had attended the dawn rite with Imarra and the healers, and broken fast with them afterward; and then she had packed together her few belongings in readiness for the journey home.

Rhysana knew that the war was over, and that her usefulness in Arrandin had come to an end. She had watched for herself – with the aid of Morvaan's observing spell, still maintained in the long gallery in the Arrand palace – while the Easterner clans withdrew from the Khôrland vale, and were herded east and north along the road toward the final border of the river ford. And then Morvaan had returned to the city the previous evening, bringing his own tale of the peace made with the Vengru, and of the clearing of the Khôrland manor house.

Morvaan had come back to the Môshári house that morning, to say goodbye to the departing magi, and was sitting with the Archmage Ellen in the shadowed gallery adjoining Rhysana's guest chambers. Dhûghaúr had been dispatched downstairs to wait for Hrugaar and Torkhaal in the small temple shrine, into which they would most probably make their magical *leap* of return. Rhysana herself was drifting up and down the gallery, looking out through the open windows at the scented shadows of the garden below and the clear blue of the morning sky above, and chewing her way absently through a second breakfast of sweet almond biscuits.

'With an appetite like that, you are bound to be an archmage one day,' Morvaan told her.

'We do not all eat as much as do you,' said Ellen. 'Besides, Rhysana is eating for two. You never had that excuse, as I recall.'

'I'm an active man,' Morvaan protested, though with the air of a man who knows that he is fighting on sinking ground. Ellen looked down her nose at him.

There was a ripple of laughter from the direction of the stair, and Hrugaar came bounding into the gallery. Behind him fol-lowed the darker figures of Torkhaal and Dhûghaúr. Ellen and Morvaan stood up to greet them. Rhysana hurriedly finished her mouthful of biscuit – just in time before Hrugaar caught her up in a rather boisterous hug. There was a salt freshness about him, as though he had come from the sea shore rather than the inland plains; so that she felt breathless and a little dizzy when he released her into the gentler warmth of Torkhaal's embrace.

'It is good to see you again, Ru,' she said, holding her husband's arms around her.

'Even if he does seem to have forgotten what little courtesy he ever learned,' said Ellen.

Hrugaar answered her with a very graceful formal bow. Ellen nodded, raising her hands together in a sign of *Aeshta* blessing. Morvaan chuckled.

'And now we can go home,' said Ellen.

'But have you no tidings to tell us?' cried Hrugaar.

'Not as such, no,' she said. 'You have come from where the tidings are, Hrugaar. And we shall soon outstay our welcome here, I think.'

'With the Môshári, or with the Emperor?' asked Torkhaal.

'Not yet with the Môshári,' Ellen allowed. 'But Rhydden would not be sorry to see the back of us; nor others in the city, perhaps.'

'And the work does not end with the war,' said Morvaan. 'We must take thought for the Colleges and the Council – and a new Prime Councillor, very soon.'

'But how fares Kierran of Arrand?' Hrugaar persisted; 'and the songmaster Rinnir? And what has the Emperor been doing?'

Ellen sighed wearily and sat down again, with Morvaan beside her. Rhysana and Torkhaal settled themselves on a cushioned bench seat, facing them, and Hrugaar and Dhûghaúr sat down on the polished boards of the floor at their feet.

'Kierran is mending well enough,' Rhysana told him. 'He was taken back to the Arrand palace, and his mother and Lienna had the care of him there. He was full of questions about what was happening at Khôrland, and I think that it irked him considerably to have been left behind. But his good humour is unsinkable.

'With Rinnir,' she sighed, 'the news is less good. You saw how badly he was burned; and the shock of that – and of Salbaar's death – has run very deep. Imarra now has him in her special care. He lives, and he seems to be healing slowly. Whether he will sing or play again, even Imarra can not yet say.'

'We did what we could at the time, in Fersí,' said Hrugaar. 'Yet perhaps it would have been kinder to let him die.'

'The gods, in their wisdom, saw fit not to take him,' said

Ellen. 'You showed him kindness in this life, as you thought best. We can still hope that one day he will learn to thank you for it.'

Hrugaar looked down at the floor, and did not answer.

'Mage Councillor Drengriis came back last night,' said Dhûghaúr. 'Foghlaar brought him to the palace, but I think he has gone to Ellanguan now. The mist around the Tollund manor house has gone.'

'Then the forest folk have left,' said Hrugaar.

'How was Drengriis?' Torkhaal asked.

Dhûghaúr shrugged. 'A little pale, nervous and awkward. He seemed to be relieved to be here in the city. But I do not know him that well.'

'That sounds much like the Drengriis I know,' said Morvaan.

'And who are the forest folk?' Dhûghaúr asked Hrugaar. 'Do you mean the Fay?'

'No,' Hrugaar smiled; 'though one or two of the Fay were there. They were mostly spirits of trees and stone, and of course the fauns. They are wilder than the Fay, and much less fond of humankind. It is small wonder that Drengriis would seem nervous to your eyes, if he has been many days in their company. He is a creature of libraries and writing desks, with no taste for the world beyond human walls.'

'Then why were the forest folk there, if they do not like humankind?' asked Dhûghaúr.

'One of the Fay was with us,' said Hrugaar. 'He called them, I think. He is a friend of Kellarn.'

'And of my daughter Corollin,' said Morvaan.

'And besides,' Hrugaar went on, 'this was not simply a war between men. The forest folk remember the ancient wars, and the days of the Bright Alliance. They know the greater perils of the creatures that the Easterners could summon. And by this we know that Drengriis is indeed safe. For had they seen any trace in him of the evil spirit that once possessed him, they would have torn him apart.'

'Some might consider that a kinder fate than returning

to Ellanguan, with Sollonaal and Rinnekh there,' observed Ellen drily.

'But that is the world Drengriis knows,' said Rhysana.

'Still, I wonder what young Faerbran Tollund made of it all,' said Morvaan. 'I hear he has been summoned to appear before The Arrand and the Emperor, to make his peace with them after the treachery of his kinsmen – probably with a hefty fine paid into the imperial coffers, knowing Rhydden.'

'Let us hope it is no worse, for Bradhor's sake,' said Ellen.

'Bradhor paid dearly for Arisâ's betrayal,' Rhysana explained. 'When word came for the Easterner prisoners to be sent to the border, the Emperor was loth to let them go. He said that it was an insult to Arrandin – and to himself, of course – to send them away unpunished, when they had brought slaughter and ruin upon his people. So he commanded that half their number were to be killed, and the other half sent home; and he required Bradhor to choose who should live and who should die, as proof of his loyalty to Lautun.'

'But Bradhor was no traitor,' said Hrugaar.

'It sounds like something out of the Wars of Power,' Torkhaal growled.

'Or the Interregnum,' agreed Morvaan. 'It seems unnecessarily savage, even by Rhydden's twisted standards.'

'It grows worse,' said Ellen. 'The twenty-odd that Bradhor chose—'

'Twenty-three,' said Rhysana.

'The twenty-three,' Ellen said, 'that Bradhor chose to live were the ones that Rhydden then had put to death; and the others – whom Bradhor thought would die – were released. Thus the Emperor thought to remove all doubt of a continued conspiracy between House Arrand and the East.'

'Bradhor took it very hard,' said Rhysana; 'and The Arrand was furious, as I have never seen him before. But they refused to give Rhydden the satisfaction of seeing them broken. They still play the courteous hosts, while he is a guest in their house; and Rhydden seems to think that he has won the point and has made no mention of it since, that we have heard.'

There was a gloomy silence. After the brief distraction of the war, the internal problems of the Six Kingdoms loomed before them again as large as ever.

'Has anything else happened in the Emperor's household?' asked Torkhaal.

Rhysana knew that he was thinking of the plight of Brother Sarin, and of the fear of the priests of Mairdun that there was a hidden danger among Rhydden's personal attendants.

'Nothing out of the ordinary,' she said; 'and His Eminence seems to have been quiet the last few days. It is possible that whatever danger Carstan feared remained behind in Ellanguan. But there has been no news of anything in Ellanguan – other than that Rinnekh has managed to make some sort of peace with the Southers.'

Hrugaar snorted. Ellen sighed and stirred, and got to her feet again.

'You mentioned something about not being welcome in the city?' Torkhaal asked her as they all rose.

'Well, in some quarters, perhaps,' said Ellen. 'I suppose it is only to be expected. In short, Torkhaal, less than a week ago we were the heroes of the hour. We saved the city – and the whole empire – from certain death and ruin. But now that the enemy has gone away, and they are stuck with wading through the loss and wreckage of it all, those same people who sung our praises now tune their voices to a different theme. They have seen us wield great power in their defence, and now they fear it – as if we would turn it against them. Also, they cry, if our power was so great, why did we not protect them more? Or do this to save them, or do that to confound the Easterners? And even though Telghraan and Ranzhaar and the rest are helping to rebuild the city, their labour is taken as no more than just repayment, for having failed to defend it properly in the first place. Not by all the citizens, of course, but by far too many. As if they could have done a better job of defending against the Easterner wizards themselves. Or as if they did not have the choice of leaving before the city was surrounded.'

It was evident that Torkhaal had struck a point of irritation with the Archmage; and that her scratching it only made it worse.

'But where would they have gone?' said Rhysana gently. 'This is their home. They blame us only out of frustration and grief.'

'Or selfishness,' said Ellen. 'They see only their own little world, their own present hardship, regardless of the fact that the whole of the Six Kingdoms might soon have been suffering a far worse fate if the Easterners had not been turned back here. One might call it ignorance – but they can hardly plead ignorance when twenty thousand Easterners and a few demonic creatures have been battering at their doors only a few days past. Their memories can not be so short.'

'Memory changes many things,' said Morvaan. 'We mould the past to protect ourselves.'

'It was much the same with the borderlanders,' said Hrugaar. 'I grew very tired of being told that I did not understand – that I could not understand. I am not altogether stupid. I understood perfectly well how they felt, even if I did not choose to share the same approach to life for myself. Yet I think that perhaps that defiance was their last defence; as though, for them, the mystery of being misunderstood – and thus being hard done by – was in some way how they defined themselves. Humans seem to need to lay the blame on someone else, or something else, rather than themselves.'

'Or else they blame themselves for a fault which is not of their own making,' said Rhysana.

'And is The Arrand held to blame by the city?' asked Torkhaal. 'Or the Emperor?'

'Or Dortrean?' added Morvaan. 'Already Erkal has been brought into question for how he ended the war. And with Kellarn finding that darned Vengru necklace, Dortrean is being blamed by some for starting it. But had Kelmaar found it, Kelmaar would have been to blame; or if the Emperor, then the Emperor. As if the whole war could be pared back to one simple root and cause.'

'Wars have been fought over lesser trifles, in the past,' Ellen reminded him. 'But no, Torkhaal. The Arrand is still much loved; and the citizens think no worse, nor better, of Rhydden than they did before. It is the *Aeshta* Orders and the Magi – especially the Magi – whom they now doubt; and it is not quite so bad as I have made it sound. Not yet. But the warning signs are there.'

'But the Magi have been in Arrandin for centuries,' said Torkhaal.

'Of course,' said Ellen. 'Dear gods, the Council itself has a longer history than Arrandin; and there were priests and magi of the *Aeshtar*, in some form or other, back before the founding of the First Kingdom. Love us or hate us, we have always been here.'

'But even without this threat of the ancient Enemy returning,' said Morvaan, 'the world of the Six Kingdoms is changing. And so the face of the Council changes – or at least, the face of the Council as the outside world perceives it. Under Herusen's gentle guidance, the Council became less severe and remote than it was when I was your age. Well, the turmoils of the last century had made us that way, I suppose. The great wars, the loss of the Guardians, the terrible Regency of Virkhaîl Fastbind's youth and the treacheries of the Interregnum. We had hoped that we were coming to better times. But now a new Prime Councillor will have to chart a new course to see us through these present troubles. It will be no easy task.'

'And which of you two will that be?' asked Dhûghaúr.

'Neither, we hope,' Ellen answered. 'Archmagi do not make good Prime Councillors, as a rule. Too eccentric.'

'Still, the choice must be made soon,' said Morvaan. 'We shall hold a general assembly within the next few days; and then you, Dhûghaúr, along with the rest, can have your say. And then we must endeavour to win back some measure of confidence from the people of the Six Kingdoms. Either that, or perhaps we may have to withdraw again for a time.'

'Yes,' said Rhysana, 'Herusen has spoken of that before.'

'But if the demon captain is soon to return,' said Dhûghaúr, 'surely we can not afford to lose the good will of the Court Noble?'

'It galls me to say it,' sighed Ellen, 'but Sollonaal may prove a popular choice in the assembly chamber. Whatever one may think of him personally, he does seem to have found favour with the imperial nobles, and with the Guildmasters of Ellanguan.'

'At a price,' muttered Hrugaar.

'If he can achieve the same with the Court Noble and in the other cities,' she went on, 'it might make our position more secure than it now is. Who knows, we may even come to be thought of as respectable citizens of the Empire.'

'I hope,' said Hrugaar, 'that I shall never have to become respectable. I had rather have the free spirit of the old Six Kingdoms.'

'That's treasonous talk, young Hrugaar,' said Morvaan; 'though I must concede that the idea has a certain attraction.'

'For myself, I am not certain that Sollonaal would be a wise choice,' said Ellen; 'I simply foretell what many of our fellow magi might say. And you, Councillor Hrugaar, shall never be quite respectable. That is one of your more endearing qualities. Now we must be gone.'

'And we can fetch Taillan and go home,' said Rhysana to Torkhaal.

'I had thought that you might want to rest at Telún for a few days,' he ventured.

Rhysana shook her head. 'I need to go home, please,' she said. 'I have done little enough while you have been gone.'

That last part was not entirely true. What she meant was that she had spent enough time watching and waiting, and that any further delay at her brother's manor house of Telún would only serve to increase her frustration. She needed to get back to the familiar routine of College life, and of caring for their son; and then she might feel better placed to tackle the many problems now facing the Colleges and the Council. She also needed to get used to life in the College without Herusen – an ordeal which she thought best to encounter sooner rather than later.

'No one will force you to work for a while, if you want to rest,' she added.

'If you are sure,' said Torkhaal.

'I shall go to Ellanguan for a few days, and leave you two in peace,' said Hrugaar. Rhysana smiled at him gratefully.

'I trust that you are not planning mischief against the Steward?' said Morvaan.

'Not this time,' Hrugaar grinned; 'though I need to find out what is happening with the Southers. But I want to go through the early records in the Book Halls, to see if there is any mention of – of the Enemy's return, now that we have heard what the Easterners have foreseen.'

'What did they say?' asked Dhûghaúr.

'That he would reappear somewhere within the Six Kingdoms, I think,' Hrugaar answered. 'I was not permitted to ride with Erkal's escort, and heard it only by report.'

There is none who can stand against the Master when he comes in glory, quoted Morvaan. *'He will rise in the very heart of your petty empire. Your strength will crumble, from the centre to the rim.* That is what the wizard said, anyway. I was there.'

A shadow of memory fluttered at the back of Rhysana's mind, and was gone. She frowned, and made a mental note to hunt it down later.

'Oh,' said Dhûghaúr. 'That doesn't tell us much more than we knew, does it?'

'Not much,' Morvaan agreed.

'That reminds me,' said Ellen. 'When Kellarn of Dortrean was here, he seemed to think that he should have recognised the symbol of the Enemy, on the talisman that he had found. Has he had much to do with the priests of the Sun Temple of late? Or how else would he have known of it?'

'Kellarn and my daughter found the shrine to the Enemy

in the Holleth Woods,' Morvaan explained, 'a couple of sum-
mers back.'

'I had thought that that was Boldrin of Levrin,' said Ellen.

'Boldrin was there later, when it was destroyed,' he told her.
Ellen nodded, and prepared to go.

'I do not suppose,' said Hrugaar, 'while we are here, that
you could show me how you work the matrix for the city's
defences?'

'No,' said Rhysana and Ellen together.

'But Torkhaal can share his memories of the matrix with you,'
Rhysana offered, 'if he has not already done so.'

Hrugaar blushed and turned his head away. It was clear that
Torkhaal had.

'And I am sure that Dhûghaúr can tell you more about it,'
she added, 'when you are in Ellanguan.'

'I had not planned to go to Ellanguan,' said Dhûghaúr shyly.

'Well, whenever,' said Ellen. 'This goodbye has lasted quite
long enough. I shall expect to see you all at the next assembly
– very soon.'

II ELLANGUAN

Chapter Seven

The Lord Steward Rinnekh made a show of reading to the end of the document before him, while everyone else waited. Then he handed it off to the almoner, pinched the man's sagging buttocks merely to put him out of countenance, and half rose from his seat to acknowledge the arrival of his unwanted guests.

'Can it wait, Lauraï?' he murmured, settling himself down again. 'I ought to see Lord Solban first, on the Emperor's own business.'

He did not wish to see either of them, if the truth were told; any more than he wished to be sitting at his desk looking at endless figured inventories of the Southers' requirements, or listening to tedious reports of minor offences within the city. Rinnekh could think of far more enjoyable pursuits for a fine summer morning.

'Lord Solban has kindly allowed me to speak first,' said Lauraï, moving round so that the long desk stood between them. 'I have asked him to be here with me – and Master Trigharran also – so that I am not misrepresented, either to the Emperor or to the city.'

There was no due deference in her manner. She might have been reprimanding one of her own household rather than addressing her rightful overlord; and her temper was clearly rising. With an effort, Rinnekh controlled his own impatience. He leaned back in the chair, crossed his legs elegantly, and looked her up and down with a slow, smirking grin.

The Lady Lauraï Raudhar of Renza was a little younger than him, tall and pale and slender, with fiery red hair coiled into a plaited crown about her head; and even by right of birth, in the neutral theatre of precedence by Blood Noble, she would have ranked considerably lower than Rinnekh himself. Had her late husband Torreghal Renza been still alive, he would have been the preferred successor before Rinnekh to the Stewardship of Ellanguan; and Lauraï might now have been Lady of Ellanguan. But – fortunately for Rinnekh – Torreghal had met his death at the hands of an ambitious kinsman; and so Lauraï had instead become joint Regent of the Watchful Isle of Renza until her only daughter Kerraïs came of age, more than a decade hence; and Regents with her were Torreghal's sister Broneïs and his mother Melissaë. Broneïs had married a lesser kinsman of Renza blood, and now had an infant son of her own. Though there was no love lost between Rinnekh and the widowed Lauraï, he had not ruled out the possibility – in his own mind, at least – of marrying her himself, in the hope of gaining control over the Watchful Isle and allaying any future challenge from Renza for his Steward's throne.

Lauraï's wisdom in her choice of witnesses that morning was debatable, he thought; though their presence might certainly hinder him from using some of his more persuasive tactics, and Trigharran's quivering nose would no doubt sniff out any active use of the enchantments from Rinnekh's golden horsehead brooch. Master Trigharran of Kelmaar – shrunken and wizened, and well over eighty if he was a day – was the oldest and most venerated tutor of the Kelmaar School in Ellanguan, and much respected among the heathen followers of the *Aeshtar* within the city. He disliked the new Lord Steward every bit as much as he did the Empire, or as Rinnekh disliked him; but Trigharran's poor opinion of all members of the female sex was legendary.

The Lord Solban of Dortrean was an even more unlikely choice. He had joined the cadets of the Imperial Household Guard shortly before Rinnekh, and had worn the golden livery ever since; and had now risen to the rank of Lieutenant General. With his dark eyes and hair the colour of rich earth, Solban was quite unlike the other members of Erkal's family; so that it amused Rinnekh to wonder whether Karlena had played her husband false in the getting of their elder son, to secure some deal or other. Solban's loyalty to the Emperor and to the Guard was beyond question – but that in itself, in a son of Dortrean, made Rinnekh wary of him. Solban would put the Emperor's interests first, before either Ellanguan or Renza. He had arrived here the previous evening, on the imperial warship sent from Lautun to help keep an eye on the dealings with the Southers. By report, the ship had passed by the Watchful Isle, a day's sail east of Ellanguan; and Lauraï had asked to be taken aboard to make the last leg of the journey with them.

'—out of the question,' Lauraï was saying, 'and as foolish as it is presumptuous.'

'Is there a point to all this?' Rinnekh sighed, as though he had been listening.

'Of course there is a point,' she returned hotly, placing both hands flat on the desk and leaning forward toward him. 'One moment the Southers are wreaking havoc along the coasts, and the next we have some foolish errand boy of your household commanding us to open our harbour to the Souther warships and furnish them with the supplies they need.'

'Only enough for them to repair their storm damage, to make safe journey home,' said Rinnekh. 'That's common kindness, Lauraï. And you know that we are at peace with the Southers now.'

He reached forward and rested his right hand over Lauraï's left. She pulled away as though stung.

'Ellanguan is far better equipped to cater for their needs,' she said; 'or Rebraal, or Lautun. But that is beside the point. The Watchful Isle is guarded and secret, an outpost for defence against attacks from the sea. Previous Lords Steward of Ellanguan have understood the wisdom of preserving its secrets, whether in times of war or peace. Few enough even of the sailors from our own Six Kingdoms are ever permitted ashore.'

'Our friendship with the Southers is vital to the Emperor,' he told her; 'and there are more problems with the new God-King than I can begin to explain. It should be enough for you that Ellanguan requires Renza to do this small service. Do I have to enforce this as a command?'

'Renza answers to Ellanguan only in outside matters,' she replied, undaunted. 'The Isle itself is our private domain.'

'You are only a Regent by marriage,' he sneered, 'appointed by the Court Noble.'

'And you are only the Emperor's whipping boy, ill grafted on to a far worthier line.'

'And your father of Raudhar is a retainer of Ellanguan, and far below the Solaní.'

Lauraï drew herself up to her full height, taller than anyone else in the room. Her eyes flashed dangerously.

'Renza holds the Watchful Isle in ancient trust from the sea fay,' she said. 'In the end, we alone are answerable to them for what befalls there. Even the Emperor himself can not set foot upon our shore unless the Lords of Renza permit it.'

'And I suppose you would defy even him,' said Rinnekh.

'That is not what I meant,' she snapped.

'Lord Steward – my Lady,' said Solban quietly. 'May I speak?'

Lauraï folded her arms as if holding herself in check, and nodded tightly. Rinnekh flung himself back in his chair.

'Go ahead,' he said.

'The Emperor is Lord Paramount of the Watchful Isle,' said Solban. 'The Lords of Renza have sworn fealty to him, and will no doubt honour his commands, and those of his chosen servants.'

Lauraï's eyes flared as though she might burst with fury. Rinnekh smirked in triumph.

'I am informed that His Highness approves of this peace with the Southers,' Solban continued, 'and that they should be permitted to repair their ships here in Ellanguan for their voyage home. My own orders were to come here to ensure that this happens peacefully. However, I am unaware that the

Emperor has granted permission for Souther ships to make harbour in any other port – not even in Lautun or Farran, where there is greater military strength for the provision of the defence of the Empire. So for the security of the Empire, the Guard deems it best to confine the presence of the Southers to Ellanguan alone.'

Lauraï's relief and thankfulness were palpable on the air in the wake of her fiery temper. Solban's tanned face remained impassive and serious as ever, but his dark eyes twinkled with humour. Rinnekh hated the pair of them.

'My harbours can't hold the entire Souther fleet,' he protested crossly.

'They will not have to, Lord Steward,' Solban told him. 'On our voyage here, we saw nor sight nor sail of a Souther vessel until we reached Ellanguan. So the whole question of Renza having to give them room was largely academic in the first place.'

Rinnekh did not fail to catch the glance exchanged between Solban and Lauraï. He scowled irritably, and stood up. He would not have put it past them to have conspired together beforehand, simply to make him look ridiculous. Well, let them enjoy their petty triumph while they could. When the Emperor returned, they would see who held the greater weight of favour.

'You have your answer, Lauraï,' he said, smiling fiercely. 'Now will you excuse us?'

Lauraï bowed and went away, the guard opening the door as she approached. Trigharran also bowed, clutching his gnarled staff, and let his grey-clad attendant lead him out.

Solban watched them go, his gaze perhaps more on Lauraï than on the old man of Kelmaar. It occurred to Rinnekh to wonder what else the Lieutenant General and the Regent of Renza had spoken about on their voyage here, and whether he could use that against them.

'A fine woman,' he said aloud, 'if rather headstrong. Do you think I could persuade her to become my Lady of Ellanguan?'

213

The look of startled surprise on Solban's face was reward enough – for now.

'Perhaps not this morning, my Lord,' said Solban, recovering himself.

'Perhaps you fancy your own chances better?' asked Rinnekh, with deceptive good humour.

'I am sure that the Lady has her own opinion on such matters,' Solban answered. 'Now if you will permit me, my Lord? I do not wish to keep you long.'

After so many goodbyes, Kellarn's mood was rather subdued as they rode out from Samsar that morning. Lord Drômagh had insisted that Erkal take an escort of four knights of the Imperial Household Cavalry, since there was still the chance that a few small bands of Easterners might be hiding out in the hills along the road to Fersí. Kellarn thought it just as likely that the knights were under orders to keep an eye on his father, Corollin and himself; and Erkal seemed to share the thought, and kept them to a brisk pace in spite of the heat of the day.

'Do you think,' Kellarn asked him, as they came out on to the more open ground to the south of the Khôrland vale, 'that the Emperor will help Lord Zhertan to rebuild his manor?'

'Perhaps,' said Erkal. 'More likely he will require The Arrand to do so, as Khôrland's proper overlord. No doubt His Highness will make provision for that in whatever funds he grants to The Arrand for the repair of Arrandin.'

The Earl's tone was casually neutral, as if his mind were more occupied with other things. To Kellarn's ears, it was a signal that he would not get a straight answer out of his father in present company.

'I had heard, your Grace,' said one of the knights, 'that Khôrland blames Dortrean for causing the war, and hopes that Dortrean might make amends for his losses.'

The speaker was Lord Mataún of Fâghsul, nephew to the War priest Môrghran. Mataún was a little younger than Kellarn, taller and more powerfully built, and too obviously held a high

214

opinion of his own good looks and prowess. His presence alone among their guard escort would have been enough to warn Dortrean that they might be being watched.

'We did not cause the war, Mataún,' sighed Erkal, 'we merely played our part in helping to end it – as has been explained to Lord Zhertan. But in truth, were I to offer anything to him now – not implying any fault on our part, but simply as a gift between friends – I would have hard work to persuade him to accept it. Zhertan Khôrland is a proud man, and he is The Arrand's man. He will accept payment where it is his due, from his own overlord or from the Emperor. He knows it is not Dortrean's place to stand in their stead unbidden.'

'Your Grace forgives much,' said Mataún, laughing. 'I can't say as I don't grow tired of these stubborn borderlanders, myself.' Kellarn wondered whether he had understood much at all of Erkal's answer.

They rode on in silence for some while after that, apart from the occasional low comments or jokes between the escorting guards. Away in the distance they could see small troops of the Emperor's armies moving hither and thither across the land; but all that morning no one else came near the road.

By early afternoon they had climbed up among the more rolling slopes at the edge of the Tollund lands. The breeze had picked up a little, though there was still little chance of shade from the high summer sun, and the Earl did not slow his pace. Kellarn felt that he was sweating more than his borrowed horse. The face of Mataún of Fâghsul was scarlet.

As they rounded a bend in the road to turn more southwest, another band of riders came into view just ahead. There were six horsemen, all clad in the golden livery of the Imperial Household Guard; and they were escorting some twenty or more Easterner prisoners marching on foot. The Easterners had been stripped of their weapons and war gear, and looked tired and resentful in the afternoon heat. Yet to Kellarn's eyes, even their few days of captivity in Arrandin seemed to have left them healthier and more at ease in their bearing than the

215

warriors he had seen leaving Khôrland; so that he wondered how much greater hardship the Easterner armies might have had to endure.

Erkal signalled a halt, and they moved aside off the road to let the captives pass. The guard leader saluted as he drew level with the Earl, with one gloved fist clenched against his breast.

'Were there no more than this to be released?' Erkal asked him.

'These are the ones who were fit enough to travel, Sir,' said the man, staying his mount. 'There are more in the city, to follow later.'

Erkal glanced along the marching line, and then back at the guard, and nodded. 'Is Lord Brodhaur still in Fersí?'

'He is, Sir.'

'Well enough,' said Erkal. 'Let Lautun lose no honour in our treatment of these men.'

The guard saluted and moved on. When all the Easterners had passed, the Earl led his own company back on to the road, and they set off again at a slightly gentler pace. By Kellarn's reckoning they were still a good five leagues away from Fersí village, and he guessed that his father wished to reach there by the end of the day, to speak with Lord Brodhaur. From Fersí it would be another full day's ride to Arrandin – if he returned to Arrandin. The further west they came, the less inclined Kellarn was to go near the Emperor at all. The presence of their unwanted escort, even here in the wild border country, was reminder enough of the dangerous whims of the imperial Court.

'What will happen after you have seen the Emperor?' he asked his father presently.

Erkal looked at him, and chuckled. 'What kind of a question is that?' he said.

Kellarn grinned back, a little awkwardly. His face flushed redder as he tried to think of a tactful way to ask what he wanted to know, with Mataún's ears wagging close by. His father took the problem from him.

216

'I doubt that His Highness will stay in the city long,' said the Earl, 'now that this war with the East has been settled. He will no doubt wish to return to Ellanguan, to satisfy himself of the peace made between Rinnekh and the Southers; and then there is the Summer Court to be held next month, in his own palace in Lautun. The greater part of our armies will soon be sent north again, once the borders are secure, since the Emperor can not keep a standing army of such size here indefinitely against the Easterners' return. But he will leave one or other of his commanders – Lord Brodhaur, or Drômagh perhaps – to arrange that with The Arrand.'

'And what about you?' asked Kellarn.

'I shall go where the Emperor commands,' said Erkal simply. 'He may want me to speak with the Souther Ambassador; and His Highness will most likely want me to attend the Summer Court.'

His father made no mention of where Kellarn might be, or what he might intend to do. But by that he meant that Kellarn was free to choose, and that their imperial escorts did not need to hear about it.

They rode on west along the road, and came to the long southward stretch where their armies had been ambushed only a few days before. The green slopes to either side were still blackened and scarred in many places, although most of the battle debris had now been cleared away – either by Brodhaur's troops, or by other folk from the surrounding Tollund lands. They passed another group of horsemen there, out on patrol; but those were in the blue and white livery of House Kîrnal, and there were no Easterners with them.

The late afternoon heat was turning to balmy early evening when they came down to the river crossing at Fersí, though the sun was still well clear of the mountains and hills to the northwest. The village was busy with much activity, and already the first of the new fences and shelters were in place; and there was the lowing of beasts and the clattering of tools, and the bright colours and chatter of the warriors and villagers at work amid the blacks and greys of the recent ashes. The tents and gear of the troops were mostly to the north of the village on the farther shore; but once they had forded the cooling river waters, Erkal and his escort were directed to the shaded comfort of the Fersí inn.

As they rode into the stableyard, the guards who were waiting to take their horses and gear were dressed in the purple and white livery of Brodhaur's own retainers of Levrin. The Commander himself came down the worn stone steps beside the mounting block to welcome them. Brodhaur's right arm was still in a sling, and his waddling gait was even more pronounced than usual, but he seemed his normal, cheerful self. He dispatched Mataún and the imperial knights off to the camp outside the village, tipped Kellarn and Corollin a wink, and ushered Erkal away indoors. Left more or less to their own devices at last, Kellarn and Corollin tarried just long enough to see the horses safely settled, and then went through into the long common room at the front of the inn.

The common room was still quiet at that hour of the day, with only a few warriors and guard captains sitting in small groups in the dim shadows. Though the place had been scrupulously cleaned since the fires of the Easterners' assault, and although a delicious smell of roasting meats and other wondrous foods was already drifting in from somewhere further back in the inn, there was still the faint memory of smoke and ashes on the air; and the dark stained wood of the panelled walls and heavy tables seemed more gloomy than comforting.

They were brought ale and fresh bread before they thought of asking, and the young lad who served them seemed cheerful and friendly enough, and far more amenable – to Kellarn's mind – than the borderlanders in Samsar had been. But the boy was soon called away to other duties; and it was not long after that before one of the senior women of the Levrin guard came in to show them upstairs to their rooms. They took the bread and ale up with them.

They discovered that they had been given a suite of rooms

on the western side of the inn. The panelled walls and furniture were of the same dark stained oak that they had seen in the common room; but the bed hangings and drapes and cushions were of rich brocades worked in many colours, and with the evening sunlight flooding in through the windows the effect was much more homely and welcoming. There were sweet scented rushes on the floor, and the rooms seemed untouched by any memory of the recent battles. Kellarn supposed that the suite of rooms was set aside for the wealthier merchants and travellers who passed through Fersí, and he wondered briefly whether Lord Brodhaur or one of his senior commanders had been obliged to move out for their own benefit. But there were no telltale signs that anyone had stayed here recently.

As soon as the woman had shut the door and gone away, Kellarn went across to the nearest of the wide casement windows and looked out. Below was a sheer drop to the cobbled ground of a wagon yard, surrounded by a high wall and with heavy gates at the far right end. There were a handful of carts and wagons at the inner end of the yard, and in the open gateway stood two men in the blue and purple of the Tollund livery and a black-clad knight of the Hyrsenite Order. Beyond the wall were the remains of the western outskirts of the village, and the road leading off through the Footstool Hills toward Arrandin.

Kellarn sighed and turned back to face the room. It would not be the first time that they had tried to slip out of an inn by a back way, to shake off unwanted pursuit; and though the windows did not offer an easy route, it was perhaps not altogether impossible. His greater concern was their lack of horses. Their borrowed mounts had been lent only for the journey to Arrandin, and Kellarn did not intend to be accused of horse stealing by taking them elsewhere. The theft of horses of any kind was a serious offence, since the people of the Six Kingdoms loved their horses as much as their own kinsmen – or even more so, in some cases. Trying to barter or borrow other mounts would only draw attention to themselves with so many imperial warriors around; nor were there likely to be any decent beasts here in Fersí that had not already been commandeered for the use of the Emperor's armies. It was not that Kellarn and Corollin could not travel perfectly well on foot; but simply that should Mataún or anyone else wish to follow them, they would doubtless be on horseback and could overtake them with ease. Assuming, that was, that they were being watched at all. Kellarn had to concede the possibility that his dislike of the imperial Court and its endless political tangles was driving him to imagine danger in every shadow.

Corollin was standing in the middle of the main living chamber, her head bowed and her eyes closed in concentration. She looked up at him and smiled as he turned around.

'We are safe, for a few minutes at least,' she told him. 'You do not want to go to Arrandin, do you?'

Kellarn shook his head. 'It would be harder to leave there unnoticed than here.'

'But easier to find horses and supplies,' she said. 'It depends on where you want to go.'

'Well, not to see the Emperor, at any rate,' he muttered, glancing back out through the window. 'The problem with the Southers seems to be largely working out peace treaties, for now. And the Magi and Orders are probably better placed to keep an eye out for problems in Rhydden's household than I would be. I can't see that staying with Father will do much good. I think we really ought to be doing something about finding the – you know.' He was reluctant to speak openly about returning to their search for the artefact, even though she had just assured him that they were safe here.

'That was my thought, too,' Corollin nodded.

'But where do we go next?'

'Kôril said that he would wait near the Tollund manor for us, or until we sent word to him,' she told Kellarn. 'That is only a few miles away. We can go there tomorrow and speak with him, before we decide.'

Kellarn hummed his approval. Though Kôril probably knew

no more than they did about the return of the demon captain, nor where to hunt next for the artefact which they hoped might defeat him, he was still one of the Fay; and the elvenfolk had access to sources more ancient and obscure than perhaps even the Council of Magi might have dreamed of. And the simple prospect of getting away from the human politics of the Court Noble and back to the wider world of their own companionship and adventures was comfort enough.

'I don't suppose—' he began. Corollin held up her hand in warning, turning her left ear toward the outer door. After a few seconds Kellarn could hear the tread of booted feet in the passageway beyond. He scooted forward, placing himself between Corollin and the doorway. The footsteps came to a halt just outside, and then there was a quiet knock.

Kellarn glanced back at Corollin, relying on her exceptional senses to warn of any danger. There was a look of puzzled surprise on her face, but she nodded and gestured for him to open the door. He lifted the latch, and swung the door open enough to look through – and discovered the face of the Abbot Commander Carstan Mairdun smiling back at him from the dim lamplight of the passage.

'If I might intrude for a moment?' Carstan ventured.

'Of course,' said Kellarn, pulling the door wider to let him inside. 'Come in, and welcome. I had not realised you were still here. In the village, I mean.'

'For a few more days, I think,' said the Abbot. There was no one else with him, so after a quick glance outside Kellarn shut the door again.

'Is there any news of Rinnir?' asked Corollin.

Carstan spread his hands in an open gesture. 'He was taken back to Arrandin, with most of the other wounded,' he replied. 'The healers of your *Aeshta* Orders there will no doubt be able to tend him better than we could here.'

Corollin's eyebrows went up.

'Isn't that heresy, my Lord Abbot?' she teased.

'No, practicality,' Carstan countered. 'The most that any

221

of us could manage here was little better than brute battle surgery. His Grace – your father – is still with Lord Brodhaur, I take it?'

'He is, I'm afraid,' said Kellarn.

'Well, no matter,' said Carstan. 'This was just a courtesy visit, one might say – unless there is something you wish to tell me?'

The Abbot's manner was relaxed and unpressing, but Kellarn felt suddenly cornered. He knew nothing more of the possible enemy hidden within the imperial household, other than what Torren of Mairdun had told him. How much Carstan might know about the whole question of Lo-Khuma he could only begin to guess – though probably a good deal, given the Hyrsenites' unusual interest in the doings of the heathen *Aeshta* Orders. But he did not know Carstan well enough to risk broaching that subject. He felt the colour rising to his cheeks as the Abbot watched him.

'Not really,' he managed. 'Why?'

'I noticed that you had four golden shadows riding in to the village,' said Carstan quietly. 'Unlikely for the Lords of Dortrean. It struck me that you might be wanting to give them the slip.'

Kellarn felt himself blush even deeper.

'Knight Commander Drômagh thought we might need an escort on the road,' he said. 'I'm not sure if he meant all the way to Arrandin.'

'Ah,' said Carstan. 'And are you going to Arrandin?'

Kellarn risked a quick glance at Corollin. Her expression was carefully neutral, waiting to take the lead from him. But that in itself, he thought, must mean that she could sense no immediate danger from the Abbot Commander. And Mairdun had put themselves out on more than one occasion in the past to help Dortrean.

'What we really need,' he said, 'is three horses, and food for several days.'

'Done,' said Carstan. 'Will the morning be soon enough?'

'But – but I can't pay you for them,' said Kellarn, surprised by his swift success.

'No need,' Carstan assured him. 'You can have them as a gift.'

'But—' Kellarn protested again. Wealthy though the Hyrsenites might be, three horses was a costly gift; and one which he felt less than worthy to receive.

'Their own riders will have no more need of them now, where they are gone,' said Carstan. 'But I am not Abbot Commander of my Order for nothing, my Lord. I see the need, and labour to fulfil it in good conscience.'

'Well, I shall hope to return the favour some day,' said Kellarn.

'No,' said Carstan. 'That would make it seem like a bribe, rather than a gift. I expect nothing in return – except, perhaps, the pleasure of watching you succeed.'

'Succeed in what?' asked Kellarn.

'In life,' said the Abbot easily.

He smiled at Kellarn, and Kellarn smiled back; and by tacit agreement they said no more upon the subject.

Carstan went away after that, before his visit should be discovered – though with promises that the horses would be ready by first light, a little way west along the road beyond the village.

'There was one other thing,' he said, as he reached the door, 'I don't suppose you happen to know who the Emperor's inquisitors are these days?'

The question was far from comfortable, given Kellarn's worries about being watched. But he had no real idea of the answer.

'His Eminence, perhaps?' he suggested. 'Or some of the *Vashta* priests.'

'That was my thought, also,' Carstan nodded. 'Go in peace.' Then he lifted the latch and slipped out quietly, without further explanation.

They made arrangements to bathe and have their supper

brought upstairs, rather than venture down to the common room again. The Levrin guard herself brought them up a platter piled with slices of roasted ox heart in steaming gravy. Corollin looked at it guiltily.

'How can they manage to give us this, when their village is half ruined?' she said.

'Food must be found for the troops, though the land starve,' said Kellarn.

'I am not one of the Emperor's warriors,' said Corollin.

Kellarn shrugged. 'One mouth more or less won't make much difference,' he told her. 'Besides, they probably salvaged this from what the Easterners butchered. Now eat! It may be the last good meal we get for quite a while.'

Erkal was back from his meeting with Lord Brodhaur within the hour, but he also seemed intent on bath and supper and bed after their long day's ride. The meeting had gone well, he told them, and although the Easterners had caused much damage, the Six Kingdoms armies had already made better progress setting things to rights than he might have hoped. The Emperor should have little cause for displeasure when Erkal made his report.

They made a point of saying goodbye to him properly before they went to bed, since there would be little time in the morning.

'Well I shall miss your company,' said the Earl; 'though I know that we haven't seen much of one another, the past few days.'

'When do we ever?' Kellarn laughed ruefully.

'Not often,' Erkal allowed. 'Still, I understand your not wanting to see the Emperor. Whether His Highness will want to see *you* is another matter. He may require your attendance at the Summer Court.'

'He has to find me first,' grinned Kellarn.

'Don't tempt the gods,' said his father; 'and don't tempt Rhydden, either. If he calls, you were best to show up.'

'Well don't put the idea into his imperial head, please,' said

Kellarn. 'Or try to dissuade him, if you can. We're trying to find out more about the threat of this demon – and we can't do that if we're stuck in the imperial palace.'

The simple explanation was true enough. Kellarn had not gone into the details of what they were trying to do, and Erkal had wisely not pressed the point.

'Isn't that a matter better left to the priests?' Erkal wondered.

'I've already spoken with the Môshári,' Kellarn told him. 'And I expect we shall visit the Sun Temple sometime soon.' Which was true enough, though he had no idea exactly when.

'And Carstan must have guessed something of what we are about, I think,' said Corollin. 'It seemed that he came here with the purpose of helping us in whatever way he could.'

'Mairdun have shown much support to the Sun Temple, and to Dortrean, of late,' Erkal nodded. 'Karlena thinks highly of Carstan. Just be careful, the pair of you.'

Kellarn let himself be hugged goodnight, and Erkal kissed Corollin on the forehead; and then he took himself off to bed. They packed their gear together quietly, in readiness for their early start, and then went to bed themselves.

They slept deeply for several hours – which was perhaps tribute to the fine food and ale of the Fersí inn, and the chance to sleep in a real bed again – and it was Erkal himself who wakened them. It was still pitch dark outside, save for the dim glow of campfires to the north and the summer stars overhead. Kellarn tugged the bedclothes and wondered whether it was worth all this trouble just to shake off an imperial tail. But his father would not let him go back to sleep.

They dressed and readied themselves in the main chamber of the suite, where the windows were shuttered and the curtains drawn, by the light of a single candle; and then they crept out along the lamplit passage, and down the stair into the entry lobby beside the common room. Erkal came with them, in case there were doors or windows to be secured behind them after they had left the inn.

The common room was in darkness; but there was a faint light seeping across the floor from beneath the door to the scullery and kitchens beyond, and they could hear the muffled noises of the inn folk setting about the work of the day. The front door was still locked and barred, as they had expected. The small door at the inner end of the entry lobby was already unbolted and on the latch, and opened without murmur to let them out into the stableyard.

The sky overhead was turning to grey as they went down the stone steps beside the mounting block. The stables were quiet, though candlelight winked down at them from one of the small loft windows. They hugged the wall and crept round into the shadow of the gate tunnel, and then waited at the heavy wooden doors while Corollin focused her mage's senses to discover if there was anyone outside. The coast appeared to be clear. So they hugged Erkal goodbye once more, and let themselves out through the small portal gate of the doors into the dim light of the village street.

With the war over and the lands around them cleared of enemies, there were very few guards on duty. They could see a couple of watchpost fires on the eastern side of the village, beyond the river. Kellarn guessed that there would be more sentries up around the camp; but that was well over a furlong away, and with the campfires there the men would be hard put to see them at this distance in the darkness.

They had little difficulty following the grey line of the street in the gloom, keeping close to the shadowed walls and ducking beneath darkened windows. At the edge of the village, the street became the road again; and there they met their first check. A short distance off to the right of the road, hidden from their sight until the last moment by a cluster of cottage buildings, were two guards standing duty beside a small brazier fire.

Kellarn and Corollin shrank back into the shadows at once,

but their movement had alerted the guards. Kellarn fumbled for his sword hilt, though he did not want to start a fight. Corollin shifted her grasp upon her staff, as though preparing to use magical means to prevent their discovery. But as the guards turned, the glow from the brazier revealed the unmistakable tailed stars of silver and gold upon their dark surcoats.

'Mairdun,' Kellarn breathed in relief. Carstan had been quite thorough in his provision of help.

The nearer of the two guards came over to them – a round woman, rather heavily built, but so light upon her feet that even watching her they could barely hear her approach. She nodded once in greeting, and then signed for them to head toward a dark blur of tree shadow to the south of the road, perhaps a quarter of a mile away across the open grazing land of the valley. She did not offer to go with them.

They nodded their understanding and their thanks, and set off along the southern edge of the road, crouching low as they went. The border road was very old, and had been paved a few times over the centuries; and though it was in better repair here than it had been out by Samsar, many of the flagstones were cracked and broken, so that one had to watch out for loose pebbles and jagged rocks underfoot. The one advantage was that – given the frequent flooding here in the river valley – the villagers had delved drainage ditches to either side of the road, and banked up the earth into low hedgerows at the edge of the meadows. Thus by keeping to the ditch, although the going was slower and more difficult, the hedgerows provided them with extra cover from the watchful eyes of the imperial troops.

By the time that they drew level with the small copse of trees, the eastern sky was turning to pale amethyst behind them and the valley was filled with the sound of carolling birds. Kellarn's ankles and the backs of his legs were beginning to ache, and Corollin seemed to be crawling on all fours. They rolled over the low hedgerow, and lay outstretched for a few moments in the soggy grass. Behind the birdsong, and the sighing of the leaves on the nearby trees, they could hear the familiar noises of the stirring camp carried down on the mountain breeze. Kellarn rolled over on to his stomach, and tapped Corollin's leg to signal that they should move on. They set off again at a crouching run, and reached the safety of the trees with no obvious sounds of an alarm being raised.

Another of the knights of Mairdun was waiting for them, whom Kellarn felt he should have recognised. The man was tall and dark-haired, and broadly built, and perhaps nearly twice Kellarn's age; and there was something about him that put Kellarn in mind of the Lady Idesîn, wife of the Lord Patall Telbray, so that he wondered whether he was a Truthsayer, or perhaps a holy knight of their Order. He was clad in tunic and breeches of plain black, and wore a long sword at his side; and he introduced himself as Halvar of Mairdun.

Halvar had in fact brought four horses with him, for he himself was bound for Arrandin. His own mount was a heavy destrier, carrying a fair amount of gear. The other three were Farási coursers – less sturdy than the great warhorses that Kellarn was used to riding, but more suited for speed and covering long distances with ease. There was a spirited bay gelding, named Rúnfyr, whom Kellarn chose; and a smaller gray mare, Mistwise, who went to Corollin. The third horse, a bay mare called Lanaë, they took with them on a leading rein, for Kôril to ride later.

They walked the horses back to the road, partly because of the dim light, and partly so that they could remain hidden behind them. When they reached the road, Halvar mounted and led the way; so that if any imperial eyes did see them, they might take it as no more than one lone rider leading three horses back toward Arrandin – and Halvar was too big and broad to be mistaken for either Kellarn or Corollin, even at that distance.

When at last they had rounded the first hill spur to take them out of sight of the village, and the eastern hills were already aflame with the dawn beneath a brilliant sky, Halvar drew rein and let them mount up. His grey eyes sparkled with good humour in the morning light.

'West and a little north lies your way,' he told them. 'Though I expect you already know that.'

'Thank you,' said Kellarn. 'You have all been very kind.'

'Not really,' said Halvar. 'Just following my Lord Abbot's orders.' His broad grin seemed to give the lie to his words; and the directness of his gaze seemed to convey hope and blessing that were at once encouraging and yet faintly unsettling. Kellarn was certain that Halvar must be a holy knight, and perhaps possessed of exceptional mental powers akin to those of Idesîn and Carstan – and Corollin. He felt relieved when Halvar looked away again, pointing to the route that they could take up into the hills.

The knight waited on the road for some minutes, watching as they rode up the green slope amid the dawn shadows. Then with a final wave he turned his horse west and went on his way toward the city.

'How much do Mairdun know, do you think?' asked Kellarn, when Halvar was safely out of earshot.

'They know of the prophecies of the Sun priests,' said Corollin; 'and probably what the Easterners said at Khôrland. They would not presume to read the hidden thoughts of our minds, without our consent – nor I theirs.'

'They seem to be going out of their way to help us.'

'Carstan is a powerful priest,' Corollin reminded him. 'We can only guess what his goddess might have shown him. Or perhaps they are just being kind.'

'Why does that worry me?' said Kellarn.

'They are a *Vashta* Order,' she offered. 'And they are caught up in the politics of the Court Noble, which you love so well.'

'Like the plague,' Kellarn grinned. 'Let's hope we can leave that behind now.'

They rode west and north through the hills, taking care to keep well down from the higher ridges that might still be glimpsed by the troops around Fersí. The Footstool Hills were gentler farming lands than the border hills of Herghin, though still mostly given over to grassland and pasture on this eastern side, with many small groves and stands of trees and only a few tilled fields and small farmsteads. For the first hour of their journey there were many signs of the Easterners' passing – the churned and trampled ground, hewn branches and burnt scars upon the hillsides, and the scavenged carcasses of slaughtered beasts. But as they drew closer to the Tollund manor house, the signs of damage lessened.

They had come perhaps two leagues from Fersí, and the manor house lay little more than a mile ahead of them, when they realised they were being followed. Looking back though the hills, shielding his eyes against the morning sun, Kellarn caught sight of two horsemen clad in the tawny gold of Lautun cresting a distant ridge. They were riding swiftly, coming straight toward the manor.

'Bother,' said Kellarn. 'I might have known we couldn't be so lucky.'

'They may have nothing to do with us,' said Corollin. 'If Lord Brodhaur is securing peace around here, the Tollund and Tormal manors are the obvious places for him to send messengers, aren't they?'

Kellarn gave a hollow laugh.

'Why should they really be that keen to follow us?' she asked.

'I killed the enemy leader, and talked to the dragon who cleared Arrandin,' said Kellarn. 'I freed the Herghin manor, and we found the necklace that clinched the peace with the Vengru. You freed the Tollund manor. Take your pick. The Emperor can't abide that kind of competition, outside of his own household guard – and especially not in a son of Dortrean.'

'But not the bars?'

The bars. The three small metal bars which were – they believed – the first three parts of the artefact that might be used to combat Lo-Khuma when he returned. The gathering of them was a secret which they had told no one, except for some of their friends among the Fay; and now Heruvor held them safe at Starmere. How to find the other missing pieces of that artefact – wherever they were, and however many there might be – was the task that now lay before them; the task which Kellarn had felt compelled to keep secret even from his father and the *Aeshta* priests. He doubted that the Emperor could have any knowledge of it. And yet they had known, even from the start, that someone else might be searching for it.

'No,' he said aloud. 'But we'd better not talk about that, until we're a long way away from here.'

Corollin shaded her eyes and gazed back at the two riders as they disappeared down into a dip.

'Should we wait and confront them?' she asked.

'No,' said Kellarn again. The last time he had confronted one of the Emperor's men, it had been Reïkjan of Kôan; and when Reïkjan had turned up dead shortly afterward, Kellarn had been held to blame. 'Let's keep moving. It shouldn't be that hard for us to shake off an imperial tail.'

They urged their horses forward at a canter, and covered the last stretch to the manor house in a matter of minutes. Having visited there a few years before, Kellarn was startled at the transformation. The high walls and towers were covered in glossy-leaved creepers that danced and whispered in the summer breeze; and the blue slated roofs were almost entirely hidden by mosses and lichens of many different colours. The outer gate was framed with honeysuckle and columbine, and the lancet windows of the towers were garlanded with sweet briars; and within the courtyard stood four birch trees, each a good ten feet tall, where none had been before. The open ground before the manor house was covered in daisies and buttercups and clover in wide swirling patterns. The guardsman who came out to meet them at the gate looked almost apologetic.

'The forest folk preferred it this way,' Corollin told Kellarn quietly. 'I'm glad to see that the Lord Tollund has not changed it.'

'He hasn't had much chance,' said Kellarn.

The young Lord Faerbran Tollund, they learned, had ridden

out for Arrandin barely half an hour since – probably, Kellarn thought, to make his peace with The Arrand and the Emperor after the treachery of his kinsman. But his wife, the Lady Naëra Kilgar of Tollund, came down into the courtyard to greet them. Kôril was not there.

Naëra was a little older than Kellarn, and truly great with child beneath her waistless blue gown; and she carried her firstborn son – named after his father, and not yet two years old – balanced against her left hip. Her pale red-gold hair was plaited into one long, fat braid, which the boy clutched protectively while darting shy glances at the visitors with his dark brown eyes.

She recognised Corollin at once, and greeted them with rosy cheeks and wide smiles. Unlike the guardsman, Naëra seemed quite delighted with her changed surroundings – though in a bemused, rather dreamy sort of way. Kellarn wondered if the ordeal of the past few weeks had been too much for her; or whether she was wishing in her heart that the forest folk had stayed.

They discovered that Kôril had gone away with the forest folk, but that he would be waiting for them at the edge of the Holleth Woods. He had clearly expected them to come this way. Naëra invited them inside for breakfast, and seemed a little disappointed when they declined. Kellarn explained that they were in a hurry, and had a long ride ahead of them.

He felt awkward about leaving Naëra to face their imperial pursuers alone – though of course she was not entirely alone, having several of her own household around to protect her. He did not want to ask her to lie about their having been here; nor did he feel it was fair to stay at the manor house and risk a showdown with the imperial guards. Tollund had enough troubles of their own. So he thought it best to ride on as soon as possible; and then Naëra could say whatever she would to the Emperor's men, in all innocence; and hopefully they would leave her alone and continue the chase. Then it would simply be Kellarn's and Corollin's problem to lose them.

Before they could leave, little Faerbran insisted on being held by Corollin, and then by Kellarn himself. Kellarn glanced anxiously out through the gate as he kissed the boy's blond head, but there was still no sign of their pursuers. Then it became a labour in itself to remove the boy from his arms – hardly helped by the laughter and cooing of the two women – as he knotted his little fists into Kellarn's red surcoat and wailed in protest. But at last they managed it, and said hasty farewells; and then they scrambled back into the saddle, and rode out through the gate and away west up the broad green slopes beyond.

They still had a distance of some three leagues to cover between the manor house and the Holleth Woods. The hillsides grew steeper as they went, pressing closer together as the great cliffs of the Knees of the Mountains swept south toward them; and before long, the whole of the northern sky was filled with the glitter and shimmer of ice and mist, and the shifting hues of the blue-grey mountain rock. The sun was climbing higher, and the day was growing warm.

Corollin took the lead from the manor house, since she had come this way before with the men of Holleth and had a better idea than Kellarn of where Kôril might be waiting for them. She followed a winding course, veering slightly to the south, and trying to keep a steady height once they had come down from the first ridge. But the going was slow, with few places where they could break into a trot or canter. The number of trees and bushes was increasing as they drew closer to the woods – which afforded them better cover, but slowed their speed further. Though Kellarn trusted her judgement, he began to grow anxious at the delay.

They had been riding for about an hour before they caught sight of their pursuers again. Corollin had called a halt beneath a bank of pink-flowered broom, to rest the horses and check her bearings in the hills. Kellarn stood stroking Rúnfyr's neck, and looking back the way that they had come. The two horsemen had paused atop a high spur ridge, little more than two miles away to the northeast. Their golden livery burned bright as a double beacon in the clear sunlight. Kellarn guessed that they had lost the trail, and were trying to catch sight of their quarry among the hills.

'We've got company,' he warned.

Corollin was at his side at once, focusing her mage's sight in the direction he pointed.

'I can't see them,' she said after a moment. 'Not clearly. Some sort of shielding spell, I think. They're just a blur.'

Kellarn swore beneath his breath. Rúnfyr reared his head and shied.

The two imperial horsemen urged their mounts forward, careering straight down the hill spur toward them.

'They are punishing their horses,' said Corollin disapprovingly. 'They'll break a leg at that rate, on this ground.'

'We've got to move more quickly,' said Kellarn, swinging himself back up into the saddle.

Corollin nodded, and turned to vault lightly onto her gray. 'Come on, then,' she said. 'But we're going to leave a trail a blind goose could follow.'

She led the way down the slope on to more level ground, letting the horses have free rein to canter across the open turf. They followed the line of the dip for about half a mile, and then turned up across the far slope, slowing to a trot as they neared the crest of a narrow shoulder between two hills. The imperial horsemen were hidden from view.

They went down the far side of the shoulder, slowing to a walk as they waded through bracken and broom, and skirted round a hazel thicket to reach clearer ground. Their trampled trail was all too visible behind them.

They continued in this way for perhaps a quarter of an hour, moving swiftly where they could, but following a more up and down trail in a fairly straight line west. On two occasions Kellarn glimpsed the bobbing gold markers of the horsemen. The first time, they seemed to have gained nearly half a mile; but on the second there appeared to be little change in the distance between them. Then at last they came through a gap in the hills, and the mountain cliffs curved away sharply to the north, and a wider view of gentler slopes spread down before them, scattered with clumps of trees and bushes. The eastern eaves of Holleth Woods stood waiting barely a mile ahead, whispering greeting in the mid-morning sunlight.

Corollin drew rein at the head of the slope, and looked to left and right.

'We need to be further south, I think,' she said, gesturing with her left hand.

'Let's just head straight for the trees,' said Kellarn. 'We can work our way down from there, once we're out of sight.'

'That was what I meant,' she said.

They urged their horses forward again, glad of the easy run and the wind upon their faces. The narrow belt of green shadow beneath the trees grew swiftly broader; and soon they could make out the darker pillars of the ancient trunks, and the blue and white flash of a jay's wings against the branches, and the calls of many birds in counterpoint to the rhythmic drumming of their horses' hooves.

They slowed to a walk as they rode in among the first of the trees, but went on for about a stone's throw before turning to look back. There were no horsemen to be seen.

'Let's keep moving,' said Corollin quietly.

Kellarn nodded his agreement. They began to edge their way south, picking their way with care between the few tangled bushes and spreading undergrowth, and keeping a weather eye for low branches overhead.

They had not gone far before the two golden riders emerged from the hills and paused to look around. Corollin signalled a halt.

'That's Mataún's horse, or I'm no judge,' said Kellarn. 'I don't recognise the other one.'

The two guards came down the slope at a trot, more or less toward the point where Kellarn and Corollin were hidden. Their horses indeed looked weary now.

'So what do we do?' asked Corollin. 'Stay here? Move? Or hit the open ground and ride like the wind?'

Kellarn grinned at the suggestion, but he was not sure how well it would work. He would not put it past Mataún to use bowfire to bring their horses down, if he could get close enough; or simply to command Kellarn to halt in the Emperor's name. Refusal to obey an imperial officer in the course of his duties was an offence punishable by law, and one which no doubt Mataún – and Rhydden – would take great delight in holding against him. He was not about to give them the chance.

'Can you do something to hide us?' he asked.

'If it were just the two of us, perhaps,' said Corollin. 'I don't think I could manage the three horses as well. Kôril is better at that sort of thing.'

'Wherever he is,' said Kellarn. 'Let's move further in, then. We must be able to lose them in here.'

They slid down from the saddle, and Corollin led the way deeper into the woods, searching for natural cover big enough to hide the horses. Kellarn came behind, leading Rúnfyr and Lanaë as quietly as he could, and peering back between the trees to try and see where Mataún and his sidekick were going.

It soon became clear that the imperial guards knew exactly where they were heading. Corollin dragged the protesting Mistwise into a thicket of young birches, and tethered and calmed her as swiftly as she could. Kellarn manhandled Rúnfyr in with even greater difficulty, nearly frantic at the noise; by which time Lanaë had slipped his grasp and cantered away through the trees. There was no time to chase after her. Kellarn lashed Rúnfyr's reins around a slender birch trunk, gentled the horse with his left hand and squinted out between the leaves.

Mataún of Fâghsul came to halt about fifty yards from where they were hidden. His great black warhorse was stamping and blowing irritably. The second rider drew up alongside – a slightly older man, dark haired and scowling. Kellarn vaguely remembered having seen him before, though he could not put a name to the face.

'They can't be far,' said Mataún. 'Why couldn't the little bugger have just ridden to Arrandin, as he was meant to?'

'Perhaps he *is* going to Arrandin,' said the other. 'We were only meant to escort him – not follow him to the edge of the world.'

'If we lose him, there'll be five hells to pay,' said Mataún.

'Erkal did not seem worried about him.'

'Exactly,' said Mataún. 'I don't trust any of Dortrean further than I can stick them. I want to know what's he's up to.'

There was a low whinny from somewhere nearby, and the sound of hooves.

'Gotcha,' Mataún grinned. He pulled his horse round to the left and began to move off. Kellarn turned his head to try and see where Lanaë had gone.

The next moment, the imperial riders cried out and their horses screamed. Rúnfyr reared and tugged in answer. Kellarn grabbed him by the halter, trying both to shut him up and to find out what was going on.

The forest floor seemed to have sprung to life around the two guards and their mounts, with ivy and bindweed snaking through the air and tangling around them like cast nets, dragging them down. Half a dozen or more dark figures had sprung into view, and were capering around with hoots and calls, and snatches of wild music from unseen flutes or pipes. Mataún was bellowing in fury.

'The fauns,' said Corollin, wriggling forward out of the thicket before Kellarn could stop her. He hesitated for a moment, then left the horses and scrambled after her.

The sight before him as he approached might almost have been funny, had it not been so frightening. The two warhorses and their riders now lay in an awkward heap upon the forest floor, held down by a tight web of creepers and plaited stems that appeared to be rooted rather than pegged into the ground. The horses' eyes rolled white and bulging in terror. Mataún had finished bellowing, and his face was now turning from red to purple as stout bindweed coiled about his throat and tried to grow in to his open mouth. The other man's face was hidden behind a mail-clad elbow.

There were eight fauns that he could see. Three of them were gambolling delightedly in a circle around Corollin. Two others were bounding toward Kellarn himself. They were no bigger than human children, being somewhat less than four feet tall; and from the waist up they resembled young men, more lithe and slender than the stocky folk of the *noghru*, and with short beards or no beard at all. Below the waist, their haunches and legs resembled those of a goat or sheep – complete with wagging tail – all covered in thick, glossy curls of a rich chestnut hue, or black. The hair on their heads was much the same, and two stubby horns peeped out from among the curls above their foreheads. As far as Kellarn could tell, they were all male. The tallest of the fauns, who seemed to be their leader, had a hunting horn slung from a green cord at his waist; and he had a broad-bladed spear, the tip of which now rested at the base of Mataún's throat.

Kellarn clutched hold of his sword before the fauns reached him, though he did not draw it. He remembered that they were as inquisitive as hungry squirrels, and had a passion for bright and sparkly treasures in particular. He resigned himself to the fact that the fauns would probably be rummaging through all the gear on their horses within a matter of minutes. But they were not going to get their hands on his precious sword.

The leader said something to Corollin in a very deep bass voice. To Kellarn's ears it sounded more like a sustained growl, though he could tell that there were some words in there somewhere. Corollin shook her head, and answered in the more liquid tones of the elven tongue of Starmere. The leader snorted, and pressed the blade of his spear harder against Mataún's throat.

Kellarn found himself being dragged forward by the two fauns, rather than plundered – though they had checked his pockets and knife in the space of seconds. They very wisely kept their hands well clear of his sword. But even as he reached the edge of the small clearing where the prisoners were being held, there was a clop of hooves and Kôril rode into view, already mounted on the bay mare Lanaë.

The fay nodded with a half-smile to Kellarn and Corollin, though his manner was as serious as ever. The fauns left off their antics and stood almost still. Their leader lifted his spear and gave a bobbing bow, and spoke again in his strange language. The fay answered him in the same growling tongue.

'They're not going to kill them, are they?' Kellarn asked anxiously. Mataún appeared to have stopped struggling now; but his face was swollen horribly, and the gurgling rattle of his breath was growing fainter.

Kôril looked down across the clearing toward him, his dark hair drifting like shadowed leaves beneath the branches. Then he spoke with the leader of the fauns again, and there was a brief debate between the two of them. Kellarn glanced at Corollin, but she seemed to have no clearer idea than he of what they were saying.

'They will not die, since you ask it,' Kôril told them at last. 'But all memory of this day will be washed from their minds – and of the next few days, until we are safely away. The fauns have promised this.'

'Then they won't remember following us here?' asked Kellarn.

The fay nodded. 'We should go now,' he said, and turned his horse away.

Kellarn looked down at the twitching pile of bodies and undergrowth. The faun leader trotted toward him, studying the sword in its red scabbard as he approached, and then looking up into Kellarn's face with beautiful deep brown eyes.

'Thank you,' said Kellarn uncertainly.

The faun replied in what sounded like the elven tongue, though all Kellarn could catch of it was the word for *forest*.

'He says that guarding the woods is their business,' Corollin explained, appearing at his side; 'and the sword is yours. Come on.'

She bowed and smiled to the faun, and led Kellarn away firmly by the hand. The fauns bounded around and ahead of them, diving into the birch thicket to fetch the horses. They performed the obligatory ritual of checking the packs and gear of their visitors for unwanted items, while Kellarn and Corollin stood patiently by; and then they let them mount up and ride away south with Kôril, and vanished behind the trees.

With no imperial guards to chase their heels, the three companions went back to the edge of the woods, where they could ride more easily on the open ground. They planned to follow the line of the trees south and then west; and then to take the Old North Road through the woods to Holleth and beyond.

'I still feel a bit guilty about Mataún,' said Kellarn presently.

'Why so?' said Kôril. 'He went where he should not, and escaped very lightly.'

'Perhaps,' sighed Kellarn. 'I suppose he was just following orders.'

The fay made no reply. Kellarn had to admit to himself that it sounded a rather lame excuse, from the forest folk's point of view.

When they reached the southern side of the woods they stopped, so that Kellarn could strip off some of his heavy gear and stow it away on his horse. It seemed to be the hottest day yet, and even the breeze from the hills felt too warm upon his face. They checked the contents of their packs and saddlebags, to see whether the fauns had taken anything. As far as they could tell – though they had no certain knowledge of what the Hyrsenites had provided for them – nothing of any importance was missing.

As the day wore on they passed along the borders of the farming lands of Brodhaur's kinsmen of Levrin. There were signs here and there of where the Easterner armies had felled trees or raided barns and storehouses, but the damage was far less than it had been elsewhere. They saw people working among the hills further to the south, and once or twice thought that they might have glimpsed the distant towers of the Old City of Arrandin; but they did not really want to be within view of the city, and were fortunate enough not to meet anyone at close quarters along the way.

By the end of the day they had reached the place where the road ran in to the woods, and made their camp under the cover of the trees. They took turns to keep watch, as was their habit, but the night was free from trouble. The next morning they allowed themselves a more leisurely start than they had had leaving Fersí, knowing that they would still be on the road well before anyone could reach there from Arrandin.

'Where *are* we going, by the way?' asked Corollin, as they strapped the last of their gear back into place.

'To Starmere, I think,' said Kellarn. 'We could stop by the monastery in the Hauchan valley on the way. Unless you have any other suggestions?'

'Starmere,' Kôril nodded.

'And Ellanguan?' ventured Corollin.

'I'm not sure I want to go there, just yet,' said Kellarn. 'But we can talk about that later. I'd rather get through the woods first.'

'Has there been any trouble in the woods?' Corollin asked.

'None since the Easterners left,' answered the fay.

'What about the caves, where we found the priests and the shrine?' asked Kellarn.

That had been their first adventure together, and the beginning of his friendship with Corollin – and their first run-in with the followers of Lo-Khuma. They had little dreamed at the time of the danger which now rose to threaten the Six Kingdoms; nor that they themselves would be drawn in to a quest to guard against Lo-Khuma's return.

'The caves are still sealed,' said Kôril. 'No servants of the Enemy have returned that way. The forest folk have been watching.'

'Good,' said Kellarn.

They set off along the road, and reached the village clearing of Holleth before noon without mishap. They passed three separate wagon trains coming east, carrying goods and supplies down to Arrandin in company with guards and other travellers. But Kellarn had left off his mailshirt again for the day, and was clad only in his linen shirt and breeches, and nobody seemed to recognise him. Kôril managed to vanish on each occasion, to reappear quietly a little distance from the road once the wagons had rolled past. He would then ride parallel to the road, through the trees, until the passers-by were safely out of sight.

Among the guards of the third wagon train was the woodsman Dalgarn, who had been in Tollund with Corollin, and had thereafter been to Fersí with Salbaar and but recently returned to his own village of Holleth. Dalgarn recognised Corollin at once, and stopped to talk with her for a few minutes and to hear her news of what was happening further east. It did not take him long to guess who Kellarn was, and he gave him a gruff nod of approval. They knew that they could trust him to keep quiet about having seen them. But Dalgarn had no news of his own to tell them, other than that more wagons were expected to come down the road over the next several days; and that there was precious little of anything to spare in Holleth at the moment, thanks to the demands of the Emperor's armies and the damage suffered in Arrandin. And then he had to ride off, to return to his duties.

When they reached the edge of the broad meadow clearing that surrounded the Holleth village, they drew rein and let Kôril dismount. Though the ordinary folk of the village might have welcomed the sight of one of the Fay, rather than feared it, there would too likely be other people around, making it unwise for him to travel openly there. He faded back into the tree shadows; and then there was a clap of wings, and a large wood pigeon flew up and out into the clearing, leading the way ahead.

Kellarn and Corollin rode on, taking the bay mare with them. They passed straight through the stockaded village – which was less busy than they had feared from Dalgarn's tidings – and out through the west gate and across the wooden bridge over the

Galloppi Stream; and then on up the road to the far side of the clearing, where Kôril was waiting for them. And then the three of them travelled on together, north and west along the road; and by late afternoon they had come to the far borders of the Holleth Woods.

Not far to their north, a jumble of twisted hills piled down from the heights of the Grey Moors. In the distance ahead, the first grey bluffs of The Steeps loomed dull and shadowed before the light of the westering sun. So they made their camp beneath the trees, waiting till morning before they began the long climb.

Chapter Eight

Rhysana glided across the darkened lobby toward the open doorway of the assembly chamber, her feet treading the path more by habit than from conscious will.

'High Councillor.' A whispered voice stopped her just before she reached the threshold. The hooded outline of the Archmage Merrech stepped closer in the blackness to her right.

'Your pardon, Eminence,' said Rhysana, nodding to him. 'I am a little tired.'

Tired was an understatement. Though Taillan had been happy enough with their kinsmen at the Telún manor, he had understandably missed his parents during their prolonged absence with the war. He had played up ever since their return to the College, clinging and craving attention, perhaps punishing them a little in his own young way. None of them had slept well with the city heat. Even the sea breeze had been too warm, and the brief storm that afternoon had done nothing to clear the air. Torkhaal and Rhysana had shuffled lecturing and parental duties between them. Nor had either of them found it easy to deal with Herusen's absence from the familiar College buildings. And now she had to sit with the High Council, and debate the choice of Herusen's successor.

'Of course.' The Archmage bowed. 'I have been studying your defence matrix in the Arrand palace. Your achievement is most impressive.'

'Others built it, and others raised it,' she said. 'I merely helped to find and analyse what was there.'

'The Emperor is impressed.'

'He would be,' said Rhysana. 'Shall you come in?'

'One moment,' he demurred.

He had not used a holding spell on her, but she felt compelled to stay. The focus of his attention surrounded her like a net, and there was the familiar sensation of sliding coils about her throat.

'Shall you be making your working notes available to the Council?' he wondered.

'I have already informed the Council of my basic findings,' she replied. 'Given the complexity and power of the matrix, the High Council may deem it wise to restrict other details.'

'Quite so,' he purred. 'As with the summoning of dragons.'

Rhysana did not answer. He gestured for her to precede him through the doorway.

The crystal dome of the great assembly chamber was dark overhead, since the night sky outside was blanketed in cloud. The only light came from a pale golden glow of power limning the arched recess of the Prime Councillor's seat on the far rim of the chamber – probably Morvaan's doing, Rhysana thought. It symbolised the focus of the coming meeting, drew attention to that one empty seat. In the dim glow, the white recesses of the High Council seats hung down like drooping lilies from the pale encircling wall above. The black hollows of the other seats were lost in shadow.

Rhysana took up her place on the second High Council seat to the left, smiling absently to Morvaan in the next seat along. Merrech circled on around the chamber, passing in front of the glowing Prime Councillor's seat to take his accustomed place directly opposite her. Most of the other councillors were already in position, but Morvaan appeared to be waiting for latecomers. Rhysana settled herself comfortably in her cushioned recess, breathed deeply to calm her mind after the unexpected exchange with Merrech, and focused her thoughts on the matter in hand.

Though it was true that most of the High Council seats

246

in the assembly chamber were technically taken, the possible candidates for the next Prime Councillor were few. Of the fourteen surviving members of the High Council, fully half had passed their three score years. Iorlaas and Drôshiin of Sêchral had already retired from College life; and Maëghlar of Kelmaar – oldest of all, except for the Archmage Merrech – was in poor health, and had for several years lived in virtual seclusion, devoting himself to a life of mystic contemplation and prayer. The two Trialmasters, Ekraan and Foghlaar, were similarly reclusive and rarely put in an appearance at Council assemblies; and High Councillor Rikkarn was absorbed in his work with the craftsmen of Telbray and Farran, researching the making of magical artefacts, and had never shown much interest in Council affairs.

Of those who remained, Morvaan and Ellen were the two most suitable choices, to Rhysana's mind. But since by tradition it was held that good Archmagi made poor Prime Councillors, it seemed unlikely that they would be proposed. Rhysana hoped that no one would even consider proposing Merrech. Lirinal of Dregharis, like herself, was still too new to the High Council – too young, and too inexperienced, to be entrusted with the care of every mage in the Six Kingdoms.

Thus to Rhysana's reckoning, at this early stage before the debate began, there were but three members of the High Council likely to be chosen as Herusen's successor: Asharka, Ferghaal and Sollonaal. Asharka of Braedun had proved most capable as the Principal of the College of Magi in Farran, and took a keen interest in the running of all four Colleges within the Empire; and she had besides brought up four children of her own, the oldest of whom was already married. But she was not herself of noble blood, and had had little enough experience of dealing with the Court Noble – which, given the present difficulties in that direction, would probably count against her. Asharka's brother-in-law Ferghaal, by contrast, was Head of the Braedun Order in Farran and had a good deal of experience in the complex games of the imperial Court; and of course he had been one of the principal commanders in the defence of Arrandin and the war with the East. Ferghaal was a strong and capable leader. But he did not have Asharka's knowledge of the workings of the Colleges; and his obvious ties with the *Aeshta* Order of Braedun might prove a stumbling block to his role as Prime Councillor of the neutral Magi.

Rhysana's train of thought was interrupted by a dark green shadow blocking the light, and she realised that the Archmage Ellen was standing in front of her, bowing in greeting. She raised her hands quickly in a sign of answering blessing, mindful that Ellen was a stickler for formal courtesy. Ellen opened her mouth to speak; but then – perhaps because of the near perfect acoustics of the chamber – she changed her mind again. She favoured Rhysana with a rare smile, and moved on to greet Morvaan and Asharka.

And then, Rhysana thought, there was Sollonaal – already Prime Councillor of the Ellanguan Magi, and thus by tradition the most likely person to take Herusen's empty seat. Sollonaal had been Senior Lecturer at the Lautun College before his move to Ellanguan, and had behind him a distinguished academic career. He also appeared to have succeeded in ingratiating himself with the imperial nobles, and with the merchants and citizens of Ellanguan – though at what cost to himself or to the Magi was still far from clear. Rhysana did not trust Sollonaal any more than she liked him, personally; and Ellen and Morvaan clearly held similar opinions of him. But given the limited alternatives, she had a sinking feeling that Sollonaal might end up carrying the vote.

Morvaan stood up and called the assembly to order. The great ebon doors swung shut.

'If I can begin,' he said. 'High Councillors Ferghaal and Rikkarn are unable to be here, but hope to make the general assembly tomorrow when the election should be made. I have been unable to reach Drôshiin of Sêchral. Everyone else is here, I think.'

'We are all grateful to you for organising this assembly, Archmage,' said Sollonaal from his seat in the South.

Morvaan glanced at him, a look of mild irritation flitting across his face.

'To explain, for those unfamiliar with the process,' he went on; 'any High Councillor may stand for election to the Prime Councillor's seat. All candidates for election must be proposed and seconded by other members of the High Council; and it is the High Council alone that makes that final vote, when all those who wish to speak on the matter have done so.

'The purpose of this meeting tonight is really no more than a chance to prepare ourselves; to see who might be willing to take on the burden of leadership, and whom we might consider suitable; and to think ahead to some of the questions that may be raised by members of the Greater Council in the assembly tomorrow morning.'

'Do the candidates have to be proposed tonight?' asked Lirinal.

'They don't have to be, no,' said Morvaan. 'It is entirely possible that the mage councillors tomorrow will name their own suggested candidates – which is permissible, provided that those candidates are members of the High Council, and that other High Councillors are prepared to ratify the nomination with formal proposal and seconding. It is also quite likely that the other councillors will come up with awkward questions on any number of subjects. So our meeting tonight, as I was saying, is really a chance for us to do our homework together, in preparation for tomorrow's debate. When everyone has had their say, then the High Council will withdraw to make the final choice. Hopefully we can decide that tomorrow, although such elections have been known to drag on for days.'

There was a heavy sigh from somewhere to Rhysana's right – possibly from Ekraan, though she could not be sure.

'Is everyone clear about the process, then?' asked Morvaan. The magi signalled that they were.

'In that case,' he said, 'to save embarrassment, perhaps we

could start by a show of hands from those of us who would prefer *not* to be proposed as candidates – or not at this stage of the game, at any rate.'

Rhysana held up her own hand, and looked around the assembly chamber. As she had expected, almost everybody else did the same, including the Archmage Merrech. Only Asharka and Sollonaal did not.

'Well, to put it another way then,' said Morvaan, 'who would be prepared to accept the burden of leadership if more than half the High Council entreated them to do so?'

Rhysana hesitated, and then brought her hand down into her lap. With Taillan still so young, and another baby on the way, she could not make such a commitment. And besides, she thought it unlikely that she would find herself in such a situation. There were far more capable and experienced people here who would be chosen before her.

Ellen and Morvaan both lowered their hands, and so did Maëghlar of Kelmaar. Merrech kept one pale hand raised, but there was a mocking irony in that. Everyone else put their hands up, except for Ekraan and Lirinal.

'Thank you,' said Morvaan, returning to his seat. 'Now, remembering that election speeches are for tomorrow, perhaps we could consider some of the more immediate problems which our new Prime Councillor will have to face. Sollonaal, as Prime Councillor of the Ellanguan Magi perhaps you would care to start us off?'

The discussion lasted for well over an hour, but Rhysana found that there was little in it that she had not already known or guessed. Having been in Arrandin, she knew as much as anyone else in the chamber about the situation with the Easterners. She had heard of the peace with the Southers; and all that the Ellanguan magi could add was that the Souther warships were still being refitted, and that more of the Emperor's troops had arrived from Lautun to keep an eye on the proceedings. The tensions between the Council and the Court Noble – and the Emperor – were well trodden ground; though discussion on that subject was somewhat restrained because of the presence of the Imperial Counsellor, the Archmage Merrech. There were now the added complications of the strength displayed by the Magi in the defence of Arrandin, and of Herusen's summoning of the dragon, neither of which could go wholly unmentioned.

'Far be it from me,' said Sollonaal, 'to question the wisdom of the last Prime Councillor, or the valour of those magi who gave themselves extravagantly to save thousands of lives – and indeed, to ensure the safety of the whole Empire. But the fact remains that the open display of such great power has reminded the ordinary people of the Empire – let alone the Court Noble – that they have cause to fear us.'

'Would you rather have us as a bunch of political academics,' asked Ekraan, 'with no real power to serve any purpose?'

'Better that, perhaps, than a return to the atrocities of our forebears in the Wars of Power,' said Sollonaal, 'when terrible power was unleashed without control. Or the barbaric rivalry between the Easterner wizards, with their patron demons. To the ordinary man, the use of such great magic makes us something other than human.'

'I do not agree,' said Iorlaas. 'Fear of power goes hand in hand with respect for it. The proper fear of the power they wield is a basic principle taught to all our students, along with the need for control. The people of the Empire can surely be taught to respect our power without hating us for it, or thinking us monsters. They respect the powers of the priests.'

'The priests are more obviously the vessels of the gods,' said Ellen. 'We have not that respectability of divine sanction behind us.'

'Whether the priests are respectable or not,' quipped Foghlaar.

'Sollonaal does have a point,' said Maëghlar of Kelmaar. He was sitting alone on the southwest arc of the chamber, just as Merrech sat alone in the northwest – since, by coincidence, all other High Councillors present sat in the eastern half of the circle, according to the mystical Quarters of their divine patrons. They turned their attention toward him and waited in patient courtesy. This was the first time that he had attempted to speak at all during the evening.

'The Easterners,' said Maëghlar at last, his voice creaking like a willow in the wind, 'are seeking the great demon. Our own priests have foreseen his return.'

Well, someone had to mention it, I suppose, said Morvaan. Rhysana realised that he was speaking privately to her, mind to mind, by virtue of the High Council seats in which they were sitting. They had skirted round the subject of Lo-Khuma when speaking about the Easterners earlier.

'Forgive me, but I fail to see the connection,' said Lirinal. 'And which great demon is this?'

Maëghlar sighed. 'The demon captain defeated by the Bright Alliance,' he explained. 'Not heathen myth, young Councillor, but dreadful history. When he returns, we face a far worse calamity than the Wars of Power.'

There was a tense silence. Maëghlar did not speak again.

'If he returns,' said Sollonaal, like a man scrabbling for dry ground, 'is it not more a matter for the priests to turn him back?'

Maëghlar did not answer.

'The *Aeshta* Orders are preparing themselves,' said Morvaan; 'and perhaps the *Vashta* Orders will do so, according to their own conscience. If, or when, such a threat should come against the Empire, the Council will look to us for guidance; and the Emperor may call upon the High Council for a response, as he did when the Easterners attacked. We must consider the possibility, rather than be caught unprepared.'

'And the next Prime Councillor should be aware of this,' said Ellen, 'even if the Greater Council is not. He is our representative to the outside world, and must secure the relationships we need to enable us to work freely – on our own terms – when the time comes. It will be no easy task.'

'Another side to this problem,' ventured Asharka, 'is that our numbers have been badly depleted by the war; and we have lost some of our more promising young magi, as well as more seasoned ones. We are all aware of the present difficulty of staffing the Colleges. Yet the fact remains that even with the Colleges running normally, it could take us several years to rebuild the strength which we had only a month ago.'

'Having said that,' said Morvaan, 'there are two young mage councillors whom I think we should seriously consider for admission to the High Council in the near future – namely Torkhaal and Hrugaar. Torkhaal, in particular. His contribution to the defence of Arrandin was invaluable.'

'With all respect for their work,' said Foghlaar, 'are we not in danger of becoming a little top heavy? There are less than fifty councillors left, by my reckoning. Put two more on the High Council, and we shall count for more than a third of the entire assembly. Given their youth, could it not perhaps wait a little?'

'And given the fact, Archmage,' put in Sollonaal, 'that they both happen to be *Aeshta* magi, and star pupils of yourself and Herusen.'

'Admission to the High Council is determined by achievement and insight,' said the Archmage Merrech. 'Personal favour or religious persuasion is of no consequence here.'

'There is also the question of testing for new students with magical potential,' said Rhysana, anxious to turn the conversation away from Torkhaal and Hrugaar – especially since the Imperial Counsellor was showing an interest in them. 'That needs to be arranged before the Colleges go down.'

'But not tonight, I think,' said Ellen. 'If no one has anything of immediate importance to add, may we please bring this assembly to a close?'

When Rhysana returned to her own chambers, she found her son stretched out in the middle of the bed next to Torkhaal. Both were soundly asleep. She shook her head, undressed quietly and lay down on her own side of the bed, careful not to disturb them.

She awoke to find Taillan sitting astride her and tugging at her left shoulder with his small hands, and giggling *Ma-ma-ma* in her ear. She looked up at him with one eye, and smiled. His silver-gold hair was newly washed and not quite dry – and quite visible in the daylight coming in through the open doorway. She could hear Torkhaal moving around close by.

'Up, up up,' said Taillan. His father lifted him away, laughing.

'Yes, I am coming,' said Rhysana.

When she opened her eyes again, everywhere was quiet. She must have been asleep for some time. Rhysana dragged herself out of bed, tugged a robe around her, and hurried into the long living chamber. The room was clean and tidy, and basking in the mid-morning light. Nobody was there.

Her first thought was that Torkhaal had taken the boy with him to his morning tutorials – not an ideal practice, but one which her husband might well have chosen so that Rhysana could sleep on in peace. Her second thought, more disturbing, was that His Eminence the Archmage Merrech had shown a renewed interest in herself and Torkhaal the previous night. But before she had the chance to grow truly alarmed, the unmistakable sound of her son's bubbling laughter floated in through the open casement windows. She pulled the loose robe more properly around her, and went to look outside.

Taillan was trotting across the grass in the cloister garden down below, reaching up with both arms toward a brightly coloured ball that bobbed like a butterfly in the air ahead of him. Hrugaar was crouching down nearby, clad in shimmering robes of grey-green; and Dhûghaúr was sitting on the far side of the garden, his legs stretched out before him and his black-booted feet tapping together. Rhysana remembered that the two of them would have come here for the Council assembly at noon. Torkhaal had evidently taken advantage of their early arrival.

Such merriment was hardly the expected decorum for the College cloisters, right at the feet of the high squared towers of the library building. Nor would it be the first time that

Hrugaar had been told off to behave himself. But with the clouds crowding together overhead, and the warm wind strong enough to reach down and set the late wisteria dancing above the pillared walkways, Rhysana thought it more probable that the weather would drive them indoors rather than any of her irate fellow lecturers. Content that Taillan was safe in Hrugaar's care, she turned her back on the window and clapped her hands to summon the *chaedar* to draw her bath.

Rhysana had no intention of attending the full assembly herself. She knew that she would be called upon afterward to join the High Council in their final deliberations, and she though it only fair that Torkhaal and Hrugaar should have their chance to take part in the main debate. So she would stay behind with Taillan, and then they could inform her of any important developments upon their return, before she went up to the assembly chamber. Not that she expected to hear anything that had not already been discussed among the High Council. But with their fellow Magi, one could never be wholly certain.

Torkhaal reached the assembly chamber shortly before the noon bell rang, with Hrugaar and Dhûghaúr just behind him. More than half the surviving members of the Council were already there before them, sitting in their seats or standing and talking quietly in small clusters around the patterned floor. The crystal dome was dull grey beneath the brooding clouds; but as they entered, a flicker of distant lightning traced the filigree lines of the facet edges with white and blue, and then faded.

The three magi circled round to the southwest side, where Hrugaar would sit as a mage of Sherunar. The two bursars, Drengriis of Româdhrí and Breghun of Lanvar, were just taking their places on the carved misericord seats. Both, Torkhaal remembered, had been kept perforce in the Tollund manor house while the forest folk were there. Breghun's barrelled waistline did not seem to have suffered from the ordeal.

Drengriis' pale face was unusually rosy and glowing beneath his thatch of sandy-fair hair.

'Councillor Hrugaar,' said Drengriis, standing again to bow. 'I still owe you a proper apology, I think. For the, um—'

'There is no need,' Hrugaar broke in quickly. 'Let us both be glad that we suffered no greater harm, in the end.'

Drengriis nodded, clearly still embarrassed by what had befallen him at Tollund. Yet he also seemed to be uncommonly pleased about something – quite unlike his usual, serious self. Torkhaal thought that he recognised the look.

'Do not tell me, Councillor Drengriis,' he said, 'that you are soon to become a father?'

Drengriis' face glowed even brighter, bursting into a triumphant grin.

'I only found out when I came back to Ellanguan,' he replied.

There was scattered applause around the chamber, and several cheers and calls from those who had overheard. Torkhaal gave him a playful punch on the shoulder, in congratulation. Then they left Hrugaar to sit down, and he and Dhûghaúr went over to the northern arc, as magi of Earth.

He was sure that he could feel Merrech's gaze following him as they moved across the western side of the floor; though the hooded archmage remained motionless, no more than a grey silhouette within the white arch of his High Council seat. Rhysana had warned him that His Eminence had taken an interest in her again last night – and that that interest might possibly extend to Torkhaal himself, and to others who had been in Arrandin with them. But if Merrech was watching, he made no move to engage them; and by the time that they reached the Archmage Ellen in the North, the feeling of danger had passed.

Ellen was arrayed in her high councillor's robes of apple green and russet brown, but with her heavy bronze hair tidied away in a black corded snood, so that there was a rather homely formality about her. Torkhaal and Dhûghaúr bowed to her, placing their hands together before their chests in traditional Council greeting, and she returned the familiar gesture of *Aeshta* blessing. Then Torkhaal sat down two places to her left, with Dhûghaúr beside him.

More magi were coming in through the ebon doors, and hastening to take their seats before the assembly began. Khôraillan of Môshári escorted the raven-haired Tiennaï to her seat in the West, and then came over to join them and sat down to Dhûghaúr's left. He was favouring one leg a little as he walked, but otherwise appeared to be hale and fit again.

All told, Torkhaal could count forty-two magi present when the assembly was called to order. Under normal circumstances, even a count of thirty would have been considered a remarkable turn-out. All of the High Council were there, apart from Rhysana. From what Torkhaal could reckon, there were perhaps only half a dozen other mage councillors still left alive in the Six Kingdoms who had not attended – either because Morvaan and the Colleges had been unable to contact them in time, or because other circumstances prevented them.

The debate for the choice of a new Prime Councillor was led – or at least opened and occasionally prompted – by the Council Secretary, Oghraan. Torkhaal had no greater opinion of Oghraan than did most of the other councillors. There was something slimy and unwholesome about the man, so that Torkhaal had often wondered why Herusen had permitted him to continue as Secretary at all. But Herusen's answer had been that Oghraan did a job which no one else particularly wanted. The next Prime Councillor, Torkhaal thought, might not endure him so patiently.

Oghraan stood while he explained the procedure by which the election would be made, and named the three candidates proposed by the High Council so far – Sollonaal, Ferghaal and Asharka. He then handed over to Sollonaal, as Prime Councillor of Ellanguan, and waddled back to his place by Herusen's empty seat.

Sollonaal then spoke at some length, his hands held all the

while palm outwards on either side of his face in the prescribed manner for speech within the assembly chamber. The tenor of his speech was apparently much the same as that of the one which he had made at the New Moon Assembly – as recounted afterward by Telghraan to Rhysana, who had in turn told Torkhaal. Councillor Telghraan, Torkhaal noticed, was not present that morning. Presumably the young Earth mage had been called away to Arrandin, or had been detained by some College business in Ellanguan.

Torkhaal was familiar with Sollonaal's oratory style, which could have given weight and persuasion to a library index, let alone a political proposal. But although Sollonaal spoke with conviction, and took himself very seriously, not all the magi who heard him were impressed. He spoke again of the continuing threat from the East, and of the uncertainty of the peace with the South; and he urged the Council to learn from the lessons of the recent war – the failure of the rash attempts to defend the border manors, and the success of working together with the army commanders in Arrandin. What was needed, he said, was an established procedure for the Council to deal with the Emperor and his commanders, to be able to provide effective support for the defence of the Empire without running the risk of another calamity such as had befallen them at Herghin. And that in turn might help to regain the confidence of the ordinary people of the Empire, if it were made clearer that the formidable power of the Magi was being deployed with the Emperor's approval.

There were the usual rumblings of protest at the idea of imperial intervention.

'What we saw in Arrandin,' said Ranzhaar of Stanva, 'was a few magi who chose to work together with The Arrand and his commanders. They were not deployed as a military unit, nor sent nor even chosen by this Council. So their undoubted success is no argument for a procedure such as High Councillor Sollonaal would appear to be proposing.'

Ranzhaar was sitting a few places beyond Ellen, to Torkhaal's right, and had been snorting and muttering beneath his breath at regular intervals throughout Sollonaal's long speech.

'The people of Arrandin did not fear the magi who fought alongside them,' said Tiennaï. 'It is only now, when the shock of their grief and loss comes upon them, that they look for somebody to blame. Had the Magi not been there, they would blame somebody else.'

'Had the Magi not been there, Arrandin would have fallen,' put in Hrugaar.

Torkhaal would have liked to add that having an artefact as powerful as the city's defence matrix effectively under the Emperor Rhydden's control was hardly a comforting thought for anyone. But he thought it best not to say so with the Imperial Counsellor listening.

'It is also the case,' said another voice, 'that the defence we provided for Arrandin is peculiar to the city, and not of a kind that we could reproduce elsewhere – except, perhaps, here in Lautun or in Ellanguan. If the Easterners return and summon creatures from other Realms, is it not more likely that the religious Orders will be better suited than our own Order to deal with such things?'

Torkhaal looked around, and discovered that it was the scarlet and grey figure of High Councillor Rikkarn who was speaking. He was seated on the far side of the assembly chamber, not far from Hrugaar.

'The *Aeshta* Orders are preparing for another Easterner attack, with that in mind,' said Ferghaal of Braedun.

'In which case,' Rikkarn continued, 'should this Council not remain aloof from that war, and encourage our members not to take part unless there is once again a clear instance of where our own skills are the most suited?'

'Yet there are those magi who will wish to take part regardless,' said Eralaan, the Senior Lecturer from the Ellanguan College. 'Surely it would be in their best interests, especially in the case of the journeymen, for us to advise them to place themselves

259

under the command of the army leaders – for their own protection.'

'It must still be their free choice,' said Morvaan. 'From the dawn of the Golden Age, it has been the task of this Council to protect any mage from being constrained to use their powers against their will.'

There was a general murmur of approval, yet not as strong as Torkhaal could have hoped. It seemed to him that several of those present might have sided with Eralaan, at least in principle, had it been put to the vote just then.

'But High Councillor Rikkarn has a point,' said Asharka of Braedun, pitching her voice a little higher to make herself heard. 'This last war cost us many good magi. I believe there is some wisdom in remaining aloof, to rebuild our strength and to ensure that our learning is passed on to future generations. As a Council, the welfare of our own Order should be a priority. Now that the armies and the religious Orders are better prepared to defend the Six Kingdoms against a second attack, we should trust them to perform the tasks for which they were trained; and not engage in the conflict ourselves until, or unless, it becomes clear that only our own arts can make the vital difference necessary to achieve victory.'

'The Council can not forbid magi to take part in the next war, High Councillor,' said Oghraan, smiling unpleasantly, 'any more than it could command them to do so.'

'The trouble is,' said Sollonaal, 'that the strength our fellow councillors displayed in the defence of Arrandin was very great – such as has not been seen, perhaps, since the days of the Golden Age. The Court Noble and ordinary citizens alike may need more definite assurance of our good will toward the Empire; and that can hardly be achieved by withdrawing our help and hiding behind our College walls.'

'I have not read that the folk of the Golden Age required any such assurance,' returned Ranzhaar of Stanva. 'They trusted the Council to govern its own magi equably.'

'Though that trust is somewhat undermined, perhaps,' came

the silken voice of the Archmage Merrech, 'when the Prime Councillor appears to go against the basic precepts of his own Order by summoning a dragon.'

A distant roll of thunder could be heard in the silence that followed. Torkhaal felt his heart pounding in answer against his chest, and echoing in his ears. Though he knew that the subject had been broached at the New Moon Assembly some days before, none of those who had worked closely with Herusen had been here to defend him then; and to some of the magi present this tale would have been little more than whispered rumour until now. It was all too clear that this would be a sensitive subject, touching as it did upon the good reputation of the late Prime Councillor. It was also clear that Merrech was intent on stirring trouble.

Torkhaal looked at Ellen, to see if she would make reply. Her handsome face was set like flint, staring out into the open space ahead of her. On the far side of the chamber, Hrugaar sat poised as a sculpture in ice; but the glitter in his eyes echoed the flicker of lightning on the faceted crystal dome.

'I was there,' said Torkhaal, his voice too loud inside him. 'It was not like the summoning of the Easterner wizards' spells. It was more like a priest calling upon a messenger of the gods – or perhaps some right of authority granted to him, as Head of our Order.'

The silence broke into uproar on all sides. He seemed to have done more harm than good. No doubt that had been Merrech's purpose.

'So is there to be one law for the Council,' said a voice, 'and another for the Prime Councillor?'

Torkhaal could not see who had spoken. More than half the magi were all talking at once.

'The magi in Arrandin were working with the *Aeshta* Orders,' said another; 'and with The Arrand, and Dortrean. Is that not the real reason why the Empire now mistrusts us?'

'Peace!' said Morvaan, holding up his hands. The assembly fell quiet almost immediately.

261

'Every House and Order in Arrandin worked together,' he told them, 'regardless of faith or political differences. Our goal was to turn back an invading enemy. It would be unwise to make distinction between our allies in that common cause.'

'Yet others may make that distinction, all the same,' said Kharfaal of Vaulun. 'The Court Noble has a history for that.'

'The Court Noble,' said Hendraal of Tarágin, 'should at least remember that Dortrean also has a long history of distrusting this Council. We should make most unlikely allies.'

The bitterness of his tone was enough to remind the assembly that Hendraal himself was a case in point. House Tarágin were retainers of Dortrean, but their bloodline had a knack of producing very competent magi. Hendraal had thus been obliged to spend more than half his life in effective exile in Ellanguan.

It was of course true that the magi in Arrandin had worked closely with Erkal Dortrean and the Môshári for the defence of the city – that relationship being focused mainly through Herusen and Rhysana, and to a lesser extent through the Archmage Ellen and through Torkhaal himself. But with Merrech there in the assembly chamber, and with almost half the councillors present being *Vashta* magi, Torkhaal thought that the last thing they needed was the suggestion of secret pacts being made between members of the High Council and some of the Emperor's most likely adversaries within the Court Noble. It was just the sort of excuse that Rhydden would pounce upon to make trouble. Coupled with Herusen's questionable action of summoning the dragon – even in the manner of an *Aeshta* priest – it might also prompt a backlash to swing the Council more heavily in favour of electing the *Vashta* candidate, Sollonaal.

'The Council – and the Court Noble – must bear in mind,' said Ellen, 'that the Earl of Dortrean came to Arrandin at Rhydden's own request, because of his skills in dealing with Easterner envoys. The Braedun Order were likewise commanded by the Emperor to help provide the first defence of Arrándin, until the main host of his armies could get down there. Thus the magi in Arrandin simply joined forces with those whom the Emperor had chosen. Had His Highness sent another of his commanders, or appointed other troops to hold the city, then we would have worked with them instead.'

'There can be little doubt of that,' Kharfaal acknowledged. 'But as most of us know all too well, Archmage, what this Council may know and what the Court Noble may choose to believe can be very different things. Convincing the Court of our neutrality, let alone our good will, has never been an easy task; and it is perhaps even harder now than it has been for many years.'

'Ironically enough,' said Morvaan, above the murmurs of agreement to Kharfaal's words, 'in times of war or civil strife, the Court Noble is less particular about our neutral standing and much more interested in having our help. During the Interregnum – as the older ones among us still remember – the face we presented to the outside world was severe and distant. The High Council then held that we had to be so, to avoid a return to the anarchy of the Wars of Power.'

'So are you suggesting,' said Drengriis, 'like High Councillor Asharka, that we should build walls instead of bridges?'

'In the Golden Age,' said Maëghlar of Kelmaar, 'the people of the Six Kingdoms held the *Aeshta* faith, and knew the wisdom that all things – no matter how different or contentious – work together in the great harmony of the dances of the gods. Now the Court Noble and the Empire follow the gods of the *Vashtar*, and have a different understanding of harmony and strife. So the world changes. As a Council we should hold firm to our precepts, as we have always done. If the world outside does not accept us, it is they who build the walls.'

There was another general outcry in the assembly chamber, particularly among the *Vashta* magi.

'With respect, High Councillor,' said Sollonaal, holding up his hands for peace in much the same way that Morvaan had done earlier, 'not all followers of the imperial gods of the *Vashtar* are so intolerant and contentious as you might suppose. There are now many *Vashta* magi within our Order, and some of us are trying to work together with the outside world to build bridges of understanding.'

'You mean that your head is so far up Ellanguan's backside that it would take a surgeon to get you out,' said Foghlaar.

The wry humour in his voice prompted several splutters and chuckles, even among the more imperially minded magi. Hrugaar doubled over in his seat, and then flung himself back into his cushioned recess with a peal of merry laughter. The tension on the air broke and fell apart in easeful mirth. Sollonaal managed to force the semblance of a smile into his face – though it probably cost him a good deal of effort.

'Secretary,' ventured Dhûghaúr, as the noise died down; 'fellow Councillors. I should like to propose the Archmage the Lady Ellen of Raudhar for our next Prime Councillor.'

Torkhaal looked at the little mage beside him. Dhûghaúr had shifted forward in his seat, as though half minded to stand, and he was trembling with nervous excitement beneath the ample folds of his black robes. Perhaps three or four other magi around the chamber were voicing their agreement. Torkhaal doubted whether Ellen would accept the proposal; but he raised one hand briefly, and hummed his own support.

'You may make the suggestion,' Oghraan allowed; 'but of course all candidates must be proposed and seconded by members of the High Council.'

'And I should like to suggest High Councillor Iorlaas,' said Corrimaer. 'He is, after all, the most senior *Vashta* mage among us, and well respected in the west for his long experience and wisdom.'

Corrimaer was one of the younger members of the Council, and nearing the end of her first term as Junior Lecturer at the College of Magi in Farran. She was sitting just to the right of Iorlaas on the northeast arc of the assembly chamber; and Mage Councillor Stellaas, appointed Mage in Residence in the city of Telbray, was seated to Iorlaas' left. In their matching robes of laurel green, the three were quite obviously the representatives of the *Vashta* goddess Serbramel, Lady of Justice, within the Council.

'I do not wish to be put forward for election,' said Ellen.

'What of it?' countered Ekraan. 'Unwillingness to lead is often a sign of true worth – of one who is likely to be more mindful of the burden of their responsibility.'

Ekraan was enthroned in the High Council seat between Ellen and Iorlaas, his midnight-blue robes bordered with lightning strokes of silver thread, and his long white hair and beard flowing down around him like mountain mist. No one seemed minded to argue with him upon this point. He was as eccentric as Morvaan, and every bit as formidable as Ellen; and as Trialmaster, he had put many of those present – including Torkhaal himself – through the perilous ordeals which had earned them their place upon the Council.

'The Archmage Ellen,' Ekraan went on, 'has shown great dedication to her work and to the welfare of this Council; and the value of her recent contribution in Arrandin speaks for itself. I shall indeed propose her as a most suitable candidate for election.'

His proposal was seconded both by Rikkarn and the frail Maëghlar. Sollonaal then proposed High Councillor Iorlaas – though to Torkhaal's mind that was but simple courtesy, and Sollonaal gave no sign that he feared any great competition from that quarter. Ellen in turn seconded his proposal, and Oghraan wrote down the names in his records.

Torkhaal glanced at Ellen in surprise, and she turned her head to look back at him. So far as he could read the expression on her face at all, she seemed to be intrigued by the thought of Iorlaas as a possible candidate. He supposed that that was partly because Iorlaas offered another *Vashta* choice, apart from Sollonaal. It also subtly underlined her determination not to be chosen as Prime Councillor.

'We were talking about building bridges, I believe,' said Oghraan. 'Prime Councillor of Ellanguan, if you would care to continue?'

Sollonaal nodded, amid the murmurs and sighs of the other magi. 'As High Councillor Maëghlar has reminded us,' he said, 'for good or ill the world outside has changed. In the days of the Six Kingdoms there were several rival powers within these lands, and the Council stood upon neutral ground in their midst – a central pillar, one might say, for stability. But now those kingdoms are united in the one Empire, and the Emperor has become the centre of stability and power.'

'The Kingdoms acknowledged one High King, as I recall,' put in Ranzhaar of Stanva. 'The High Kings of Lautun, who were the forefathers of the later Emperors.'

'But they were still divided,' countered Sollonaal. 'Now the Empire has itself become the centre, while we are on the outside, as it were. We must be able to adapt to this change in our standing. It would be pride, even arrogance, to assume that we alone should be the arbiters of the use of power, now that all others have joined together in harmony within the Empire.'

'I should hardly describe the Court Noble as a haven of peace and harmony,' said Kharfaal of Vaulun.

'What we need,' said Sollonaal, with measured weight, 'is an established protocol for working together with the Empire in times of crisis or war. When the threat of war comes from outside of the Empire – as it does with this question of the Easterners' return – that need not alter our neutral standing with regard to the internal politics of the Empire.'

It sounded, Torkhaal thought, much the same as the speech which Telghraan had reported from the previous assembly; and reasonable enough, given the immediate problems facing the Six Kingdoms. But he found it hard to believe that Sollonaal could have overlooked the long-term pitfalls of such an alliance – the tyrannous ambition of the Lautun Emperors, and the dangers of delivering the considerable power of the assembled Magi into the hands of any one political leader – and the great difficulties of guarding against them. More disturbing was the evident support that this latest speech received from many members of the Council.

The Archmage Merrech raised long white hands on either side of his grey hood. 'The precepts of this Council,' he said, 'are not to determine the ends to which power is put; only that that power itself should be mastered with proper control. We have seen no evidence to suggest that this was not the case among the magi defending Arrandin. Nor – unless those precepts be changed radically – will the next Prime Councillor have authority to command individual magi as to what they should or should not do in time of war. That is a separate political consideration.'

Again a wary silence followed Merrech's words. The Magi were habitually cautious when reminded of his sinister presence – and the more so when he appeared to be upholding the very core of Council tradition. By instinct they misdoubted his purpose.

The crystal dome flared iridescent, and then faded back to grey.

'Yet the Prime Councillor is in some measure answerable for the actions of all Magi,' said Ferghaal of Braedun. 'Not in the same way that an army commander is accountable for his men, nor the leaders of a religious Order, nor even the Head of a House Noble. But still, the Prime Councillor is the leading figure to whom the outside world will look; and he or she must be able at least to keep political channels open with the Emperor and the Court Noble, and to sustain some measure of confidence in our Order – if only to prevent the actions of a few individual magi turning the whole of the Six Kingdoms against us.'

The unspoken thought behind Ferghaal's words was clear to most of the listening magi. One of Herusen's most difficult tasks over the years had been to preserve some semblance of the good reputation of the Council in the face of Merrech's unrivalled position of political influence as the Emperor's closest advisor. But unfortunately, Torkhaal realised, the comment might also be taken to refer to the actions of those of them – including Herusen himself – who had taken part in the defence of

Arrandin. It seemed so unfair that Herusen's final act of sacrifice could so swiftly be turned against him.

What they really needed, Torkhaal thought, was another Prime Councillor as kindly and dependable, and as wise, as Herusen had been. Morvaan might have made a reasonable successor; though he had not yet been proposed as a candidate, and he was perhaps a little too quirky and boyish to be wholly reliable. Asharka had the administrative competence, but lacked the personal presence to be able to handle the great and vicious among the Court Noble. Sollonaal was too obviously political, Iorlaas too remotely ascetic and severe. Ferghaal was a natural leader for a military Order, but Torkhaal was not sure how well he would adapt to the political role required of the Prime Councillor, nor how patient he would remain with the frustration of having no direct control over the other magi; and the Court Noble would in any event find it hard to believe that Ferghaal's election did not signify some hidden alliance between the Magi and the *Aeshta* Orders.

The only other candidate at present was Ellen, who held that Archmagi made poor Prime Councillors and who seemed to have no desire to be elected. Like Hrugaar and Dhûghaúr, Torkhaal personally thought that Ellen would make a very good Prime Councillor – though more austere and slightly less approachable than Herusen had been.

In his heart, he really favoured Rhysana as the best choice of all. But Herusen had left too soon. As a young mother, Rhysana would refuse to take on the added burden of leadership – not while those whom she respected, like Ellen and Morvaan, were still alive and capable of doing so. And even without the children she might have refused, on the grounds that she had not the wisdom born of age and experience; though at least, Torkhaal thought, she would have felt more free to choose. But they had made their own choices together; and as with so many other things, they had now to face the consequences.

*   *   *

Kellarn lay back on the scrubby turf, glad to stretch out after their long morning's journey.

'You are not to go to sleep,' said Corollin's voice from nearby.

'I'm not,' he said.

To prove the point he rolled over on to his side, propping himself up on one elbow to look around.

Kôril was standing a short distance away from them, beside a low outcrop of rock; watching while the horses drank from the little stream, and keeping a weather eye for any sign of approaching danger. His grey garb seemed to blend with the blue-grey of the mountain stone, and his dark hair drifted like the shadow of an ancient tree, long fallen and forgotten.

The ominous cliffs of The Steeps were now well behind to their southwest, and the ragged crests of their upper ridges were hidden from view beyond the rise and swell of the moorland slopes all around. It had taken the first half of the morning to make the torturous climb through the knotted hills that spilled down between the Knees of the Mountains and the first buttressed flanks of the cliffs themselves; and though they had not been challenged by any of the evil or magical creatures that lurked among the rocks, they had felt the gaze of many eyes upon them and caught the whispering of strange voices on the eddying breeze.

After that long climb, the ride north over the high ground of the moors had been relatively easy. Though the heat of the sun had grown as he rode up through the summer sky behind, the air was clearer here, less fraught with peril; and all around the larks were hovering and twittering above their hidden nests. Away to the west the land softened into a haze of grey and gold, with piled white clouds gathered down toward the distant coast.

'You have the look of a man who has come home,' said Corollin, sorting through the contents of their saddle bags as she sat cross-legged beside him.

'Or a boy who has escaped,' Kellarn grinned. But it was true – he did feel more at home here, high up, close to the mountains on the wild open ground. He looked down at the grass between them, with the tiny, star-shaped orange flowers on their wandering stems, and then up at the clear sky overhead.

'Do you know?' he said. 'That was the most time for a long time that I have spent with my father.'

'We were with him in Dortrean less than two months ago,' she reminded him.

'That was different,' he said.

Dortrean was home. Not that either of his parents were so very different in their bearing toward him personally, wherever in the Six Kingdoms they might meet – more discreet, of course, in the Emperor's presence or at formal Court gatherings, but never less affectionate. What Kellarn meant, he supposed, was that these last several days had been the first time for a couple of years that he had been with his father when the Emperor and so many other nobles were around. Erkal, like Karlena, thrived on his work with the Court Noble, and had a natural instinct for its complex and often eccentric politics. Kellarn himself was far less comfortable in the world of the Court, and was glad to have left it behind; and yet somehow it struck him that he had found it a little easier to cope with this time. He wondered whether he was becoming more like his parents; or whether it was simply because the war with the Easterners had drawn most of the Court's attention away from itself.

Corollin gave him a questioning look, but he found that he did not want to talk about it any more. He shrugged, and returned another grin.

She smiled and went back to her work, pulling out a pouch from beneath the safety of her leather tunic. Though Kellarn had seen her do this dozens of times before, he watched again in idle fascination as she took out a rough-cut crystal like a pale amethyst, about an inch across, and held it up in the sunlight; twirling it back and forth between supple fingers until she found the angle that she wanted. She held it still for a few moments, and Kellarn half fancied – as he had done on a few other occasions in the past – that he glimpsed a flicker of light from within the crystal itself. Then she breathed a soft sigh of satisfaction, and shifted the crystal down into her left hand.

'Shall I hold it for you?' he offered. It was still magical and strange, and he felt his heartbeat quicken at the suggestion. But at least – so far as he knew – the enchantment upon the crystal served but one purpose, and was safely under her control.

He curled his legs beneath him and knelt up, and Corollin handed the crystal to him and showed him which way up to hold it. Then she picked up a blanket roll and lowered it end-on toward the crystal. The air above Kellarn's hands blurred into a small whirlpool coil, and he felt the familiar answering swirl of vertigo and excitement in the pit of his stomach as the blanket roll sank down, shrinking with dizzying speed, and vanished. Corollin reached back and picked up a second roll.

The amethyst was a treasure from an older age of the world. Corollin referred to it simply as her *crystal casket*, and it was a most useful means of storing and carrying their gear on their journeys together. They had found it by chance on their travels through the Low Mountains, far to the south of Arrandin; though it had been Heruvor of Starmere who had first recognised it for what it was, and shown them how to use it. Or at least, he had shown Corollin and Kôril. The magic of the crystal required some mental gift or discipline which Kellarn himself did not possess. For once, he had found his inability to use a magical object strangely disappointing.

The grey figure of Kôril appeared beside them as they packed.

'We should move again, soon,' said the fay, still keeping his eyes on the land around.

'Trouble?' asked Kellarn.

'Not near by,' said Kôril; 'yet perhaps not far off. We should put the high moors behind us before dark if we can.'

The suggestion was no more than common sense. Though less perilous than the cliffs of The Steeps, the Grey Moors had a grim reputation of their own. Many creatures, wild and strange, strayed down there from the nearby mountains; whether great cats or goblin folk, or hawk-headed lions – evil mockeries of the true gryphons which, in Six Kingdoms legend, dwelt on the heights of the Black Mountains far to the west – or other things, fraught with magic and malice toward humankind. Over the long years of Six Kingdoms history, many attempts had been made to tame the moors for human habitation; and the ruined stones of forgotten homes and towers could still be found here and there, where those attempts had failed. The nearest surviving manor lands to their north were those of the Lords of Telún, on the very border of the moors themselves. If they made good speed, with no unwanted delays upon the way, Kellarn supposed that they might reach there by the end of the day.

Kôril did not drop his gaze from the distant slopes. Though by habit more quiet and remote than his two companions – or than just about anyone they had ever met – his bearing these past few days seemed even more withdrawn and preoccupied than usual; so that Kellarn wondered whether something was troubling him. He caught Corollin's eye and frowned a silent question. She gave a slight shake of her head in answer, as if warning him to leave well alone.

'What do you think now, about going to Ellanguan?' he asked aloud.

'I am not sure,' she said. 'That is where we were first drawn in to this quest, when the Librarian gave us the map last summer. And the Book Halls do hold some of the oldest records, from the early days of the Six Kingdoms.'

'But I thought that the whole point of the artefact was that there *were* no records,' said Kellarn. 'Only the makers themselves knew of it; and each one knew only where his own part of it lay hidden, and was under oath not to reveal it.'

'They must have left some clue or other,' said Corollin. 'The map led us to the first bar – the Ellanguan part – down beyond Valemur. Then in the labyrinth beneath Hauchan we found Ferrughôr's book, which told us of the purpose

272

behind the making of the artefact, and how and why it was hidden.'

'The book didn't tell us how to find the Hauchan bar,' Kellarn pointed out. 'It was just hidden close by. And we only found them by chance. I mean, we were sent to Hauchan because the Vengru woman was there, weren't we? We had no map to take us there.'

'That was more than chance, I think,' she said. 'The hand of the gods was in it. Perhaps the Easterner woman was also drawn there, if her kinsmen serve the dark Enemy.'

Kellarn felt the prickle of renewed sweat break out across his forehead.

'That's one of the reasons why I wanted to avoid Ellanguan,' he said. 'The Librarian who gave you the map was terrified that someone else was hunting for it. Perhaps the Easterner priests were after him.'

Kellarn himself had never met the Librarian, while he was alive. Shortly after the poor man had entrusted Corollin with the map, he had been hauled away by the Ellanguan city guard – supposedly for being out in the streets after curfew. When they had tried to rescue him from the cells of the Steward's palace, he had been shot down by Rinnekh's bowmen. At the time they had had no idea what the map might lead to, only that it was important; and given the mood of the city, they had assumed that the upstart Steward was behind the Librarian's fear. It was only later, in Hauchan, that they had discovered the true nature of their quest. With hindsight, they knew that the servants of Lo-Khuma had been abroad in the Empire well before then, and it seemed all too likely that some of them could have been in Ellanguan.

'Might he then have lived, had we left him in the Steward's palace?' asked Corollin.

Kellarn shrugged awkwardly. 'Probably not. And if Rinnekh had questioned him, he would have found out about the map, even if he didn't know about it before. At best, we have to assume that Rinnekh has found out something of what was going on by now. And I'd rather not have his men breathing down our necks in the Book Halls, either, unless we *really* have to go there.'

Corollin took the crystal back from him, and held it up while she focused on the closing spell to seal it. Kellarn got to his feet.

'Anyway,' he said, 'we found the third bar without any written clues. The moon fay of Starmere showed you where it was, in a vision.'

'They may not be able to help in that way again,' Kôril put in.

'But without the records in the Dortrean Manor,' said Corollin, 'we could not have found the way to the ruins of Khêltan, to retrieve it.'

She tucked the crystal away in its pouch and stood up.

'The other three kingdoms,' she said, 'were Lautun, Cerrodhí and Farodh. Of those, Cerrodhí and Farodh have been lost for centuries; and searching in the imperial city of Lautun might prove even more difficult and dangerous than returning to Ellanguan. We have learned a little in Starmere about where their old palaces and temples once stood. I had hoped that the Book Halls in Ellanguan might perhaps tell us a little more – whether any of the early kings made any great journeys, as Falladan did when he hid the Ellanguan bar; or whether later travellers stumbled across their treasures, as happened with Khêltan. But I suppose you are right. Perhaps it is best to visit Starmere first.'

'In Starmere the memory of many ancient things lives on,' said Kôril. 'Though the making of this artefact was kept hidden from them, the Fay know stories of your Old Kingdoms long forgotten among humankind. It may be worth the risk of asking them.'

'What risk?' asked Corollin.

'The hearing of the tale may change the listener,' said Kôril. 'Especially when the Fay are the tellers.'

'Is it not a little late to warn us of that now?' she smiled.

'And Ferrughôr of Hauchan married Hirulin, the daughter of Heruvor,' said the fay; 'and so she was estranged from her own kin. Though the folk of Starmere have aided us in this quest, for them the memory of your old kings brings its own sorrow. If you speak the name of Ferrughôr too often, you may risk facing Heruvor's wrath.'

'Better that than Ellanguan,' said Kellarn.

It was early evening before the High Council assembly finally came to an end. The clouds had rolled away again, and the air in the cloister garden was limpid and vibrant with the mingled perfumes of the rain-washed flowers. The college martlets were darting and chattering around the shadowed eaves, and a single gull flashed white and grey as it floated overhead.

Rhysana invited Ellen back to her apartment, and they found their three menfolk waiting there for them. Torkhaal was half asleep in his chair beside the hearth, and Hrugaar and Dhûghaúr were standing together looking out of the window at the far end of the living chamber.

'So who is it to be?' Hrugaar demanded, remembering to bow to the Archmage Ellen.

'In a minute, Ru,' said Rhysana, stooping to kiss her husband on the forehead. 'I just want to look in on Taillan.'

'I only put him down a few minutes ago,' said Torkhaal.

'I shall be very quiet,' she promised.

'I need a drink,' said Ellen, as Rhysana headed for the door.

'Does that mean that you won?' asked Dhûghaúr.

'More like that Sollonaal did,' said Hrugaar glumly.

Ellen said nothing. Rhysana slipped through the doorway to check on her son in the dim light; and having reassured herself that he was comfortably asleep, she crept through into the bathroom to freshen herself before rejoining the others. She might have been tempted to change out of her formal high councillor's robes; but they had been sitting in council for hours, with only one brief recession, and she was now so hungry that her insides felt as though they were devouring themselves.

When she returned to the living chamber, Ellen was sitting at the end of the long table with Hrugaar and Dhûghaúr on either side. A silver jug bobbed in the air as one of the unseen *chaedar* poured pale yellow wine into the silver goblets before them. Rhysana saw that two large loaves of bread had already been brought in, and dishes of honey and butter, and a blue bowl filled with pickled herring. She went straight to the table and sat down. Torkhaal dragged himself out of his chair and came over to join them.

'So who is it to be?' asked Hrugaar again. 'Ellen said that we had to wait for you to tell us.'

'Iorlaas,' Rhysana said simply, reaching for the bread knife.

'What?' cried Hrugaar and Dhûghaúr together. Torkhaal sat down more swiftly than he had intended.

Rhysana hushed them with a warning frown, and a nod of her head in the general direction of the sleeping Taillan.

'May we ask why?' asked Torkhaal softly in his deep, purring voice. 'Or is that a High Council secret?'

'Ellen?' Rhysana began to carve her way into the first of the loaves.

'Not entirely secret,' Ellen allowed. 'When Iorlaas makes his first formal appearance as Prime Councillor, at the next Full Moon Assembly, some introduction will no doubt be made.'

'If he survives the Rite of Ascent,' said Rhysana.

'And what is that?' asked Dhûghaúr.

'The ritual of his investiture as Prime Councillor,' Ellen explained. 'We inherited the term from the religious Orders, I believe.'

'But can you not tell us the reasons now?' pleaded Hrugaar.

'You could work it out for yourselves,' said Ellen. 'In brief, Ferghaal was probably the best choice of the three *Aeshta* candidates; but his strong links with the Braedun Order were a problem. And the High Council felt that a *Vashta* mage might be better suited for dealing with the imperial Court at this time.'

'I still think you would have made the best Prime Councillor,' put in Dhûghaúr.

276

Ellen turned her head to fix him with a warning look, then sipped her wine and continued.

'Of the four *Vashta* magi of the High Council,' she said, 'two are of blood Noble – Drôshiin of Sêchral and Lirinal of Dregharis. Neither, as you will recall, was proposed as a candidate. Lirinal is still comparatively young, and it is less than a year ago that he joined the High Council. He also comes from a lesser branch of a Merchant House Noble; and though the merchant nobles are well versed in the shifting alliances of the Court, he is too little known – and thus unpredictable – to take on the role at present.'

'He is also very much under the shadow of Sollonaal,' said Rhysana.

'Drôshiin is that much older, and of greater precedence by blood,' Ellen went on; 'but he is kinsman to the new Empress – albeit not that close – and of no good reputation. To put it bluntly, the man is morally bankrupt. Which leaves us with the two proposed candidates, Iorlaas and Sollonaal.'

'Sollonaal will soon be morally bankrupt,' said Hrugaar. 'He has the soul of a merchant.'

'Iorlaas has served on the High Council longer than anyone, now,' said Ellen, ignoring him, 'except for Morvaan and His Eminence, of course. He is the most senior of all the *Vashta* magi; and he is a follower of the goddess Serbramel – the most popular of all the *Vashtar* among the people of the Empire.'

'Serbramel,' Hrugaar sighed. 'The Reverend Mother Kaïra will be delighted.'

'Perhaps not,' said Torkhaal. 'I do not recall him visiting Telbray very often; and Kaïra is not that popular, even among the other members of her own Order. She may not have any influence with Iorlaas at all – which would infuriate her all the more.'

'Iorlaas is an ascetic,' said Rhysana, between mouthfuls of bread and honey; 'and apt to be severe. But he does have a sense of fair play – which Kaïra, I believe, does not.'

'Anyway,' said Ellen, 'Iorlaas has a decade on Sollonaal;

and given the combination of his strict adherence to Council tradition and his *Vashta* faith, he seemed to be the better choice. With Iorlaas, one is more aware of the tradition than the man. Sollonaal relies more on personal reputation and presence – which may do well enough among the Council or the merchants of Ellanguan, but in the games of the Court Noble would be too great a risk.'

'Especially with the speeches that he has been making about imperial alliance,' said Torkhaal.

'Was Sollonaal very upset?' asked Dhûghaúr.

'He took it fairly well, in the end,' said Ellen. 'Better than I might have expected – though I suspect that it irked him a little that he had been rash enough to propose Iorlaas himself, out of courtesy, without weighing up the possible danger to his own cause. But Sollonaal knows that time is on his side. He can still hope to be Iorlaas' successor.'

By now the *chaedar* had brought in a large plate of fresh sardines, some cheeses and a bowl of summer fruits. Rhysana had avoided the pickled herring, but she fell upon the sardines eagerly. She would have spread honey over them, had it not been for Ellen's horrified expression as she reached for the spoon; so instead she helped herself to a wedge of cheese, and plenty of bread and butter. The three men had eaten earlier, but Torkhaal joined Ellen in attacking the bread and cheese.

'Yet how will Iorlaas fare,' asked Hrugaar, 'when the demon captain returns?'

'Or even the Easterner wizards?' Dhûghaúr agreed.

'That was held to be of lesser importance,' said Ellen. 'Remember the debate. We still have several *Aeshta* magi – thank the gods – who can deal with the *Aeshta* Orders; and it is not the place of the Prime Councillor to command or forbid them to do so. But the Prime Councillor is the face of the Council when dealing with the imperial Court. It was felt that Iorlaas would have a better chance of standing his ground over Council tradition, while still appearing favourable to the new imperial philosophies and ideals.'

'So Iorlaas is to be a political delegate, rather than a spiritual leader,' said Torkhaal.

'In essence, yes,' Ellen nodded. 'Though not all of the Council may think so.'

'Some of them will still wonder why you did not choose Sollonaal,' said Dhûghaúr. 'He did seem the more obvious choice.'

Hrugaar shook his head. 'Sollonaal is too hungry for power.'

'Do you think so, Ru?' asked Rhysana.

'Not true power, magical power, as we know it,' he explained. 'In fact, it seems to me that Sollonaal has grown afraid of that kind of power, since the Easterners attacked.'

'His mastery and academic insight have never been called into question,' observed Ellen. 'His reputation as Senior Lecturer here in Lautun was well deserved, from what I recall.'

'Perhaps,' Hrugaar shrugged. 'Yet to me it seems that he has turned aside from that path, and now tries to seek strength through political influence.'

'Like the Imperial Counsellor?' ventured Dhûghaúr.

'No,' said Rhysana. 'His Eminence uses both kinds of power. He is far more dangerous.'

'Sollonaal is dangerous,' returned Hrugaar, 'in other ways.'

'Have you heard something in Ellanguan?' asked Torkhaal.

'Not as such,' said Hrugaar, dropping his gaze. 'I should have told you ere now, if I had. But the air in the city has changed. It feels as though you can hardly draw breath without being watched.'

'The Southers are still in the city,' Ellen reasoned, 'and likely to be there for some weeks yet. Even with the strict curfews – and the added advantage that most of the Souther sailors are slaves tied to their ships – it must be a nightmare for the city guard to keep the peace. With the Empress in Ellanguan, and a shipload of the Imperial Household Guard, I doubt that their task is made any easier.'

'Yet there is something else, I think,' said Hrugaar. 'The Book Halls are more closely guarded than ever. It seemed that whenever we turned a corner we would bump into one of the librarians, or one of Rinnekh's men.'

'Even in the Book Halls of the Magi we felt that we were being watched,' added Dhûghaúr; 'and in a way that discouraged us from working at all.'

'But is this Sollonaal's doing,' asked Rhysana, 'or Rinnekh's?'

Hrugaar shrugged. 'I suppose that I am none too popular with either of them,' he sighed. 'Yet it seemed that the librarians were watching everyone.'

'But what would they be afraid of?' asked Torkhaal. 'Do they think that someone will turn up another defence matrix in Ellanguan, like the one in Arrandin?'

'Possibly,' said Ellen. 'As we have been saying for the last several days, the power that we displayed in Arrandin has made many people wary of us. But it is not good that any mage should be hindered in his private research. The High Council must look in to that.'

'Can they not see that we might be trying to help the Empire?' grumbled Dhûghaúr.

'Ah, but have you approached the correct imperial authority?' Torkhaal grinned.

'Bugger that,' breathed Ellen, reaching for the silver wine jug.

'Have you asked the Warden about references to the Enemy's return?' suggested Rhysana.

'This afternoon,' Hrugaar nodded. 'He named a few manuscripts in the libraries here which might be of help, and a couple more in the Book Halls of Ellanguan; and he seemed to think that Ellanguan might be the better place to look – which leaves us little better off than where we started.'

'What about asking one of the lecturers from the Ellanguan College to help?' offered Torkhaal. 'They might have more freedom to move around the Book Halls. Though it is difficult to know whom to trust, with Sollonaal as Principal there.'

'Let us see what the High Council can do, first,' said Ellen.

'It occurs to me now,' said Hrugaar, 'that Corollin –

Morvaan's daughter – was researching the earliest days of the Old Kingdoms. That was last summer, I think. Though of course her work may have had little enough to do with this.'

'Kellarn did not mention anything of it to me,' said Rhysana.

'Nor either of them to us,' said Hrugaar. 'But they seem as concerned as we are about the Enemy's return. It might do no harm to ask Corollin what she turned up.'

'Will they still be in Arrandin?' asked Torkhaal.

'I shall find out in the morning,' said Hrugaar.

'Speaking of Dortrean,' said Ellen, 'which we were, in a roundabout way, I see that Erkal's other son, Solban, is in Ellanguan with the Imperial Household Guard.'

'Karlena will be pleased to see him, I expect,' said Rhysana; 'but what of it?'

'My niece Lauraï is also in Ellanguan,' said Ellen.

'That is Lauraï Raudhar of Renza,' Hrugaar explained for Dhûghaúr's benefit. 'Torreghal's widow.'

Ellen glanced at him, and then went on. 'From what Lauraï tells me, Rinnekh has already managed to cause a rift in the traditional alliance of Ellanguan and Renza – although I suppose that was inevitable, from the moment that he was chosen as old Gradhellan's heir. Rinnekh commanded Renza to let the Southers make harbour at the Watchful Isle, and the Regents of Renza rightly refused.'

Rhysana stopped chewing, though she was unable to pass comment because her mouth was too full. Hrugaar's eyes flashed green as if from personal insult.

'The interesting point,' said Ellen, 'is that Solban of Dortrean apparently sided with Lauraï against Rinnekh, overruling the command for obvious reasons of defence. And now Lauraï is staying in Ellanguan, awaiting the Emperor's return; and Solban is most diligent in visiting her each day, showing personal concern for her welfare. He was there when I visited the Renza house myself, yesterday afternoon.'

'Solban is still the Emperor's man,' said Hrugaar. 'Is he not trying to sweeten Lauraï's temper for the Emperor's purposes?'

'Quite possibly,' Ellen allowed; 'though I had the impression that they have taken a great liking toward one another.'

'Is not Solban Erkal's heir?' asked Dhûghaúr.

'He is,' said Rhysana. 'And an alliance of friendship between Dortrean and Renza at such a high level – even if it come not to marriage – is likely to cause a few ripples in the Court Noble.'

'Yet would the heir of Dortrean be permitted to marry the widow of the Lord Renza?' wondered Hrugaar.

'It is not without precedent,' said Ellen.

'But when Solban becomes Earl,' said Dhûghaúr, 'would that not just put Dortrean and Renza in the Emperor's pocket, if his loyalty is to Lautun?'

'Not if Lauraï has any say in the matter,' said Ellen.

'Nor Kellarn,' Rhysana added. 'Nor Solban himself, I think. He may embrace the ideal of a single Empire, and have risen high in the Household Guard, but he has no love for oppression and tyranny – and he is not one of Rhydden's personal favourites. Mellin Carfinn still trusts him. He may yet surprise us all.'

'But if there is a dispute between Ellanguan and Renza,' said Torkhaal, 'with whom will the Emperor side?'

'Neither, if he has any sense,' said Ellen. 'Still, I do wonder what may come of it.'

Chapter Nine

Kellarn did not catch sight of the Telún manor house before the end of the day, though they had managed to put the higher parts of the Grey Moors behind them, and he guessed that the low stone croft nestled into the hillside in the middle distance ahead belonged to one of Telún's outlying tenants. The clouds had moved up from the west, and the late afternoon had become overcast and dully oppressive. Twilight came early.

They settled for the night under the lee of a small stand of hawthorn trees, close to a mountain rill that tumbled north and west down through the rocks and heather. Corollin thought the place safer than most on the moors, but she lay down with her staff close beside her. Kellarn kept his sword on the blanket beside him, ready to hand.

He slept deeply for some hours, and then stumbled awake through an uneasy dream. He dreamed that he stood in the grey shadows of an empty street, with a sense of danger nearby. A man came out of the shadows to greet him – friend, rather than foe. At first Kellarn thought that it was his brother, Solban. But then the man's face shifted in the twilight, so that he had the look of Kierran of Arrand.

'Sun and Moon, Col,' grinned Kierran. 'What are you doing here?'

Kellarn's heart stirred within him; joyful, yet suddenly shy. He found that he could not answer.

Kierran came forward and took Kellarn by the shoulders in cheerful embrace – and then staggered and slumped against him. Kellarn flung his arms around him to catch the weight.

His hands met the warm slickness of fresh blood; and it was no longer Kierran that he held but a stranger, wild and ragged – the Librarian from Ellanguan.

Kellarn opened his eyes and sat up, his heart pounding. The night air was close and damp, and the moon and stars were hidden. The thorn leaves whispered behind him on the moorland breeze. The sky overhead flared and faded again, telling of lightning somewhere high up in the Blue Mountains.

He reached back and found the hilt of his sword, straining for any sound of danger nearby. There was only the gurgle of the stream, and the night noises of the horses, and the murmur of the trees. It felt as though it was well past midnight, and time that Kôril should have woken him for his turn on watch.

There was no sign of Kôril in the darkness. But as Kellarn looked around a tiny fountain of starlight sprang up beneath the deeper shadow of the hawthorn trees, revealing the fay's sombre face. Kellarn crept over to join him, careful not to wake the sleeping Corollin. The fay brushed one hand through the fountain, and it scattered and faded.

'The moon has gone down,' said Kôril softly. 'You should sleep. I can keep watch.'

Kellarn sat down beside him, resting his sword on the ground. He was now wide awake, and still unsettled by the memory of his dream. He had no idea who the Librarian was, nor what his purpose had been – only that he had once worked in the Book Halls of Ellanguan, and that Corollin had met him during the course of her studies. Corollin had not thought him to be one of the Magi. And then the memory of Kierran unsettled him in different ways, so that Kellarn regretted not having visited him again in Arrandin. But it had not seemed right at the time. He hoped that Kierran was not in any danger.

Kôril sat still and silent as ever beside him. There was a brooding tension on the air, which seemed to have little to do with the mountain storms. Kellarn remembered that the fay had been closed in upon himself for days, and wondered again what might be troubling him. Though Corollin had hinted that he should leave well alone, he thought that there might be no great harm in asking. At least, he thought that he should try.

'What is it?' he asked.

Kôril shifted in the darkness, though Kellarn did not think that he was looking at him. There was another dull flare across the clouds overhead, and then a silence for several heartbeats.

'I killed a woman,' said the fay simply.

'At Tollund?' Kellarn prompted.

'No,' said Kôril. 'Not Arisâ.'

He offered no further explanation. Kellarn frowned, wondering who else might have made such an impression upon his friend, if the death of Arisâ had not.

'The Vengru woman?' he asked.

'No,' said Kôril. 'Another, older than she.'

Kellarn said nothing, waiting; and at length the fay sighed and spoke again.

'It was after you had left Ellanguan,' he said. 'My own studies led me to a forgotten hiding place on the shores of the Great River. Wizard's Steep, men call it; though the story behind the name has now faded from memory. I had hoped to find there some insight into the powers used of old among humankind, in the early days of your kingdoms – such powers as Ferrughôr and the first kings might have used in the forging of the artefact which we now seek. Yet that hope proved void.

'There I found a square chamber, unvisited by any save myself, I think, for many lives of men. And in the midst of that chamber was a dome of power – that kind of power which bends light around itself, so that it can not be seen when you look straight at it. Only from the corner of the eye can you glimpse it, as a grey blur of blindness. But that is of no matter. My scrutiny, or perhaps my presence alone, disturbed the spell; and it ended. And there, where it had been, stood the woman.'

Kôril paused, as if looking back in his mind's eye. 'She was beautiful once, I think,' he said, 'and her jewels and robes must have been very splendid. But she was faded and withered, like a flower gone to seed. Hate alone sustained her. She railed at me in one of the old kingdom tongues, calling me a liar and a fool; and when I stood in her way she tried to destroy me. She failed.'

'But who was she?' asked Kellarn.

'I know not,' Kôril answered. 'A woman from the past, by her speech and dress. In her own age, her power must have been very great – a match for any of your Council of Magi now, I guess.'

'Then how did you survive?'

'I am a son of the Fay,' said Kôril simply. 'It was a sore challenge; but her strength, like her beauty, had withered. She perished in fire. Only the twisted metals of her jewels now remain.'

He fell silent again. A low rumble of thunder echoed in the distance.

'Were you hurt?' asked Kellarn. It was not exactly what he wanted to ask, but he was still struggling to understand the strange tale – how the woman had come to be there at all, if she belonged to another age in Six Kingdoms history; and whether that was the reason why her death had had such a profound impact on his friend.

'A little,' said Kôril. 'But her death still troubles me.'

'She was trying to kill you,' Kellarn reminded him.

'I know. Yet there was another power at work there, too subtle for my understanding. I fear that I may have stumbled upon a greater pattern in the dance of life; and the tale of the world now changes – though how I can not tell. I must seek the wisdom of Starmere in this.'

'The *Aeshtar* are the Lords of the dance of life,' said Kellarn. 'Why should we fear to tread the patterns they have prepared?'

It was a confidence he did not altogether feel. Mere mortals, like himself, had cause to feel awe, or simple terror, when they glimpsed the great purposes of the gods at work in their lives. But Kellarn had always thought the elvenfolk of the Fay to be closer to the gods, in mystic harmony with the patterns they

286

wove. If Kôril was troubled by what he had done, how great a calamity might come of it?

'We can ask Heruvor about it,' he said, when Kôril did not answer. 'Perhaps you should try to rest.'

'Perhaps I should,' said the fay. He stood up and moved away. Kellarn shivered in the damp air, and went to fetch his blanket before settling down to keep watch.

The storms were gone well before morning, though the sky remained full of clouds, and as the day wore on the sun galloped in and out of view behind them. The three friends rode down through the tamer hills of the Telún lands, and up into the broad gap of the Hauchan valley. Neither Kôril nor Kellarn made mention of their conversation from the night before.

The countryside around them was now green again – a spread of rolling grassland and scattered farmsteads and fields, with lush meadows and pastures down near the river, shaded by elms and alders and pale willows. But though less wild than the Grey Moors, the Hauchan valley had still something of the feel of a borderland about it; a gateway *from* the Blue Mountains, perhaps, rather than a way in to them. The ruined city of Hauchan – where Ferrughôr had ruled as High King some fifteen centuries before – lay at the upper end of the vale, and was rumoured to be haunted; and at times strange creatures from the mountains would come down to make their home there. The valley folk seldom took their herds so far up that way; and in harsh winters they might have worse things to contend with than wolves and bears and bad weather.

A little after noon they came to the fords of the Great River – in the midst of the valley, but at a point where the many winding curves of the river's course brought it close to the northern side. The ruins of old Hauchan were still some ten miles further to the east, hidden by the lie of the land and the cloud shadows; but they did not plan to go that way. Straight ahead, about a mile beyond the fords, the towers of the Monastery of Maësta stood out clear against the high cliffs in a patch of sunlight.

The Monastery of Maësta more resembled a fortress stronghold than a cloistered temple. Like Kellarn's home, the White Manor of Dortrean, it was built atop a sheer spur out-thrust from the great cliffs of the northern valley side; and the smooth walls and squared towers seemed to rise up from out of the blue-grey mountain rock itself. As far as Kellarn knew, there had been a temple here since the dawn of the Golden Age of the Magi, and perhaps even before; and for centuries it had been a place of pilgrimage for followers of all the *Aeshta* Lords of Water – Maësta and Sherunar, and the Moon Maiden Haëstren. Though not themselves followers of Water, Kellarn and his friends had been well received at the monastery on their previous visits, according to the tradition of harmony between all the Lords of the *Aeshtar* and their servants. Given that the priests had until recently had the Vengru necklace in their care – and since, like the Sun priests, they had foreseen the danger of Lo-Khuma's return – Kellarn thought it might do no harm to talk to them.

They rode on to the trading village at the foot of the cliffs, and left their horses at the inn. Then they made their way on foot up the narrow road which climbed across the cliff face to reach the monastery gate, several hundred feet above the valley floor.

With most of the active priests and knights of the Kelmaar Order called away by the war, and with the contemplative members caught up in the daily observances of their Rule, nearly an hour went by before anyone was free to speak with them; by which time guest chambers had been prepared for them, and they had abandoned all pretence of expecting to travel farther that day.

At last they were led into a small fountain court, not far from the temple doors; and then a silvered trellis gate on the far side was unlocked, and Maëra of Kelmaar came out to receive them. Maëra was a scholar and priestess – a woman well into her middle years, with steel grey hair swept back into a loose-coiled bun, and a pleasant but rather excitable manner. Her grey robes bordered with silver were not those of a Chosen Priestess of her Order; but apart from that, Kellarn had little idea of her ranking among her brethren. They had met once or twice before, on previous visits here, and she was clearly delighted to see them.

Since Hrugaar had come to the monastery little more than a week ago, to fetch the Vengru necklace, the priests had already learned much concerning the end of the siege and the departure of the Easterners. Through means of their own they had also gathered more recent news from Arrandin. Maëra told them that the Emperor had left the city the previous day, with his own escort and a small number of troops taken from the Six Kingdoms armies, and was now riding north along the road toward Ellanguan. Kellarn's father was still in Arrandin, and expected to remain there for several days. The Arrand himself was far from well.

Of the Vengru necklace, Maëra could only repeat what Hrugaar had already told them – that there had been no power or enchantment upon it that the priests of Kelmaar could find, merely the lingering memory of its former owner, which had been washed away with simple ceremony. The few other belongings which the Easterner woman had had with her – her staff and flail, and her tusked silver amulet – had but confirmed that she was a servant of the Keeper of Souls, the White Lady of Death in the Easterner faith. There had been no sign that the Vengru woman had been a follower of Lo-Khuma like her kinsman.

Drifting in and out of Maëra's conversation there was also a good deal about the business of Ellanguan – which was only to be expected, given that Ellanguan had always stood foremost in the hearts and minds of the Kelmaar Order, before any other city or kingdom in all the waking world. Rinnekh's provisional treaty with the Southers still held; but though the Emperor might be pleased with it, the Steward was already at odds with Renza and more than half the city over the question of the fitting of the Souther ships. Then again, Rinnekh had been at odds with most people long before he had clawed his way on to the Steward's throne. There had been some minor troubles involving the Souther sailors within the city, and now stricter curfews were being maintained. A division of the Imperial Household Guard was there, under the command of Kellarn's brother Solban; and Kellarn's mother, the Lady Karlena, was still with the Empress.

Those of the Kelmaar Order who remained in Ellanguan watched all this from the lists, and waited. Being no longer welcome in the Steward's palace – and with the greater part of their strength still south and east beyond Arrandin, or far to the west in Farran – there was little more they could do. Maëra herself seemed unsettled by the news, as though she feared that worse trouble might yet come of it.

'Do you wish to go to Ellanguan now?' Corollin asked Kellarn. He shook his head once, doubtfully.

'Fire in the water,' nodded Maëra, watching them. 'That could make matters worse.'

'But the Lady Karlena is there,' said Corollin.

'The *Vashta* lay brother,' said Kellarn, 'the one who met the Emperor on the harbour front. Did anything more come of that?'

'Sarin is dead, by his own hand,' Maëra answered. 'Or so we have heard. There has been no other news concerning his vision.'

'Oh,' said Kellarn.

It would have seemed foolish to say that he was sorry for Sarin's death, since he had never met the man, and Maëra herself had probably had nothing to do with him. And yet, after a fashion, he was saddened by the news. He supposed that it was simply the nature of Sarin's plight – a young man driven by a vision from the gods, only to end up tortured and broken, killing himself in his madness. Kellarn wondered whether all such visions granted by the *Vashtar* demanded so terrible a price; and then it struck him, rather uncomfortably, that perhaps their own service to the more kindly Lords of the *Aeshtar* might yet make demands upon them just as difficult to bear. As a warrior, he had considered the possibility of dying in defence of faith or of kinsmen. But this seemed somehow different.

He lost the thread of the conversation for a moment. When he brought his attention back, Maëra was confirming the likelihood – given the nature of his madness – that Sarin had indeed been responsible for his own death.

'And there is no news of the power of the Enemy at work within the city?' asked Corollin.

'Nothing certain,' the priestess sighed. 'With all her conflicts and tensions, Ellanguan has become like a muddied pool. It is hard to tell what is happening.'

She took her leave of them soon after that, and went away again beyond the silvered gate; and one of the junior guards came and led them to their chambers high up in the guest tower. They rested there in the lazy afternoon heat, and then washed and had supper together before going down to hear the sunset rite in the outer temple.

But when Corollin and Kôril had gone to bed for the night, Kellarn sat alone on the broad sill of his open window, glad of the cool mountain wind upon his bare skin. Far below, the Hauchan valley was flooded with moonlight, dipped and rippled with many cat's paws of deep shadow.

The memory of his dream from the night before had returned to trouble him – not of Kierran, nor of the dead Librarian, but of that first brief glimpse of his brother. Though he and Solban had grown apart over the years, each choosing very different lives and ideals, there was still a closeness of sorts between them when they met; enough for Kellarn to wonder whether the dream had been a sign that his brother was in danger – or whether perhaps Solban's likeness had appeared to warn him of his own danger, if he should return to Ellanguan.

On the other hand, he reasoned, the dream might have been nothing more than the confused images of his own fears. Kellarn had to admit that he was afraid of going to Ellanguan; and Maëra of Kelmaar had apparently shared his misgivings, for whatever reasons of her own. It occurred to him that perhaps it might be best to face that fear head on, and ride to Ellanguan instead of Starmere. Yet every instinct he trusted told against it.

He looked up at the high mountain peaks and the moon-dappled clouds, but no inspiration came. And then at last he flung himself down on the cool linen of his bed, and slept soundly until Kôril came to wake him.

They left the monastery at first light, and walked down through grey mists to collect their horses from the village. There was no mention between them of going to Ellanguan. They rode west slowly through a shrouded world, the noises of horse and harness sounding louder than usual in the muffled silence. Corollin led the way, keeping closer to the line of the mountain cliffs than to the river as far as Kellarn could tell, though he could see little of the valley around them. Kôril rode behind them, looking back over his shoulder at times as if trying to pierce the mists with his keen eyes. But there was no sign that they were being followed.

The third hour of the morning was passing before the air began to clear; and then above and to their right loomed the broad shoulders and sheer sides of Koritalla – the out-thrust mountain peak that stood sentinel at the entrance to the Hauchan valley on this side. High up beyond the northern face of that mountain, Kellarn knew, lay hidden the Valley of Two Waters, where Corollin had first begun to study the forgotten lore of Zedron; and somewhere at the feet of Koritalla, in centuries past, there had also once been a gateway to the realm of the Redbeard dwarves of the Blue Mountains. But the Redbeards had quarrelled with the men of Ellanguan, and the gate had long ago been shut. Nor was there a path to the Valley of Two Waters from this side.

Their spirits lifted as the day brightened, and the horses picked up their pace. They skirted the familiar spurs of Koritalla and turned northward again, with the sun now growing hot upon their backs.

For most of that day their way lay over open grassland and

gently rolling hills. The mountains filled half the sky to their right, and to their left the land lay basking beneath a peaceful summer haze, with only an occasional hawk or mountain bird drifting overhead. From what Kellarn could remember, this broad stretch of land between the mountains and the Old North Road – some five or six leagues away to their west – was a hinterland estate belonging to the Lords Steward of Ellanguan, and by tradition a home for the lesser kinsmen of that House. But he did not recall much use being made of it in old Gradhellan's day; and he doubted that the upstart Rinnekh had ever come here.

As the afternoon wore on they drew level with another valley entrance – nearly as wide as the Hauchan vale, though a good deal less deep, and filled with a smooth green rise running in between the broken cliffs. There were wagtails bobbing in the grass, and many brightly coloured flowers scattered in waves across the rise; but the general air of emptiness and neglect seemed more focused there. The place was named Deadmen's Green, after some battle or other in Ellanguan's long history; and like the upper reaches of the Hauchan valley it had a sinister reputation in Six Kingdoms folklore.

On the far side of the Green, and straying for some miles across its northern borders, were the first trees of the Whispering Forest. Already the long line of the woodland eaves filled the horizon ahead like a huge mountain shadow left behind from early morning; and yet the Whispering Forest was but a slender arm reaching down from the Great Forest of Cerrodhí, which spread north and west for over fifty leagues and had once been a kingdom in its own right.

Whether the Whispering Forest had ever been part of the old Fifth Kingdom of Cerrodhí, Kellarn did not know. In his own mind he thought of it as the realm of the moon fay of Starmere; and certainly, when he had been here before, the paths he had used had been made by the elvenfolk themselves. The Fifth Kingdom – always remote from the doings of the other human kingdoms – had not survived beyond the end of the Golden Age of the Magi; and now, like all forests in this part of the world, it remained dark and dangerous. Those few humans who lived and worked along the forest edge – woodcutters and charcoal burners, swineherds and huntsmen – rarely ventured further than a few miles inside.

They slowed to a halt as they rode in among the first outlying trees; though their way still lay for the most part along clear grassland runs, open to the sky, and the deeper forest shadow was perhaps a mile or so ahead of them. Corollin sat up in the saddle, looking forward and back at the high mountain cliffs to gain her bearings. Kellarn did the same, but the best that he could hope to manage would be a rough guess. When he had come this way before it had been a wintry landscape of snow and cloud and bare, ragged branches. The lush growth of summer put him quite out of reckoning.

Kôril nudged his bay mare forward a few steps, and dropped lightly to the ground. After a few moments he pointed ahead and to their left with his free hand.

'We need to move a little further west, I think,' he said.

Corollin and Kellarn nodded their agreement, and the two of them dismounted.

Even with the fay to guide them, it took the better part of an hour to find the beginning of the forest path; by which time the tree shadow had grown deep around them, and the early evening sky was all but hidden behind the thick canopy overhead.

The start of the path was marked by two large oak trees, whose gnarled branches and snaking roots twined together to form a natural archway and threshold. From a short distance away, there was nothing remarkable about them to distinguish them from any of the other oaks or elms or chestnut trees that stood around, all of great size and age; nor was there any sign of a path. But when they stood before them, looking through the archway, a clear avenue opened up through the trees, running more or less straight ahead into the forest.

Kôril led the way beneath the arch, his bay mare walking

quietly beside him, and Corollin and Mistwise followed behind. But when it came to Kellarn's turn, Rúnfyr shied and reared in sudden protest, and pulled away. Caught off balance, Kellarn found himself half dragged, half stumbling after him, clinging to the reins.

He soon got his feet under him and pulled the gelding to a halt; and then gentled him and led him back again. But as soon as they reached the outer branches of the oaks, some distance from the archway itself, Rúnfyr kicked down his heels and pulled backward, his eyes rolling white in frightened warning.

'I know it's magic,' Kellarn told him, struggling to calm him again. 'But they're good people. Elvenfolk. You'll like them.'

Rúnfyr was unconvinced; and for all Kellarn's strength and pleading, he could scarce drag the horse any further. Corollin left her own mare behind and came out to help, but the presence of two humans only seemed to make matters worse.

After two more attempts, and a particularly wild tussle in which Kellarn was hurled aside, Corollin grabbed hold of the gelding's halter and yanked the great head around, staring him straight in the eyes. Rúnfyr went suddenly still, all fight taken out of him.

Kellarn climbed grumbling to his feet, wary of how long this latest truce might last. Corollin was walking backward toward the archway, now leading Rúnfyr with both hands upon the halter, still holding him with her gaze. Her eyes flared wide as the horse's, the rich blue of jasper rimmed with white like glittering frost. Kellarn felt a dull queasiness in the pit of his stomach.

Corollin moved on between the oak trees; and Rúnfyr followed, picking his way over the twining roots as though clearing a low hurdle. Kellarn came behind them, watching the ground carefully.

Some twenty yards further in, Corollin loosed her hold on the gelding's halter and pulled forward his reins to tether him to a sturdy branch. Then she tossed her hair back from her shoulders, and flung an accusing glance at Kellarn. Her eyes had returned to their normal size again; but her forehead glistened with sweat, and she was clearly in no good humour.

The forest around them appeared much the same as it had before – except that perhaps the shadows were now a little deeper to either side. The line of the path stretched on ahead of them. Kôril handed the reins of the other two horses to Kellarn, and went back to look at the oak tree arch.

'Sorry,' said Kellarn to Corollin.

'It's Rúnfyr who needs the apology,' she returned crossly. 'I hate having to do that.'

'It's not my fault,' he rejoined. As a rule, horses were very good with him.

Corollin looked away.

'I'm sorry,' Kellarn told Rúnfyr. The gelding took no notice.

Kellarn did not ask Corollin what it was that she had done. It was clear to him that she had used some sort of magic to control the beast; and just as clear that this was not the best time to talk about it. He turned to see what Kôril was doing.

The fay was crouched down between the two oak trees, stroking one pale hand through the grass. After a while he stood up and shrugged.

'I sense no danger here,' he told them, coming back along the path. 'But other folk use this way, apart from Heruvor's folk of Starmere. Kellarn, you had better take Lanaë for now – I can handle Rúnfyr. We should move deeper in to the forest ere we rest. Is that all right?'

This last question was addressed to Corollin more than Kellarn. She wiped the back of one hand across her brow, and nodded.

'What other folk?' asked Kellarn.

'None that may harm us, if we keep to the path,' said Kôril.

Corollin patted Kellarn's arm as she took Mistwise's reins, to show she was not really angry with him. Kôril untied Rúnfyr and led the way ahead. The gelding followed him quietly, as though nothing had ever troubled him.

Rinnekh Ellanguan strode irritably into the small antechamber, glancing across to check that the window shutters were firmly closed against the evening sky. Then he stopped and turned, watching while the guard captain shut the panelled door through which they had entered. In the soft candlelight the panels of the door blended with the rest of the wall, masking its presence completely.

'Give me one minute, Turill,' Rinnekh told him.

The guard bowed his head, clasping his right fist across his chest in salute, then crossed the chamber to the main doorway – clearly visible with its handles and fittings of silvered steel. Rinnekh dismissed him from thought without waiting to see him go. He tugged at the high collar of his pale blue tunic, then folded his arms tightly across his stomach.

'Bother Trigharran,' he said aloud to the empty room.

He felt better for saying it, even if it might help little in the coming interview. The presumptuous Trigharran of Kelmaar – as bold as he was undoubtedly ancient – had all but demanded an audience with his Lord Steward; a private audience after the sunset curfew, when the watchful eyes of the city of Ellanguan were all safely indoors. Rinnekh had doubted Trigharran's motives at once. But given the old man's strength of influence among the heathen followers of the *Aeshtar*, both in the city and among the Lords of the Court Noble, he had felt obliged to see him.

Though the messenger from the Kelmaar School had claimed no knowledge of what Master Trigharran might wish to say, it seemed likely enough that it would be about the Southers. It had occurred to Rinnekh, later that afternoon, to wonder whether Lauraï of Renza had put him up to it, to strengthen her cause before the Emperor's return; and whether Solban of Dortrean had supported her.

Solban himself posed a more pressing problem to Rinnekh than did either Trigharran or Lauraï – or even the Lady Karlena, who mercifully was away from the palace for much of the time keeping the Empress out of mischief. Ever since Solban had arrived with his division of the Imperial Household Guard, Rinnekh had had the growing impression that he was now a prisoner in his own city. Though the Lieutenant General had taken pains to work alongside the city guard and the Steward's household, he had made it clear from the start that he was here to serve the interests of the Empire rather than of Ellanguan. Trying to keep anything in the palace hidden from Solban had become a major undertaking – which was why Rinnekh had given instructions for Trigharran to come through the guardhouse gate, as though visiting prisoners, and then to be brought up by a back way to this little used chamber in his own private apartment. True, Solban might know of Trigharran's visit already. But then again, there was the chance that he did not.

Rinnekh's growing fear was that Solban might be one of Rhydden's Black Destriers – the Emperor's most loyal and secret spies, and among his most deadly agents. Rinnekh was himself a Black Destrier, of course, being an imperial favourite; but he had never yet been called upon to do anything really dangerous or adventurous in his Emperor's service, and knew the identity of only one other Destrier – the Lord Priest Môrghran of Fâghsul. As a son of Dortrean, Solban was hardly the most likely choice for one of the Emperor's most trusted servants; but to Rinnekh's mind that only served to make the choice more probable. Solban's loyalty to the Empire was well proven. And if Rhydden did not trust Rinnekh to govern Ellanguan in his absence without Solban to watch over him, then Rinnekh's future favour with his Emperor might now rest in Dortrean's hands. The thought was far from pleasant.

A knock sounded, and Turill opened the door to admit a short man in robes of scarlet and white – the Truthsayer Baelar from the Temple of War. The man bowed before he approached, and Rinnekh unfolded his arms and held out one hand for him to kiss.

He had discovered Baelar while still heir designate to the

Steward's throne, and the man's services as Truthsayer had proved invaluable in Rinnekh's everyday dealings with the merchants and the business of governing Ellanguan. He had used him more rarely in dealings with other Lords of the Court Noble, or with the Southers, since it was tantamount to insult to question the word of one born of noble blood. Rinnekh had hesitated before deciding to command Baelar's attendance this evening. His presence alone, coupled with his priestly service to the *Vashtar*, would prove a goad to Trigharran. But Rinnekh doubted Trigharran's purpose, and had to be sure that he uncovered the whole truth of it.

'You are to read the truth in his words, not mine,' he reminded Baelar.

'My Lord,' said the priest, bowing again in acknowledgement.

Rinnekh motioned for him to stand behind a high-backed chair to the left of the hearth. Baelar pulled his hood forward over his face, so that only his cropped dark beard was visible beneath.

Rinnekh barely had time to take up his own position in front of the chair before the door opened again, and Master Trigharran came in. A young man in the grey of Kelmaar was guiding him from behind – the same man, Rinnekh realised, who had served as messenger earlier that afternoon. Turill stood watching in the doorway, until Rinnekh signalled for him to go outside and stand guard.

'Seldom do we come here now,' said Trigharran; 'and less welcome than of old.'

Though grown frail in body, his voice was clear and resonant as ever. Rinnekh scowled at the memories it conjured.

'There is a chair here waiting – Master,' he replied, gesturing to a seat across the hearth.

Trigharran wagged his head slowly from side to side, as if he were sniffing the air rather than trying to see with his milky blind eyes. The scant white hair drifting across his bald pate was fine as a young baby's. His wizened face was every bit as ugly as a baby's too, Rinnekh thought.

At length the old man tapped the heel of his grey staff on the floor just ahead of him, and his attendant brought out a small three-legged stool from behind his back and set it in place there. Then there was the brief ceremony of getting Trigharran seated comfortably on his stool, and arranging the grey shroud of his old robes around him. He sat there clutching his staff, watching blindly as Rinnekh himself sat down. The young attendant went down on one knee at Trigharran's side, his head bowed so that his face was hidden behind a heavy fall of dark hair.

'The Emperor is returning,' said Trigharran.

'Yes,' said Rinnekh carefully.

So much was known throughout the Steward's palace. Rhydden had left Arrandin three mornings since. Solban had informed him, but Rinnekh had already learned the news from High Councillor Sollonaal.

'The lay brother of the *Vashta* Order of Serbramel is dead,' said Trigharran.

'Yes,' said Rinnekh again.

News of the death of Sarin had also reached him – from those whom he had commanded to arrange it. He wondered whether Trigharran had guessed at the truth.

There was a stubborn silence between them. Rinnekh shifted in his chair, chill fear and smouldering impatience stirring within him.

'Is this all you have to tell me, *Master*?' he sneered at last. 'Or am I supposed to draw some imagined connection between these two facts?'

'He had a vision,' said Trigharran. 'Have you betrayed the Emperor?'

'Since when have the heathen Orders concerned themselves with the visions of the *Vashtar*?' Rinnekh countered. 'Besides, Sarin was clearly raving. And there is no question of my loyalty to the Emperor. That loyalty, if you recall, was your chief objection to my accession to the Steward's throne.'

'And the Southers?' prompted Trigharran.

'His Highness approves the peace,' said Rinnekh, 'and himself instructed me to achieve it. The Imperial Household Guard are here to ensure that it is kept – in support of my endeavours.'

'Then you have made no secret treaty of your own?'

The old man's voice was gentle, but slid deep as a knife straight into Rinnekh's heart. Rinnekh sat transfixed for a moment, breathless.

'Don't be absurd!' he snapped.

Trigharran turned his head toward the empty hearth.

'I have seen it,' he sighed. 'In my own meditations. You have set your hope in the strength of the Southers, against a time when Rhydden's love shall fail.'

'Their strength is vital in the cause against the Easterners, yes,' said Rinnekh hotly. 'But I serve Lautun, not the God-King. It is you, with your heathen lies, who are trying to drive a wedge between the Emperor and me. I don't doubt that the madman Sarin was your witless tool.'

Trigharran sat unmoved on his little stool – like an old speckled gull, ragged and wind-ruffled on his chosen perch.

'It is not too late to turn back,' he said quietly. 'I will say nothing outside this room.'

'Turn back from what?' Rinnekh scoffed.

Trigharran did not speak, but Rinnekh knew the answer. Nor could he deny to himself the truth of what Trigharran was saying. Though his own position in Ellanguan had grown strong in the past few years, should Rhydden turn against him, that strength would not be enough to save him. The Souther T'Loi and his warships, by similar token, had no guarantee of favour when they returned home to the God-King. The treaty and friendship between Rinnekh and T'Loi had thus largely been precipitated by their common need to survive. Rinnekh had no wish to betray his beloved Emperor – but he had begun to take thought of how to survive without him.

How much Trigharran knew from his dubious heathen arts, or how much he was still guessing based on long experience and cynicism, Rinnekh could not tell. What concerned him more at that moment was the fact that Trigharran had offered to remain silent. From the first, Kelmaar had objected even to the very notion that Rinnekh might hold the Stewardship of Ellanguan. They would hardly cast aside such an opportunity to discredit him in the Emperor's eyes – unless they thought it to their better advantage to hold the threat of exposure against him, like a knife to the throat.

'You say you will not spread these lies further,' he said scornfully. 'But no doubt this silence comes at a price?'

'There is no price,' said Trigharran, shaking his head. 'It is not too late to turn back. For the sake of Ellanguan. For your own sake. Others of my Order do not know of this yet. Kelmaar does not seek her own gain. I have come in secret, so that your choice may remain a matter between the gods and yourself alone.'

'And you,' Rinnekh pointed out. 'Though I could have you killed here and now, to put an end to this.'

The young attendant jerked up his head, his face made curiously more handsome by the flare of anger and defiance. Trigharran rested one hand on his arm.

'It is not too late,' he repeated calmly.

Rinnekh frowned. Trigharran's quiet confidence unsettled him – which put him further out of temper, and made him hate the old man even more than usual. The conversation was going nowhere.

'So what do you suggest I do?' he said. He let exasperation and frustration roughen his voice, with a note of helplessness that was not altogether feigned. Perhaps by showing weakness he could lull Trigharran into revealing how much he really knew.

'What you must, to serve Ellanguan,' Trigharran answered unhelpfully.

The old man signalled to his attendant and clambered slowly to his feet. Rinnekh stood up and clapped his hands twice. Turill appeared in the doorway.

Trigharran nodded in Rinnekh's direction, and turned to go

without further ceremony. His grey-clad attendant sketched a more formal bow, and then hastened to guide the Master safely out of the chamber. Rinnekh stood still and watched them go, clasping his hands together as if still torn by uncertainty. He dropped the pretence the moment the door was closed.

'Did he lie about Kelmaar not knowing of his errand?' he demanded.

'He believes what he has seen in his own meditations, my Lord,' Baelar answered. 'He believes that none other knew of this visit, nor of its purpose – save for ourselves, and the youth that accompanied him.'

The hidden door in the panelled wall had already opened again. The Souther Ambassador T'Loi came in, his golden robes fluttering like windblown flames.

'Good,' said Rinnekh. 'I want them both dead before they reach the Kelmaar School.'

'My Lord,' said Baelar, bowing.

'A pity,' said T'Loi. 'A few more days, and their deaths might have been put to better purpose. But to hold them would not do. There would be questions.'

'This serves *my* purpose,' said Rinnekh pointedly.

'There will likely be questions anyway,' Baelar ventured.

'Then we'll have something to talk about tomorrow,' said Rinnekh. 'Now go and tell Turill.'

The Truthsayer hurried away. Rinnekh tugged at his collar again, trying to arrange it more comfortably over the small pendant and chain which lay hidden beneath.

'Will this Kelmaar Order cause trouble, do you think?' asked T'Loi.

'When don't they?' Rinnekh gave a mocking laugh. 'But trust me – they will find nothing to link the old man's death to us.'

'And if others receive this vision from his gods?'

'Then we scuttle their ship and burn it,' said Rinnekh. 'No one who fears the Emperor would dare piss on them to save them.'

*　　*　　*

303

Karlena of Dortrean was not fully dressed the next morning when there was a knock at her door and a flustered Lisella came hurrying in.

It was not particularly early. Beyond the latticed windows of the Dortrean apartment the pearled grey of the overnight sea mists had all but vanished from the upper city, and the day was turning fine and warm; and Karlena – though not formally attired for waiting on the Empress – was already quite presentable. She had bathed, and put on a dressing gown of creamy white satin, edged with deep borders of full-blown roses embroidered over a leafy tracery of fine Telbray lace.

A single, deep-voiced bell was still sounding from the great dome of the Temple of Sherunar, further to the west. But the dawn rites there should have been long finished, and the continued tolling had made Karlena restless. Fearing that some death or misadventure had befallen through the night, she had sent her serving woman out to gather news. It seemed that she had found her answer sooner than expected.

Close at Lisella's heels – and hardly waiting for the house-hold woman to announce her – followed the Lady Melissa of Vanbruch. Karlena closed up the small codex that she had been reading and laid it on the table beside her, wrapped in its protective silk shawl. She rose to greet her guest.

'I was not certain that you would still be here,' said Melissa, pausing briefly to make courtesy before sweeping forward to kiss her.

'The Empress does not sleep well of nights, in the city heat,' Karlena explained. 'I have the luxury of a few hours to myself before my presence is required.'

She was not as fond of kissing as Melissa, but she did not make an issue of it that morning. Melissa was arrayed in the formal black of her house, rather than her preferred pinks and greys – a sober gown, adorned only with two small winged horses worked in copper thread upon the high collar.

'Then you have not heard the news?' Melissa demanded. 'Old

304

Trigharran has been found – murdered in the street, and his guard with him.'

'Murdered?' echoed Karlena. Lisella gave a little gasp of dismay.

Before Melissa could answer there was the sound of booted feet on the stone floor, and Solban of Dortrean came in through the doorway. The flash of brown and gold behind him warned of other imperial guards in the outer chamber.

'You will excuse us, Lady Melissa,' he said.

Melissa glanced at Karlena. But Solban's stern manner would brook no argument.

'I shall not keep you long,' Karlena told her quietly.

Melissa made her a courtesy and went away, dropping a second courtesy to Solban as she passed. Karlena signalled for Lisella to go with her.

'To what do I owe the pleasure of a visit from my son?' she said. 'You are on duty, I take it?'

'I am,' Solban nodded. 'I shall try to keep this as pleasant as possible.'

He shut the door firmly, so that the two of them were alone. Karlena sat herself down again.

'A lovely creature, Melissa,' she said. 'I should not have minded having her for a daughter, had either of you been minded to ask.'

'Her heart was set on Kellarn, I recall,' said Solban. 'But that is beside the point.'

'Then what is the point?' asked Karlena. She gestured to a nearby chair, for him to be seated. 'Are you here to tell me about Trigharran?'

He showed no surprise that she had heard the news. He knew his mother too well. He moved toward the chair, but remained standing.

'Not exactly,' he said. 'The Emperor is expected, either tomorrow or the day after. I am here to ask you to leave the Steward's palace.'

'To leave?'

Karlena had considered the possibility, and even the advisability, of withdrawing from Rinnekh's palace. But that had been some days ago, before the arrival of Solban and the Imperial Household Guard had served to make her own position more secure. It was not a request that she had expected to hear from her son's lips.

'I have spoken with the Lord Steward,' Solban told her. 'Under the circumstances, he has agreed that it might be best for you to stay with friends or kinsmen in the Nobles' Quarter for the next several days. He sends his apologies.'

Karlena snorted. She could well imagine that Rinnekh would jump at any opportunity to be rid of her.

'What circumstances?' she asked. 'Rhydden has his own apartment here. Or am I to be turfed out for one of his army commanders?'

Solban sighed. 'An envoy from the Northern Lands is approaching Ellanguan,' he said aloud – almost, Karlena thought, as though he expected someone outside to be listening. 'They will be guested here in the palace. With the presence of the Southers, the Lord Steward can not spare the guards to ensure your safety.'

'And I should be safer in the Nobles' Quarter than in the Steward's own palace?' Karlena countered.

Solban said nothing. It was a lame excuse, and they both knew it.

'Elmirra has offered me the use of the Ercusí house,' she offered after a moment, 'though few of her own people will be there. Or did you have it in mind that I should stay with the Empress?'

'Her Serene Highness is provided for,' Solban returned. He hesitated, shifting his weight on his feet.

'Actually,' he added, in a much lower voice, 'I thought that you could move to the Renza house.'

Karlena smiled, and gestured again for him to sit down. Her son's regular visits to the widowed young Lady of Renza had not entirely escaped her attention, and she could read his moods as easily as his father's. He had grown fond of Lauraï; and with the death of Trigharran, he was clearly more concerned for Lauraï's safety than her own. To Karlena's knowledge, Lauraï had brought no guards with her. Renza and Kelmaar were traditional allies; but for Lauraï to take shelter with the priests of Kelmaar might only place her in greater danger. Nor was it prudent to bring her into the Steward's palace when she was already at odds with Rinnekh. Solban had few enough guards of his own to spare. Thus his readiest answer was to send his own mother to look after her.

'What strength of defence does the Renza household have here?' she asked.

'None to speak of,' said Solban. 'A few of her father's people of Raudhar, at best.'

Karlena nodded. There was also the possibility that Lauraï's aunt, the Archmage Ellen of Raudhar, might be prevailed upon to watch over her niece. But Karlena knew little of Ellen's doings, or whether she was even in the city; and besides, she thought it was Lauraï's business to approach the Magi for help, should she choose to do so.

'Then perhaps,' she said, 'I should move to the Vanbruch city house. I am sure that the Lady Melissa will be agreeable. She is well provided with armed guards. And I have no doubt that if the Lady of Renza wishes to join us there, she would be made most welcome.'

Solban's face softened further, into a shy smile of relief.

'Thank you,' he said.

'So what can you tell me about Trigharran?' prompted Karlena. 'Are we all in danger?'

Solban shrugged, and his face grew serious again.

'Not much,' he said. 'Not yet. The city guard found him last night, lying dead in the street just beyond the Old Temple Square. There was a young man of his Order found with him. The Steward has commanded a full enquiry – and I expect Kelmaar are asking questions of their own. At the moment it appears that the two of them were abroad after the sunset curfew, and that they were fell upon, murdered and robbed.'

'But that is terrible,' said Karlena. 'Who in Ellanguan would do such a thing?'

'Quite,' Solban agreed. 'Two holy men of Kelmaar are no target for an Ellanguan thief – and even the meanest street urchin might have spared one as old as Trigharran, even if they did not recognise him. There are already rumours that it was the work of hired killers. And not a few tongues have been quick to voice the thought that we have a harbour full of Southers at present. That puts an added strain on the whole business of this agreement with T'Loi, just before the Emperor arrives. And if the city takes it into its head that the Southers are responsible, we could have a riot down at the harbour front – or even at the palace doors.'

'But not in the Nobles' Quarter,' Karlena nodded.

On the other hand, she thought to herself, if this were in truth the work of the assassin brotherhoods, then nowhere in the city would be truly safe for the next appointed victim.

'I shall speak with Melissa at once,' she said, rising. 'But poor Trigharran! This is a sad day in the long history of Ellanguan.'

'Let us pray that it gets no worse,' said Solban. He hesitated a moment, and then came forward to kiss her.

'There is rumour,' he murmured quietly in her ear, 'that Trigharran came to the palace last night. Had you heard?'

Karlena shook her head as they parted. The trail of her son's thought was clear. It was possible that Trigharran had tried to meddle in Rinnekh's affairs, and so come to an untimely end. The same fate might befall Lauraï, or anyone else who crossed the Steward's path. It was a danger that Karlena had acknowledged ever since the Emperor had left Ellanguan on the eve of war; but this was the first proof of how close that danger might really be.

'I shall speak with Melissa,' she said again. 'But I shall expect you to come and visit us, when you are off duty.'

Solban went away again, taking his guardsmen with him.

Melissa, who had been hovering anxiously nearby, came hurrying back with Lisella. She was relieved to discover that Karlena was in no great trouble, and seemed only too pleased to have the Countess stay at her city house – especially when she learned that neither Rinnekh nor the Imperial Household Guard would be likely to hold it against her. Karlena left Melissa to arrange the move with Lisella and the Vanbruch household. It was agreed that Lisella should also go there. From her evident distress at the news of Trigharran's death, Karlena wondered whether the serving woman might have stronger sympathies with the heathen *Aeshta* faith than her mistress of Ercusí realised.

More than an hour had passed before Karlena was fully dressed and ready to attend the Empress. She had put on her high-collared gown of mulberry linen, and Melissa had provided her with a sash of deep grey silk to wear in token of mourning for the departed Trigharran. Karlena was not altogether surprised to find that an armed guard had also been provided to escort her to the Emperor's city house, clad in the copper and black of the Vanbruch livery. The temple bell was still tolling.

The Empress' household was a hive of activity when Karlena arrived, busy with preparations for the Emperor's return and buzzing with speculation over the morning's news. Grinnaer herself was in her preferred circular turret room, playing with a small honey-coloured spaniel pup – a recent gift from one of the Ellanguan merchants. Her mood was distracted and difficult. She blamed the heat, and a poor night's rest. She blamed the puppy for a chewed, soggy circle in the primrose silk of her loose-fitting gown. She blamed Goshaún for the newly scrubbed patch on the floor where the puppy had become over-excited and messed himself; and she blamed Karlena because Solban had been so gloomy and serious with his Empress over the whole business of Trigharran. The fact that Trigharran had been murdered seemed to be of little consequence to Grinnaer – but then she was not in the habit of venturing out into the city streets after dark herself, nor was she troubled by an over-active imagination.

Karlena had not been there long before the Empress grew tired of the spaniel and told Goshaún to take him away; and once Goshaún had gone, she gestured irritably for her remaining household women to make themselves scarce. Then she drew Karlena over to the deep window seat on the eastern side of the room, and they sat down.

'I'm late,' she said.

Her voice was low, furtive. Karlena had no need to ask what she was talking about. Ever since Grinnaer's marriage to the Emperor the previous winter, all the Empire must have been waiting for news of just such a sign that Rhydden was indeed to be blessed with another heir. Her eyebrows went up in silent question.

'How late?' she asked practically.

'Three or four days,' Grinnaer shrugged. 'Or five or six weeks. I missed the last one.'

Her mood seemed more apprehensive than elated – but then, given her position, that was perhaps only to be expected.

'Did you say anything, the last time?' Karlena asked her.

'To my household women,' Grinnaer nodded. 'And one of the priestesses of Hýrsien – Tannaïa, I think – came to look at me. They said I had just missed a cycle. It has happened before.'

From her dealings with the previous Empress, Karlena had no great faith in the skills of the *Vashta* priestesses when it came to the business of motherhood and childbirth. But there were women enough of good experience within Grinnaer's household, so that she supposed they would have had the right of it.

'And there have been no other signs?' she wondered. 'No sickness, or increased appetite? Dizziness—'

The Empress sighed and turned her head away, looking out through the window. 'I thought that perhaps it was just the city heat,' she said uncertainly.

Karlena followed her gaze toward the great round tower of

the Ercusí house, further along the street, and to the bright green ridges of the Tumbling Hills peeping above the many roofs and turrets of the Nobles' Quarter. The Emperor would be riding back through those hills in the next few days, returning from Arrandin and the aftermath of the war. Whether Grinnaer would be much comforted by her husband's return was a very debatable point – though if she were now carrying his child, Rhydden might at least make the effort to show her some simple kindness and attention, which had thus far been sadly lacking in their marriage.

To an extent, Karlena pitied the Empress' plight – craving affection from a husband unwilling, or unable, to give it to her; anxious to provide him with the heir for which he had so evidently married her. Desperately afraid that she might fail. Perhaps afraid, also, of the unknown ordeals of being with child and giving birth for the first time. Indeed, it seemed to Karlena that Grinnaer was almost looking for reassurance that she could *not* be with child. The implications of that thought were unsettling. Karlena hesitated for several heartbeats, uncertain how to proceed.

'Grinnaer,' she said gently, 'when did Rhydden last visit your bed?'

'A while ago,' answered the Empress, in a very small voice. 'Three, four months, perhaps.'

Karlena covered Grinnaer's pink hand briefly with her own. It was not impossible that Grinnaer now carried Rhydden's child. Other daughters of the Court Noble had been known to carry almost to full term with scarcely an outward sign to betray their expectant motherhood; and Grinnaer was perhaps inexperienced enough not to be able to guess for herself with any certainty. Karlena thought it less likely that the Empress' serving women and the priestess of Hýrsien would have missed the pregnancy, if they had examined Grinnaer when she missed her last monthly cycle. Unlikely, but not impossible. She would have set greater weight on the judgement of an *Aeshta* priestess in such matters.

The other possibility, now growing rapidly in Karlena's mind, was that it was not Rhydden's child that Grinnaer thought she might be carrying. Why else, after all, would they be having this conversation? And she could already guess who that other father might be.

'Is there someone else?' she demanded, looking straight at her.

Grinnaer began to shake her chestnut head. But then she bit her lip, and nodded once in confirmation.

'Not—?' Karlena glanced meaningfully at the doorway where Goshaún had gone out only a short time ago.

Grinnaer had at least the decency to hang her head in shame. Though not altogether surprised – and upbraiding herself for not having recognised the warning signs the sooner – Karlena was still shocked that her guess had proved correct.

Such union between brother and sister was of course not unheard of among the low-born of the Six Kingdoms – nor even among those of Blood Noble – though it was held unwise for the getting of children. The Blood Laws which governed the succession of the Houses Noble sternly proscribed any marriage between such close kin. The priests of the *Vashtar* condemned it as loathsome and unnatural.

Grinnaer was hardly the first wife in the Six Kingdoms to play her husband false; but as Empress she was courting treason by doing so. Karlena had the fleeting, whimsical thought that should Grinnaer indeed give birth to Goshaún's child, at least the false parentage would not be readily apparent, in that the baby would simply be deemed to take after its mother's family. But the whole notion was appalling. And should Grinnaer try to pass her brother's child off as Rhydden's – thus supplanting the ancient imperial bloodline with her own – she could only be doubly damned in the eyes of the Court Noble.

Karlena could imagine how Rhydden's neglect of Grinnaer had driven her to seek comfort in a lover's arms; and she could in part understand why she might have turned to Goshaún. But whomever Grinnaer might have chosen, Karlena's present need would have been the same. She must discover the full truth of the matter at once, and put a stop to it.

'How long?' she demanded.

'Only since the Emperor left for Arrandin,' Grinnaer told her. 'And then not for a few days. It's too soon, isn't it?'

Karlena frowned, thinking. Rhydden had been gone barely three weeks. Too short a time for even a priestess of the Môshári to be certain – unless Grinnaer had in truth been carrying Rhydden's child for three or four months, with no one the wiser. She would have to find someone suitable to look at Grinnaer, as soon as possible; and persuade Grinnaer to let herself be examined.

'This will have to stop, you know,' she said, as kindly as she could. 'If Rhydden finds out, he'll have both your heads for it.'

'You wouldn't dare tell!' said Grinnaer, suddenly fierce.

Try me! thought Karlena, with answering force.

'You'll go down as well,' added Grinnaer spitefully. 'You were the one who was meant to be watching over me.'

Karlena did not bother to point out that there were many servants in the imperial household who probably saw and heard far more of the Empress' doings than Grinnaer might have given them credit for, and some of whom would no doubt be all too eager to whisper her shortcomings in the Emperor's ear; so that whether Karlena herself kept silent or not might make little enough difference. What Grinnaer had said was undoubtedly true. It would give Rhydden a lawful excuse at last to have Karlena's head for treason, if it suited his purpose. Whether she sought to save Grinnaer or to denounce her, her own head was already upon the block. She wondered whether Rhydden had foreseen this, before he entrusted the Empress to her care. Or if not Rhydden, then his scheming Archmage. It had the feel of one of Merrech's moves. How could she have let herself be caught so easily, after so many years of working against him?

Whatever the frailty of their position, Karlena had mixed feelings toward Grinnaer. She found her a weak creature, too self-absorbed and lacking in moral strength to fulfil her role as

Empress Consort; so that one might hardly blame the Emperor for wanting to be rid of her. Yet mingled with the disdain was pity, and some measure of affection. The gift of motherhood – to Rhydden's children, not Goshaún's – might be the making of Grinnaer. Karlena could not find it in her heart to deny her the chance to prove herself.

'I want a priestess to examine you properly,' she told Grinnaer, 'so that we know where we stand. Will you permit that?'

There was a final flicker of defiance in the Empress' eyes. Then she quietened down, and nodded sulkily.

'And what if I am – with child?' Grinnaer faltered.

Karlena took her by the hand again. If it were Rhydden's child, there would be no problem. If not – it was not altogether unheard of for the healers of the *Aeshta* Orders to end a pregnancy in the very early stages, if the well being of the mother depended upon it, and if they could do so in clear conscience before the gods. What effect the loss of Goshaún's child might have upon Grinnaer, Karlena could only begin to guess. She would have to speak privately with the priestess beforehand.

'Let's not borrow troubles before we have them,' she replied. 'It may be nothing more than the summer heat.'

The door opened, and Goshaún slipped quietly inside. He slunk across the room toward them with his head down, trying to avoid Karlena's gaze. It was clear that he knew what they had been talking about; and looking at the pair of them, Karlena guessed that they had made the decision together to tell her. She was not sure that she found the thought comforting.

'For now,' she told Grinnaer, 'we need to get the Emperor back into your bed as soon as possible, so you can at least have the chance of providing him with an heir. If we can persuade him to like you, so much the better.'

There was an element of deception in the plan which Karlena did not like; but she set it aside, persuading herself that it was only right for the Emperor to sleep with his consort.

They could worry about any other complications as and when they arose.

Grinnaer's eyes brimmed with tears, now looking desperately forlorn. Goshaún also looked far from happy.

'But how?' Grinnaer asked.

Karlena had no ready answer.

'We could get him drunk,' suggested Goshaún, trying to sound lighthearted.

It occurred to Karlena that there might be a better chance of getting Rhydden into the Empress' bed if Goshaún were lying waiting beside her. But she also put that thought firmly out of her mind.

'And you,' she told Goshaún, 'will stay well away from your sister. If that means getting on the next ship out of Ellanguan, then you do it. Is that understood?'

His half-hearted grin faltered, and his eyes filled with tears.

'Oh can't we just die and get it over with?' wailed Grinnaer.

'No,' said Karlena firmly. 'We are not dead yet.' She reached out, and took Goshaún by the hand also. 'This is but the Realm of Shadows. The pain will seem unbearable, and the grief inconsolable. But we shall fight, and we shall come out alive.'

She looked from one to the other, willing them to accept her strength; and then she pulled Goshaún down beside her, so that the three of them sat huddled together on the window seat.

'But how can we survive?' asked Grinnaer.

'Hush now,' said Karlena. 'We'll think of something.'

Chapter Ten

When Kellarn awoke, the only light was the pale creamy gold of Corollin's magic. The forest all around was in darkness. He crawled out of his blanket wrappings and stood up, trying to shake the chill stiffness from his arms and legs. Corollin and Kôril were moving about quietly, and already there was the rustling and calling of birds greeting the new day overhead.

They saw to the horses as well as they could, and ate a meagre breakfast standing, and then set off again through the deep forest shadow. None of them was much in the mood for talking. Kellarn took Rúnfyr again, since he seemed more settled now, and Kôril led the way with the bay mare Lanaë.

The path had been made by Heruvor's folk of Starmere and was used by them, and Kellarn supposed that they must tend it after their own fashion; but it was less well kept than most paths in the Six Kingdoms, and not suited for heavy horses. At times it seemed little more than an old badger trail, picking its way over tree roots and under ground elder, all but hidden in the gloom. Then at other times the trees would draw back and it became a broad track, where they could mount up and ride for a short way before having to climb down and lead the horses again. All in all it was slow going.

They had been travelling for some hours when they fought their way down a last, difficult bank, thick with hazel bushes, and came into a narrow dell with a small stream running west across the line of the path. The sky overhead was now a deep summer blue, and the upper branches and treetops shone bright as green flame in the mid-morning sunlight; and in the shaded hollow of the dell, the borders of the stream were rich with rushes and grass and garlanded with large buttercup flowers of yellow and gold.

As if prompted by some common instinct, the three horses shouldered their way to the right, toward a patch of clearer ground with pebbles and rocks at the water's edge. Kôril was content to let them go. It was a journey of some seven leagues or more from here to the Blue River which flowed down from the vale of Starmere, and there would be few enough chances to find clean water along the way.

They stopped to rest, and filled their waterskins from the stream. Kellarn sat down on one of the larger rocks, stretching his legs out before him. Corollin stepped over to the far bank and wandered a little way upstream.

From here, Kellarn knew, they could follow the winding course of the stream eastward, back up to the valley cleft where it leaped down from the heights of the Blue Mountains; and climbing up to the head of that valley would bring them to the mountain path which led south and east above Deadmen's Green, and then on at last to the hidden Valley of Two Waters. Corollin had been studying in that valley when the war with the Easterners began; and although she had agreed to come with him to Starmere, he wondered whether she might now be wanting to change her mind.

He kept watch on her discreetly as she stood gazing east toward the mountains, her white staff clasped lightly between her two hands. She stood there for some minutes, as if lost in her own thoughts. Then she smiled and gave a half bow – though Kellarn had no idea to whom, or to what – and came back down across the stream to join him.

'What is it?' asked Kôril, before Kellarn could think what to say.

'Fond memories,' said Corollin, 'nothing more.'

'You're quite happy to go to Starmere?' Kellarn asked her.

'Of course,' she laughed. 'Why should I not be? Besides, going back to the valley would be of little help just now. We need to hunt for the bars.'

'Yes,' said Kôril. 'To find each of the artefact pieces so far, a time of roughly ninety days has passed. If the pattern holds true, we should find the next before this present moon grows old and dies.'

'That doesn't give us much time,' said Kellarn.

'Neither will the old Enemy,' said Corollin.

'And yet, if the pattern holds after that,' said Kellarn, frowning, 'it would be another six months before we had all six bars – that's if there are six bars to find, one for each of the old kings. That seems an awfully long time.'

'But less time, perhaps, than it would take the Easterners to raise another army,' said Corollin. 'All we can do is search hard, and trust the gods to set our feet on the right paths.'

'I suppose so,' said Kellarn.

He stood up, dusting the moss from the seat of his breeches.

'And when we've found all the pieces,' he said, 'shall we be able to use them?'

'I do not know,' Corollin answered. 'That is another reason why we need to speak with Heruvor.'

They collected the horses and set off again, crossing the stream and climbing an easier bank overgrown with tall mallows on the far side of the dell. After that the path ran clear for a good while; though they were back in the green shadow of the forest, with no glimpse of the sky through the thick canopy overhead.

Their mood had lightened after reaching the familiar landmark of the dell. Corollin was now more lively and alert, like a child counting the miles on the last lap of the journey home. Kôril also seemed brighter, and somehow more focused; though since he was concentrating on following the path it was difficult to tell.

Kellarn himself had begun to feel that curious inner churning of joy and terror which usually came to him before any meeting with the elvenfolk of the Fay. It was true that he seldom felt it now with Kôril, except at odd, unexpected moments; and at least he had the comfort of having met with Heruvor before, and being assured of his good will toward them. Nevertheless, the feeling was something more akin to the excitement of riding out to battle than to the joy of coming home.

The path now led them up and down across gentle slopes for a couple of miles, with the ground climbing fairly steadily over the hidden roots of a mountain spur. Near to the stream there were signs of many forest creatures – wild boar and polecats, squirrels and all kinds of birds. But as they moved further north the forest around them grew quieter, and the trails of passing animals became more scarce.

At one point Kellarn caught sight of what he guessed to be a flock of birds, away to the right of the path. They were large and dark, with the flickering flight of bats, and silent as hunting owls. He asked Corollin what they were, but she had no better idea than he; and when they asked Kôril he replied simply that they should keep their eyes on the path.

The day outside wore on, and the air beneath the trees grew heavy and damp. The path grew narrow again, though it kept to its straight course up and down the rolling folds of the land. Apart from their own footfalls and the noise of the horses, the only sound was the endless stirring of the breeze through the tree tops high overhead.

It was the sound of the wind through the leaves – so Kellarn had been told – that gave the Whispering Forest its name; and it held a hidden peril for the unwary traveller. The constant ebb and flow of the rustling leaves lulled the hearer into a sense of peace, or into the forgetfulness of a daydream, in which it would be all too easy to wander away from the path and become lost. At times he overheard Corollin humming to herself – strange, discordant melodies, which he guessed she was using to rally her own thoughts against the distraction of the whispering leaves. But when he tried to do the same, it only seemed to make matters worse.

Kellarn's greatest help, in the end, came from the horses. The forest seemed to have calmed the beasts to the point of making them slow and sluggish, so that they showed little interest in moving at all. The effort of leading Rúnfyr forward, matching the horse's stubbornness with his own, somehow lent Kellarn the strength of will to carry on.

Whether Heruvor himself had commanded the whispering magic of the leaves, or whether it was a natural defence of the forest itself, Kellarn did not know. What he did know was that after they had reached the Blue River, they would encounter many spells of beguiling and enchantment woven by the moon fay among the trees. The folk of Starmere referred to those magics simply as the Nets, and they formed a defensive barrier perilous to humankind.

Without Kôril to guide them, and the good will of Heruvor himself to let them pass, Kellarn and Corollin might have had little hope of finding their way through the Nets. In the long history of the Six Kingdoms only a handful of humans had ever reached the secret lake of Starmere, though many more had tried in vain. Those who failed returned disappointed to the world outside, if they were fortunate; or else wandered witless through the forest until starvation – or some worse fate – overtook them.

Torkhaal balanced the small codex on his knees and flicked through the pages with deft, gloved fingers. A stack of four or five other bound volumes lay waiting on the table beside him, and Dhûghaúr was now returning a similar number to their proper places on the golden oak shelves somewhere at the far end of the Lower Library. They had proved to be of no use. In his own mind, Torkhaal was not sure that any of the books here would be of much use in their search for references to the ancient Enemy, or to his foretold return. But for Hrugaar's sake he had agreed to help Dhûghaúr that afternoon, once his lecturing duties were over.

Hrugaar had already checked the few texts to which the Warden of the College Libraries had directed him; devoured them – mentally, rather than physically – found nothing of help beyond that which they already knew, and then moved on to forage through the reserve collection in the *aumery* library upstairs. But though the *aumery* was rich pasture for studies concerning the Council of Magi and their Art, it offered scant pickings on the subject of a demonic adversary banished from the world even before the founding of the Old Kingdoms. Or at least, if anything was there, it had eluded him. So now they had widened their search to include the diverse treatises and protocols, collections of lore and fable, and even heroic romances, held upon the shelves of the Lower Library.

He was disturbed from his work by the sudden appearance of a shrouded figure, directly across the table from him. With the familiar outline of dark hooded robes, Torkhaal might have thought it was simply Dhûghaúr or one of the shorter magi – but the prickle of hairs rising on the back of his neck warned him otherwise. He flicked his gaze up quickly, shifting the weight of the codex to one hand. But then the figure lifted back her hood to reveal a cascade of soft golden curls, shimmering in the late afternoon sunlight. It was Ilumarin of Aranara.

'What are you doing here?' he demanded, scrambling to his feet.

It was hardly the correct manner in which to greet a Chosen Priestess. But visitors to the College were seldom left unattended, and never whilst they were within the hallowed confines of the libraries. Ilumarin seemed not to mind.

'Your Warden knows of my presence,' she assured him, bowing in greeting with a sign of *Aeshta* blessing. 'Besides, I am not truly *here*, within the waking world. Only in your thought.'

She glanced around wistfully at the many coloured books upon the shelves, like a child in the feast hall before the guests arrive – permitted to look, but not to touch. Then she made a diffident gesture with her left hand, as though she would feel more comfortable if Torkhaal sat down again. After a moment, he did so.

'*Why* are you here?' he asked carefully.

It side-stepped the question of *how*, which was still unsettling him. The College buildings – and the libraries in particular – were wound about with many spells to prevent such visitations. He would have to ask the Warden about it later.

'You have heard about Trigharran,' she said.

'Yes,' said Torkhaal. Hrugaar had gone down to Ellanguan that morning to help the priests of Kelmaar in trying to discover the truth about Trigharran's death, and was to stay there for the Rite of Burning at sunset. He had returned, briefly, at noon to report that most of the answers still eluded them; and that even though the priests had spoken with Trigharran himself, as he tarried in the First Realm of the Dead, the old man had refused to say anything concerning the manner of his departing.

'I can tell you no more of that,' said Ilumarin, following his thought; 'and that is not my errand.'

'Which reminds me,' said Torkhaal, 'how did you know about Hrugaar, when last we met?'

'I did not know,' she answered. 'We knew that Tinûkenil was nearby, and that he might have the skill to heal him; and that Hrugaar might – or might not – make the choice to return to the waking world. There was a possibility. *All foretellings are vague, and their interpretation uncertain.*'

She wrinkled her nose in a playful grin. She had a very pretty nose, Torkhaal thought.

'You sound as though you have been talking with Carstan Mairdun,' he growled.

'When we sought for news of Trigharran,' said Ilumarin, 'other tidings found us. She whom you name Illana has but recently entered the First Realm of the Dead.'

'Illana?' cried Torkhaal. 'But how is that possible? She should have died a thousand years ago.'

Ilumarin shrugged, but made no answer.

'It is feared,' she went on, 'that rather than journey forward, as is fitting for the Dead, she may seek to return; or perhaps even to be born again into the waking world, bringing the memories of her last life with her. And whilst she tarries in the First Realm, there are those who might try to reach her and question her with their arts, for no good purpose.'

Torkhaal thought at once of the Archmage Merrech. Illana had been one of the most gifted magi in all the history of the Six Kingdoms, and one of the most evil; and His Eminence seemed all but obsessed with Illana and the unsolved mysteries of her greatest work, the *Argument of Command*. Merrech's personal conflict with Rhysana had first come about when Rhysana herself had begun to study Illana's lore.

'This knowledge could prove perilous,' Ilumarin nodded, 'should it fall into mischievous hands.'

Torkhaal glanced around the library. There was no sign of Dhûghaúr, nor sight nor sound of anyone but themselves – not even, he thought, the *chaedar*.

'And why are you telling me?' he asked.

'You are Rhysana's husband,' said Ilumarin. 'My errand was to her. But she is with your son. And besides, in her condition, the shock of the tidings should be broken gently. You were the better choice.'

In her condition. The words triggered the memory of something she had said only a short time before. His stomach knotted in sudden panic.

'Our baby—' he began.

'No,' she assured him quickly. 'Only a few weeks can have passed in the waking world since Illana first arrived in the Realms of the Dead. You gave life to your child long before that.'

'And why are you telling Rhysana?' Torkhaal was still uneasy.

Ilumarin dropped her gaze to the table between them.

'We debated long before agreeing to do so,' she said. 'As with the Fay, those who have dealings with us often find themselves changed, and grow estranged from those around them.'

She had taken the question in a way other than he had intended; but Torkhaal sensed that he would get no further with her upon that point. And already she was lifting her hood again, and turning to go.

'My Lady,' he said, calling her back. She turned her face toward him.

'We have been looking for older foretellings of – of the Enemy's return,' he said awkwardly. 'You seem to have knowledge of such things. Can you help us in this?'

Ilumarin tilted her head slightly as she considered the question.

'So much I may say,' she said at last. 'In one sense, the Enemy already has returned – in that his own power has grown again, and he now has servants who call upon him and give him a first foothold in the waking world. True, the power that he grants them now is only a shadow of the power and terror he would wield, should a way be opened for the Enemy himself to enter the waking world again. But as long as he has servants with any means of power, that danger remains.'

'So the servants are the problem?' he asked.

'Perhaps what you are looking for is not what you seek,' said Ilumarin. She smiled, and faded from his sight.

Torkhaal leaned back in his chair, suddenly tired. He drummed his fingers irritably on the forgotten codex.

'Still no luck?' asked Dhûghaúr, appearing at his elbow. He made no mention of Ilumarin's visit, and Torkhaal did not think that he had been aware of her.

'No,' Torkhaal sighed, pulling himself upright again. 'I am beginning to wonder if we are barking up the wrong tree.'

'Perhaps we shall know what we are looking for, when we find it,' said Dhûghaúr.

Twilight came early beneath the boughs of the Whispering Forest, and for the last hour or more of their journey Kellarn and his friends had to rely on the pale golden light shining from Corollin's staff. With the endless murmuring of the leaves and the tired stubbornness of the horses, Kellarn had lost track of how far they might have come; but Kôril seemed unhappy with their slow pace, and had urged them to one more mile before they stopped for the night. At least it would shorten their journey the following day.

They made a small fire on a clear patch of ground, with four large beech trees standing at their backs and as fair a view as they could manage ahead and behind along the path. Kellarn chewed his supper with little interest, trying to bring some sense of order to his drifting thoughts.

'What happens if we can't use this thing, when we have found all the pieces?' he asked aloud.

'Let's not borrow troubles before we have them,' said Corollin. 'And as I said before, that is something which we can ask Heruvor when we see him.'

'It has been given to us to find some of the pieces,' said Kôril. 'It may be given to others to find others, and perhaps other hands again will wield this thing when it is made. We play but a small part in the great pattern woven by the gods.'

Kellarn found the answer strangely irritating.

'You mean we'll have to give it to the Magi,' he said, 'or to the priests?'

Kôril shrugged.

'The priests are perhaps more likely,' said Corollin. 'As far as we know, the powers of the *Aeshta* Orders are closer to the magics used by the founders of the Old Kingdoms. The arts of the Council of Magi have changed much more over the years. The early kings seem to have been like priests, or holy knights, with great powers of mind and will; but much of what they did still remains a mystery. I am hoping that Heruvor can tell us more about it.'

'Though their powers were other than those of the Fay,' Kôril reminded them.

'What about the lore of Zedron?' asked Kellarn. 'Has that taught you any more about it?'

'I do not know,' Corollin sighed. 'Zedron came five hundred years after Ferrughôr, at the end of the Wars of Power, and his lore is different again. He makes mention of the *syldhar* as his source – a magical race, more like dragons than anything else, from what I can tell. But even less is known about them.'

'Besides, even Heruvor can sense no magic in the three bars that we have found,' said Kôril. 'It could be that the object which they make is no device of power at all. It might be a weapon to wield in the hand – perhaps even a sword for Kellarn.'

The fay smiled in the firelight. In spite of his misgivings, Kellarn found himself grinning back; and the mood of the camp grew easier again.

They settled to sleep soon after that, lulled by the song of the leaves. If Kellarn dreamed, he did not remember it. When Kôril woke them, several hours later, the night had grown old and the murmuring of the trees had faded almost to silence on the cool air. The fay had kept watch alone while they slept, but he showed no sign of weariness.

They broke their fast with hot tea and hard oatcakes, and then set off in the darkness, guided once more by the light from Corollin's staff. The path now ran down again into a broad, shallow vale, and the trees grew tall and straight, with lofty aisles stretching away upon either side. The forest floor was thick with old fallen leaves, and few bushes grew there; but the line of the path was clear, on firm ground, and the going seemed easier than the day before.

The darkness faded to grey twilight as they climbed the far side of the vale, and the whispering of the leaves grew stronger with the new dawn in the world outside. There was also the welcome sound of birds again nearby – the clear calls of blackbirds and thrushes, and the rattling chuckle of magpies, and other pipes and trills to which Kellarn could not put a name.

They paused for breath at the head of a steeper rise, where the smooth mountain rock broke surface beneath their feet and they could glimpse the early morning sky overhead. Kellarn was just stretching up on his toes, trying to catch sight of the mountain tops to the east, when Rúnfyr tugged hard at his own reins and gave voice to a deep whinny.

Kellarn let go the reins and caught his balance; then spun around on the spot, reaching for his sword. The others were also moving.

He saw first the hand, light against the greying bark of the old birch trunk where it rested; and then the arm running down to the elbow, and back up to the shoulder behind; and then a face popped round the side of the tree, to rest its cheek beside the hand. A handsome face and merry, set with bright green eyes above a generous smile, and with slanting golden eyebrows flicking upward in amusement.

'Galden!' cried Corollin, laughing in delight as she ran forward to greet him. The visitor stepped out from behind the tree, raising both hands to the horses' noses as they also ambled forward.

Kellarn relaxed his guard and smiled. Galden was one of the golden fay – most noble and rare of the elven kindreds who still walked in the Middle Lands. He was tall, with short golden hair, and skin tanned to a pale golden brown; and he was of slightly more muscular build than Kôril or the moon fay to whom Kellarn was more accustomed. He wore a simple grey shirt and brown breeches, and went barefoot on the ground; and there was a wild freshness of Earth about him that stirred the passions and senses. Galden dwelt alone in the Valley of Two Waters, where Corollin went to pursue her studies, and a close friendship had grown between the two of them.

'But what are you doing here?' Corollin asked him.

'We heard news of your approach in Starmere,' said Galden. 'I am sent by Heruvor to meet you.'

He made no mention of why he had been in Starmere at all, nor why Heruvor should have thought it necessary to send him. He grasped arms with Kellarn in brotherly welcome, and then gave a bobbing bow to Kôril.

Kôril bowed more formally in answer, and did not smile. He seemed less pleased than the others to see Galden – though, as far as Kellarn could remember, they had got on well enough in the past.

The four of them set off at an easy pace, the horses causing no problems now that Galden was with them. Their way lay up and down again, the path running straight over a series of folded ridges in the land. The whispering of the leaves was still all around them, but mingled with birdsong and somehow subdued. Kellarn wondered whether the presence of the golden fay made it so. But then he had always found Galden attractive, and found himself awkward and distracted whenever Galden was around. So though the arrival of the fay might have solved the difficulties of the forest's enchantment and the horses' moods, it gave rise to other complications. Fortunately Galden spent most of his time chatting quietly with Corollin, allowing Kellarn to tag along behind in peace.

The middle morning was passing when they reached the brow of the last ridge and began the long descent into the Blue River valley itself. The path still held to its northward course, angling at a gentler slope to the right and down across the steep valley side. But here the trees seemed to press closer again, with more bushes and undergrowth straying on to the narrow trail, and blue bugle flowers and feathery ferns glowed bright amid the deep green shadow. The noise of the river grew louder as they came down toward the valley floor, and presently they began to glimpse pools of sunlight and sparkling water in the distance ahead.

At last the path took a wide curve to their left and ran out to lose itself in the rich grass and rushes of the river shore. Kellarn stood blinking in the bright summer noon. The sky overhead was clear blue again, with plumes of white cloud trailing around the high mountain peaks to the north and east; and the river banks were a haze of blue and white and purple where great flag lilies waved among the reeds. The heat of the day surprised him.

They left the horses to browse along the shore, and found a drier patch of ground to sit down for their own midday meal. Then Kellarn and Galden went down to paddle in the cool shallows at the water's edge. Corollin brought over the waterskins for them to refill while they were there.

'Shall we cross the river here, or farther up?' she asked.

It was no idle question. The Blue River flowed swift and cold, and was still swollen at this season with the melted snows from the high mountains. Though the path had brought them here, and the river was perhaps no more than twenty yards across at this point, it did not look to be an easy crossing.

'Oh, here,' Galden nodded. 'We shall follow the path north and east through the Nets. But the horses will not come with us. Some of Heruvor's folk will lead them further up river, by another way.'

Kellarn shaded his eyes and looked around. He had seen no sign of the moon fay as yet; but given the arts of the elvenfolk, that did not mean they were not near by.

On such a fine summer's day, with the warmth of the sun and the cool water playing pleasantly about his feet, he was less than eager to face the shifting shadows of the Nets – not even with the prospect of Starmere beyond, or the company of Galden along the way. But he supposed they had better get on with it. He sighed, and splashed his way back up on to the shore.

'Could we not all go up river?' Corollin asked.

'We could,' said Galden. 'But that way is a little longer; and we should still have to pass through the Nets.'

'I never understood why there had to be so many defences around Starmere,' said Kellarn. 'I mean, I know they want it to stay secret and hidden. But do they fear it might come under attack?'

'Perhaps,' said Kôril. 'Few humans have ever understood us; and many now fear us, and mistake our secrecy for guile and treachery. And then there are the shadowfay, and evil creatures from above and below the mountains. For all their merriment, the moon fay of Starmere are mindful of the perils around them.'

'Yet it is also true,' said Galden, coming out of the water to join them, 'that the Fay keep themselves hidden for the sake of others. Think of your own priests and magi. They guard their mysteries with great care, for they have knowledge which would

330

be dangerous for other humans to know, until they are ready to learn it. So it is with the elvenfolk of the Fay. Humans who have dealings with us set their feet upon a different path, and often grow estranged from their own kind. So until they show the readiness and the strength of will to seek us out, we try to keep out of their way.'

'We are hearing much golden fay wisdom this day,' observed Kôril.

For answer Galden grinned, and then gave a loud whistle. The three horses pricked up their ears and came trotting toward him. Three moon fay also stepped out from among the trees – shorter than Galden, and with long dark hair, and clad all in green and grey.

They loaded their gear on to the horses again, and handed them to the moon fay. Kellarn recognised one of the three as Sîlgon, a border warden who had guided them once before. The other two were not unlike Sîlgon in appearance; but they spoke few words in any human tongue, and Sîlgon did not name them.

Kôril kept hold of Lanaë, twining his pale fingers in her mane.

'I shall take the longer way, I think,' he told them. 'I need time to gather my own thoughts ere I speak with Heruvor. Galden can see you two safe through the Nets.'

There seemed little purpose in arguing the point, since they would no doubt see each other again soon enough, and since the strange tension between Galden and Kôril would not have made their journey any the easier. Kellarn remembered the conversation he had had with Kôril on the edge of the Grey Moors a few nights before, and wondered if the death of the unknown woman was still playing on his friend's mind.

They said their farewells, and horses and fay slipped away into the trees and were quickly lost from sight. Kellarn shouldered his pack, and picked up his boots and socks.

'Can we really ford here?' Corollin asked Galden uncertainly.

'Of course,' laughed the fay. He bounded across the grass ahead of them, and crouched down at the water's edge with his hands flat upon the ground.

He stayed there, still as stone, while Kellarn and Corollin joined him. For several seconds nothing happened. Kellarn looked down at him in question, but Galden's gaze was focused out across the river. The long toes of his right foot were drumming up and down in excited rhythm on the muddy grass.

Then the sound of the water changed, and the blue-grey rock of the river bed began to break surface in three or four places ahead of them. The waters swirled and surged, turned aside from their course as more rock continued to rise. Before long a solid causeway stretched the width of the river before them, with the water running swift but shallow over the surface and churning through deep, narrow channels at either end.

'Now we may cross,' said Galden, standing up again. He took each of them by the hand. His grip was gentle, but very strong, so that they felt no need of a rope to bind them together. Kellarn felt self-conscious at the fay's touch – and foolish for doing so. He kept his head well down, and paid close attention to where he was putting his feet.

It was still a difficult crossing, for mere humans, and both Kellarn and Corollin nearly lost their footing at some point. But they reached the far bank with no great loss of dignity; and then Galden sent the river bed back down to its proper place, while they dried their feet and caught their breath.

They found the path at the edge of the trees, and soon it began to veer to the right, climbing up on to higher ground away from the river. Galden led the way, with Corollin and Kellarn in single file behind him. The trees pressed close around them again, and even the shadowed air seemed heavy with growth. The noise of the river faded, and the calls of the birds were left behind; and soon they were back among the endless whispering of the leaves, with the knowledge that danger lay not too far ahead.

From what little Kellarn understood of the Nets of Starmere

– or from what others had tried to explain to him – the most likely danger was that of simply getting lost. The trees seemed to move around if you looked away from them, and even the lie of the land might shift and change between one glance and the next. The thickly woven branches made it all but impossible to take bearings from the surrounding mountains, or from the sun or moon; nor was it much help trying to following the line of the path or the river. The elvenfolk of the Fay seemed untroubled by this enchantment; or perhaps their closeness to the life of the world enabled them to see through the ruse as nothing more than a juggler's trick or sleight of hand. But for a human traveller – even with one of the Fay to guide him – the sheer effort of concentration to keep to a chosen course, and to keep moving, was very tiring. It was held unwise to stop for rest whilst travelling through the Nets.

There was also the danger that the enchantments of the Nets could let loose the deepest buried passions and frustrations, and give visible shape to hidden hopes and fears. Kellarn and his friends had escaped this danger lightly enough on their previous visits to Starmere; but it had been known to cause lasting madness in those who dared the Nets and failed.

He comforted himself that perhaps knowing the nature of these perils was the first half of the battle to be able to overcome them. Yet that in itself was not enough. It occurred to him that it might be thought cheating to rely on Galden to take them safely through. But Heruvor in his wisdom had sent Galden to them; and if Kellarn had learned anything from the Fay at all, it was that he should have the sense to accept help when he really needed it.

They had come less than a mile from the river when Galden called a halt. He fished out a grey pouch from somewhere inside his shirt, and took from it an orb of deep blue crystal perhaps two inches across – small enough to sit comfortably in the palm of his hand. He passed his free hand over the surface of the orb, and a flicker of stars swirled in the dark heart of the crystal, and then flared to life with a brilliant silver-blue light.

'This is an elf lamp from Starmere,' said Galden, holding it up. 'You may have seen them before.'

Kellarn and Corollin nodded. The forest close around them now seemed to be bathed in the mingled light of moon and stars; though further off, beyond the reach of the lamp, the green shadows grew deeper.

'The lamp should show us the veils of power with which the Nets are woven,' Galden told them. 'It has no virtue to protect us – other than to show us that power is at work.'

'Can the magic of the Nets work on you?' asked Kellarn.

'I can find a path through them easily enough,' Galden answered. 'But the Nets were woven by Heruvor and Neriel, both great among the moon fay; and even the Fay must take care when passing through them. They are a snare for the unwary, or the over-confident.'

'Neriel?' wondered Corollin.

'The mother of Tinûkenil, whom you have met,' said Galden.

They set off again, still climbing for a while as they left the river valley behind. Then the ground levelled out and the trees drew further apart – mostly oaks and chestnuts of great age and girth – and presently they began to glimpse wisps of mist trailing among the branches or drifting over the mounds of fallen leaves, silver-grey in the light from the lamp.

'We have come to the Nets,' said Galden quietly, pointing to the mist. 'Stay close.'

Corollin grasped her staff in both hands – focusing herself to calm, rather than preparing for a fight. Kellarn found his own hand straying to his sword hilt. He moved it away deliberately, and quickened his pace a little to close the distance between himself and the fay.

They continued for a long while in silence after that. The silver-grey mists grew thicker, draping down from the branches in billowing veils or rolling like sea waves over the spreading roots and scattered banks and hollows. For the most part Kellarn tried to keep his eyes on Galden's back, and the lamplit ground just ahead of them, and not to look at the mists at all. But at the edge of sight he was still aware of constant movement – of trees and shadows shifting and changing, and of half guessed forms and faces taking shape from the eddying mists and then fading away again like wandering dreams. The thought came to him that Kôril had mentioned other folk that used the forest path, and that the Nets served as defence against other creatures apart from humankind. Kellarn pushed that thought gently aside. He kept reminding himself to stay calm, to let such things pass and pay them no heed.

They must have travelled in this way for well over a league – keeping more or less to a straight course as far as Kellarn could tell – when the path began a slow arcing curve, dropping down and to their right. The forest shadow seemed deeper that way, and the mists of power lay thick across the line of the path.

'Are you sure we want to go this way?' asked Corollin doubtfully.

Galden glanced back over his shoulder, his face lit by an untroubled grin. 'Quite sure,' he answered. 'We need to be heading east now.'

They went on down the slope, and the thick wall of mist drew nearer. Kellarn and Corollin kept close to the fay, trying not to think what might happen when the mist surrounded them, nor even to consider the possibility that they might lose sight of one another. But that fear proved unfounded. Though the power of the Nets was made visible by the elf lamp, it did not hinder their sight as an ordinary mist might have done. As they breasted the first wave of mist, it was simply as though they were bathed in a flood of silver light. It was cool to the touch, and Kellarn felt his skin crawl uneasily; and it cost him some effort not to believe that it might eat away his flesh, or unhinge his mind and send him berserk. He kept his eyes fixed on the back of Galden's neck, and steeled himself against the fluttering panic; and then the mist was behind them, and he found that he could breathe easily again. He felt the sweat trickle cold across his temples.

He looked sideways at Corollin, to see how she had fared. She returned the look with a nod and a half smile of encouragement

– as though she were more concerned about Kellarn than herself. But then he supposed that she was more used to dealing with magical energies than he was.

After that the veils of mist grew thinner, but more numerous, with many strands woven like great webs between the trees. Yet few came near the path, and most could be dodged under or passed through with little effort. The ground was more uneven here, and Galden was leading them by a winding course past steep earth banks and bushy hollows. Kellarn's legs began to ache, and Corollin was breathing more heavily on the upward slopes. Galden was glancing back over his shoulder more often, drawing them on with the strength of his quiet confidence.

At last they trudged down a gentle slope, thick with leaves, and came to a narrow stream. The clear water bubbled merrily as it tumbled over rocks and roots, flowing away out of sight to their right on its journey toward the Blue River. Tiny flowers of pale indigo and white grew close to the water's edge among the stones; and though they could not see the sky overhead, the air seemed fresher and easier.

Galden paused beside the stream, kneeling down and resting one hand flat upon the stones. Corollin came to a halt and leaned her weight upon her staff, taking long deep breaths. The very sight of the stream made Kellarn thirsty. He drank instead from his waterskin, and then offered it to Corollin.

'We have come the right way,' said Galden, standing up again. 'One of the moon fay has been here recently.'

'How can you tell?' asked Kellarn.

'The stones remember,' answered Galden simply. 'And the flowers are her handiwork.'

He took his turn at drinking from the waterskin, and passed it back to Kellarn. Then he turned and sprang lightly across the stream.

Kellarn crouched down to look more closely at the flowers. They were much the same shape as snowdrops, with long bladed leaves. They did not appear to be newly planted, nor could he tell if any had been picked. He wondered whether they had been put there by magic; or whether *recently* in golden fay terms could be measured in months and years. He tried touching one of the flowers, and it felt real enough.

As they moved away from the stream the air grew more oppressive, and the sense of lurking peril seemed somehow stronger than before. From what he could remember of the Nets, Kellarn hoped that there could not be much more than an hour's journey left before they came out on the other side. But then time and distance seemed to have little meaning here. You simply had to keep moving until it was over.

He supposed that it was part of the test of readiness and strength of will that Galden had mentioned down by the Blue River – though it seemed that Corollin was better able to cope with the magics of the Nets than he was. When he thought about it, they were here more for Corollin's sake than his own. And for all that the Fay were supposed to keep themselves hidden until humans were ready to meet them, it seemed that they had gone out of their way to ensure that Corollin and Kellarn made it safely through the Nets to reach them.

Of course it was true that he was eager to see the Fay; and he had learned to accept help when he needed it. It irked him that he should need it, but he still accepted it. And the Fay, for whatever reasons of their own, accepted him – much as the Father of All Dragons had accepted him. Though, as with the Fay, the dragon had perhaps more truly come to him. Kellarn had neither the right nor the power to summon Ilunâtor.

'He is not a tame dragon,' he said aloud, 'to come at your call.'

'No,' said Corollin and Galden together.

But their *no* meant something other than he did. There was a new coolness on the misty air around them; and above and behind him he could feel the gathering weight of a huge *presence*. Corollin had already turned round, her face filled with dismay.

Kellarn whirled round instinctively. A silver sword was in his hand. But instead of the dragon's face, a tall man was standing there. He was clad all in white and gold, with a long mane of ebon hair, and a golden diadem upon his brow. At first glance he looked like the Emperor Rhydden. But he seemed to grow taller and broader before Kellarn's eyes, and his face shifted and grew ever more painfully beautiful and bright. A blade of dark fire sprang to life in his hands.

Kellarn leaped forward in challenge. Their blades clashed and sheared apart in a scream of power, and a shower of sparks fell all around.

'Collie, no!' commanded Corollin.

He turned around – he found he had no strength left to resist her. She stood there clasping her staff before her, and angry lightning flared iridescent about her head. The trees shone like white marble, backed by a veil of pale blue.

Then a burst of gold slammed into him from behind, knocking him face down upon the ground. His chest burned, suddenly winded, and his sight blurred briefly into darkness.

The grass swam in to view again. He found that Galden was kneeling beside him, with his hands upon Kellarn's shoulders.

'Yes' said the fay. 'Feel the firm earth beneath you. You are with us now.'

'What happened?' Kellarn groaned.

'You were beguiled into a waking dream,' said Galden. 'We should not speak of it here. I had to knock you down. Yet I think you have suffered no great hurt.'

Kellarn dragged himself to his hands and knees, and Galden helped him to stand. Though still merry, there was anxious concern etched in the fay's handsome face. Corollin was watching them both intently.

'I'm sorry,' said Kellarn, piecing together what had happened in his mind and then setting it aside for later.

'You were tired,' said Galden. 'Come! It is not much further.' He brushed Kellarn's hair back with his fingers, and blew softly on his forehead. Kellarn suddenly felt much better.

They moved on again by the light of the crystal lamp. Kellarn grinned sheepishly at Corollin; but she also was tired, and managed no more than a half smile and a nod.

Before long the forest floor began to level out, with more open space beneath the tangled boughs. They still seemed to be climbing slowly. The mists of power revealed by the lamp grew finer, drifting and curling in lazy billows at the edge of sight; but the sense of lurking peril still hung heavy on the air. Kellarn worked hard to stay alert, mindful of the mists for what they were, and concentrating on the route that Galden was taking. Corollin had withdrawn into herself, fighting her own private battle to keep moving.

They continued in this way for a mile or more, with the forest around them ever shifting and the ground beneath their feet seeming ever the same. Then without warning the air grew lighter and easier, and a good deal warmer. The mists drew back behind them, and ahead between the trees the twilight of the forest shadow gave way to patches of apple green and pale gold. The carolling of birds greeted them, and the excited chatter of squirrels; and there were the first faint stirrings of a mountain breeze.

Galden led them a short way further before calling a halt. Corollin flopped down on the ground, exhausted, and laid her staff among the leaves beside her. Kellarn tugged off his own gear and sat down.

'We have reached the vale of Starmere,' said Galden, tucking the elf lamp away again inside his shirt. 'Here we can rest in safety. It is only a short step now to the lake.'

Kellarn leaned back and closed his eyes, letting the warm air wash over him with its mingled scents and sounds; and for the first time in a long time drifted into carefree sleep.

Erkal Dortrean had barely returned to his borrowed chambers in the Arrand palace when there came a knock at the door. He swore under his breath, in no mood to be disturbed.

'Shall I send them away, your Grace?' offered Kierran.

The Earl managed a lop-sided smile. 'Better find out who it is first,' he said.

Kierran went over to the door and slipped outside. There was a whispered conversation on the landing beyond, and then he came back in again. The mail-clad figure of Boldrin of Levrin followed him.

'Forgive me, your Grace,' said Boldrin. 'I was wanting news of The Arrand. They told me you had just been to see him.'

Erkal waved him forward, propping himself on the edge of a cluttered table – the paraphernalia of reports, inventories and general information that he had promised to look at later that evening. Boldrin did not sit down.

'How is he?' prompted the knight, after a moment.

'I have seen him better,' Erkal allowed. He looked at Kierran, and signalled with his head for him to speak.

'Mother always worries more than she should,' began Kierran awkwardly. 'But the siege was a great strain, and the Emperor's visit didn't really help. Father let his blood get overheated once too often. He tried to hide it while the Emperor was here, of course; but now we are all paying the price.'

He looked down at the floor, rocking one foot sideways and back.

'His leg is swollen, and giving him great pain,' he shrugged. 'He can use his arms again, a little, though mostly he just lies in bed. Speaking is an effort, and he gets muddled with his words. Lienna and the Healers say that they are pleased with his progress. There is not much we can do, except keep him comfortable, and wait.'

'And how are you, Kierran?' Boldrin asked him.

'Oh, right as rain,' he laughed. 'I was mostly bruised, but not much worse. I felt rather a fraud, staying in bed as long as I did. Like my father, I make a very bad patient.'

'I meant, how are you about your father?' said Boldrin gently.

Kierran sighed. 'All right, I suppose,' he answered. 'As I said, there is nothing much we can really do. I dare say he would be glad to see you – and Mother would, too.'

'And how is Bradhor?' wondered Boldrin.

Kierran shrugged again.

'Better since the Emperor left,' said Erkal. 'He has taken charge of the city and the guard, and taken some comfort from keeping himself busy. I have offered him help where I can. Bradhor is a worthy man, as you know, but I confess I find him less easy to work with than his father. Still, he has good commanders and advisors, and the good opinion of his own people – and a good family to support him. And I dare say that my daughter Ellaïn will try to find him a new wife, when she returns.'

Boldrin chuckled.

'No, I have no great worries about Bradhor now,' Erkal concluded. 'The Arrands are a hardy breed.'

That last was true enough, though he had said it partly for Kierran's benefit. He still had some private misgivings about Bradhor's anger with the Emperor, and his sense of personal betrayal over the treachery of his late wife. But Bradhor had always struck him as a straightforward man, not given to lengthy brooding. If he could weather the worst of it now, busy with setting things to rights after the siege, then hopefully the rest would clear away with no lasting damage.

Boldrin looked at Erkal with his piercing blue eyes, as though he guessed that there was more which remained unsaid; but he did not pursue the point. Nor did he make any move to leave.

'Was there something else?' Erkal asked him.

'A small matter,' the knight nodded. 'You hear more news in the palace than I do, no doubt. But there have been some rumours of late amongst the Emperor's armies which may not have reached your ears.'

'Since when have we listened to rumours?' asked the Earl.

'All the time,' Boldrin grinned. 'We might not believe them, but we are well advised to be aware of them.'

Erkal raised one hand in token of defeat.

'Mataún of Fâghsul showed up in Fersí a few days ago,' said Boldrin. 'There was another man with him, a War priest – one

341

of Môrghran's brood, we think, though he serves in the Imperial Household Guard. They were under orders to escort your son Kellarn safely to Arrandin.'

'Mataún rode with us from Samsar to Fersí,' Erkal nodded. 'I have not seen him since. I do not recall the priest.'

'They had found themselves up near the Tollund manor,' Boldrin went on, 'with no memory of how they came there, nor what they were doing there at all. There is no news of Kellarn – except that he is no longer in Fersí. I take it he did not come back with you?'

'We left the village separately,' said Erkal. 'I do not know where Kellarn is.'

'But you do not fear for his safety, I see,' said Boldrin. 'That is good. Well, there have been strange doings up at Tollund, with the forest folk there; and Mataún has had the butt end of many jokes among the Guard, which will probably do him no harm. But the twist in the tale is less welcome. Or the fork, perhaps I should say; since there are two tales that have come of it, and both – like the serpent's tongue – are perhaps coated with falsehood.

'The first is that Kellarn has been spirited away by the forest folk, and is now either their prisoner or in league with them against the decent folk of the Empire. Knowing your son – and knowing Morvaan's daughter Corollin, who I believe was with him – I think that that tale may be slightly closer to the truth. Or at least, it might explain how Kellarn got away, and what happened to Mataún.'

Erkal said nothing, though he was inclined to agree with Boldrin's judgement.

'But the growing rumour,' Boldrin sighed, 'is that Kellarn doubled back to join the Easterners. There are many among the Emperor's men who feel cheated of a fight at Khôrland, and that the Easterners escaped far too lightly and without proper retribution. And of course there are those who now say that Dortrean, or the Magi, or the *Aeshta* Orders, have made a secret treaty with the East; or that Kata Aghaira has put a spell on our commanders, or on The Arrand himself; and that the Easterners will achieve by treachery what they failed to achieve through strength of arms.'

'That's ignorant talk,' said Kierran scornfully.

'It is,' said Boldrin. 'Yet it is spreading. A gathered army with no one to fight will breed its own enemies. The sooner they can go home, the better.'

Erkal hummed his agreement. There was nothing new in such rumours of treachery – though for Boldrin to mention them they must have been stronger than usual. He had heard report of similar discontent within the city, blaming the Magi for the damage suffered, and blaming both Dortrean and the Emperor for not calling the Easterners to proper account thereafter. But he held that when people settled back into their everyday lives again, the resentment would fade.

'They will not be here much longer,' he said. 'The Ercusí and most of the Ellanguan forces are due to pull out in the next day or two. Kelmaar and Eädhan have already gone – and Româdhrí. They are more worried about the Southers now, I think. Lord Brodhaur will send the rest home as soon as he can.'

'And when will you be gone?' asked Boldrin.

'Soon,' Erkal answered. 'Perhaps I should have left before now, but The Arrand had need of me here. The Emperor will want me back before the Summer Court – and that is only a few weeks away.'

'I shall see you before you go?'

'Of course,' Erkal promised.

Boldrin went away, and Kierran closed the door behind him. Erkal wandered over to the window and looked out at the Old City in the late afternoon light. The buildings there had survived unscathed, and were as they had always been; but the hills beyond were a shifting wave of colour with the troops returning from the eastern borders. It reminded him sharply of the early days of the siege. Arrandin was not the place it once was. His friend The Arrand was dying.

343

Kierran appeared at his side – too tall and grown up for the little boy he remembered. A familiar stranger now.

'When you go,' said Kierran, 'may I come with you?'

'Your place is here,' said Erkal. 'Your father needs you.'

'No,' said Kierran.

Erkal turned and looked at him.

'He has Bradhor, and Mother, and half the household,' said the boy defensively. 'There is nothing I can do here, except play nursemaid to Bradhor's boys or ride patrols with the city guard.'

'Both very useful,' the Earl pointed out.

'But other people can do that,' protested Kierran. 'I want to go to Ellanguan with you. The Southers are there, and the city could be in danger. You could be in danger. You have no household here with you. If you take me along, at least you'll have one person you can trust to defend your back.'

Erkal smiled. 'I am honoured by the offer,' he said seriously; 'though I hope I do have one or two friends left at Court, all the same.'

'Well then you would have one more.'

Erkal considered the question. He was moved by the offer; and had The Arrand been well, he thought that there might have been no great objection to his accepting it.

'And don't say you have to ask Father – or Mother,' said Kierran. 'You always say that.'

Erkal did not answer, as he might have done, that he would still have to ask Bradhor's permission as Acting Head of the Arrand House. But Kierran's forward passion – bordering on presumption before an anointed Earl – prompted another thought in his mind.

'I can not promise that Kellarn will be in Ellanguan,' he said.

Kierran blushed and ducked his head, like a child caught scrumping apples. Then with an effort he looked up again.

'I know that,' he said steadily. 'But you shall be there.'

Erkal hesitated a moment longer, then gave a cautious nod. Kierran's face flushed even brighter red in gratitude.

'I trust that you are not planning any mischief?' warned the Earl.

'Not yet,' Kierran answered. 'It depends what happens with the Southers.'

When Kellarn opened his eyes again, Corollin's face was looking down at him and smiling. The tree canopy overhead was a shade darker, but busier than ever with the calls and flutterings of the birds.

'You've been crying,' he told her.

'That is because I am happy to be here,' she said.

Kellarn did not bother to think about that too deeply. He rolled on to his side and got up. Galden came over to join them.

They moved on swiftly through a woodland rich with bushes and flowers and glades of soft turf. The air grew sweeter, alive with excitement. Then suddenly they stepped out on to the open shore, and the lake of Starmere was before them.

Away to the left, the lake stretched beneath sheer bluff cliffs of grey – so high that they seemed to hold up the northern sky. To the right, the waters narrowed into a wedge, and thence spilled out into a stream, winding away south past deep meadows and withy bushes for a mile or more to join the Blue River. On the near shore, the trees grew close to the water's edge; but on the farther side the land lay open in fields and pastures, and low vineyard slopes basking in the last of the sunlight. To the south and east, the valley was flanked by the Blue Mountains, climbing rank on rank to their snowy heights beneath the deepening sky; and above them floated the newly risen moon, already grown near to the full.

The folk of Starmere dwelt in low wooden buildings on the eastern shore, close to the feet of the grey cliffs. Galden stood and pointed to where the first lamps of evening glittered in the long shadows.

'See, where the boat comes to meet us,' he said.

Kellarn looked, but at first he could see only the clear waters of the lake, mirroring a deep blue sky scattered with summer stars – though the sky overhead was still just too bright for the first stars to peep through. Then slowly his eyes made out the familiar shape of the small elf boat gliding without sail or oar toward them, its smooth timbers shimmering silver grey, and the carved likeness of the Panthress of the Heavens rearing triumphant at its bow.

Chapter Eleven

Heruvor came down to the harbour to meet them, tall and silver-haired and merry as ever. His kinswoman Ferunel was with him, clad all in white beneath her mantle of twilight grey; and a handful of their household stood round, calling soft welcomes with their musical voices.

Kellarn and Corollin were lifted ashore, and Galden sprang lightly on to the timbered wharf beside them. Then they were led away up the green bank, beneath the rustling willows, and out on to the smooth lawn beyond.

The house of Heruvor stood on a low promontory at the feet of the grey cliffs, divided from the open meadowland of the eastern shore by the narrow harbour inlet. To Kellarn's eyes it more resembled a small group of wooden buildings all joined together, with covered porches and steps here and there, and two squat round towers at the nearer end. Since the moon fay must have dwelt here for at least fifteen hundred years, he had often wondered why they had not made for themselves more permanent dwellings of stone. But when he had asked them about it, they had only laughed.

On the far side of the promontory ridge a long hall stood alone, and there Kellarn and his friends had stayed on their previous visits to Starmere. But now Heruvor led them in to his own house, to the upper floor of the northern wing. He bade them welcome as his guests, and left them to rest and refresh themselves after their long journey. Ferunel went away with him.

They did little more than eat and sleep that evening, glad of the soft beds and the dark beamed roof over their heads. In the morning Heruvor was not there, but they bathed with Galden in the cool waters of the mere, and then the moon fay brought them breakfast on a wide porch close to the shore.

The moon fay seemed to know much of the news of the outside world; of the wreck of the Souther fleet, and the departure of the Easterners, and of the roles that Kellarn and Corollin had played. They showed particular interest in Kellarn's sword, and in his meeting with the dragon, and seemed disappointed that he had so little to tell them about either one. Galden was more interested in the magical defences of Arrandin, of which Kellarn could tell him even less. No one spoke of the demons summoned by the Easterners, nor of the reason for their visit here.

Their horses and gear arrived soon after that, brought by Sîlgon and the border wardens. Kôril was not with them. Sîlgon explained that Heruvor had come out to meet them, and that he had taken Kôril away to speak privately. The moon fay seemed quite untroubled by the fact, so Kellarn thought no more of it.

They whiled away the better part of the morning with laughter and easy chatter, enjoying the warm sunlight and the fragrant air, sitting or strolling along the promontory shore. Their errand seemed somehow less urgent, now that they were here. But at length Ferunel came down from the house to find them. The three of them scrambled to their feet and bowed.

'Have you come to tell us to stop wasting time?' Corollin asked.

Ferunel gave a rippling laugh. She was almost a head shorter than Heruvor, and her hair was a paler silver, closer to white gold. She had cast aside her grey cloak and was clad only in her simple white gown; and one large, moon-like pearl hung from a silver chain about her throat.

'Where there is joy among friends, I should not call it a waste,' she replied. 'But no. The moon will be full on the third night from now, and then we shall have a feast. Then there will

348

be talk of many things, and we shall speak of the errand which has brought you hither.'

Kellarn felt his heartbeat quicken. It had been Ferunel who had shown them the vision which had led to the third of the jewelled bars, during another feast at Starmere. But Kôril had warned that they might not receive such help again.

'Alas, no,' said Ferunel, seeing his thought. 'Seldom does such help come twice. Yet what aid we may offer you, in memory or foresight, we shall.

'And that is the reason I am come here to find you now,' she said, brightening. 'Though the strength of Starmere may be in clear memory, or so it is said, we have also the written records and maps within our house. Heruvor has said that I may show them to you again – if you truly wish to shut yourselves away on such a fine summer day.'

'I think that we better had,' said Corollin.

Ferunel led them back inside, and through into the eastern wing. Heruvor had in fact a sizeable collection of books and scrolled maps, though nothing on the scale of the library in the White Manor of Dortrean, let alone the vast Book Halls of the cities in the world outside. Kôril and Kellarn had spent some time here the previous winter, looking for mention of the old kingdoms and any clues as to the places where the remaining pieces of their artefact might be hidden, while Corollin had been at work on her study of the lore of Zedron. Or at least, Kôril had searched through the texts, with Heruvor's guidance. Kellarn had less skill in such matters, and little knowledge of the strange words and letters, and had spent more time looking at the maps. Corollin now wished to see these things for herself, in the hope that fresh eyes might bring fresh insight. Ferunel remained with them, answering their questions when she could, but more often watching with interest as Corollin and Galden went about their search.

Their first thought was to read about the Great Forest of Cerrodhí, which lay close at hand to the north; but there were few written records of Cerrodhí in Heruvor's house, and only the vaguest maps of its vast, pathless ways. Ferunel herself could tell them little more. She knew that there were some among the moon fay who could lead them to where the halls of the kings had once stood, or to the groves of Temrbrin. But the humans of that kingdom had had more dealings with the wood fay than with the folk of Starmere; and the wood fay had fled to the west when the forest fell under shadow.

The next closest kingdom in their search, after Cerrodhí, was Lautun; but none of them much liked the idea of tackling Lautun while there were other choices left. They turned instead to the old Sixth Kingdom of Farodh; and there the search proved more fruitful, for the priest-kings of ancient Farodh had been servants of Haëstren, *Aeshta* lady of the Moon, and Ferunel was able to guide them to at least half a dozen places where there was mention of that land and people, in the days before their city was lost and the kingdom abandoned to the spreading marshes. Though the moon fay had had few dealings with them personally, they seemed to have shown an interest in them from a distance.

The drawback to Farodh, in Kellarn's mind, was that it lay beyond the western borders, on the far side of the empire. Though the long journey did not trouble him, and it would put a welcome distance between himself and the imperial Court in Lautun, it also meant that he would be on the other side of the empire from Ellanguan if the treaty with the Southers failed. True, he had considered that unlikely when he decided to ride to Starmere; and he had to admit that Ellanguan was not a place where he now wished to be. He comforted himself that at least they were doing something worthwhile here; and that it was foolish to assume that he was the only person in all the Six Kingdoms who could make a difference against the Southers.

The Emperor returned to Ellanguan late that afternoon with great fanfare but little ceremony. An agreeable number of citizens turned out to give him a victor's welcome home.

Solban of Dortrean rode with him along the last straight mile to the gate, giving a brief account of what was happening in the city in his usual sober manner. A more detailed report would follow later. Much of what he said was already known to Rhydden; and after the hardship of the long ride north from Arrandin, the Emperor let his attention wander a little while his Lieutenant General droned on.

One piece of news of which he did take note was that more Souther ships had been sighted further to the south, a long way off the coast. Solban's early reports suggested that these ships showed no sign of storm damage, and were on course for Ellanguan. The other piece of news – or more a warning – was that the Empress was waiting to greet him outside the Steward's palace. Neither prospect pleased Rhydden greatly.

They came down the chalky road, with the river estuary stretching wide beyond the sloping green bank to their left, and the Tumbling Hills now behind and to their right. Several score of common folk were gathered in the shadow of the grey-green city walls, dressed in their brightest festival clothes; and through the open gate Rhydden could glimpse many more thronging in the square and streets beyond. The gate arch itself was flanked by several guards in the blue-green and white of the Steward's household, with tall pole arms ready to hold back the surging crowds.

Rhydden had only small show of strength for a returning hero, though adequate for the afternoon's needs – a select escort of two dozen mounted knights, with their attendant staff trailing in their wake. Solban had also provided a detachment of guards on foot to clear a way through the city, and their golden tunics shone like beacon markers at regular intervals ahead.

The Emperor rode through the gate to a fanfare of trumpets and emerged into the sunlit warmth of the square. He had dressed for the occasion in his mailshirt of black steel, draped about with cloth of gold; and he favoured the crowd with his most radiant smile of benevolence. He had no great affection for these people, ever stubborn and independent, but they did not need to see that. They needed a show of strength and confidence, an image that they could trust.

The cheers came on cue, re-echoing from the surrounding buildings. Rhydden raised one hand in salute as he rode forward. There were a few cries of complaint, mostly about the Southers or the harshness of the present Steward; but Rhydden ignored them, and Solban saw to it that they were swiftly silenced.

The Lord Steward Rinnekh was waiting at the inner edge of the small square, ready to lead his Emperor through the city streets. He was arrayed all in white over silver-washed mail, with his white steel circlet on his brow; so that from a distance he cut a more dashing figure than the Emperor himself. Rhydden could not find it in his heart to hold that against him – though he made a mental note to think of pleasurable ways in which he could pay him back later.

They rode on down the wide street, borne along on a wave of noise: the shouts and cheers and the clatter of hooves, and the calling of horns ahead and behind, and the cries of the sea birds overhead. They passed the crossroads where gawping youths had clambered up on to the old crown monument – a curious relic from the earliest days of Ellanguan, when it had perhaps seemed more likely that the heirs of their first king Falladan would return to claim the throne. And then at last they turned to the right, and climbed the narrower strait of Wainwrights' Street to reach the Upper Square on the western side of the Steward's palace.

The Empress was amongst those waiting on the pillared steps to greet him, beneath her golden canopy. She had contrived to make herself more handsome than usual, and was clad in a mailshirt borrowed from one of the women of the Guard, with tunic and leggings of gold. Her chestnut hair hung down across her left shoulder in one long, heavy braid. Rhydden wondered whether the change in her appearance was more practical than symbolic, given the presence of six armed guards hedged tightly about her, and the presence of both the Souther T'Loi and the Northern Envoy – at a suitable distance from one another –

further along the steps. Nevertheless, he had to admit that for the first time in many months he found Grinnaer almost attractive.

There were other women of the Court clustered behind her, and various nobles and merchants to right and left in their costly finery. The Renza widow, Lauraï, stood tall among them. Rhydden was a little surprised to see her here, though the presence of the Souther warships was reason enough to explain it. He did not recall Solban having mentioned her in his brief report.

'We have not observed your Lady mother,' he said to Solban as they dismounted.

'The Countess is with the Envoy from the Northern Lands, Sire,' Solban answered; 'there upon our right.'

Rhydden let his gaze flick that way as the horses were taken from them.

The Envoy was a tall young man, clad in black and deep blue, with curling dark hair cropped short. He had the build and stance of a powerful warrior, though he bore no weapon or gear of war that afternoon. The coppery head of Karlena of Dortrean barely reached to his shoulder; so that his face was turned down toward her as she gestured discreetly, presumably telling him who was who and what was happening. There were two other young men with them, like enough to the first to be his brothers or close kinsmen. Rhydden did not recall seeing any of the three before.

Not being obliged to speak to any of these people, the Emperor kept his fixed smile and allowed Rinnekh to precede him up the steps and through the great west doors into the welcome shade of the palace.

The Imperial Counsellor the Archmage Merrech had arrived before them, to satisfy himself that the Emperor's chambers were secure. His dark shadow hovered behind the two golden liveried guards whom Solban had set to watch the outer doors of the apartment. Rhydden's squire Zhiraún and other attendants were also there, having left the main procession at the East

353

Gate and hastened to the palace by a shorter way. Solban and Rinnekh withdrew to allow the Emperor time to refresh himself.

Rhydden strode through into his dressing chamber, and suffered himself to be divested of his mailshirt and sword and heavy gear. He would bathe later in the day, when the air was cooler; so they towelled down his chest and back, and gave him a fresh linen shirt and silken slippers. Then he sent all but the tow-haired squire away.

He threw the boy face down across the narrow side table and had his way with him – more because it had become expected between them than from any sense of urgent passion. Then he went back through to the outer living chamber.

'You shall spoil that boy, Sire,' said his Counsellor.

'For whom?' Rhydden scoffed.

The Archmage handed him a goblet of wine.

Rinnekh was at his door well before the Emperor thought of sending for him. The guards showed him in, and Rhydden granted him time for private reunion and the exchange of news. In particular he wished to hear more concerning the Souther warships sighted further down the coast.

'They are friendly to T'Loi, Sire,' said Rinnekh; 'or so he says. With the changeful tides of the God-King's Court, it is impossible to be certain. Since T'Loi is my hostage here, they are supposed to be coming to confirm our peace treaty with the God-King.'

'And should they prove unfriendly,' said Rhydden, 'how do you propose to defend Ellanguan?'

'We still hold T'Loi,' Rinnekh answered; 'and five of their warships, with troops and crew; and T'Loi's own ship, with all its gold and jewels. Even if they refuse the peace treaty, they are likely to bargain first before they attack.'

'How seaworthy are those ships now?' the Emperor wondered.

'Not very,' said Rinnekh. 'Not for battle on the open sea. The refitting has begun, but it will be a couple of weeks before they are ready to leave. I told our people to drag their heels over the work, until we had surer guarantee of peace. Lieutenant General Solban seems to think I should have done otherwise.'

He did not bother to disguise his contempt as he sneered Solban's name and rank. Rhydden's eyebrows went up in amusement, suspecting a little jealousy between the two of them.

'The security of the city – and of our Empire – is his main concern,' he said. 'That is what he was trained for, Rin. Solban will strive to keep the peace, as he is able, while those above him determine the greater policies by which he is governed.'

He raised his goblet in a toast, and Rinnekh grinned at the flattering praise.

'Besides,' added the Emperor lightly, 'we understand that there has been some unrest within the city of late.'

The Steward's smile turned brittle.

'Something about old Trigharran,' Rhydden prompted.

'The old fool was stirring trouble against the Southers,' said Rinnekh. 'And Lauraï of Renza has been sticking her oar in too. You know what Renza and Kelmaar are like. And of course Solban was delighted, because it suited him to keep the Southers under closer guard and strengthened his argument to send them packing as soon as possible. Apart from the fact that he seems to spend half his time these days drooling over Lauraï.'

'Indeed?' said the Emperor. He was intrigued by the outburst, sensing that there might be food here for further thought. 'Yet slowly, Rin. Let us go back to Trigharran. What was it that he was saying, exactly?'

He did not need to look at Rinnekh to sense his discomfort; and apart from his own hold over his young favourite, Rhydden knew that the presence of the Archmage Merrech would suffice to tease the full truth out of him.

'He claimed that I would deliver Ellanguan into enemy hands,' said Rinnekh awkwardly. 'And that I would betray you, and make my own treaty with the Southers.'

'And did you?' asked Rhydden.

'No, Sire!' Rinnekh cried. 'I secured the peace treaty, as you required. No more.'

'Of course.' The Emperor smiled. Upon that point he was minded to believe him; nor was there signal from the Archmage to suggest otherwise. 'Now what more has been discovered of Trigharran's death?'

'Nothing much,' replied Rinnekh, more calmly. 'The priests of Kelmaar have been using their heathen arts to try to work it out, and Solban's men and mine are still working on it. I expect it will be in Solban's report. His murderers seem to have used some sort of magic, possibly of Easterner or Souther origin. So his death only served to make the problem with the Southers worse.'

Rhydden nodded. 'So how did you do it?'

Rinnekh dropped his gaze. He reached for his goblet, but found that it was empty.

'With the help of some of T'Loi's people,' he said. 'It was a gambit for both of us, but it seems to have paid off.'

'And you pulled the hood over Kelmaar's eyes? Well done.' Rhydden drained his own goblet, and signalled for him to fetch more wine.

'So what can you tell us about Solban and Lauraï?' he asked next.

'She took passage with him from Renza, on His Highness' own warship,' Rinnekh answered, coming back across the chamber. 'I do believe the young widow has turned Solban's head. He has visited her every day since their arrival; and Lauraï and Karlena are now both staying as guests in the Vanbruch house.'

'Interesting,' Rhydden mused. 'We had not given much thought to an alliance between Dortrean and Renza. Yet if Renza take up their claim to your Steward's throne of Ellanguan, that would make a powerful alliance indeed.'

'Lauraï's brat is barely walking,' Rinnekh argued. 'Their claim is still years away. Would Solban think so far ahead?'

'Karlena would,' Rhydden countered. 'Besides, Lauraï is a

356

Regent of Renza. Should anything happen to you, she might become Regent for the heir of Ellanguan.'

'Renza are producing heirs,' put in the hooded Archmage, 'while the Lord Steward of Ellanguan is not. The skill of Karlena may be less than rumour makes it, but she would seize such a chance if it were set before her.'

'Bastard Solban,' Rinnekh cursed.

'Yet would you consider, Rin,' said the Emperor carefully, 'that Solban's interest in the Lady Lauraï has swayed his judgement when dealing with the Southers?'

The Steward would clearly have loved to denounce his rival on the spot. But the Emperor fixed him with his bright gaze, and he sighed and shook his head.

'Not yet,' he allowed sullenly.

The Emperor nodded, half to himself, and reached for his wine.

'We shall have to speak with T'Loi,' he said presently. 'Given that we have his ships and his men, and his complicity in the death of Trigharran, it might perhaps prove useful to send him south, to meet with these new warships before they reach Ellanguan.'

'But what could we gain by that, Sire?' asked Rinnekh.

'I don't know, Rin,' Rhydden sighed. 'By all reports, it seems likely that the Easterners will return. Dortrean bought them off for us this time, but the cost to our own strength of men in this war was high. We can not hope to withstand another such assault – not if the Easterners decide to pass Arrandin by, and strike straight at the heart of our Empire. The Magi's artefact of power can defend Arrandin alone; and if the rest of our Empire fall, then the city stands to little purpose. The Easterners must know this. We have won peace with the Southers; but what we now need is an alliance of war with the Southers against the East. It is our hope that T'Loi can achieve it.'

Rinnekh looked doubtful. 'T'Loi has less favour with the new God-King, Sire,' he reminded him. 'And what if the Southers agree to send their troops, but then, when they land here, they turn traitor and attack us?'

'We have considered the possibility,' Rhydden allowed. 'One solution would be to garrison their troops well to the south; so that if they betray us, we may hope to turn them back at the line of The Steeps. The Braedun *commanderie*, down beyond Levrin's lands, comes to mind as a suitable place.'

'Braedun?' gasped Rinnekh. His face was a mixture of astonishment and spiteful glee.

The Emperor nodded.

'But – can we afford to have the *Aeshta* Orders turn against you, Sire, with the threat of war still at hand?'

Rhydden twirled his goblet slowly in his hand.

'Braedun can move their remaining troops to Arrandin for a while,' he said. 'We trust that they will see the wisdom in manning the city with our own people, rather than keeping a strong Souther army there. What grounds can they have to turn against us, when we are simply requiring them to provide for the defence of our Empire in her hour of need?'

He put on a smile of beatific innocence. Rinnekh laughed.

'Then again,' said the Emperor, 'from what we have learned in the past few weeks, we must now face the very real possibility that the heathen Orders will turn against us.'

Rinnekh gulped his wine. 'Will they ally with the Easterners?' he asked.

'Perhaps,' said Rhydden. 'During the siege of Arrandin, the perceived threat was from outside the Empire; and so they rallied to the defence of their home ground. But at the final parley with the Easterners at Khôrland, the chieftains invoked the name of an ancient enemy of the *Aeshta* Orders; and one of their wizards claimed that this enemy would rise in the heart of our own empire, not among the Easterners themselves.

'Thus the heathen priests – and some of their friends among the Magi – are now preparing in earnest for a holy war. They may need no great excuse to start a witch hunt through every household in the Empire that does not hold to the *Aeshta* faith.

And to that end they may seek alliance with other Easterner clans to rise against us – or perhaps even to approach the God-King for help, if we do not get there first.'

'And how likely is that?' asked Rinnekh.

Rhydden sipped his wine deliberately.

'Dortrean agreed the peace with the Easterners,' he said after a moment. 'He was also very thick with the Easterner loremaster in Arrandin, who seemed to oppose the chieftains; and he worked closely with the Magi and the *Aeshta* Orders in the defence of the city. And Kelmaar supplied the jewel which bought the Easterners off – which, apparently, they had received from Erkal's younger son Kellarn. We know that Dortrean favours the heathen Orders, and has more skill than most in dealing with foreign envoys. It is all too possible that he might support a holy war; and that he may even now be making secret treaty with the Easterner clans. And where Dortrean leads, other Houses Noble may follow.'

Rinnekh swore under his breath.

'Has Karlena had much to do with T'Loi?' the Emperor asked him.

'Very little,' Rinnekh answered. 'And very cool. She has made no treaty behind our backs. I managed to keep her away from the Northern Envoy until this afternoon.'

'Why is he here?' asked Rhydden.

'To pledge support against the Easterners – and against the Southers, if necessary.'

'Good,' said Rhydden. 'So long as that support comes to ourself, and not to Dortrean. We shall speak with him soon. But first we must endure our Lieutenant General's report. You were best to leave us now, Rin.'

'So what will you do about Dortrean, Sire?' asked Rinnekh, standing up.

'Nothing as yet,' said Rhydden calmly. 'We are keeping close watch upon them. We shall be ready to strike when the time is right.'

'And there is other news stirring, which even Karlena may

not have heard,' said the voice of the Imperial Counsellor.

Rinnekh and Rhydden exchanged glances in the silence that followed. Rhydden shrugged and smiled. If Merrech chose not to elaborate, then even imperial command would not break his silence.

Rinnekh bowed and kissed the Emperor's jewelled ring, and Rhydden tousled his head fondly; and then the Steward went away again.

'So what was this other news, Counsellor?' asked Rhydden, when they were left alone.

'I confess that I lied, Sire,' purred the Archmage. 'I thought it prudent to remind Rinnekh that he should not assume that he knows everything. I would not, of course, lie to you.'

'Of course,' said Rhydden.

For once, he was not sure that he believed Merrech; and the thought unsettled him. Merrech was not in the habit of lying, even if he uttered the truth in a manner misleading to the point of equivocation. But then, if he were lying about not lying—

Rhydden flicked the side of his goblet irritably, refusing to be drawn into one of the Archmage's mental games.

'Was there more news from Arrandin?' he asked aloud.

'The Arrand is sinking slowly. That was a skilful move, Highness, to wound the father by striking the son.'

'We had the best tutor,' Rhydden smiled. 'Though I am still not convinced why you thought it necessary. The old Arrand was weak, but at least he was experienced.'

'He was too independent,' the Archmage demurred. 'With Bradhor, fear and the inexperience of youth will persuade him to obey orders.'

Rhydden gave in gracefully.

'Have you heard the report of our Destrier yet?' he asked.

'Before you reached the palace, Sire,' Merrech confirmed. 'His account tallies with what we have just heard.'

'And has Rinnekh uncovered him?'

'Not yet. He still believes that the man whom he knows as

Baelar is entirely his own discovery, and he is very pleased with him. Other than that, your Rinnekh seems to have performed better than I had expected.'

'Though not, perhaps, with Lauraï,' said Rhydden. 'We shall have to think on that.'

Kellarn and Corollin had gone back to their rooms when Kôril came to find them. The fay brought with him the three bars that Heruvor had had in his keeping, and the grey book found in Hauchan which Ferrughôr had written. He had come to say goodbye.

'I shall go to the King of the Elves of the North,' he told them. 'Heruvor agrees with me on this.'

'Is something wrong?' asked Corollin.

Kellarn kept his head down, and busied himself with taking out the bars from their white silk wrapping. He had told Corollin privately about Kôril's worries over the death of the unknown woman, because he thought it right that she should know. Kôril himself had not yet told her.

'Not really,' said the fay. 'I have been too long among humans, I think – even you!' He laughed.

'But shall you return?' she demanded.

'Perhaps,' said Kôril. 'The King of the Elves of the North is wise, and sees much of what passes in the world from his high mountain home; and I shall abide by his counsel. It may even be that he can help us in this quest for the hidden bars. I hope that I may return, ere long.'

'Must you go now?' asked Kellarn.

'It is better so, I think,' said the fay. 'You can look after one another while I am gone.'

Corollin said nothing. Kellarn balanced the three bars side by side along his forearm. They were made of a metal like white steel, about the length of his index finger. The ends of each sloped in beneath, and the lower face curved up into an inward arch; but the upper face was flat, and set with a precious stone cut into a smooth half orb. The Hauchan bar had a grey-blue star stone, and the Ellanguan stone was a very deep sapphire blue; and both of these bars were engraved with the likeness of two circling hawks. The third bar, rescued from buried Khêltan, held a gemstone as red as wine, flanked by two chasing hounds. The hounds reminded him of the patterns on his sword.

'I'm sure that these are meant to fit around something,' he said aloud, changing the subject.

'Or in to something, perhaps,' said Kôril. 'The other pieces may be a very different shape.'

'So we don't even know what we're looking for, let alone where,' Kellarn sighed.

'So it would seem,' said Corollin. She took the bars away from him, and wrapped them back up in their silk scarf. No more was said about Kôril's leaving. They knew that they would not change his mind.

The next morning dawned grey with mist, paling later to a thin, drizzling rain. Kôril was gone before they awoke. Corollin and Galden spent much of the day poring over books and maps again, aided now by Sakhîrlan, one of the senior loremasters of Heruvor's household. Kellarn looked in on them from time to time, though he knew he was not much help. He looked at his sword, and thought about it; and then practised with it for a while in the large empty hall beneath their guest rooms; and then later in the day he took himself off for a long run around the lake and back, once the rain had passed. But most of the time he was content just to sit and talk with the elvenfolk, when they were around; or to sit and watch the vale of Starmere itself, when they were not. He did not see Heruvor and Ferunel that day. The moon fay told him that they were busy with another guest, and they seemed to think that there was more news stirring. But they would not tell him who or what it was; and Kellarn had not the skill – nor felt the need – to hunt for the right questions to draw it out of them.

The third day dawned misty again, but soon turned fine and clear. The moon fay were busy making ready for the evening feast. Corollin and Galden set aside their studying, and the

362

three of them took the horses and rode out around the green meadowland of the vale and down to the banks of the Blue River. They filled the day with easy laughter, with no thought of the troubled world outside. Then as the sun sank down among the western trees, they bathed in the mere once more and went inside to get dressed.

Heruvor's folk had laid out fresh clothes for them in their rooms. For Corollin there were hooded robes of a soft strawberry-gold hue. For Kellarn there was a creamy white linen shirt, and breeches and cloak of a deep Dortrean red. When Galden came to fetch them he was dressed all in meadow green, with a green cloak bordered in gold; and a garland of leaves and yellow flowers was twined across his brow.

Kellarn did not recall having seen him dress so finely before, and the sight took him by surprise. It brought to mind that their merry friend was also one of the golden fay, of great stature and power. He bowed, a little awkwardly. But Galden laughed and raised him up, and the three of them went downstairs together.

The great feast hall was in the midst of the house, with lesser halls opening on either side, so that the whole house seemed filled with music and song and the light of many coloured lamps. More than a hundred moon fay were gathered there; and there were songbirds and tabby wildcats, and huge hounds with silky grey coats and deep blue eyes.

They made their way through the throng and in to the middle hall. The lords of the house rose to greet them as they entered. Heruvor was clad in white and grey, with a diadem of clear gems glittering about his head; and Ferunel now wore a violet cloak, sewn with silver and many jewels.

At Heruvor's right hand stood a sombre elf, with long dark brown hair tinged to bronze in the firelight. He wore tunic and breeches of darkest green, and his great black cloak was overlaid with a lustre of blue and green like the sheen of magpie feathers; and there was a sense of dread power about him, or dark brooding. Kellarn's first thought was that he might be one of the shadowfay – and yet somehow he knew that that was not so.

The dark fay turned his face toward him, and Kellarn found himself gripped by the strength of his gaze. The fay's eyes flashed bright amber, burning right through him, and he had the impression of huge wings buffeting the air – like, and yet unlike Ilunâtor. For one brief moment he glimpsed a huge chasm opening before him, down which he could trace the memory of countless years, back to a time before time when the first mountains reared their heads and reached toward the newborn stars; in which the history of his own small kingdoms was but a brief candle, guttering in the dark. And then the moment passed, and the face of the fay softened toward a smile.

'I am not of that kindred,' he told Kellarn; 'though some of them came from the stone fay, who are my kin. And you are Kellarn of Dortrean. Well met.'

The music and laughter blurred into life around them again. Galden put his arm around Kellarn and drew him forward. Kellarn leaned against him gratefully.

'This is Sarnîl,' said Heruvor, introducing them. 'He has come from the Black Mountains of your home. And this is my kinswoman Losithlîn, the sister of Ferunel, who has also joined us for the feast.'

Losithlîn was standing to her sister's left, clad in simple green and black, with flowers of white and green and pale indigo woven in her silver hair. Though much like Ferunel in appearance, her beauty seemed more shy and fragile. She nodded to them in greeting, but did not speak.

They sat down at the round table, with Galden next to Sarnîl, and Kellarn beside him facing Heruvor and Ferunel. Corollin sat to Kellarn's right, next to Losithlîn. The moon fay brought them fruits and breads of many kinds, and pale wine which seemed to clear the head and heart rather than cloud them. Yet the feast seemed to be quite as much about songs and tales as it was about eating.

Kellarn sat quietly in his chair, content to watch and listen while he ate. There were hymns to Haëstren, and songs of the Moon Maiden and the Lord of the Sun; and a song about the Antlered Man, the wild huntsman of the gods, who had been Haëstren's consort before Torollen wooed and won her. And then there were songs of the ancient realms of the Fay, now lost or changed with the passing years; and Ferunel sang of the kingdom of her father Nerentor, west beyond the Black Mountains, now drowned beneath the waves. Though Kellarn understood little of the elven tongues in which all these were sung, they brought to his mind visions of mountains and forests, and white shores washed by a moonlit sea; and the flight of birds, and the secret lives of creatures that roamed the land or burrowed beneath it.

There was not much talk around the table at first – or what there was seemed to be part of the songs, and flowed in and out of them. But at length the music seemed to drift farther off, and Kellarn realised that most of the fay had gone through into other halls for dancing and merrymaking. Heruvor set down his cup, and spoke to them again in the human tongue of their own kingdoms.

'I understand,' he said, 'that you wish to know more about the powers used by your first kings?'

Kellarn glanced around the hall, and then looked at Corollin. There were still a handful of other folk lingering nearby, and Sarnîl was at the table. Though he supposed that they should trust Heruvor's judgement, he was not sure how open she wished to be about the nature of their quest.

'That is so,' Corollin answered. 'I need to know exactly how they differed from the powers that the Six Kingdoms use now, or how they are alike, and whether the lore that was used to defeat the enemies of the Bright Alliance is still known to us; and how the lore of Zedron fits in, which I am studying.'

'That is a long subject,' Heruvor laughed, 'and we might sit here till Kellarn's beard grows grey, and still come no farther than the first debate. None in Starmere could make you a full account – not even Sarníl, I think.'

'I have not the knowledge,' said Sarníl. 'Humans have not been my study.'

'Nor I,' said Galden.

'Yet I can answer you in brief,' said Heruvor. 'Enough, perhaps, to guide you toward the answers that you seek. It is still a long tale, for power springs from the life of All that Is, and that is no small matter! But to understand the strength of the old kings, and of the Enemy they stood against, it is well to know where both came from in the beginning.'

He spoke then of the conflict between the *Aeshtar* at the dawn of the world, which was afterward known as the Wars of the Gods, when the Lords of the *Aeshtar* strove to express themselves each according to their own nature and purpose, and the great harmony between them had yet to be achieved. In that age the first of the Fay were born, who were the children of the *Aeshtar*; and each was like a spark of the life and power of the *Aeshtar* housed in bodily form. As the Fay grew and multiplied they became the agents of the gods to find harmony among themselves, and thus to bring order and balance into the created world. So their long task was begun; and it was held among the Fay that when their earthly bodies perished, their spirits would take up their place on the outer borders of All that Is, sustaining the harmony of the created world with their song until the last purpose of the gods is complete.

In that age also were born the unicorns, the great Guardians of the World, and the first of the dragons, and the messengers of the gods; and in the flares of power overflowing from the strife between the *Aeshtar* many other creatures took shape, both beautiful and terrible. And then the first harmony was achieved, and the Sun and Moon danced together in measure through the sky; and it was said afterward among the Fay that at that time the firstborn of humankind set foot upon the created world.

'Your first fathers were like to the Fay,' said Heruvor, 'in that the life of one of the Lords of the *Aeshtar* flowed true in them. But that was after the gods had found harmony among themselves, and so the life of all the *Aeshtar* was also housed within them in some measure; and as the years passed, and humans married and multiplied among themselves, the natures of all the gods within became mingled and perhaps lessened. Though still there are those born among you in whom the life of one of the *Aeshtar* flows more strong and clear than all the rest, who will become magi or priests or holy knights, according to your customs.'

'Was the magic of the first humans like yours?' asked Corollin.

'In part,' Heruvor nodded. 'Or so I am told. But unlike the Fay, humankind are not bound to the very life of the world. Few other creatures are. They die and are reborn within the circles of the dance, moving ever toward their own fate, which is other than our own. They may love and serve the created world, or strive against it, but they can never be simply one with it as we are. So we taught them of the *Aeshtar*, and of our own ways; but their powers grew and changed thereafter, according to their own nature and purpose.'

He spoke then of the first human realm – as the Fay reckoned it – far to the east beside the Grey Mountains. In those days, although the first harmony had been achieved, there were still many dreadful creatures and powers abroad in the world following the strife between the gods, and the paths between the waking world and other Realms were more open. The lords of the Fay befriended the humans of the Grey Mountains, seeing in them the hope of bringing greater harmony and peace; and they taught them the ways of the gods, and the beauty and strength of the light that was within them. But many of the Fay then turned aside from their first purpose, seeking to subdue the created world and rule it according to their own thought; and they rejected the life of the *Aeshtar* within them, and allied themselves with the powers of destruction and chaos that yet remained in the waking world; and so they fell into the corruption and malice of the shadowfay. Then there was war, and bitter conflict, with humans and fay on both sides; and even the home of the golden fay, east beyond east, was assailed.

Heruvor sighed. 'There were long battles, with many deeds of great bravery and sorrow. The human lords were more like us then, and the strength of the golden fay was glorious and unstoppable as the dawn. But in short, the dark allies of the shadowfay were destroyed, or overthrown and cast out of the waking world; and the veils between Realms were drawn shut to hinder their returning. And when the last battle was done, the Wars of the Gods were held to have come to their full end. Then the shadowfay fled and hid themselves, and would not be reconciled to their kin. But the first realm of men had also been destroyed, and so the humans who remained went south, beyond the Stormrider Sea, and found new lands for themselves; and their children were the forefathers of the horselords, who became your first kings.'

'So their magic might have been much the same,' said Kellarn.

'Perhaps,' said Heruvor. 'Yet you must remember that those human realms to the southeast have a long history of their own. They had some dealings with the havens of our kindred on the Stormrider Sea; but my own people came west, hither to the Middle Lands and beyond, watchful for the evil creatures that had fled here. The men of those realms marched down their own paths for close on two thousand years before the darkness returned, and their descendants came north over the Low Mountains to join us in the Bright Alliance.

'Their use of power had changed – and it differed amongst themselves, even as their language and stature differed, for more than one clan had come north. Yet all had a love for the *Aeshtar*, and they held to the old ways as they remembered them; and in that, they told us, they differed from many of the clans whom they had left behind. Still, there was much that we could teach them. In those days they were eager to learn.

'You have heard the tale of the Bright Alliance, and

Ferrughôr himself wrote of it in the grey book that you found. The horselords fought side by side with the elvenfolk of the Fay, and with the Redbeard dwarves of the Blue Mountains. Together they drove the darkness back across the Endless Plains, where your city of Arrandin now stands; and Furghollan and many of the human lords whom we loved were slain in those battles, for the enemy captain emptied his hordes from every burrowed pit beneath the Middle Lands and sent them against us. But at the last, the Enemy himself was brought to battle before the cliffs which you now call The Steeps; and Ferrughôr and Falladan, the sons of Furghollan, were among those who overthrew him. The body which housed him in the waking world was destroyed, and they shredded the power from his naked spirit; and then they thrust him out of the waking world, and drove him back beyond the veils of the other Realms to the uttermost limit of their knowledge and strength.'

'But why didn't they destroy him completely?' asked Kellarn.

'Nor human nor Fay has such power, that I have heard,' said Heruvor. 'Not to snuff out the final spark of life from his undying spirit. Few even among the most ancient of the great creatures, from the earliest days of the Wars of the Gods, could do so.'

Kellarn thought of Ilunâtor, but said nothing.

'Yet you asked about the powers of the first kings,' said Heruvor. 'The taller folk, who were the people of Furghollan, were possessed of great strength of mind and will. They saw the life of the *Aeshtar* within the very fabric of all that is, and within themselves, and grasped and moulded it to their purpose. That was a skill which we had taught to their ancient forefathers, though they had honed and polished it after their own fashion in the long years that lay between. It was with that strength – together with their great strength of arms – that they were able to withstand the power of the Enemy, and to overthrow him. Furghollan's sons then founded the kingdoms of Hauchan and Ellanguan; and their kinsman Llaruntôr rode further west and founded the Third Kingdom of Lautun.

'The shorter folk, who later dwelt in Cerrodhí, Farodh and Khêltan, also saw the life of the *Aeshtar* within all that is. But they saw deeper into the great patterns of the dances of the gods, and the harmony that they weave, and sought to move in measure with them; to serve, rather than to control. In that, they were more like to what your priests and holy knights have now become; and in that also, perhaps, they came closer to the heart of the Fay.'

'So one human of each kind, joined together, might come closer to the nature of the power of the Fay?' asked Corollin.

The elvenfolk laughed delightedly, and Ferunel clapped her hands.

'Alas, no,' Heruvor answered. 'The paths of human and fay are long estranged, and even your great priests are not one with the life of the world as we are.'

'Yet Corollin has a point,' said Galden. 'In *effect*, or at least in outer form, might not the two together come closer to our work than is usual among humankind?'

'Perhaps,' Heruvor allowed. 'Yet still they would begin from a different place. Indeed there were some among the lords of the shorter humans, such as Halgan of Khêltan, who had also great strength of mind and will; and yet were other than we are.

'It was Halgan who pressed north and west from The Steeps, hunting down the fleeing remnant of the enemy host while Ferrughôr sat triumphant in Hauchan. Perhaps even then he foresaw that the Enemy would return; for Halgan was a man of vision, and knew well the measures of the dance of life and the lore of the Realms beyond the waking world. Had Ferrughôr sought his counsel at that last battle, it may be that they could have bound the Enemy more securely in the Realms beyond, preventing his return. Who now can say? With Ferrughôr, the wisdom of foresight came later.'

The gathering at the table fell quiet. Kellarn guessed that they must all know the story of how Ferrughôr had married Heruvor's daughter Hirulin, and he wondered whether that might also count as a lack of foresight in Heruvor's eyes. After

Ferrughôr's death, Hirulin had gone away; and her daughter – born of the union of man and fay – had been lost soon afterward when the city of Hauchan was overthrown. Whether the people of the Old Kingdoms loved the Fay or not, it seemed that they did not like their rulers to have fay blood in them. Except in Renza. But then the people of Renza had always been something of a breed apart.

'Did the taller lords become the Magi, then?' Corollin asked.

Heruvor shook his head. 'I should not put it so. Both kindreds then dealt with the raw energies of life, face to face, and moulded or shaped them according to their understanding and purpose; and their gift of sight extended into the workings of the mind and of the heart – the life within, as well as the life without – as does your own. Those skills enabled them to challenge the power of the enemy captain and his demons, and to prevail. For myself, I should call one who used such powers a *wizard*, rather than a mage; though I use the word in a sense other than that which you use for the wizards of the east. Few among your Council of Magi now have such sight, I think; and among those who do, the gifts are perhaps lesser than they were of old.

'In the Wars of Power which followed, the boundary between priest and mage was still not clearly drawn. Many of the wizards, as I shall call them, had still the gifts of the old kings; and many had the insight of the priests into the dances of the gods and the life of the Realms beyond. But many – like the shadowfay, alas – overreached themselves in their ambition. And then Caraan called the first Council of Magi, to bring them under control.'

Heruvor laughed softly to himself. 'It was that desire for control, though in itself of good purpose, which worked against the Magi. You might say that they mistook wise counsel for command. So fond did they become of rule and rote, of tried and tested method, that they grew apart from the true source of their power. Instead of wrestling with the raw energy of life face to face, as their forebears had done, they snared it at arm's length with learned rites. There are those, it is true, who are still born with the sight of the old kings; and there are those who dare to cross the bounds and embrace the life of the *Aeshtar* within them with passion, and so become Archmagi. But most are now scholars and pedlars – brave and dedicated, and masters of no small power in their own way, and yet blind to the life all around them.'

'Or to put it another way,' said Galden, 'they have built themselves a strong fortress of stone against the storms and perils of the world. But when the rock beneath it crumbles, it will not save them.'

'The priests of the *Aeshta* Orders,' said Heruvor, 'have kept closer to the ways of the old kingdoms; though, as with all humans, their strength lessens as their blood mingles, and some of their skills have been lost or forgotten down the years. They have kept the mystic vision of the dances of the gods, and their wisdom still runs deep. But few now have the strength of mind and will that once belonged to the old kings; or for those who do, the lore of how to use that strength has mostly been forgotten.

'Yet be not mistaken. The lords of the lesser kingdoms – of Khêltan, Cerrodhí and Farodh – were priests as well as kings. They loved the *Aeshtar*, and delighted in the patterns of the great dance; and they strove ever to understand those patterns and to move in measure with them, which is a path of great wisdom. And be assured that among the people of your Six Kingdoms it is that joy and passion which has sustained and defended them through the years – not their strength at arms, nor the wealth of the land, nor their skill at making treaties, nor even their great love of horses! You yourself have that gift of passion, Kellarn. You love the gods, whether or not you hope to understand them; and you love our people of the Fay. Though we slay you, yet would you love us for it.'

'But I have no power or wisdom!' Kellarn protested. 'I can't even do the simplest magic. All I can do is fight.'

'That but proves your worth,' said Losithlîn, speaking for the first time in her soft, liquid voice. 'You love the *Aeshtar*, and the world that is theirs, with or without great hope of return. That is a precious gift.'

'Magic springs from the heart, and flows through the mind,' said Ferunel. 'That is perhaps where your Magi fail.'

Kellarn ducked his head, blushing fiercely. Everyone seemed to be looking at him.

'You have not spoken of the Guardians,' said Corollin, coming to his rescue; 'yet the *Aeshta* Orders held that they were central to their faith and power.'

'That is so,' said Heruvor.

There was silence around the table. Then Losithlîn spoke again.

'At first they were like to the priests,' she said; 'but they walked apart, and their lives grew to many times the length of humankind. Their study was the life of the dance itself, and the ways of all the gods; and the mysteries of Osîr, the Lord of the Stars, the First Father of all the Lords of the *Aeshtar*. The great priests of your Orders would at times seek them out, for wisdom and insight. But their power was different – more like, perhaps, to the lords of the first human realm in the east, beside the Grey Mountains.'

Until the Emperors butchered them, thought Kellarn.

Losithlîn said no more. If any of the fay perceived Kellarn's thought, they did not speak of it.

'What about the Easterners?' he asked aloud. 'And the new gods of the *Vashtar*?'

'Of the Easterners I know but little,' Heruvor answered. 'In the long years after the end of the Wars of the Gods their forefathers built a great kingdom in the northeast. Some say that they were descended from the humans who had fought beside the shadowfay against us. Others tell that they came from further to the north, over the mountains, or from the east across the sea. The Fay had little to do with them, and that kingdom foundered in the evil days which shook the world before the Bright Alliance. They follow strange gods, and have dealings with many creatures from many Realms. At a guess, I might hazard that their magics now are not so different from those of your own kingdoms in the latter days of the Wars of Power. But I only guess, I do not know.

'With the *Vashtar* of Lautun it is early yet to tell. Some say that they are but new masks for the Lords of the *Aeshtar*, moulded to the purpose of the human priests. Others hold that they are beings of power from other Realms, like the gods of the Southers; or perhaps the empty likeness of gods created by men's thought, which creatures from other Realms might then fill, masking their true nature and purpose.'

Kellarn's stomach turned cold. 'Like—?'

'Like the enemy captain, yes,' said Sarnîl. 'Or others, perhaps worse than him.'

'There were worse?' Corollin cried.

'In the Wars of the Gods,' Sarnîl nodded. 'It is to be hoped that they will never trouble the waking world again. Yet he was the most beautiful, perhaps; and the most cunning at beguiling others to his will.'

Kellarn shivered. Though he had no love for the servants of the *Vashtar*, he would not have wished such a terrible deception even upon them.

The elvenfolk sighed and stirred. The great feast hall was now empty, save for themselves. Heruvor stood up and led them out through a lobby on to the wide porch, where they could see the light of the full moon shining upon the mere. The valley air was cool and still, and the music and laughter of merrymaking came only faintly to their ears from the house behind.

'There remains the lore of Zedron,' said Corollin presently. 'From what you have told us, it is perhaps closer to the powers of the old kings than I had thought. Zedron refers to his powers as *gifts*, and groups them broadly into gifts of *seeing*, *shaping*, or *command*. Like the Guardians, perhaps, he seems to refer to the harmony of all the *Aeshtar*; but then the texts of lesser spells of the Magi that I have seen rarely confine themselves to just one of the gods, so I suppose that there is no great argument in that. There should be more of his work recorded elsewhere, or so he claims, but I have yet to find it. It may be that he never wrote it down.'

'You have studied him, not I,' said Heruvor. 'How then should I advise you?'

'Zedron also speaks of the *syldhar* as a source for his lore,' said Corollin. 'But apart from the name, he says very little of them.'

Heruvor returned no answer.

'There is a folk tale in the northern part of Lautun,' she went on, 'which links the name with shapeshifters from the mountains, or dragons disguised in human form. And in Dortrean the name is linked with the tale of the white horses that usher down the snows from the Black Mountains.'

'Is it?' said Kellarn. But her words had reminded him of his dream of the dragon, many days ago, with Corollin and the moon fay, and half a dozen human figures ranged behind them.

He felt Sarnîl's gaze upon him again. He dared to stare back, and the fay gave a half smile.

'I am of the stone fay,' he told Kellarn. 'Though I have taken the shape of a dragon, from time to time.'

'Have the Fay no knowledge of the *syldhar*?' asked Corollin.

Galden stirred at Kellarn's side. 'It is said among the moon fay west of the Black Mountains,' he told her, 'that the *syldhar* were the first children born of the harmony of the gods; or that perhaps, like the star fay, they are the children of Osîr. But that does not quite seem to fit. They are like to the Fay, and yet unlike.'

'You never told me that before,' she said.

'You never asked,' said Galden simply.

'Of the *syldhar* I know little,' said Heruvor. 'It was long after the Wars of the Gods were ended before we heard of them. They seem few in number. But they are a secret folk, and dwell in their own Realm, and seldom walk in the waking world.'

'Perhaps Zedron wrote more of them, elsewhere,' Galden offered.

'So do they change into dragons?' asked Kellarn.

Galden shrugged.

Losithlîn twined her long hair through her fingers. 'There is a tale,' she said quietly, 'that the first Guardians sat at the feet of Ilunâtor, and learned wisdom of the *syldhar*.'

'Then might the lore of Zedron be closer to that of the Guardians?' Corollin wondered.

'I can not answer that,' said Losithlîn. 'I have no knowledge of Zedron's work.' She went and sat on the porch rail, gazing out over the moonlit waters.

Kellarn sat down on a bench by the door. He felt suddenly tired and confused.

'The question is,' said Corollin, 'if we find all the pieces, would the *Aeshta* priests be able to use this artefact of power? Or one who had mastered the lore of Zedron?'

'You have read Ferrughôr's book,' answered Heruvor. 'This thing was devised by the kings alone. Since he calls it an artefact of power, we must assume that it was a power that the kings themselves could use. But since the pieces are now being gathered together, having lain scattered and hidden for so long, we may hope that one who can use that power will also be found. If you wish for my advice, I would say find the pieces first! And then take thought about who may use them.'

'That seems to be the trouble,' said Corollin. 'Knowing where to look. For each of the three bars that we have found so far, we have had guidance of some kind. But now I am at a loss. I was hoping that by coming here we might find some clue to lead us to the fourth.'

Heruvor bowed. 'If the moon fay can help you, we will,' he said.

'Perhaps you have already found what you need, but do not know it,' said Ferunel. 'Such is often the way with the dances of the gods.'

Corollin studied her hands in silence. Kellarn sat forward, trying to think. There seemed to be something else that the Fay were not saying – or perhaps they were waiting to be asked. It also puzzled him why Sarnîl was here at all.

'You mentioned earlier,' he said, 'that there were worse things in the Wars of the Gods. How were they defeated? And was the Enemy defeated then?'

'Heruvor has already told you,' Sarnîl answered. 'The strength of the golden fay was far greater then; and we had the aid of others, greater than ourselves – the unicorns and dragons, and high messengers of the gods. But now they, like the Enemy, have withdrawn into their own Realms. Even were we to find them and call them back to help us, they could still be driven from the waking world by one who had the strength. If the Enemy were here in the waking world, he could drive them out. In the age of the Wars of the Gods, the ways between the Realms were not closed as they are now.'

'But if they were here first, surely they could drive him back,' Kellarn reasoned.

'Perhaps,' said the fay. 'Indeed, that is where we now stand.'

'It was Sarnîl who drove the Enemy back last year,' Heruvor explained, 'when he tried to return in the Black Mountains.'

'You?' cried Kellarn. 'But – but I thought it was the Sun priests.'

'Torriearn was there,' said Sarnîl, 'and Tinûkenil, and others. Between us we closed the door, as you might say, and barred his way in to the waking world. The Enemy may have been a little bruised, and confounded for a time, but no more than that. He will not go away. He will seek another door or window to come through. And so the danger remains, until his power is destroyed. And in truth, Kellarn, his power is even now on both sides of the veil. For there are many who call upon his name and worship him, and his thought and power spread like a sickness through the waking world, or like a blight upon the land.'

'Is that what the words on the sword mean, then?' asked Kellarn. '*You shall burn the illness that blights the land.* Tinûkenil thought it came from the *Lay of the Sun and Moon*, or something.'

'The gods forbid that I should question the word of Tinûkenil, in the house of Heruvor,' said Sarnîl wrily. 'But what sword is this?'

'My sword,' said Kellarn, reaching to the empty space where it should have been.

'Shall I fetch it?' offered Galden, and was gone before anyone could reply.

'It's a holy blade of Hýriel,' Kellarn explained. 'Or so Tinû said.'

'I see,' said Sarnîl.

Kellarn had the uncomfortable feeling that Sarnîl's words meant more than they seemed to say. As they waited quietly for Galden to return, he began to wonder whether he should have mentioned the sword at all.

'Would destroying his power in the waking world, among his servants, be enough to weaken the Enemy or drive him away?' Corollin asked then.

'No,' said Ferunel. 'Such creatures do not go away, nor cease to be, simply because there is none found to believe in them. It is true that he might choose to bide his time, until he could rebuild his strength here. Yet the Enemy needs but one servant in the waking world, with the knowledge and power to open a way in; and when he steps through, a great host could follow behind him from the Realm beyond. So it was the last time that he came, in the days before the Bright Alliance.'

'Then how can he be destroyed?' asked Corollin.

'With your artefact, perhaps,' said Heruvor.

'But if we can not find it, or use it?' she pursued.

'He is but a creature of the dance, spawned in the churning powers of the strife of the gods,' Heruvor answered. 'There are still those in the waking world with the strength to resist him, for a time. Whether they can break his gathered strength and drive him powerless from the waking world again, or prevail against him unaided, remains uncertain.'

'The *noghru* of the Black Mountains,' said Sarnîl, 'held the Enemy to be a corruption born of Earth and Fire; even as they believed their diamonds to be the highest mystic union of those two powers. That describes him well enough. And it is true that the powers of Earth and the Sun show the better strength in defending against his evil hosts. That is one reason why I offered to help Torriearn rebuild the Sun Temple.'

Kellarn opened his mouth, but no sound came out.

'And so did I,' said Galden, returning. 'Though I played a lesser part.'

'It will serve as a beacon,' said Sarnîl, 'both to strengthen the hearts of your human kindred, and to draw the Enemy's gaze away from other things.'

'What other things?' asked Kellarn.

'You, for one,' Galden grinned, handing him his sword.

Kellarn carried the sword out on to the porch steps before he unsheathed it. The elvenfolk gathered round him. The blade shone pale silver-grey in the full moon light, and the patterned tracery seemed only a faint grey shadow tinged with bronze. It reminded Kellarn suddenly of his vision while travelling through the Nets. He shivered.

'Here,' said Galden, resting one hand over Kellarn's without touching the hilt of the sword. A warm golden light flowed down along the blade, and the runes and twining creatures shone clearly again. The memory faded, and seemed to become less terrible.

'Thank you,' said Kellarn gratefully. Then he drew a clear breath and repeated what Tinûkenil had told him about the sword, and what was written upon it.

'The dogs' heads remind me of the two dogs on the Khêltan bar,' he added.

'Yes,' said Heruvor. 'It does seem to be a Khêltan blade; or perhaps from the early years of Dortrean, which came after. They befriended the dwarvensmiths of the Black Mountains, and some of their metalwork was very fine. The verses, I think, are spoken by Hýriel to her son Torollen in his youth, as it is told in the *Lay of the Courtship of the Sun and Moon*. This would indeed have been a blade forged for a knight of Fire or the Sun, to hunt down the servants of the Enemy.'

'And the Enemy himself?' Kellarn wondered.

'Perhaps,' said Heruvor. 'But I would not counsel you to go looking for that battle too soon. You shall find other trials enough along the way.'

'With the Southers?' asked Kellarn.

'You humans and your wars,' said Sarnîl. 'It is as with the shadowfay. Ever it seems there are squabbles between them, to rule all things as this one or that one desires. They bring grief and sadness, yet all their striving serves but to lead them back into the measures of the dance that the gods themselves devise. And now they are caught up in a greater struggle, which could bring ruin upon us all; and still all but a few do not understand it, and are blind to the world around.'

'Don't you like humans?' Kellarn asked him.

'Some I like, some I dislike,' said Sarnîl. 'Much the same as do you, Kellarn of Dortrean.'

'The elvenfolk of the Fay love humans as we love all true creatures of the dance,' said Galden. 'But most often humans seem to want to be loved above all other things, or else they doubt that they are loved at all.'

'Ferrughôr was much the same,' said Heruvor. 'He showed wisdom as a ruler of men, urging them to peace among themselves. Yet he put humankind first, deeming them heirs to the world and the one great hope of the dance. I liked his father better.'

'Yet not all humans are thus,' said Ferunel. 'And among your people, those who yearn to return to the ways of the Old Kingdoms perhaps long – whether they understand it or not – to see themselves again as but part of the great dance, delighting in their kinship with all other creatures of the gods. The lords of the lesser kingdoms had that vision. The great priests of your *Aeshta* Orders still cherish it.'

Kellarn sighed and sheathed his sword.

'But if the Enemy is part of the dance,' he said, 'and bound by its laws, as we are, then surely he must also tread the path that the gods choose. Or has he the power even to break the harmony of the dance itself?'

Heruvor shook his head, but it was Ferunel who spoke.

'He has not that power, Kellarn,' she said; 'and there is indeed hope in what you say. Yet he has the power, given time, to lay waste the waking world; to ruin all that we love, and enslave all that he does not kill; and to tear the veils between the Realms. Then there would be battles such as have not been seen since the days of the Wars of the Gods. Though he can not stand against the gods themselves, or against their highest servants, yet the world thereafter would be wholly changed. It may be that the *Aeshtar* would permit such trials of death and loss, and forge new wonders of life from among them. Yet it is our hope also that they may spare us, and offer us the means to turn this horror aside. And behold, the wisdom and joy of the gods! For though the name of Ferrughôr brings sorrow to Starmere, yet in this hour of need it also brings us hope.'

Heruvor turned his face toward her, his silver hair flickering in the moonlight. Then he smiled again, and gave voice to clear laughter.

'Which brings us back to your quest,' he said, 'and whither you shall go next.'

Corollin looked at Kellarn and Galden.

'I vote for Farodh,' said Kellarn. 'It may be covered in marshes, but it is a good deal smaller than the Great Forest, and at least we could see where we're going. And we do know a bit more about it.'

Corollin nodded slowly.

'Cerrodhí is still closer,' she said; 'and there may be fewer places there to look.'

'One of our people may be willing to guide you through the forest,' Heruvor offered. 'If that is where you choose to go.'

'I have sought the counsel of the Moon in this,' Ferunel told them then; 'and this much I have seen. A metal bar, like to the three that you have found, now lies hidden where the Realm of the Moon touches the waking world.'

Kellarn felt his heart leap at her words, and a broad grin spread across his face.

'That may not help you much,' she said, smiling kindly at him. 'It holds true even of the moon fay themselves; for our life is in both Realms at once, though our thoughts turn more often to the waking world. But it also holds true of many places that are holy to Haëstren, or where her power is strong; and I think that perhaps it will be a place, rather than a person, that you seek. The Moon had temples and shrines in Farodh.'

'Once again the Moon blesses us with new hope,' said Corollin, bowing.

'I don't suppose,' said Kellarn, 'that the Moon mentioned any other pieces?'

Ferunel laughed.

'The full moon spoke to me of one,' she answered. 'If she knew aught of any others, she kept her own counsel.'

'Perhaps there were only four,' said Galden. 'You have found Air, Water and Fire. The fourth could be Earth.'

'Or there may be five, for the great lords of the *Aeshtar*,' said Ferunel. 'Or seven, if we count the Sun and Moon.'

'Or six for the Six Kingdoms,' said Heruvor. 'Yet surely the news of one is enough to keep you searching, Kellarn? The rest will follow after.'

'Yes – thank you,' said Kellarn, blushing.

'And when shall you start?' asked Sarnîl.

The question was addressed to Kellarn; but it was more truly Corollin's quest than his, and he looked to her to make answer.

'Soon,' said Corollin. 'I had hoped that Kôril would come with us, but I have no idea when he will be back.'

'He may be gone for a while,' said Heruvor. 'Kôril has his own business, and his own paths to follow. You shall find him again, when you have need of him.'

'Will he be all right?' Kellarn asked.

'Oh yes,' said Heruvor. 'He just needed to step back for a time, to see more clearly.'

'But not for too long, I hope,' said Sarnîl. 'The power of the Enemy is spreading. I must go back to the mountains.'

'And I to the valley,' said Galden. 'I have been too long away; and the shadowfay are stirring.'

Sarnîl bowed to Heruvor and the elvenfolk, and then to Corollin and Kellarn. It seemed that he was going at once. A ring on his left hand flickered green and gold as it swept through the air, so that Kellarn's eyes caught and followed it without thinking.

'It is a pretty thing, is it not?' said Sarnîl, watching him. 'It came from one of the human servants of the Enemy, in the Black Mountains last year.'

'Is it safe to wear it?' Corollin wondered.

'There is no power or virtue in it,' said Sarnîl; 'nor was it his to own. But it brings to mind that the Enemy may seem fair – and thus he beguiles many to his will. *Atallakûr* we called him of old, the Beautiful Deceiver. This jewel reminds me to be ever watchful.'

'And how can we guard against such deception?' she asked him.

'Look with your heart,' said Ferunel, 'and do not trust to simple reason.'

'Yet the Enemy can beguile the heart also,' Sarnîl warned.

'You have the gift of sight,' Heruvor told her. 'Look for where the power of the *Aeshtar* runs true, and where it does not.'

'But what about me?' said Kellarn.

'You have the sword from Khêltan,' said Sarnîl. 'Wield it well, and it will ward you from the wiles of the Enemy.'

The stone fay bowed again and went away down the steps. Losithlîn followed him.

'Must you be leaving soon?' Corollin asked Galden.

'Soon enough,' he said. 'Perhaps I may come with you as far as the eaves of the Whispering Forest, to see you safely on your way.'

'But not to Cerrodhí?'

'I thought that you were bound for Farodh,' Galden laughed.

'I suppose that we are,' she smiled. 'Everything seems to be pointing that way now. But I still have this niggling feeling that Cerrodhí should come next. I shall have to sleep on it.'

'What, and miss the rest of the feast?' cried Heruvor. 'The night is not yet grown so old. There is still time for music and dancing.'

'For a little while, then,' Corollin allowed. 'I don't suppose that I could get to sleep just yet, anyway.'

Chapter Twelve

Rhysana stood at the open casement window, breathing deeply of the cooler air as she watched the dawn sky beyond the towers of the library building. Down in the shadowed cloister garden a thrush was singing.

She had slept badly, her mind still wandering through the business of the Council assembly, and risen as tired as when she went to bed. But her reward had been this view of the dawn, with feathery clouds of pink-shot-grey spreading across a shimmering sky.

The Full Moon Assembly had been a backwards step – or at least a side-step, skirting the issues that had blocked their path before. As usual, they had resolved nothing. With the Easterners gone and the Emperor's armies marching home, many of the questions raised by the war had been conveniently forgotten. The Magi of the Council had turned their attention to Ellanguan – to the death of Trigharran, and the problems of dealing with the Southers. There was also the business of the end of the College term, now only seven days away; and the Summer Court, which would begin seven days after that. It would be Iorlaas' first Court as Prime Councillor, and the appointed delegates from the Council to support him must be chosen with care. Iorlaas had said little upon the subject, other than that he hoped for a time of peace for the Council to regain its strength. Sollonaal had been quiet to the point of being sullen. There had been scant mention of the return of the Easterners, or the rumours concerning Dortrean or the *Aeshta* Orders. No one had mentioned Herusen or the dragon. No one had mentioned Lo-Khuma.

Hrugaar had stayed with Taillan while they went to the assembly – Hrugaar who might best have told the Council of Trigharran's death. That, she supposed, was why he had stayed away. She had half expected him to be off in search of the sea fay under the full moon; but he seemed to think that there would have been no purpose in it just now.

The simple facts of Trigharran's death were clear. A single blow to the back of the head had been enough for the old man. His young attendant had put up more of a fight, but had been outnumbered. Both had been slain with ordinary weapons, handled with reasonable skill – but not with the swift precision of the assassin brotherhoods, who had in any event denied responsibility. Both had been robbed, and there was as yet no sign of what had become of their belongings thereafter. The attackers had used magic to conceal their identity, but no magic had been used upon the victims. From what Hrugaar and the priests of Kelmaar had been able to determine, the spells were most likely of Souther craft, drawing upon the power of one or other of their myriad strange gods.

Yet though one might conjecture many reasons for Trigharran's death, none could be proved beyond that of the killing and robbing of chance victims. It was Hrugaar's personal belief that Rinnekh himself was behind the murders. But there was no shred of evidence to support it, and to have said as much in the assembly would only have angered Sollonaal and the more imperially minded magi, and drawn the attention of the Archmage Merrech. Besides, Hrugaar's dislike of the Lord Steward was well known in the assembly chamber.

There was also the fact, Rhysana thought, that Hrugaar did not want it generally known that he had returned to Ellanguan. Dhûghaúr had gone with him, and with Telghraan's help they had taken the search for mention of Lo-Khuma back to the Book Halls in the city. The Book Halls were still closely watched, and the Archmage Ellen had decided against broaching the matter with the High Council while the Emperor and the Southers were still there. Whether Ellen herself was in

Ellanguan, Rhysana did not know. Ellen guarded her privacy fiercely, even by the Magi's obsessive standards.

Like Torkhaal, Rhysana now doubted that Hrugaar's search would bring to light anything that they did not already know. He had told of her of his conversation with Ilumarin concerning the nature of Lo-Khuma's return. They had both said as much to Hrugaar – though without mention of Ilumarin or her errand – but he had only laughed, and replied that at least it gave him something to do while keeping a weather eye on what was happening in Ellanguan.

In that respect, she supposed, the Council had the right of it. It was time to step back, to think of something else. They had thought about the Easterners and Lo-Khuma so much, and for so many days, that they had thought themselves to a standstill. There was nothing more that they could do for now. It was time to turn to other things, to regain their sense of perspective.

The same held true, if in a slightly different vein, for the question of Illana's death. Rhysana had found herself less surprised than Torkhaal by Ilumarin's tidings. Or rather, the initial alarm had swiftly tailed off into something approaching irritation, or disappointment. The fate of Illana had remained unknown for centuries, another great mystery surrounding the most notoriously enigmatic of all the ancient magi. Now that she was known to be dead and gone – no matter how she might have cheated time for a thousand years, no matter the implications of her death – she seemed somehow lessened, merely mortal.

Rhysana might almost have resented the fact that Ilumarin had told her, had not the Moon priestess clearly thought it so important that she should know. And now, standing watching the glory of the dawn, she found that she could not really be bothered with any of it – not with Illana nor Lo-Khuma, nor with the Easterners nor the Southers, nor any of the small doings of the Court and Council. The dances of the gods unfurled a larger pattern, within which all these things – and Rhysana herself – would move according to their proper time and place. She would simply hold herself ready, and face each new challenge as it came.

And then, borne upon the salt breeze from the sea, a new thought came to her; or an old thought, a mental note which she had made to herself some time ago, but which had lain buried beneath the business of College and Council until now. A new strand of the pattern flickered into light within her mind.

Rhysana did not doubt her guess. She had studied Illana's lore at length; had driven herself near frantic translating the twisted verses of the *Argument of Command* and trying in vain to interpret them. Even now she could picture the words of the text upon the page. But she needed to check, to make certain that her memory did not beguile her.

She breathed a prayer of thanks to the Lord of Air – and to the Lord of the Sun, who rode up with the dawn that had inspired her – and glided back in to the grey stillness of her bedchamber.

She picked up her shawl from the end of the bed, and went over to kiss the silver-fair head of her sleeping son. Then she went back around the bed to kiss her husband on the forehead. He stirred and gave a rumbling purr, and opened one eye.

'What is it?' he asked.

'Nothing,' said Rhysana quietly. 'I am just going over to the *aumery*, before the boy is awake. Go back to sleep.'

'Why can't you have cravings for custards, or pickled walnuts,' he growled, 'like any normal woman?'

'This *is* normal, for me,' she said. 'I shall not be long.'

She stroked his chest in farewell. Torkhaal reached one arm around the back of her legs, drawing her closer against the edge of the bed.

'Wake me when you get back,' he grinned.

'Perhaps,' she teased. 'Go back to sleep.'

She patted his chest once more, then slipped away from his grasp and went out.

The thrush was still singing as she made her way along the

pillared walkways of the cloister garden, and the first of the College martlets were chattering to one another up among the eaves. The air was like new wine, sweet with honeysuckle. Rhysana kept to her unhurried pace, both because College decorum required it and because she was remembering how to take delight in her surroundings.

She let herself in quietly through the tall bronze doors with their circling patterns, and then fashioned a small sphere of her own silvery magelight to guide her across the darkness of the lower hall and up the wide sweep of the library stair. She was hardly surprised at all when she met the dark figure of the Imperial Counsellor coming down the stair toward her. Given that Merrech usually turned up whenever she returned to the study of Illana's lore, she had almost been expecting it.

'High Councillor,' his voice hissed in the shadows around them.

'Archmage,' she nodded.

He went on past her without further comment. Rhysana felt more wary than relieved. She began to climb again.

'Rhysana,' his voice came from behind her.

At the same moment a wall of dark opalescent flame sprang up from the steps just ahead of her, barring her way. She staggered back, and nearly lost her footing; turned awkwardly as she prepared to face the worst.

'The Warden of the College Libraries serves many purposes,' he said. He was standing several steps below, facing her. 'He guards boundaries beyond which it is perilous to cross, or where the student might overreach himself.'

Rhysana breathed deeply. There was the familiar impression of unseen coils snaking about her, but he had made no further move to attack. She was uncertain whether he intended to threaten her, or to lecture her; or whether perhaps he was making some form of complaint.

'Restriction for positive ends,' she nodded carefully, not lowering her guard.

The Archmage turned and went on down the stair. The wall

of his power vanished. Rhysana waited until she saw him go out into the cloister garden, and the bronze door had swung shut behind him.

She gained the landing without further incident, and circled round past the door to the Lower Library and on up the *aumery* stair. The Warden was there waiting for her when she reached the smaller landing at the top.

'Mistress,' he said in his flat, mechanical voice.

'Good morning, Warden,' said Rhysana. She bowed as gracefully as she could, a little breathless from the climb.

If she was at all worried that the Warden might have barred her way – given Merrech's unexplained comment on the stair below – that doubt was swiftly laid to rest. Even as Rhysana straightened herself up, the unseen hands of the *chaedar* were pulling open the low door to the *aumery* library. The Warden stood motionless in his grey hooded robes, allowing her to proceed.

He made no mention of the Archmage Merrech, or what he might have been doing there that morning, though he would surely have been aware of their encounter on the stair. Nor did Rhysana wish to offend him by questioning him upon the matter. The Warden respected the right of all magi to privacy in their personal affairs.

She went through into the library and the *chaedar* closed the door behind her. The Warden remained outside. It was a rare privilege granted to Rhysana that she might study the reserve collection without his direct supervision – a privilege born of her fastidious care when handling any manuscript or codex, from which the peculiar friendship between the two of them seemed to have grown.

The scarlet codex she wanted was already being lifted from its proper place on the carved stone shelves, and carried over to the faldstool desk beside the window. That was another aspect of her friendship with the Warden which both delighted and baffled her. He seemed to know – on occasions more clearly than did Rhysana herself – which texts she would find the most helpful in her work. The fact that he had instructed the *chaedar* to fetch out the *Argument of Command* thus strengthened her conviction that she was on the right path.

She settled herself at the desk, schooling herself to calm with the familiar ritual of donning her white gloves. The scale-patterned hide of the codex binding shone softly in the dawn light, as if in smug reminder of previous defeats when she had wrestled with the riddles contained within. Rhysana pushed the reminder firmly aside, hefted the book open, and turned the pages until she found the passage she sought.

She had no need of magic to decipher the snaking letters upon the page. The language of the text was that of the scholars of Lautun in Illana's day; and for one of Rhysana's academic training it took no great effort to translate the basic sense of what was written there, though the word order could prove somewhat eccentric at times. The true difficulty lay in the interpretation of the riddling verses – a challenge that had confounded even the most gifted magi of the Golden Age. Had Illana's recorded deeds in life not proclaimed her wickedness, the *Argument of Command* alone would have earned her notoriety for its cryptic perversity and malice.

The greater part of the treatise dealt with the legends and histories of the old Six Kingdoms prior to the founding of the First Council, and with the lore of creatures both natural and magical. There was some reference to the more ancient legends of the Wars of the Gods, and to the battles of the Bright Alliance; and passing mention of the demon captain – though not by name – and of the diverse ranks and kinds of creatures from other Realms that had swelled his hosts. Yet the verses that Rhysana had remembered that morning came later, in one of a small group of songs known as the *Passing of Lordship*.

'*The kings must acknowledge its glory*,' she translated aloud; 'or *his glory. He rises in the heart; strength crumbles from the centre to the rim.*'

It was not so very different from what the Easterner wizard

had said at Khôrland, as Morvaan had reported it. Close enough to suggest that he might have been aware of Illana's work; or that the two of them had had access to a common source.

Rhysana sat back, repeating the verses to herself. It had become an accepted tradition among the scholars of the Magi to render *he* as *it* in their translations; and the verses were then interpreted as a reference to Illana's own fortress citadel of Whitespear Head – which had indeed risen in the heart of the Six Kingdoms and still stood there to this day, sealed by the Council itself to guard against all intrusion. That fortress held mysteries of power as baffling as any of the verses in the *Argument of Command*.

There were also those who saw in the latter part an allusion to the terrible destruction of the Wasted Hills, north of the Lautun plains, though Rhysana thought that to be pressing the point a little too strongly. The word for *strength* could imply capability, or strength of will, as well as strength of arms or magical power.

She held it unlikely that this particular song foretold the return of the demon – though for Hrugaar's sake she determined to consider it again later, in the light of that possibility. What concerned her more at that moment was the implication that there might be any connection at all between Illana and Lo-Khuma, or the Easterner wizards who followed him. It raised new questions as to the circumstances of Illana's recent death, and what else that might signify. And it brought back into question the role of the Archmage Merrech, and how much he knew of all this.

Rhysana closed up the codex and sat quietly, setting the thoughts aside in her mind and restoring her sense of calm. She found herself wondering what she should do next.

Nothing, just yet, she told herself firmly; and then added, *Time enough, soon enough.*

The saying had been one of Herusen's, and the memory brought a sad smile to her face. She realised that she had been counting on the benefit of his wisdom in this matter, forgetting that he was gone – even though the tidings of Illana's death had apparently been intended for herself and Torkhaal alone.

The Warden was standing in the doorway, his hooded robes a soft pewter grey in the dim light.

'Is all as it should be, Mistress?' he demanded.

Rhysana did not know how to answer him, so she returned a question of her own.

'Do you miss Herusen, Warden?'

'Herusen, Prime Councillor of All Magi,' he recited. 'Flower of the Staff. His memory is with us, Mistress.'

Rhysana nodded absently, and rose to her feet. She supposed that the Warden might be able to help her with this latest discovery. But she needed time to think first, before she mentioned it.

'How did the Chosen Priestess Ilumarin manage to speak with Torkhaal, in the Lower Library?' she asked.

The Warden had already vanished. Rhysana sighed, though with no great sense of disappointment. Torkhaal had asked him the same question before now, and come no nearer to receiving an answer.

She lifted the scarlet codex from the desk, and put it away in its proper place on the stone shelf. Then she straightened the shawl around her shoulders, glanced once around the *aumery* to check that all was as it should be, and went out.

Kellarn slept late that morning, and awoke only when the sunlight slipped through the window shutters to dance across his pillow. The house was quiet again after the merriment of the night before. Corollin had already gone downstairs, and was busy gleaning tales of Farodh and the Old Kingdoms from Heruvor and some of the other moon fay.

He went and listened with her for a while, and then swam in the mere with Galden, and lay on the grass to dry himself in the sun. But the shadow of parting now fell cool across his heart, and even the Nets of Starmere could not wholly keep back the call of the world outside. He knew that they must soon be leaving.

The memory of his vision in the Nets had also returned to trouble him, though it seemed faint and remote beneath the bright summer sky. He had thought to ask Heruvor privately about it; but the lord of Starmere was in a circle of other folk, so instead he asked Galden. The golden fay nodded, as if he had been waiting for him to talk of it.

'From what I understand of the Nets,' he told Kellarn, 'they can let loose the hopes and fears of the human heart. So it was with this waking dream of yours, I think. The enemy captain is your great fear, and the dragon both fear and hope; and in the dream the two came out and flowed together in confusion.'

'I thought at first that the Enemy looked like the Emperor,' said Kellarn. 'But then he changed.'

'The Emperor is another thing that you fear,' said Galden; 'and not without cause. In human dreams, so I am told, many things may blur one into another.'

'There was the burst of golden power at the end,' Kellarn nodded. 'I could not tell whether it came from Corollin or – or the other thing; or whether it was you.'

'That was me, I think,' said Galden. 'I saw a little of what it was that the Nets drew from your mind, and knocked you down to end it.'

'Was it dangerous, then?' Kellarn asked carefully.

'In its own way,' Galden answered. 'The Nets have power of their own, and also the power that you give to the shapes that they fashion. You believed that there was danger, and so your own peril grew.'

'But it was only the Nets, wasn't it?' asked Kellarn. 'There was nothing else, from outside?'

'It was not the Enemy himself, if that is what you fear,' Galden assured him. 'It was the power of the Moon at work. But if you wish to know more of that, you must ask Heruvor himself.'

'And why did my sword turn silver?' Kellarn wondered.

'You did not draw your sword,' said Galden. 'It was a moonlight dream – no more, and no less. Let not your heart be troubled by it any further.'

They went back to join Corollin and the moon fay, and no more was said on the matter. Kellarn decided not to ask Heruvor about it.

The next morning they set out early, while the dawn was still no more than a blush of rose above the misty mountain tops behind, and the white moon sailed ahead of them high in the western sky. Heruvor came down to the wharf to see them on their way with words of blessing and good cheer.

'But where is Ferunel?' asked Kellarn, feeling strangely disappointed.

Heruvor pointed to where her slender figure glittered like a star on the farther shore.

'Ferunel has gone ahead with your horses and gear,' he told them. 'She will guide you safely through the Nets to the world outside.'

The three of them climbed down into the grey boat – Galden and Corollin, and Kellarn last of all – and it carried them in silence across the moonlit waters of the mere. Heruvor stood and watched them go, with one hand raised in farewell; and Ferunel stood waiting to greet them, with both arms outstretched in welcome.

Galden was first ashore again, and other folk of Heruvor's household came forward to help them and to hand over their horses. Mistwise and Lanaë tossed their heads with low whinnies of welcome, their breath coming in steaming plumes on the cool dawn air; and Rúnfyr was prancing merrily on his front hooves like a young colt let out to play. Kellarn felt that he was the only one who was less than eager to be going.

The moon fay said their farewells and slipped away into the shadows. Ferunel smiled and led the way west in silence. There was a light on the air around her, like moonlight reflected from mountain snow, which seemed to grow brighter as they moved in beneath the trees.

Whether through the arts of Ferunel herself, or because they were now leaving Starmere to return to the world outside, they passed through the Nets untroubled. She led them at speed, so that they had to hold to a good pace to keep sight of her; and after their first meeting on the shore she remained at a distance, glimpsed only as a ghostly figure among the trees, her long cloak rippling like quicksilver behind her. The forest around them slumbered in deep shadows of ebon and grey, paling here and there to silver mist flecked with many hues of mother-of-pearl. There was no sign of a path, nor of the little stream that they had crossed before; or if there was, Kellarn had no memory of it afterward. And then presently the grey shadows deepened to green, and the air grew sweet with the musk of earth and bough, and Ferunel stood waiting to greet them.

'Here I must leave you,' she said as they came up. 'Go now with the blessing of the Fay, and of all good creatures of the *Aeshtar*.'

'Once again we are in your debt,' said Corollin, bowing.

Ferunel shook her head with a light, musical laugh. A diadem of many jewels, clear and white, glittered upon her brow, and scattered light like raindrops all around her.

'It is we who owe much to you,' she answered. 'There is still hope in the world.'

Kellarn also bowed, though he could think of nothing to say. Ferunel darted forward and kissed him on the forehead, and then kissed Corollin and was gone. Rúnfyr stamped and snorted.

'She's getting as bad as my sister Ellaïn,' Kellarn muttered.

Galden was crouched down on the grass, his head cocked to one side as if listening for something. Then he grinned and stood up, and called the bay mare Lanaë to his side.

'Ferunel has brought us further north from the Blue River, near to the mountain cliffs,' he told them. 'West and north now lies our way, to the borders of Fystenur, the great forest – or Cerrodhí, as you call it.'

'Are we going to Cerrodhí?' asked Kellarn.

'If we followed the Blue River it would take you south, out of your way,' said Galden; 'and closer to Ellanguan.'

'Do not argue with the guide, while you have him,' said Corollin.

'I wasn't arguing,' said Kellarn; 'just asking.'

They set off again at a slower pace. The forest floor ranged up and down over many folds, scattered with rocky dells; and though the undergrowth was kept at bay by the thick tree canopy overhead, the ground was rough and treacherous beneath its mask of fallen leaves. The air grew dull and more oppressive as the morning wore on, and the sighing of the wind among the treetops was joined by the harsher counterpoint of squalls of rain beating against the leaves overhead and the steady dripping of water from the lower branches to the floor. Kellarn found himself wishing he had stayed behind in Starmere. He also fell to wondering whether Ferunel had led them through the Nets because she feared that he might have let loose a worse vision of terror than before, from which Galden might not have saved them. But watching Galden walking cheerfully ahead of them, barefoot as ever, such fears seemed rather foolish.

In the early afternoon the air grew brighter again, and the mood of the forest less gloomy; and the ground became more level, though it was still climbing steadily. The trees here were mostly elms and tall oaks, and they could glimpse patches of daylight – if not sky – high overhead. Galden picked up the pace; and his eagerness seemed to be catching, so that Kellarn forgot about being fed up over leaving Starmere and pressed forward to walk beside him. Corollin was looking around her as she went, taking everything in in her own quiet way.

In the late afternoon they crested a sudden ridge and came to a halt. The ground dropped steeply away ahead of them, and for the first time since they had left Starmere they could see the open sky. The brightness and the freshness were dizzying.

As Kellarn's eyes grew accustomed to the light, he realised that they had rounded the end of the mountain line that ran west from the Starmere valley, so that they were now facing north-northwest across the long southern spur of the great forest. To their right, the sheer mountain cliffs marched northward for many leagues. Ahead and to the left, all he could see was the leafy rooftop of the forest, stretching away to blend into a shimmering haze with the deep summer sky. Though he knew for a fact that the western edge of the forest spur could not be much more than ten miles away to his left, the brightness of the sun in that direction kept it hidden from his sight.

'Below us is the valley stream which marks the first border of Fystenur,' said Galden. 'Lachaïta we call it, though I do not know if it has another name in your kingdoms. The horses will not like the steep slope, so we shall take them round by another way. Yet I thought that you might like to see the forest from here.'

They rested there a few minutes more, listening to the wind and the birds, and drinking in the clearer air. Then they fetched the horses and retraced their steps for a way, and turned west and then north to go down into the valley.

It proved to be a longer route than Kellarn had expected, and the best part of an hour had passed before they heard the gurgle of water close ahead. Galden brought them down to where an old willow had toppled to make a natural bridge, at a height of several feet above the stream. Being full of life, the willow had put out many side branches along its upper edge to form a row of smaller trees, all twice as tall as Kellarn. It would still have been possible, Kellarn thought, to weave one's way between the row of trees and cross over dry shod. But since they had the horses with them, he supposed that they would have to pull off their boots and wade barefoot through the stream. Not that he really minded the cold water at the end of a long summer's day, but he thought that crossing the tree-bridge might have been fun.

'Are we going to cross over the stream?' Corollin asked Galden. 'Or shall we just follow it down to the forest edge?'

'I had thought to go across,' Galden nodded. 'We can rest on the far bank for tonight – and Kellarn can go and fall off the willow bridge as oft as he likes.'

'Am I that obvious?' Kellarn grinned sheepishly.

Corollin laughed. 'Galden wants to climb it too,' she said. 'You are quite as bad as one another.'

They forded the stream and set up their camp on the far side; and then Kellarn and Galden played on and off the willow tree while Corollin prepared supper, until it was too dark to see properly. And then they settled the horses for the night, and took turns to sleep and watch.

They made an early start again the next morning, loading up the horses by the creamy gold light of Corollin's magic. Kellarn was just relieving himself behind a tree trunk, in readiness to set off, when there was a sudden disturbance in the branches overhead. He reeled off a string of rude words beneath his breath, fumbling to finish up and fasten his breeches. Having Galden arrive beside him did not really help.

'There is something up there,' the fay whispered.

'I know,' Kellarn growled.

He stepped back to draw his sword, then flattened his back against the tree trunk and slid sideways into the half-light. Corollin was crouched half hidden behind the tethered horses, her short sword in her hand, scanning the branches for signs of danger.

For several heartbeats nothing happened. Then there was another rustle of movement, followed by the loud clapping of wings as a pair of birds flew out and away.

Kellarn burst out laughing, and moved away from the tree. 'Only pigeons,' he said.

Corollin stood up more slowly. A tiny grey feather drifted down from where the birds had flown, dipping and gliding from side to side on its long, spiralling journey to the ground below. Kellarn found himself watching it, entranced by its light, unhurried grace. Corollin was watching too. And then the feather dipped down to brush the ground, and the air above it swirled with many colours, and a woman of the Fay stood before them.

At first glance, Kellarn did not recognise her. Her garments were the deep green of yew leaves, and she wore a huge cloak sewn with bird feathers of every size and hue. But her long silver hair was still woven with flowers of white and green and pale indigo; and there was still the shy, untame beauty behind her queenly glance.

Corollin bowed low, and Galden knelt beside her. Kellarn found himself going down on one knee, and presenting the hilt of his sword in homage.

'Rise up, Son of the Living Fire,' the fay woman told him; and though her voice was gentle as ever, it held a wild joy as thrilling as a call to arms. He scrambled to his feet.

'Losithlîn?' he faltered.

She nodded with slow diffidence.

'I serve for the Guardian of Fystenur, on whose borders you now stand,' she said. 'There is no true Guardian for that forest now, alas. Yet still I serve, as I may.'

She gestured for Corollin and Galden to rise.

'For long years the forest has lain under shadow,' she went on. 'In that time, many treasures of the old kingdom of Cerrodhí have been looted and stolen by the creatures from the mountains, and the shadowfay covet them. But other treasures the Guardians have saved, or their servants, and gathered them together where none can harm them. Such a treasure I now bring to you. For from our speech together in Starmere, I deem that the time has now come for this jewel to be brought back into the world of humankind.'

Losithlîn held out her hand and showed him a small metal bar, like to the three that they had already found. It was set with a gemstone of bright apple green, with the image of two trees carved on either side.

Kellarn's mouth opened and shut, but no sound came out; and then he grinned so broadly that he felt his cheeks must be pushing into his ears. Corollin and Galden pressed forward to see, though they took care not to touch Losithlîn or the jewel that she held.

'Is this the one of which Ferunel spoke?' Galden asked.

'Perhaps,' said Corollin. A brief flicker of disappointment passed across her face. 'That won't make the Farodhí part any easier to find.'

'But at least we don't have to hunt all over Cerrodhí for this one,' said Kellarn.

'That would have been a long search indeed,' said Losithlîn. She handed the bar to Kellarn, and he looked at it for a while longer before passing it to Corollin for safe keeping.

'I don't know how to thank you,' he told Losithlîn.

'Finish the journey that you have begun,' she answered; 'and honour the gods who have brought you safe thus far. No other thanks are needed.'

'But still we are very grateful,' said Corollin.

Losithlîn turned her head, as if looking at the horses.

'Where shall you go now?' she asked.

'West to Farodh,' Kellarn answered. 'That was the plan.'

'Then walk with me for a while,' she offered. 'I can lead you to the old forest road, north and west from here, which will shorten your journey in the world outside.'

Kellarn and Corollin looked at Galden, and he nodded his agreement. Losithlîn called to the horses, and the beasts seemed to shake themselves awake. Kellarn realised that they had stood still and quiet for quite a long time.

They set off north from the stream, the valley slope climbing more gently on this side. The forest was dark and silent all around; but with Corollin's light and Losithlîn to guide them, they seemed to make good speed.

'Did you know about the Cerrodhí bar, when we were at the feast?' Kellarn asked presently.

'No,' said Losithlîn. 'I came to Starmere for the full moon feast, and for other reasons of my own. Then after we had spoken, I returned to the forest and looked again with new eyes at the treasures that are hidden there. But such is often the way with the dances of the gods. Our paths seldom cross without purpose.'

'Then do the gods choose our paths for us?' he asked. 'Or do we choose them for ourselves?'

'A little of both,' she smiled.

Kellarn sighed. He should not have expected a simple answer from the Fay.

'Who you are,' Losithlîn said after a moment, 'has already been shaped, in part, by the union of every man and woman through the ages who has brought about your birth into the waking world, as well as by your own choices. And who you are affects the choices that you have yet to make. The Lords of the *Aeshtar* see all these patterns unfolding, and the likely paths that you might choose, and weave them all into the dance.'

'So they knew that the old kings would make the bars,' said Corollin; 'and that some day we – or someone – would find them.'

'In a sense, yes,' said Losithlîn. 'Yet one can not measure the dances of the gods within the flow of time alone. Or to put it another way, the coming conflict with the Enemy is one of the focal points of the dance; and it might also be said that what has happened, in what we now call the past, had its root and cause in the conflict we have yet to see.'

Kellarn shook his head. The argument was carrying him well out of his depth. 'Are we living life backwards, then?' he grinned.

Galden laughed in delight, and Losithlîn smiled.

'Not quite,' she allowed.

'And after the focal point?' wondered Corollin.

'Love the *Aeshtar*, and do what you think is best,' said Losithlîn. 'All the rest will follow.'

Corollin made as if to speak again, but then held her peace. Neither Losithlîn nor Galden offered further comment.

'Do the Fay foresee as much as the *Aeshtar*?' asked Kellarn.

'No indeed,' Losithlîn answered. 'And even the Lords of the *Aeshtar* themselves can not see all things that shall be; for some things are still hidden in the unknowable mysteries of Osîr.

For us, as creatures of the dance, there are still many joys and blessings unlooked for.'

They walked on in silence for some while after that. The forest on either side still slumbered in deep shadow, much the same as when they had set out, so that Kellarn began to wonder whether he was caught in a dream; and when he thought about it, he found that he was hardly tired at all, and only a little hungry. He tried willing himself awake, but nothing seemed to happen. In the end he decided that it was either a dream or some form of Fay magic; and since Corollin and Galden seemed happy enough, he thought it best not to cause trouble by asking about it.

At length they came to a part of the forest where bushes and ferns grew more thickly beneath the trees. Losithlîn took a turn to the left, and they picked their way down a long slope on to the beginnings of what seemed to be a narrow trail. The trail soon widened into an overgrown path, with smooth stones half buried in many places beneath. Rúnfyr was less happy about the ground underfoot, and began to grumble and play up. And then they rounded a bend in the path, and beheld a clear avenue of trees running straight ahead, ending in an archway of bright daylight no more than a furlong distant. Losithlîn signalled a halt.

'Here is the old road,' she told them. 'It will lead you south, to the main road of your own kingdoms, and then whither you will thereafter.'

'Wherever that is,' said Kellarn, gripping Rúnfyr's reins tightly and glaring at him to behave.

Losithlîn stretched up on tiptoe to whisper in the gelding's ear, and he quietened down almost at once.

'You could make for the Sun Temple first,' Galden offered, 'and see what we have done there. The priests would be interested in Kellarn's sword.'

'So long as they don't want to keep it,' said Kellarn.

'But the Sun priests would know little of Farodh,' said Corollin.

403

'And only the old kings would know where they hid the treasure that you seek,' Galden returned.

'You might try asking them,' said Losithlîn.

'The dead kings?' Corollin looked dismayed.

'Not all may be in the Realms of the Dead,' said Losithlîn. 'The Guardian of Telbray Woods could tell you if any are now reborn among the living.'

'I thought that he was dead, too,' said Kellarn doubtfully.

Losithlîn shook her head. 'He left an heir,' she said quietly. 'The new Guardian may be able to help you.'

Kellarn and Corollin looked at one another. Delving the memories of the Dead was not a task that appealed to either of them.

'It is worth a try, I suppose,' Corollin sighed.

They turned back to Losithlîn, but she had already vanished. Galden was looking down at his feet.

'I suppose you'll be going now, too?' said Corollin.

'Back to the valley,' said the fay, looking up again. 'The humans of your kingdoms would not take kindly to seeing me ride with you; and I have my own work to do.'

'We shall come back to see you,' said Kellarn.

'In this life, or another,' Galden nodded, handing him Lanaë's reins.

On impulse, Kellarn seized the fay's hand and kissed it. He had a sudden fear that he would not see him again. Galden responded by wrapping him in a tight bear hug. His breath was warm and sweet around Kellarn's head, and he had the smell of newly turned earth on a fine spring morning.

'Be at peace, little brother,' Galden whispered. Then he stepped back and bowed to Corollin, and turned and sprang away swiftly among the trees. The horses tossed their heads and whinnied in farewell.

'Why do *you* always get the hugs goodbye?' grumbled Corollin.

'Because that's all I get,' said Kellarn. Then they both laughed, and felt the better for it.

They mounted up and rode out from beneath the trees. The sky was bright and clear, and the sun had barely climbed to mid-morning. The Blue Mountains were now well over twenty miles away to their east. As far as Kellarn could guess, Losithlîn must have brought them a good ten leagues north and west from the forest stream, either by her Fay magic or some power of the Guardians. He found that he did not really mind – no more than when Galden had raised the bed of the Blue River. He supposed that it was the human Council of Magi to which he objected, more than the magic itself.

The Forest Road was little more than an old green track, cutting fairly straight through open hill country. There were still many stands of trees and bushes all around, and acres of bracken and tall cow parsley, but it was far easier than finding a path though the Whispering Forest.

By noon they reached the broad paved road of the Eastern Way – the great thoroughfare of the old Six Kingdoms, which came up from Arrandin and the South and then ran west to the ferry crossing at Rebraal, and on down between the hills and the plains toward the imperial city of Lautun. They let the horses stretch their legs along the road, glad of the chance for speed and a cooler breeze upon their faces. The rain clouds of the previous day had gone, the wind had died, and the summer sun was baking.

There were few travellers on the road, and none to give them any trouble. The growing number of farmsteads on either side lay peaceful and content among the hills. Though perhaps a little quieter than usual, it did not have the feel of a land at war. But then the call to arms had been barely a month before; and if the peace with the Southers held, the warriors would be coming home again soon, well in time for harvest.

They camped just off the road that night, and reached the walled town of Rebraal in the late afternoon of the second day.

'Will they know us again, do you think?' asked Corollin, as they caught their first sight of the grey stone towers.

Kellarn made a face. They had had a run-in with the town guards a few months back, after trouble with slavers on the imperial plains. The misunderstanding between them had eventually been cleared up, but only after a whole day had been wasted.

'Probably,' he said. 'Unless the fools who dealt with us have all gone down to Arrandin.'

'They were pleasant enough to me, in their own way,' said Corollin.

'That's because you're a lovely young lady,' he told her.

'That makes no difference.'

'It does to guardsmen,' he grinned. 'I've served in a guard, remember. But they could have cleared us through in half the time, if they'd been doing their job properly.'

'I suppose,' she shrugged. 'It might help, though, if they remember us this time.'

'It might,' Kellarn allowed. 'I just don't like the idea of having the Emperor's men know where I am. But we'll have to risk it.' He knew of no other way to cross the Strong River between the forest and the sea.

The guards who stopped them at the gate were clad in the brown and green livery of the Lords of Rebraal, with mailshirts and long swords and steel-crested helms. They were red-faced and sweating, even in the afternoon shade, and more alert than Kellarn could have wished.

'Don't I know you from somewhere?' asked the younger of the two, eyeing Corollin up and down as she fished in her pouch for enough coins to pay the toll.

'I think not,' she said smoothly.

The elder guardsman was studying the three horses with evident suspicion.

'They're rather fine beasts,' he observed.

Rúnfyr jostled at Kellarn's side, and bared his teeth in warning.

'They are on loan from the knights of Mairdun,' Kellarn explained. 'We are returning them to their *commanderie*.'

'I suppose you have proof of that?' the guard rejoined.

'Well enough,' came another voice. 'These two are known to me. Let them pass.'

A third man had emerged from the gate tunnel, dressed much the same as the other two, but with green leggings instead of brown and carrying his helm under one arm. With his greying hair and dark eyes there was something of the look of a badger about him. Kellarn sighed, recognising him as the Captain with whom they had spoken at length on their last visit.

The two guards also sighed, and stepped back with reluctant grace. Corollin handed her coins to the younger man, and then they trooped through the gate tunnel into the shadowed street beyond.

'You do get around, my Lord,' said the Captain, when they were some distance from the gate. 'The last I heard, you were killing Easterners beyond Arrandin.'

'News travels fast,' said Kellarn. 'But I'm more worried about the Southers just now.'

'You're not alone there,' the man agreed. 'But we brought the news with us from Arrandin – hared back ahead of the rest, at my Lord Dernam's command, and got here last night. The Southers may have made peace down in Ellanguan, but I'll believe it when they start doing something about the damned slavers everywhere. No offence, my Lady.'

'None taken,' said Corollin. 'You are still having trouble, then?'

'Same as ever,' said the Captain glumly.

Kellarn said nothing. His memories of the slave traders were not something he wished to discuss.

They came out into the heat and bustle of the market square. To their right loomed the high walls and round towers of the Rebraal fortress, grey and solid in the afternoon sunlight. The Captain led them round to the left, toward the small stabling inn that they had used before.

'Are you staying long in Rebraal?' he asked them politely; 'or just passing through again?'

407

'Straight through, I fear,' Corollin answered. 'We were hoping to take the ferry and be out through the west gate well before dark.'

The Captain looked at them both, but then nodded without further question.

'I'll see you over myself then,' he said. 'That'll end my duty for the day.'

He led them on along the edge of the square, and then down the winding street to the riverside wharf.

The Strong River clove its way through a steep-sided gorge, starting from within the Great Forest of Cerrodhí and running all the way down to its rocky end on the coast; and as the name implied, its waters were swift and powerful. The footings of an old bridge could still be seen up near the northern end of the wharf; but the bridge had been swept away long ago, and no one had bothered to rebuild it. Most merchants and traders now favoured the coastal shipping routes between Lautun and Ellanguan, rather than the longer overland haul along the road. Travellers who chose to use the road had to take the ancient ferry – and pay their fares toward its upkeep.

The wharf was less busy than the square, with only a few barges and riverboats moored alongside. There were one or two sentries in the gold and brown livery of Lautun walking up and down, and a couple more loitering near the door of the Customs house. Perhaps because they had the guard captain with them, no one seemed to pay Kellarn and Corollin much heed. They had a wait of ten minutes or so, and more coins were taken out of Corollin's pouch; and then they boarded the squat raft of the ferry and were hauled across to the landing on the far bank.

The western side of Rebraal was older and much smaller, with the boatwrights' sheds down by the water's edge and the stone houses of the more prosperous merchants above and behind. They climbed another winding street, with Corollin and the Captain leading the way, and crossed the smaller square at the top which lay just inside the gate.

'You're sure you won't stay till morning?' the Captain asked.

'It's none too safe out there. I'm sure we could stand you a drink or two, for all that you did down South.'

'You are too kind,' Corollin demurred. 'But we really must go. We should prefer to keep it quiet about our coming north. My Lord Kellarn hates all the fuss and attention.'

'Yes,' said Kellarn, quite truthfully.

The Captain bowed in acceptance, and escorted them out through the gate; and stood and watched as they rode off along the road.

'Do you think he'll keep quiet?' asked Kellarn, when they were safely out of earshot.

'Captain Broghan? Oh yes,' said Corollin.

'Broghan,' echoed Kellarn. 'I couldn't remember his name.'

'I am not so sure about the other guards, though,' she said. 'Especially that one at the gate. Did you mean what you said, about taking the horses to Mairdun?'

'One day, perhaps,' said Kellarn. 'I still feel guilty about keeping them; and I'm not sure it would be a good idea for people to know that Dortrean had such a costly gift from Mairdun.'

'Your father did not seem to mind,' she said.

'No. But if the Emperor's spies think we are heading for Mairdun, it might keep them off our backs.'

'Are you sure they'll still be looking for us?'

'Probably,' he said. 'Let's not take any more chances.'

'You are getting too good at lying,' Corollin told him.

'It wasn't lying, exactly,' said Kellarn.

They followed the road for well over a mile, until the lie of the land took them out of sight from the walled town. Then they checked all around, to make sure that no one was watching, and turned north toward a long brake of thorn trees. They had to dismount to lead the horses in among the trees, and all three beasts made a good deal of fuss about it; but they hoped thereby to discourage any would-be pursuers from following them. When they came out near the far end of the brake, some twenty minutes later, they took care to cover all signs of their departure. By then the sun had climbed down close to the hilltops to their northwest.

Their plan was to strike north toward the western borders of the Great Forest, and then to skirt up and around the outer edge of the imperial plains of Lautun to the fords of the Rolling River – not far, in truth, from the *commanderie* of Mairdun. It was a longer route, and beset with its own dangers; and a horseman riding straight from Rebraal to Mairdun could have reached there and turned back ahead of them. But Kellarn had reasons of his own for heading north here. For one thing, the Lautun plains were the Emperor's own lands, and he had no intention of being seen going that way. For another, the lands ahead to the west of Rebraal were held by the Lords of Kôan, where he would still be less than welcome after his unfortunate quarrel with the late Sir Reïkjan. The northern route would take them instead into the domain of the Earl of Scaulun. Though Scaulun – like most Houses Noble between Rebraal and the Rolling River – favoured the ways of the Empire, they had no great quarrel with Dortrean at Court. They would also have the backbone to side with Kellarn and Corollin, should one of the Emperor's bullies show up to cause trouble on their own lands.

They pressed on between the low hills, keeping their distance from any farms or cottages of the Rebraal folk, until the sun had gone down and the twilight grew too deep to ride safely; and then they made camp beside a small stream that flowed east toward the river gorge, and took turns to keep watch through the hours of darkness. But as it turned out, there was no sign of their being followed that night, nor the next day; and so they left the Strong River behind, and passed quietly through the lands of Scaulun, and came within sight of the western eaves of the Great Forest.

The Emperor Rhydden sat back in his chair, and turned his head toward the nearby window. The last of the sunlight slanted through the latticed panes, turning the folded shutters on one side to ruddy gold. The game, he thought, was not going too badly – both the game on the *sherunuresh* board before him, and also the larger game of war and peace being played out all around. He allowed himself a small smile of satisfaction, waiting for the Archmage Merrech to make his move.

The business with the Southers was going well – well enough, at least, for Rhydden to be at ease over the prospect of leaving Ellanguan two days hence to return to Lautun for the Summer Court. T'Loi had dealt with the newcomers as asked, and now two more ships lay peacefully at anchor off the coast while the rest sailed back to the God-King. Whether the God-King would be as amenable as T'Loi in his support against the Easterners was still far from certain; but the Southers already here would go a long way to help strengthen the defence of the Empire. A long way in more senses than one. The heathen priests of Braedun had been told to remove themselves from their *commanderie*, away down beyond Levrin, so that the Souther forces could be garrisoned there. Rhydden did not trust T'Loi so far that he was prepared to leave a Souther army in Ellanguan even an hour longer than was necessary.

The Northern Envoy Hakhutt had been less pleased with the thought of Souther allies, though after a good deal of persuasion and suitable largesse he had grudgingly accepted it. He had ridden away that morning, taking Rhydden's own squire, Zhiraún, as a parting gift. The Emperor had hoped that Hakhutt might leave one of his brothers behind in exchange, but no such offer had been forthcoming. The Envoy was to bring the matter before his fellow lords in the Northern Lands, and would then return to the Court at Lautun with their considered answer. Rhydden did not expect to see him again in less than a month.

The Archmage Merrech made his move. Rhydden looked back at the chequered board.

'You are letting me win, Counsellor,' he teased, removing the Archmage's ivory knight and replacing it with his own gilded priest.

'Not quite, Sire,' Merrech replied. The golden priest vanished from the square, to be replaced in turn by the ivory figure of one of his wardens. The whole pattern of the carved pieces on the board seemed to shift, revealed suddenly in a new light. The Emperor stood up.

'Where is Solban, anyway?' he said irritably.

'He comes,' said the Archmage.

Rhydden hardly heard him. Dortrean was still the two-edged sword in his imperial hands. Erkal – now less than a day's ride from Ellanguan – had of course proved his worth in his dealings with the Easterners. Karlena and Solban, in their different ways, had proved valuable in this business with the Southers and with the Northern Envoy, and also with the Empress. But their service, like their loyalty, came at a price that Rhydden did not wholly understand.

The latest news of Dortrean was small, yet enough to leave him further unsettled. Erkal's younger son Kellarn – or a man fitting his description – had been seen passing through Rebraal the previous afternoon, taking horses to Mairdun. Kellarn who had played his own part in turning the tide of war in Arrandin, before eluding Rhydden's spies. The young woman with him was like to the woman who had ridden with Dortrean from Khôrland to Fersí; and the Hyrsenites of Mairdun had been in Fersí.

By coincidence, perhaps, it had been the Hyrsenites to whom the hapless Brother Sarin had been sent, after Rhydden had finished with him, at the suggestion of the Lady Karlena. Rhydden did not take chances with coincidence. It was one thing that Dortrean had the age-old support of the *Aeshta* Orders, and now appeared to be patching over some of their differences with the Magi – just when the Magi themselves were struggling to come to terms with the unrivalled power achieved by their own people in Arrandin. It was quite another if they were beginning to find favour with the imperial *Vashta* Orders as well.

Rhydden's solution for Kellarn was simple: he was being followed again, and they would find out what he was up to before deciding whether to bring him in. Mairdun had a history of wayward beliefs and practice, so a routine investigation for heresy should suffice to bring them to heel. Rhydden would mention that to the War Priest Môrghran, who would also be returning to Ellanguan the following day. The Lords of Dortrean themselves, however, needed a sterner reminder of their own mortality.

The door opened and Lieutenant General Solban was announced. Rhydden nodded and sat down again to hear the evening report. The hooded Archmage took a step forward, masking the small gaming table from Solban's line of sight.

There was little news to report, and for once Solban had the sense not to dwell on it. Rhydden watched him carefully. He was not sure that he liked what he was about to do. But that was no longer a consideration.

'The Souther warships,' he said, when Solban had come to an end. 'We are not content that they should remain too long in Ellanguan. How long before they may depart for the *commanderie* of Braedun?'

A cloud shadow of remembered anger passed across Solban's face.

'The two off the coast may sail for the Braedun lands as soon as His Highness wishes,' he answered. 'There is room enough for them to camp on the Galloppi shore at once. Those in the harbour could be gone within a week, at a push.'

'And what of the *commanderie* itself?' Rhydden pressed.

'With respect, Sire,' Solban bowed, 'the *commanderie* has many places and treasures that the priests of Braedun have held sacred for centuries. They can not so readily move out for the Southers to come in. Nor, if His Highness will permit me to say so, do I think it wise for the Southers to have use of such a place of fortified strength; nor well advised to bring grief upon the Braedun Order by demanding that they surrender it.'

'We can hardly expect our Souther guests to sit in the fields all summer,' returned the Emperor lightly. 'Nor through the winter, if the Easterners come not again within the year. And if the God-King does not favour our agreed alliance with T'Loi, there may be other war ships sailing up the Galloppi against them. They shall have need of a place of shelter and strength.'

'With the deepest respect—' Solban began again.

'You show us too little,' Rhydden interrupted. 'Nor did we ask for your opinion. But it is of no matter. Since the heathen priests have decided to drag their heels, we have chosen another course for the present. The Southers shall remove themselves to the Watchful Isle, until such time as Braedun is ready for them.'

Solban choked on an oath.

'We understand that the Regent Lauraï of Renza has already left Ellanguan,' the Emperor went on.

'Two days since, Highness,' confirmed the Archmage. 'She took passage on a merchant ship of Vanbruch.'

'A pity,' said Rhydden, studying Solban's scarlet face. 'She might have saved us the errand, had she still been here. But no matter. You shall go to Renza, Lieutenant General, and make arrangements for the Southers to be welcomed there.'

'This is madness, Sire,' Solban managed. 'If His Highness will consider—'

'It was not a request,' said the Emperor calmly. 'Yet since you are so evidently concerned for the safety of Renza, we are content that you shall see to this personally.'

Solban controlled himself with visible effort. He glared at the faceless Archmage.

'Was this your counsel, Eminence?' he demanded.

'Would you believe me if I said no?' returned Merrech smoothly.

'Enough,' said Rhydden. 'You are relieved from further duties, Dortrean. We expect to see you gone from here by morning.'

Solban hesitated a moment longer, then drew himself up to salute. His right hand was shaking as it clenched against his chest. Then he spun round on his heel and left.

The noise of his booted feet faded as the door was shut behind him.

'Have him taken, once he leaves the palace,' said Rhydden.

'Highness.' The Archmage bowed.

Rhydden glanced back at the *sherunuresh* board. The table top was now hidden beneath a dome of magic, like a dish cover of polished black steel. Even he, seated within arm's reach, had not noticed when Merrech had done that. He signed irritably for him to remove it.

'We should rest soon,' he said, as Merrech obeyed. 'We have a long night ahead of us.'

'The Empress has requested an audience,' the Archmage reminded him.

Rhydden snorted. Grinnaer must have made half a dozen such requests in as many days, and on each occasion been refused. If Karlena's training had improved her bearing in the feast hall, it had also made her more demanding as a consort. He would have to teach her a lesson of his own.

'She can wait,' he said.

It was long past midnight when the Emperor returned to his own apartment in the Steward's palace. The guards on the landing shrank back as he passed, and closed the doors behind him with fumbling swiftness. He threw back his head and laughed. The sound re-echoed in his ears from the surrounding walls.

He could still feel the blood pounding through his veins, burning with fiery power, bringing strength no lesser mortal could hope to bear. His senses soared, exultant. He could reach the harbour in seven strides, or swim to Renza, or fling open the doors again and slay the cowering guards with a glance.

He could still see, in the dim light of the hall, the image of Solban before his eyes – stretched naked on the stone slab, with four hooded figures standing round. The stubborn defiance in his face, and then the anguish; and then the slow rise of terror, when at the last he began to understand the true price of gainsaying his Emperor. The taste of his blood had been very sweet.

Of course Solban had been right – there was no question

of letting the Southers set foot on Renza. More than half of Ellanguan would have found good cause to kill Solban to prevent him from such an errand; and when his body turned up in the morning, and rumour of that errand had been spread, that would cloud the matter nicely. As Lord Steward of the city, Rinnekh would have a rough ride for the next several days trying to keep the peace, before giving in gracefully and conceding that the Southers should go nowhere near the Watchful Isle. But then Rinnekh had had his own revenge against Solban tonight.

Rhydden moved on through his apartment. His people were either asleep or keeping themselves hidden. He remembered that Zhiraún had gone away.

The red glow of firelight showed through the open doorway of his bedchamber. Rhydden strode in. Grinnaer was sitting upright in the bed, small and pale and naked. Like the guards, she seemed to shrink back at his approach; but her jaw held a determined look that he had not seen before.

Rhydden came to a halt near the foot of the great bed. His first thought was to have her removed. But there were other possibilities.

'Did you tell her?' he demanded. His voice was like the roar of a furnace to his ears.

Grinnaer gave a timid nod. 'As His Highness commanded.'

He had no need of her answer. He knew everything that passed within the Empress' household, better than did Grinnaer herself. But the game had to be played out.

'She fell for it at once,' said Goshaún, closing the doors behind him, and then sauntering forward. '*Oh, the pain will seem unbearable—*'

Goshaún was a poor mimic, and his voice and manner were nothing like Karlena's, but Rhydden laughed again. He tore off his robe and cast it aside, and stood tall and naked before them.

'Then you shall have your reward,' he said. 'Both of you.'

He beckoned Goshaún forward, and tugged him by the belt

when he came close, pulling him round in front of him so that they were both facing Grinnaer. He wrapped his arms lovingly around the boy's shoulders.

Then with one clean jerk he snapped Goshaún's neck. It was a trick he had learned years before, but never had he done it with such strength and grace.

Grinnaer gave a voiceless cry, clutching blindly at the sheets. Rhydden let the body fall, springing forward on to the bed, knocking her back as he bore down on top of her. He pinned her down with one forearm across her throat, tearing with his free hand at the useless sheet between them.

'Never betray your Emperor,' he warned, heedless of her choking spasms. 'Remember – your life is bought by his. This once. Now you are only mine.'

Chapter Thirteen

It was Brodhaur Levrin who told Erkal of Solban's death. Riders in the golden livery of Lautun had met them on the road in the late morning, bringing word from Ellanguan. Brodhaur was grim and grey as he recounted the news.

The two Earls rode on at once, ahead of the main body of returning troops. Kierran of Arrand rode with them, and the *noghr* priest Dharagh, and a vanguard of the best knights that Brodhaur could find. Solban's body had been found down by the harbours, ravaged and abused and prey to dark magic, and rumour ran rife through the city. Karlena was under guard in the Steward's palace. Brodhaur was expecting trouble.

They reached the gate before mid-afternoon, and drew rein to hear report from Rinnekh's guards. The wide street ahead of them was unusually quiet, with only one or two ragged figures scuttling between shadowed doorways; but from somewhere near at hand came the buzzing murmur of gathered crowds, the sound of bees about to swarm.

The guards told them that the fountain gardens to the east of the Steward's palace were full, and there were more people in the Upper Square to the west. Many of the Southers had taken refuge aboard their ships, and there had been fires started and a few outbreaks of fighting along the harbour front. With the help of the Emperor's men, the city guard had so far been able to stem the uneasy tide. Erkal himself was as like to be stoned as cheered if he came within sight of the crowds.

They rode on down the street, the stern-faced knights flanking Erkal on either side, and then turned to enter the palace through the barrack gate. Erkal dismounted swiftly in the busy yard, waving the men aside as he himself went to help the *noghr* down from his forward perch on Kierran's saddle. Kierran slid down a moment later, with a ready grin that was too much like Kellarn's.

'You are not much use to me here, just now,' Erkal told them both quietly. 'See if you can get down to the temples and find out what else is going on. And send word to the Sun Temple, if they have not done so already. There could be trouble in Dortrean. And Ellaïn has to be told.'

'She may have left for the Summer Court,' said Kierran. 'It's a long ride from Dortrean.'

'She will not have left,' said the Earl. 'Now go.'

'We might be of some use here,' Dharagh objected, patting the head of his axe. 'I should like to meet this Steward.'

'Not yet,' said Erkal.

He went inside with Brodhaur, passing through the gloomy shadows of the barrack wing and on into the austere splendour of the huge East Hall.

The hall was as busy as the yard, with merchants and guardsmen and a handful of nobles all jostling and squabbling together like feeding gulls. The Souther Ambassador T'Loi was there, clad all in white, with two burly bodyguards and a host of frightened attendants. T'Loi was speaking with High Councillor Sollonaal, while three other magi hovered close by, all robed and hooded in the blue-green of Ellanguan. The lovely Eonnaï of Gadhrai was going head to head with one of the Guildmasters of the city, backed by two of her fellow priests. Some of Rinnekh's household guards stood duty at the doors, but there was little other semblance of order.

'Gods, this is looking ugly,' Brodhaur muttered. He moved away, calling the nearest guards to attention.

Erkal made straight across the hall and up the staircase at the far end, ignoring the hurried bows and comments from those who noticed him as he passed. It occurred to him as he strode along the upper landing that perhaps he should not have sent

Kierran out among the dangers of the city streets. But then Dharagh was with him, and no doubt the *noghr* would hew the legs from beneath anyone foolish enough to come too close.

Karlena was standing by the window of their bedchamber within the Dortrean apartment. She had been looking out, but turned her head as he came in. She was clad from chin to floor in a heavy black velvet overgown, with a high aureole collar and a long sash girdle worked with copper thread; and thus arrayed, with her pale face and burnished copper hair, she reminded him more than ever of the painted images of Hýriel, Lady of Fire.

'If my dwarven priest were with me, he would fall down before you and worship,' he said.

'A *noghr* is no good to me without an axe,' she returned. 'There are heads that need to roll.'

They looked at one another a few moments more, then came together in desperate embrace. They held each other close for a long while, without words.

'You know,' said Erkal at last, 'a *noghr* is perhaps a little too short to make a good headsman.'

'Not if the guilty kneel,' she said.

They fell silent again. At length Karlena loosened her grasp and pushed him away gently.

'You are creasing my gown,' she told him.

Erkal gave a gasp of laughter, of disbelief. 'You can think of your gown, at a time like this?'

'When did you see a goddess with crumpled clothes?' she replied. 'Apart from that tart among the *Vashtar*, perhaps.'

'Eörendin?' he offered.

Karlena nodded. 'Besides, I borrowed this from Elmirra's wardrobe. You know what she is like.'

She had not let go of him completely. He did not let go of her.

'Are you ready?' he asked.

'Not yet.' Karlena shook her head. 'There are things that you should know.'

He lifted her on to the edge of the high bed, and then sat beside her with their four hands joined.

'Goshaún is also gone,' she said. 'Rhydden killed him. Or had him killed. It makes no difference.'

'Grinnaer's brother?' said Erkal.

'There was – talk,' said Karlena carefully. 'There were those who thought the Empress unnaturally fond of her brother. Rhydden could not permit that.'

Erkal looked at her.

'And was she?' he asked. Karlena did not reply.

'What I can tell you,' she said, 'is that I had one of the Môshári Healers look at Grinnaer shortly before Rhydden's return, for various health reasons. At that time, Grinnaer was not with child – whether by Rhydden or anyone else.'

Erkal nodded. 'And how is she now?'

'They would not let me see her,' Karlena sighed. 'The priestesses are with her. By report, Rhydden beat her very badly. But if she survive and mend, there is now the chance that she may be carrying his child; and for that – if for nothing else this day – I suppose we should be thankful.'

They sat together in silence again. Then Erkal tilted her face up toward his, and wiped the tears from her cheeks.

'Ready to face the dragon in his lair?' he asked.

'Where is that *noghr*?' she said.

They made their own way to the Emperor's apartment. No one seemed to have orders to stop them. They found Rhydden in the squared chamber where he was wont to hold his breakfast meetings with his commanders. Rinnekh and the Archmage Merrech were with him, and there was a mess of parchments and tally sticks spread out across the long table.

'Dortrean,' said the Emperor, his voice pitched deep with compassion as he rose to greet them. Erkal and Karlena bowed.

'Would you excuse us, Eminence?' said Erkal.

The Archmage bowed and went away in silence.

'And you,' said Erkal, turning to Rinnekh, 'get your backside into the saddle and go out and speak to the city, before they tear your palace down about our ears.'

The Steward gaped at him, wide-eyed and open-mouthed, and then looked to his Emperor for support. Rhydden nodded for him to go.

Rinnekh slammed the door behind him as he went out.

'We understand your grief, Dortrean,' said the Emperor, when they were left alone. 'We have lost sons and daughters of our own – though none, it is true, were with us for so long.'

'Where is my son, Sire?' Erkal asked.

'The priests of War have charge of him,' Rhydden answered. Erkal frowned.

'We could no longer ensure his safety within your *Aeshta* temple,' said Rhydden, 'given the changeful moods of the city. And some of the Souther commanders and T'Loi's folk are guested in the cloisters of the priests of Arts. Nevertheless, as a ranking officer in our Imperial Household Guard, and as heir designate to a Noble House Ancient, we have commanded that he shall be afforded full honour and ceremony at the Rite of Burning this evening.'

'His Highness is most gracious,' said Erkal bowing. 'But is that wise, given the present mood of the city?'

If Rhydden noticed the irony in Erkal's manner, he made no mention of it.

'Whether we give him public ceremony or not,' he said, 'there will be those who hold us to blame. For your sake, and for his, we feel beholden to afford him all due ceremony.

'Of course we blame ourself,' he went on smoothly. 'Your son was right, Dortrean. We should never have considered sending the Southers to Renza. Alas, he has paid a dear price for loyal service to his foolish Emperor.'

'Are we any nearer the truth of what happened, Sire?' asked Karlena.

Rhydden looked at her, as if noticing her for the first time.

'Truth is such a difficult word in Ellanguan,' he observed, 'where treachery breeds even among our own household. But alas, my Lady, no. The heathen Orders are whispering of demons and dark magic at work, perhaps from the Southers or an Easterner spy. There are not a few who have been quick to link your son's death with the tragic loss of old Trigharran, though we have seen no certain ground for that. It may be that your son's firm hand when dealing with the Southers did not earn him their great friendship. Yet it is also true that the *Aeshta* Orders themselves had as good a cause as any – and perhaps more than the Southers – to confound his last errand.'

'The *Aeshta* Orders would not have used him thus,' said Karlena.

The Emperor shrugged elegantly. 'Perhaps not,' he allowed. 'But one of the Magi might have done so, and made it appear like the work of others. Even the late Herusen Dârghûn, it seems, was not above breaking the rules of the Council to suit his own purpose. And there are many in the city who have no love for the Southers, and who would make trouble against them to have them sent away.

'You are well aware of the problems with the God-King,' he said then, turning his attention back to Erkal, 'and of the need for surety of peace. Given that your treaty with the Easterners appears to have brought us but brief respite before a renewed assault, you must appreciate the urgent need for this alliance with the Southers to hold good.'

Erkal made to protest, but the Emperor overruled him.

'We are no less eager than yourselves,' he said, 'to have Souther armies camped on Lautun lands. Yet nor do we consider it wise to harbour them here in Ellanguan after this latest business. We shall therefore have them remove at once further down the coast, to the Braedun lands as planned, and they shall have to refit their own ships there as best they can. As our best man for dealing with foreign envoys, you yourself shall ensure that this is achieved peacefully.'

'Sire,' Erkal acknowledged through gritted teeth.

'It is a sign of our continued favour that we permit you to do so,' the Emperor warned him. 'Or have you not heard? Many now fear that you have made secret alliance with the East, or with the heathen Orders, or both; and hold Dortrean to blame that the Southers are here at all. By allowing you to deal with the Souther commanders, we give you the chance to prove your loyalty to the Empire and her safe defence. We trust that you shall not fail us.'

'Is this much the same speech that you gave to our son,' said Karlena, 'before sending him to Renza?'

'Not at all,' said Rhydden, smiling. 'His loyalty was beyond question. But you are both overwrought. You were best to leave us now.'

Kellarn braced himself to mount up again. He had shaken off the stiffness from legs and back. His uneasiness remained.

He knew that they were being followed. They had caught sight of a lone horseman early that morning – the second morning since they had passed through Rebraal – and had at first persuaded themselves that he might be no more than an errand rider of the Lords of Scaulun, intent on other business. An hour later they had seen him again, in company with a second horseman, still keeping the same distance behind them. When Corollin had tried to use her magic to find out who the men were, it seemed that they were using their own magic to confound her.

After that they had seen them but twice in all the long day, and only brief glimpses at a greater distance. Whoever the horsemen were, they were taking great pains to stay out of sight. To Kellarn's mind they were most likely the Emperor's spies, who had picked up their trail at Rebraal. But in this part of the Six Kingdoms they might have been slave traders or outlawed thieves, or any number of unpleasant things; or even honest wardens in the service of one of the imperial Houses, keeping their own watch on travellers and trouble-makers.

'They are still there,' said Corollin quietly, from her seat on Mistwise's back.

425

Kellarn growled in answer. He did not ask her how she knew. His own instincts told him much the same.

His sense of unease had come some while before they had seen the riders. It had begun the previous night, with a dream born of childhood memories. He had been swimming in the Ringstream below the Dortrean Manor, with Mellin Carfinn and his sister Ellaïn. His brother Solban, ever the serious one, had stood on the far bank beneath the trees, trying to warn them of something with increasing distress. When Kellarn awoke in the darkness, that sense of distress had stayed with him – made keener by the chill night breeze, and the sight of the nearby eaves of the Great Forest in the waning moonlight.

At first he had feared some threat of danger from the forest; for though the moon fay Losithlîn might serve as Guardian of Cerrodhí, there were still too many half guessed eyes and ears alert within its shadowed borders, marking their progress. Then when the riders had appeared, he had reasoned with himself that it might be no more than an instinctive wariness of being followed. Yet the nagging doubt, tending now toward a dim sense of foreboding, did not seem to be that simple.

They had turned west well before noon, leaving the forest eaves behind them and riding more swiftly across pleasant grassland hills. To their right, the Highland Mountains rolled down toward the plains in the gnarled promontory of The Hocks, which divided the wooded vastness of Cerrodhí from the barren slopes of the Wasted Hills on the northern borders of the imperial plains. The tawny bluffs and hollows of The Hocks lay drowsing in the summer heat, spread with a ragged blanket of green beneath the fading gold of gorse and broom, and only a few dark specks of hunting hawks drifted lazily above the horizon.

The lands around them belonged to the Lords of Aartaús; and Aartaús – more so than Scaulun – might have looked kindly upon Kellarn had he sought their help. Minnaíra, the Arrand's wife, was close kin to their Lord; as was the new Lord Dhûlann, one of Dortrean's own retainers. Aartaús were also one of the few imperial horsebreeders willing to trade bloodstock with Mellin Carfinn of late, since House Carfinn fell foul of the Emperor. But Kellarn did not know where their manor house stood, nor had there been much sign of herds or herdsmen to point the way. He fought shy of turning aside to look for it.

By late afternoon they drew level with the last outflung spur at the western end of The Hocks – a weathered tor of ample height and girth, skirted by a folded rise of scrub and shattered stone. The sun had passed well into the northern half of the sky, climbing down toward the ridges of the Wasted Hills, now close ahead; and long purple shadows stretched toward them. Corollin called a halt.

'There is water up there,' she said, nodding toward the valley dip on the eastern side of the tor. 'It may be the last good stream that we can find, till we get beyond those hills. And it is getting late.'

Kellarn hesitated. Like Corollin, he doubted that anything they found amid the barren hills would be fit to eat or drink – though he had planned on skirting round them, rather than riding through them. It was also true that the cliffs of The Hocks would offer better shelter, and that a camp there might be more easily defended if there was trouble during the night.

'What about our two friends?' he said.

Corollin shrugged. 'They will follow us wherever we go. I am more worried about the horses.'

Kellarn frowned.

'I'm fed up with this,' he said. 'I don't want the Emperor's ferrets at my heels all the way to the Black Mountains. Let's hide and give them a surprise.'

Now it was Corollin's turn to look doubtful.

'We were lucky with Mataún,' she said. 'You were less lucky when you picked a quarrel with Sir Reïkjan of Kôan. Must you go looking for trouble?'

Kellarn did not like the reminder.

'That was different,' he said. 'Besides, if they are following us, they're likely to cause trouble anyway. I don't want to be the one caught unawares.'

Corollin sighed and gave in.

They turned and rode north into the shadow of the tor, picking their way along the lower ground as they came to the first of the gnarled spurs. After about a mile they reached the head of a small valley, and dismounted. There were a few trees and bushes growing around the place, but no sign of water; and though the slopes on either side did not look too steep to climb, Kellarn had the unpleasant feeling that they had just run themselves into a trap. But there was no use in turning back now.

At Corollin's suggestion they divided the horses, taking Rúnfyr and Lanaë up the gentler slope to the west to tether them out of sight. Mistwise, being the most even-tempered of the three, they hid further down the valley behind a cluster of evergreen oaks. They made a point of trampling the ground a good deal where they had dismounted, to give their pursuers something to think about; and then they hid themselves among the rocks on either side, and waited.

The sky overhead turned a shade deeper, and the air around them cooled. Kellarn found that he was sweating. He studied the patterns on his drawn blade, watching how the gold glowed softly in the fading light. And then the sound of hooves reached his ears, and he had his first sight of their pursuers from close to.

The taller of the two men – whom they had seen first that morning – was clad in drab riding gear of grey and brown, with a short sword hanging at his side. But though his garb was simple, he had the rich brown hair and classic good looks of many of the Lautun Houses; and the great horse which carried him was clearly as noble as his master.

The second rider, now taking the lead, was dressed in similar fashion; but his horse was of lesser stock, and the man bore no weapon that Kellarn could see. He was bent far forward in the saddle, as though studying the ground while he rode, and his long black hair hid his face from view. There was something familiar about him that tugged at Kellarn's memory in warning.

The two horsemen came slowly up the valley, until they reached the trampled ground barely twenty yards from where Kellarn was waiting. The shorter man signalled a halt with one pale hand and dropped spider-like to the ground, his arms and legs curled beneath him. His horse backed away at once, as if glad to be rid of him. He stayed crouched on the ground for several seconds, then lifted his head to look straight at Kellarn. His face was rounded and young, with large dark eyes that many might have thought beautiful. The hatred and triumph in his gaze struck Kellarn like a physical blow.

Kellarn recovered and stood up, and then walked out slowly, his sword tip pointing down at the ground before him. The dark-eyed man also stood up, and seemed to become more human. His companion dismounted to join him.

'Why are you following us?' Kellarn asked.

He managed to keep his voice level and courteous, with only a faint edge of danger. The taller man bowed from the waist, and smiled as he straightened up again. He had a very fetching smile, and soft brown eyes that danced with fun, so that Kellarn found it hard to dislike him. There was only a few years difference between them; and it struck Kellarn that in another time and place they might have got on well together.

'We did not want you to come to any harm, my Lord,' the man answered. 'There have been slave traders abroad on the plains.'

His voice was soft and deep as his eyes, and quite as playful. Kellarn resisted the urge to smile, and shifted his grip on his sword.

'I know,' he said.

'Though clearly,' the man went on, 'you are well able to defend yourselves. For our part, we mean you no harm.'

Kellarn glanced at Corollin, who had by now appeared some distance to his right. She shrugged in answer. That was a bad sign. It meant that she could not tell whether the man was speaking the truth.

'Who sent you?' Kellarn asked carefully.

The man chuckled. It was a wasted question. Kellarn might have begun this dangerous game, but he could not control it.

Then a shrill whinny sounded from the trees where Mistwise had been. There were answering calls from Rúnfyr and Lanaë. The taller man whipped out his sword and spun around, ready to face an attack. Kellarn raised his own sword in sudden doubt. The smaller man clasped his hands before his chest, whining a hurried prayer that seemed to end in a strangled shriek.

For a moment, nothing happened. Then the air in the valley fell into deeper shadow, and a chill wind stirred around them. Ahead and to Kellarn's left, about a dozen paces away, a dark mass blurred into sight. It had the likeness of fighting hounds, all grappling and tearing at one another's throats. He could make out at least three snarling maws, and too many yellow eyes in all the wrong places. But it moved with one purpose; and the ground beneath it burst and spat like water in a frying pan.

The two horses shied and bolted. The taller man gave a cry and fled. The shorter stood his ground, though shaken; and then again that slow smile of mocking triumph and hatred spread across his face. He gave a jerking nod of his head, and the seething darkness veered in its course and moved toward Kellarn.

'Collie, no!' yelled Corollin. She threw herself into a tumbling roll on one shoulder, coming up again square on her feet beside him. It was a trick that she had taught herself from the lore of Zedron, and one which Kellarn himself kept meaning to learn.

'I need you,' she said, grabbing him by the wrist. He knew better than to protest.

Corollin had no time to be gentle. The shock jarred him with the force of a whiplash as she plunged in with her mind, sucking up his strength. She had no time to shield him properly from the battle which followed.

430

Trailing in the wake of her thought, or as if looking over her shoulder, Kellarn watched as she focused on the darkness. They were thrown back by a whirlwind of clashing colours and voices, too many and too wild for her to encompass. She turned instead to their dark-eyed pursuer, bursting in upon his mind in a wave of fury, seizing control with a swiftness that left Kellarn reeling.

The swirling darkness of the unknown creature slowed, and came to a halt. It began to roll back again, drawn toward the one who had summoned it.

Though from a distance, Kellarn felt the malice and terror of the captive man – the sting of sweat, and the warm dampness where he had wet himself. Corollin now compelled him to call his demon toward him; and yet her control was not complete. She left him the free choice to undo his summoning spell, to send it back whence it had come, and thus to save his own shrinking hide.

The man wavered, defiant, still striving to evade her grip. Then the darkness was upon him, and it was too late. Corollin cut loose abruptly, leaving Kellarn dizzy and alone. He staggered and fell to his knees.

There was a high-pitched shriek, drowned out as the frying pan sizzle grew swiftly to a roar. The body of the hapless man shrivelled and burst beneath the darkness. Every scrap of him either vanished or was devoured. The demon showed no sign of departing. Kellarn swore.

He dragged his feet beneath him to stand. Corollin was leaning heavily on her staff, her breath coming in ragged gasps. He could only begin to guess what this had cost her. He stumbled forward over the scrubby ground, gathering what was left of his strength to do battle. If Corollin called after him, he did not hear.

The demon rolled toward him, a cloud of teeth and eyes and flailing claws. The wind grew bitterly cold. The pale, creamy gold of Corollin's power flickered around them, but neither paid it heed. With a desperate prayer to Hýriel and Torollen,

431

Kellarn hefted his sword in both hands and drove it straight into the heart of the swirling darkness.

The detonation was appalling. Crimson flame billowed from the blade, filling his sight and flinging him backwards to the ground. All breath was snatched out of him. His lungs burned for want of air. Corollin screamed.

Kellarn fought blindly to move, to breathe. No other attack came. Then as the fire and pain receded, a new sound reached his ringing ears – the trumpet roar of a great beast, somewhere close at hand.

He rolled on to his side and sat up, blinking to regain his sight. The wind had died, and the demon was gone. His sword lay within easy reach, unharmed. The ground all around was burned and blackened.

Corollin had moved down to stand beside him. She seemed stronger again now, alert for danger. He saw that her left sleeve had been torn away above the elbow, and there were ugly weals and scars along the length of her forearm. Her face was grubby and streaked with tears.

'There is something else out there,' she said.

'A dragon,' said Kellarn. He checked himself for signs of hurt, but he seemed to have survived unscathed. 'A dragon, but not *the* dragon.'

Corollin muttered a word that Kellarn did not know, but he guessed that it was rude.

'I think it's friendly,' he said, reaching for his sword and climbing slowly to his feet.

Why he thought so, he could not say. Dazed as he was, he had known at once that the roar had not come from Ilunâtor, Father of All Dragons. But the sound had been as triumphant and thrilling as it had been terrifying. He supposed that he meant that the dragon had not *felt* hostile toward them, whether or not it might prove to be friendly.

'Let's check on the horses,' murmured Corollin, indicating Rúnfyr and Lanaë.

They moved carefully up the western slope, staying alert

for any sign of danger. There was neither sight nor sound of anything else stirring. The two horses were wide-eyed and panicky, but not beyond gentling. They had more or less settled them when there came the clop of hooves from the valley below, and Mistwise came into view. Walking beside her was a person with long dark hair, and a great black cloak which shimmered in the dim shadows. He looked straight up to where Kellarn and Corollin were standing, and Kellarn understood.

'Sarnîl,' he said. 'Sarnîl was the dragon.'

The stone fay waved to them, signalling them to come down. They took the horses with them.

'Well met again, Son of Dortrean,' said Sarnîl as they reached him. 'Well met, Daughter of Zedron.'

Kellarn and Corollin bowed.

'I had thought you were going to the Black Mountains,' said Corollin.

'The shadowfay are abroad,' Sarnîl answered. 'There were rumours in the Great Forest. One of their changelings picked up your trail.' He pointed at the blackened ground, to where the shorter of their two pursuers had been devoured by the demon.

'The shadowfay,' said Kellarn. 'But why would they be following us?'

'They have long served the Enemy,' said Sarnîl. 'And then his human companion bore this.'

He reached beneath his cloak and brought out a long knife, carved all of grey stone. The hilt was in the shape of a winged reptilian beast, with the blade proceeding from its mouth. The beast looked more like a bat than any other creature Kellarn could think of.

'It is a shadowfay blade, fraught with their power and malice,' said Sarnîl, hiding it away again. 'Only their greater warriors would carry such a weapon – or those of other races with whom they had made solemn pact. Then also there was this.'

He showed them a small square pendant, no bigger than Kellarn's thumbnail, on a fine golden chain. It bore the device

433

of a black enamelled horseshoe on a gold field; and when the fay turned it over, they saw the familiar device of the lozenge within the square upon the other side.

'It is the sign of the enemy captain, who of old we named *Atallakûr*,' he said.

'And the horseshoe is said to be the sign of the Emperor's Black Destriers,' said Kellarn, 'though I have never seen it used until now. So the priests of Mairdun were right. There *are* followers of the Enemy in the Emperor's household.'

'And one, at least, has made alliance with the shadowfay,' said Corollin.

'What happened to the other man?' Kellarn asked Sarnîl.

'He is no more,' replied the fay. 'It is not wise to leave an enemy at your back. And now news of this battle will be slower to reach the shadowfay – or your Emperor. But we should be moving. You are hurt and weary, and there is good water not far off.'

'We?' echoed Corollin.

'I think that I shall stay with you for tonight,' said Sarnîl, 'and perhaps a while longer. I do not like the feel of what has happened here.'

'What was the thing that he summoned?' asked Kellarn.

'It was one of the *Ulhennar*,' said Sarnîl. 'A lesser terror from the strife of the gods; though one perilous to try to control, and baleful to all living things. The changeling may have overreached himself, I think. But that is a good blade, Son of Dortrean.'

'A *lesser* terror?' said Kellarn doubtfully.

'It has gone now,' said Sarnîl. 'Think no more of it for tonight.'

They moved west out of the valley, and soon came to where a clear stream ran through a rocky dell. They washed themselves and tended to Corollin's arm. They were more weary than they had realised.

Perhaps because of Sarnîl's presence, nothing came near to disturb their rest. The next morning was cloudy, and the air grew heavier with the threat of approaching storm. Kellarn's sense of foreboding had returned. Sarnîl frowned at the sky, and said that he would ride with them that day.

They left The Hocks behind them and rode south and west along the borders of the Wasted Hills. To their left, the lush green of the imperial plains of Lautun stretched away into a grey haze, which grew brighter as the day wore on. To their right the land rose dreary and brown, already parched by the summer sun. Few things grew there, and the men of the Six Kingdoms had abandoned it long ago. The bleak emptiness of the hills was a grim reminder of what the power of the Magi could do, without the proper control of their Council. Kellarn wondered whether the Eastern Domains had similar blighted places, from battles between their own wizards; and whether creatures such as the *Ulhennar* might have played a part in the ruin of the Wasted Hills. For once, he had to admit that the founding of the Council of Magi might not have been such a bad idea to begin with.

Sarnîl was poorer company than Galden might have been, nor was his silent presence wholly comforting. Like the hills, he brought to mind the perils of their quest. But it seemed that he would stay or go as he thought fit, and Kellarn did not want to anger him by disturbing him. If it came to another fight, they would be far better off with Sarnîl beside them.

The stone fay kept them to a hard pace, pushing on until sunset to get them well clear of the western end of the hills; but when they stopped for the night, he seemed pleased enough with the distance they had covered that day. He scouted off on his own for a while after they had set up camp. When he returned, he reported that there was no one close by, and that there was as yet no sign that they were being followed again.

The storm broke after midnight, south over the plains, but passed well away to the north before morning. The day dawned clearer and damp, with the promise of more rain to come. Kellarn had slept little, and the soggy start and humid air did not improve his mood.

435

They now rode straight west across open grassland, catching sight here and there in the distance of some of the magnificent horses of the Emperor's herds. In the early afternoon the level ground began to rise again into gentle rolling hills, and they drew near to the southern borders of Dârghûn. Fortunately they did not have to pass through the Dârghûn lands; for though Herusen himself might have been kindly enough at Court, the guard patrols of his home domain had always been more than usually wary of any traveller who dared to cross their borders. Kellarn doubted that that would have changed in the few weeks since the old man's death. Instead there was a broad stretch of common ground running from the plains to the fords of the Rolling River, bordered to the north by Dârghûn and to the south by the lands of Cardhási; and that was the way they took.

By late afternoon they came down into the wide green valley of the Rolling River. The nearest of the Black Mountains were now barely five leagues to their north, with their great heads hidden behind piled clouds, and the eastern arm of the Dortrean Forest curled about their feet. On the far side of the fords they could see the beginning of the Dortrean Way – not a paved road, such as those further to the south, but an ancient grass track that ran beneath the eaves of the forest and all the way to the stone bridge in the heart of the Dortrean Valley.

They rode down to the near shore, and drew rein beside a weathered stump of grey stone. It was all that remained of a tall statue of a seated horse – one of many that had long ago been set along the length of the river to mark the western boundary of the old Kingdom of Lautun; though others, mostly to the south, had been better preserved. Sarnîl sprang lightly from Lanaë's back and handed Kellarn the reins.

'Here we must part again,' said the fay. 'You shall be safer on your home ground, and I have other work to do.'

As if to echo his words, a distant flicker of lightning lit the darkening sky in the east.

'Thank you,' said Kellarn awkwardly.

'Should we take the gold pendant?' asked Corollin. 'The priests of the Sun Temple may wish to study it – or perhaps to destroy it, if they think that wise.'

'It shall be unmade soon,' Sarnîl nodded. 'But the servants of the Enemy are looking for it. Can you keep it hidden from them, as I can? And if the Sun priests see this thing, what are they most like to do?'

Corollin did not answer.

'They would start a holy war against the Emperor,' said Kellarn. 'Probably storm the imperial palace, and get themselves all killed.'

Sarnîl nodded again. 'You must choose the time carefully to tell them this tale,' he said. 'I hold Torriearn in great honour, and he is much loved by the Sun; but often his feet run ahead of his thought.'

'Torriearn fell, in Arrandin,' Kellarn reminded him.

'I know,' said Sarnîl. 'Ever the sun must set, ere it can rise. But you have no need of this thing. You shall find dangers enough along your way, without carrying another with you.'

They said their farewells and rode out across the ford. Sarnîl stood watching until they had clambered up on to the far bank. Then he waved once more, and vanished behind the grey stone.

Kellarn slid down from Rúnfyr's back and knelt upon the ground, running his fingers through the sweet grass.

'I never thought I should be so glad to be home,' he said.

'We still have a long ride ahead,' said Corollin.

'I know,' said Kellarn. 'But this is Dortrean. Sarnîl was right – we should be safer here.'

Rhysana picked up the last folded linen shirt from the foot of Herusen's bed and packed it neatly into the open chest beside her. She tucked his gold embroidered slippers alongside. There was still plenty of room in there, but they seemed to be almost done.

The College term had ended and the students had gone

away. The new Prime Councillor wanted the use of Herusen's chambers. The Archmage Morvaan had arrived early that morning to break the seal on Herusen's study door, set there by the Council after his death. Morvaan had sorted through the books and papers, most of which would now go to the College libraries. The *chaedar* had brought up the rest of the paraphernalia in the single chest beside her. It had fallen to Torkhaal and Rhysana to clear his private chambers. Hrugaar and Dhûghaúr had come to help them.

Rhysana did not know, but she suspected that Herusen himself must have sorted and cleared through most of his belongings before his last sojourn in Arrandin – as if he had foreseen all along that he would not return. Either that, or he had lived a much more ascetic life than she had realised. What remained of his life here they would carry back to the Dârghûn manor. For Rhysana, it was the nearest that she could come to saying a proper goodbye. Herusen's memory, as the Warden had said, would be always with them in the College.

Torkhaal and Hrugaar came through from the outer living chamber, carrying a gilded casket between them with a *sherunuresh* board balanced on top. Taillan gave a squeak of delight and trotted over from where he had been playing beside the window. Hrugaar deftly intercepted him as they set down their burden.

Rhysana measured up board and casket with her eye to see if they would fit into the chest.

'I thought that Morvaan was looking older,' she said aloud.

'He is old,' said Torkhaal.

'He lost Vortaar, and then Herusen,' said Hrugaar; 'and it seems like that he shall lose The Arrand too, ere long. It can not be easy.'

'Will he work so closely with Bradhor, do you think?' Rhysana asked. 'You should have brought those in before.'

She began to unpack things from the chest, to make a space for the casket. Torkhaal knelt down to help her.

'No,' said Hrugaar. 'Bradhor may heed his advice, but it will not be the same. Nothing now will be quite the same.'

Rhysana did not need the reminder. It was not just the absence of Herusen that they felt, and the loss of senior magi such as Vortaar. Those who now moved to replace them, especially the new Prime Councillor Iorlaas, were very different in character.

'How are you finding Iorlaas?' asked Dhûghaúr, echoing her thought.

'Iorlaas, hoar-arse,' said Taillan.

Hrugaar started a coughing fit to cover his laughter.

'No, Taillan, we must not say that,' Rhysana told him firmly. 'Poor Prime Councillor Iorlaas would be very unhappy if he heard you. Where you hear such things I can not imagine.'

She favoured Hrugaar with a long, hard stare.

'Not from me,' he said defensively, his face still flushed with merriment.

'The students have been saying it,' put in Torkhaal.

'Hoar-arse, hoar-arse!' Taillan sang loudly.

'All right, frosty bottom,' said Hrugaar, lifting him up. 'Enough is enough.'

The boy went quiet at once, and allowed himself to be carried back to where he had been playing with Dhûghaúr. Rhysana sighed.

'A little different from what I had expected,' she said, returning to the question. 'I thought him slow to respond to the whole business over Solban. But then it is early days yet.'

It had not been until the evening following Solban's death that Rhysana had heard the warning note at the back of her mind – sonorous and unfamiliar – summoning her to the High Council; and even then, less than half of the surviving councillors had bothered to attend. Herusen would have called them all together within an hour from when the news first broke.

'Perhaps he was waiting for Sollonaal,' offered Dhûghaúr, 'as head of the Ellanguan Magi?'

'Solban was heir to the most senior House Noble in the

439

Empire, after Lautun itself,' Torkhaal objected. 'It was not Ellanguan's problem alone.'

'Sollonaal was not in the Council meeting,' said Rhysana. 'Lirinal of Dregharis was the only Ellanguan mage there, and he was very cagey about saying anything.'

'Sollonaal is more concerned with building his own strength in Ellanguan,' said Hrugaar; 'and most of the College magi there are behind him. When last we saw Telghraan, he seemed less than happy about it.'

'Sollonaal is free to make his own choices, as are we all,' said Rhysana. 'But if he tries to drag a whole college behind him, then perhaps the Council will have to step in. How are things otherwise in Ellanguan now?'

Hrugaar shrugged. 'A little quieter. The Emperor set sail yesterday, on his way home for the Summer Court. Karlena sailed with the Empress – though I think she had small choice in the matter. Erkal has stayed to make sure that the Southers move peacefully down to Braedun.'

Rhysana nodded, her jaw tightening to hold back her anger. It appalled her that Rhydden could give an *Aeshta* monastery to the Southers without even a backwards glance. Torkhaal reached over to hold her hand.

'Yet there is little enough peace in Ellanguan,' Hrugaar went on. 'The tide of ill feeling still runs high against the Southers, and there have been more fights along the harbour front. It is well that the Emperor's armies returned when they did.'

Taillan's wooden horse went skidding across the floor and stopped in the open doorway. Dhûghaúr stood up and went to fetch it.

'And the *Aeshta* Orders?' Rhysana asked.

'They are keeping their heads down,' said Hrugaar. 'The priests of Kelmaar believe that whatever caused Solban's death – or the one who summoned it – is no longer in Ellanguan.'

'But did it leave with the Emperor's household?' asked Torkhaal.

'Perhaps,' Hrugaar allowed. 'Or with the Southers. It is said that when the death reading was done, what was left of Solban's mind was more like to the madness of Brother Sarin than to old Trigharran. The one clear thought that remained, like a word of warning, was *Kellarn was right*. Yet what he was right about they could not discover.'

'*Kellarn was right*.' Rhysana frowned. 'Have they told the Emperor's men?'

Hrugaar shook his head. 'No one outside of Kelmaar knows, except for us. And Miranda only told me last night, after I had bothered her about it a good deal.'

The news was somehow comforting. Rhysana supposed that if someone from the Emperor's household had been responsible for the madness of Sarin and the murder of Solban, then Kellarn was safer if their attention was not drawn to him – wherever he might now be. Kellarn who wielded a blade of Fire, and who had spoken with the Father of All Dragons. Kellarn who had blamed himself for not recognising the symbol of Lo-Khuma when he saw it. She wondered whether he knew something that they did not; and whether he would have told the Magi anyway, even if they had had the chance of asking him.

'Poor horse,' said Dhûghaúr. He was crouching down in the doorway, stroking the back of the toy horse that stood upright on the floor before him. 'Look, Taillan! Poor horse.'

A whisper of bronze power played across the polished wood, and then the little horse shivered and tossed its mane, and walked round in a tight circle between Dhûghaúr's knees. Taillan peeped around the curtained post of the bed, and squealed.

'There now, she will not harm you,' Rhysana told her son. 'Brin is a very gentle horse, remember?'

The boy clung to the curtain, unconvinced. Hrugaar crawled forward on all fours to sit beside Dhûghaúr. The wooden mare sniffed at his hand, then cantered out and back across the floor. Taillan scuttled over and climbed in to Hrugaar's lap.

'Do not touch, just watch,' Hrugaar told him quietly.

Rhysana smiled. Torkhaal lifted the gilded casket into the chest, and together they packed the other things around it.

'One good thing about our new Prime Councillor,' she said presently, returning to their earlier conversation, 'is that he got rid of Oghraan so quickly.'

The slimy Council Secretary had lasted barely three days under the new regime before Iorlaas had required him to stand down. His likely successor had been debated briefly among the High Council; but his was only one of many posts that would have to be filled within the next two moons, before the next College term began, and the war had left them with few enough magi to choose from.

'But who shall replace him?' wondered Dhûghaúr.

'Actually,' said Hrugaar, 'Iorlaas has asked me.'

Dhûghaúr gasped, and Torkhaal laughed. The wooden mare reared up, and then sprang away in a joyful gallop around the far side of the chamber. Taillan clapped his hands.

'Ru?' asked Torkhaal, looking at Rhysana.

'It was Iorlaas' suggestion to the High Council,' she allowed; 'which is why I could not tell you before. Whatever reasons he might have given, it seems clear that Ru is the least likely person to side with Sollonaal against him in the assembly chamber.'

'It will also pay him out for all the mischief he has caused in past assemblies,' Torkhaal grinned. 'Now he has to keep order himself. I think I am going to like Iorlaas.'

'I have not yet given him my answer,' said Hrugaar. 'I might say no.'

'No!' said Taillan, smacking his arm and laughing loudly.

'I think someone is getting overtired,' said Rhysana.

Privately she thought that Hrugaar might make a good Council Secretary; and from a selfish point of view, it would mean that he would spend more time here in the Lautun College, where they could see him. She also felt that it was important for at least one of them to be able to work closely with Iorlaas. Having been so near to the centre of Council power with Herusen in the last few years, she disliked the thought of being pushed back into the lists when so many things were changing.

She patted the last of Herusen's belongings into place, and they closed the lid and stood up. Dhûghaúr called the horse back to him, and it became a simple wooden toy in his hands once more.

'Where do you want the chest?' he asked.

'The *chaedar* will bring it for us,' she said; 'and then we shall take it to Dârghûn tomorrow, or the day after. We are hoping to test Herusen's grandson, Aidhan, for magical ability while we are there.'

'I had thought that he was to join the Môshári,' said Hrugaar. He lifted Taillan off his lap and stood up.

'He is,' said Rhysana. 'And it is true that they could test him themselves. But we have spoken with Imarra and Gravhan, and they have agreed that Torkhaal may offer to test him now. They know that we shall have need of all the new magi that we can find.

'After that, I think that perhaps I should visit Mellin Carfinn,' she added thoughtfully. 'She was fostered with Erkal's children. She may want someone to talk to, about Solban.'

'She has the priests from the Sun Temple,' said Torkhaal. 'And Ellaïn may still be in Dortrean.'

'I was thinking of Ellaïn, too,' she said.

Torkhaal growled, and took his son by the hand.

'You should not tire yourself out,' Hrugaar warned.

'Talking with Mellin is hardly tiring,' said Rhysana calmly. 'Besides, the mountain air will do me good. And we have nearly a week before the Summer Court begins.'

Two days later Kellarn rode past the double peaks of the Twin Watchers as the western sky kindled to sunset. The sun had already gone down behind the Black Mountains, and the Dortrean Valley lay under deepening shadow. The towers of the White Manor shone pale and unearthly above the gloom on their rocky spur, and the firefly sparks of half a dozen lanterns moved slowly up the cliffside at their feet.

'Who would be going to the manor at this hour?' asked Corollin.

'I don't know,' said Kellarn. 'It may be nothing – just a patrol returning.' He sounded more confident than he felt.

They had kept to the green track of the Dortrean Way ever since they left the fords, skirting south around the forest. On the second day they had glimpsed the golden domes of the new Sun Temple, away to their left, and had they turned aside they would have been there by now. But after their parting conversation with Sarnîl, Kellarn hesitated to go there just yet. The Telbray Woods lay further south and east again, beyond the Dhûlann manor lands; and they might also have ridden that way, without passing near the Sun Temple, to search for the Guardian of whom Losithlîn had spoken.

Yet though their journey on Dortrean soil had been free from trouble, Kellarn still could not shake off the uneasiness that had dogged him now for several days. For whatever reason, he felt that he needed to go all the way home to the White Manor to set his heart at rest. Corollin had agreed to this readily enough – though whether she shared his uneasiness or was simply tired of his poor company, she did not say. It would give them the chance to look at the manor library, and they could sleep in a proper bed; and at most it might only delay them by two or three days.

They rode on up the valley, and presently Corollin called up the pale golden glow of her magic around them to light their way through the shadows.

'We don't need the light,' Kellarn told her. 'This is Dortrean. I know my way home in the dark.'

'But the horses do not,' she objected. 'And I do not want to end up wading through mud down by the river.'

'That's unlikely at this time of year,' he returned. But he let her keep the light.

The fire had faded from the western sky and the first stars

were winking down at them by the time they crossed the old bridge and came to the paved road to the manor. The last of the birds were chattering excitedly to one another, making their way home to rest.

An armed escort rode down to meet them – two men of Ellaïn's household in the Arrand livery, and two of his father's household of Dortrean. The guards' faces were long and sober in the dim light, though they seemed pleased enough to see them.

'What is it, Tamas?' asked Kellarn, singling out the eldest of the four. 'What has happened?'

'It's not for me to say, young master,' the man replied awkwardly. 'The Lady Ellaïn will tell you.'

'My father is well?' Kellarn demanded.

'The last I heard, my Lord.'

'And Mother?'

Tamas nodded, but refused to be drawn further. The other guards held their peace.

They rode on as swiftly as the tired horses could manage, and passed through the manor village. A few faces appeared at doors and windows, and a woman started wailing. Kellarn began to grow more deeply alarmed; but the guard escort prevented them from stopping.

They made their way up the steep ascent and in through the double gates of the White Manor. Kellarn dismounted as soon as they reached the lamplit hall within. The *noghr* steward was there to welcome them, solid and unruffled as ever in his simple scarlet and black.

'Markhûl!' Kellarn cried, as much in relief as in greeting. 'What *is* going on here?'

The *noghr* frowned as he stood up from his formal bow. He had known all of Erkal's children from babyhood, and knew every move they might try to make. There was no easy way around him.

'The Lady Ellaïn is with guests in the lower gallery,' he told them. 'A supper is being prepared. You have time to bathe before you join them.'

'What guests?' Kellarn demanded.

His childhood awe of the *noghr* was less than the unknown fear that now drove him. He found himself moving on toward the main stair up into the manor. Markhûl was obliged to follow him.

'Mellin Carfinn,' came the reply; 'and the Lady Rhysana, Dergrin's daughter of Telún. There is news from the Court.'

But no imperial agents, Kellarn thought. His fear of immediate danger lessened; and yet the nagging unease of the last five days kept him moving, edging his temper.

The stone stair was a slow haul after a long day in the saddle. Markhûl was not far behind him.

'Where is Jared?' asked Kellarn.

'Gone to Court,' the *noghr* grunted.

That news, at least, was not surprising. The Summer Court in Lautun would begin in only a few days' time, and of course Jared would have gone. Ellaïn would stay here until the Dortrean forces returned from Farran, or wherever else they had been sent during the war – or until she was sent for.

'The children are well?' asked Corollin politely.

'Asleep – or should be,' Markhûl said.

Kellarn reached the top of the stair at last, and picked up his pace as he went through into the great square lobby with its two sweeping staircases. He had no intention of going up to bathe. He turned right and strode down the length of the throne hall. The *noghr* was now trailing behind on his short legs. Corollin was half way between them, torn between keeping up with Kellarn and the due courtesy of allowing herself to be escorted by the steward.

The throne hall of the White Manor had no raised dais and monumental seat of carved stone, as the Arrand palace had. The heavy wooden chair used by the Earls of Dortrean stood in the midst of the floor toward the far end, cloaked in its familiar dustsheets and all but invisible against the white stone all around. There were no lamps lit in the hall, but the tall windows that ran the length of the eastern wall were still unshuttered, letting in the evening starlight from the courtyard garden; and Kellarn knew where he was going. He passed the shrouded chair and made straight for the double door in the centre of the far wall.

'You should be properly announced,' Markhûl called to him sternly.

'This is my father's house,' said Kellarn.

He opened the door and went down the short stair in the thickness of the wall to the lower gallery beyond.

The three women had been sitting on the long cushioned settles away to his left, but they stood up as he came in and Ellaïn hurried forward to kiss him. She was clad all in grey, with a grey snood hiding her pretty fair hair, and her face looked pale and tired.

'What is it Ellaïn?' Kellarn demanded. 'Why will no one in this bloody manor tell me anything?'

Ellaïn burst into tears and turned away. Mellin planted herself squarely in front of Kellarn and fixed him with her bright green eyes. She was also in grey, though her face had a better colour than his sister's and her yellow-gold hair ran free. She looked more than half minded to slap him.

'Solban is dead, Collie,' she said steadily.

Kellarn stood still, looking back at her. Everything else went blank.

'The Journeyman Corollin, from Arrandin,' came Markhûl's voice in the silence.

Ellaïn wiped her eyes.

The *noghr* said something else, speaking low. The dark blue shape of High Councillor Rhysana sailed past.

'You must be Morvaan's daughter,' said Rhysana in her clear, sweet voice.

'Adopted daughter, my Lady,' answered Corollin. 'He has spoken often of you. It was you who saved Arrandin, was it not?'

'I played a part in her defence,' said Rhysana; 'as did you.'

The words flowed past Kellarn's ears unheeded. He was still looking at Mellin.

'How?' he asked, finding the thought with some difficulty. *How did he die?*

Mellin glanced at Ellaïn, and then back at him.

'He was killed,' she said. 'It – wasn't nice.'

'It never is.'

The words came out in a yelp. He had a wild desire to laugh. Mellin took him by the hand.

'Come and sit down,' she said.

'No.'

Kellarn stood his ground. A tide of thoughts and confused dreams surged up around him. The Southers were in Ellanguan. The Steward Rinnekh was not to be trusted. He had feared for his own safety going there. He had feared that his brother was in danger. He needed to face this standing.

'Tell me,' he said tightly.

Mellin looked to the other women, but they offered her no support. Ellaïn went to sit down again. Mellin squared her shoulders to face him.

'He was found by the harbours, in Ellanguan,' she said. 'He had been tortured and murdered – some say by the Southers, others not. The Sun priests say that there was evil magic involved, and a demon was summoned to slay him. He could not defend himself. Even you could not have saved him, Col.'

Somehow she had gone ahead of him, challenging the thought even as it closed upon his heart. Could he have saved Solban? Or had his brother died in his place, because Kellarn was not there?

'Rhysana can tell you more than we can,' Mellin added.

Kellarn turned around, and realised that Mellin still had hold of his hand. He tugged it free; wrapped his arms tightly around himself.

Rhysana was close behind him, next to Corollin. She turned her face aside, diffident; as though uncertain what to say, or unwilling to say it.

'Well,' he demanded. 'What will the High Council deign to tell us?'

It was less kindness than Rhysana deserved, but Kellarn could not help it. One of the main purposes of her precious Council – or so it had always claimed – was to prevent the kind of magic that had killed his brother.

'Kellarn!' cried Ellaïn indignantly.

'Oh come on,' said Mellin. 'We are all friends here. For Solban's sake – for everyone's sake – can you two please start talking to one another sensibly?'

Kellarn stood stubborn. Angry tears burned his cheeks. Rhysana smoothed a deep fold of her skirt into place, and then lifted her head to look him straight in the eye. The compassion in her face surprised him.

'There is truly little more to tell,' she said. 'But whatever demon it was that was sent against him, it left his mind in ruin. Only one clear thought remained, or so the priests of Kelmaar told Hrugaar. *Kellarn was right.*'

'About what?' he returned without thinking.

Rhysana shook her head. 'I had hoped that you might know.'

Kellarn had no clear idea of what Solban might have meant. He could not remember the last time they had spoken together, and they had differed on a great number of things over the years – mostly, of course, because Solban favoured the Empire and Kellarn did not. But he did not stop to think about it. Rhysana's tidings had kindled another thought in his mind.

'The *Vashta* lay brother,' he said aloud. 'He was driven mad. Before the war.'

Rhysana hesitated, then nodded once. 'Brother Sarin.'

'Sarin. The imperial household – damn!'

Rhysana nodded again.

'Was the Emperor in Ellanguan?' asked Corollin.

'He was,' said Rhysana. 'It is said that he had sent Solban on an errand to Renza, to prepare a way for the Southers – but Erkal has prevented that.'

Kellarn was not listening. He remembered their battle beneath the cliffs of The Hocks; and the black and gold

449

pendant which Sarnîl had found, but would not let them keep. He stepped back and drew his sword, still looking at Rhysana.

'This is Rhydden's doing,' he said thickly.

'You don't know that, Col,' Mellin warned.

'I know.' He raised the sword in both hands, and flame kindled along the blade. Mellin drew back, pulling Rhysana behind her.

'I know,' he repeated, more clearly. 'And by all the gods and this blade, I shall avenge my brother's death – on him, and on his foul Archmage, and on every demon that serves them.'

The flame flared brighter, from scarlet to dazzling gold, and went out. No one spoke. Corollin stood frozen, as if caught up in a sudden vision. Mellin was shaking.

Rhysana was watching him, her blue eyes wide and wild with imagined possibilities.

Kellarn lowered his sword. The fire had gone out of him, and he felt suddenly very weary.

'I don't even know what I'm doing here,' he murmured. 'I should have been in Ellanguan.'

He sat down where he was upon the floor, and wept.

(*Here ends the second book of the Arrandin Trilogy. The third book,* The Fall of Lautun, *tells of the end of Kellarn's quest and the calamity of Lo-Khuma's return.*)

Index of Names

Aerlan of Braedun, Lord – Chosen Priest of Telúmachel.

Aeshtar, The – ancient elemental gods revered by the Six Kingdoms; still worshipped by many within the empire, and by most of the Magi. [*gen. pl.* **Aeshta.**]

Aghaira, Kata – gifted loremaster and storyteller from the Eastern Domains.

Aidhan of Dârghûn, Lord – one of Herusen's grandchildren; son of Serinta.

Andrakhai, The – lesser clan chief of the Eastern Domains.

Antlered Man, The – wild huntsman of the *Aeshtar*; consort of Haëstren in ancient tradition.

Aranara – lesser contemplative Order of the *Aeshtar*, devoted to Haëstren.

Arisâ Levrin of Arrand, Lady – late wife to Bradhor of Arrand, and sister of Hardhen of Levrin.

Arrand, The – Head of House Arrand and ruler of the city of Arrandin; father of Bradhor, Jared, and Kierran; former member of the Imperial Council.

Asharka of Braedun, High Councillor – Principal of the College of Magi in Farran; sister-in-law to Ferghaal.

Atallakûr – name used among the Fay for the demon captain Lo-Khuma.

Baelar, Father – Truthsayer; priest of Fraërigr from the Temple of War in Ellanguan.

Black Destriers – elite and most secret body of imperial spies and inquisitors, fanatically loyal to the person of the Emperor himself.

Blood Laws – ancient and complex laws governing marriage, inheritance and title within the Six Kingdoms.

Boldrin of Levrin, Lord – holy knight and senior guard officer in the Temple of Telúmachel in Arrandin.

Borderlander – name given to the people of the Six Kingdoms living east of Arrandin or in the hills west of Farran.

Bradhor of Arrand, Lord – eldest son and heir designate to The Arrand.

Braedun, House – Greater House Noble; principals of the most senior religious Order of the *Aeshtar*, devoted to Telúmachel and the Tumbrachin.

Breghun of Lanvar, Sir – Mage Councillor; bursar and secretary of the College of Magi in Arrandin.

Bright Alliance, The – legendary alliance of humans, *noghru* and Fay in the wars before the founding of the Six Kingdoms.

Brin – Taillan's toy wooden horse.

Brodhaur Levrin, Lord – Earl of Levrin; Commander in Chief of the Imperial Household Guard; Imperial Counsellor.

Broghan – a guard captain of Rebraal.

Broneïs of Renza, Lady – Regent of Renza; sister-in-law to Lauraï Raudhar of Renza.

Brörigr – *Vashta* Lord of Knowledge and Poetic Rhetoric; Head of the House of Arts; rival brother of Fraërigr.

Camarra Kelmaar of Dârghûn, Lady – Journeyman Mage; wife to Haldrin of Dârghûn.

Caraan – legendary mage of the early sixth century; founder of the first Council of Magi.

Carstan Mairdun, Lord – Head of House Mairdun; Abbot Commander, Lord Priest and supreme head of the Hyrsenite Order of Mairdun; gifted scholar with formidable psychic skills.

Cavalry, Imperial Household – mounted division of the Imperial Household Guard.

Chaedar, The – collective name for the invisible, non-human attendants in the College of Magi in Lautun.

Col – childhood name for Kellarn; also **Collie** or **Collie-dog**.

Corollin – Journeyman Mage; adopted daughter of Morvaan.

Corrimaer, Mage Councillor – Junior Lecturer at the College of Magi in Farran.

Council of Magi, The – ancient assembly comprising all ranking magi, established to govern the ethical practice and welfare of their art.

Court Noble – collective name for all those with noble precedence, either by right of birth or conferred through achievement of rank within the religious Orders or the Council of Magi.

Dakhmaal, Mage Councillor – itinerant mage from Farran.

Dalgarn – a woodsman of Holleth.

Dergrin Telún, Lord – former Head of House Telún; late father of Lavan and Rhysana.

Dernam Rebraal, Lord – Head of House Rebraal and ruler of the lesser port of Rebraal.

Destriers – *see Black Destriers*.

Dharagh – a *noghr* from the Highland Mountains; priest of Hýriel.

Dhûghaúr of Moraan, Sir – Mage Councillor; lesser kinsman of the borderlords of Herghin.

Dhûlann, House – Lesser House Noble of Dortrean.

Drengriis of Româdhrí, Lord – Mage Councillor; bursar of the College of Magi in Ellanguan.

Drômagh of Sêchral, Lord – Knight Commander of the Imperial Household Cavalry; Imperial Counsellor; uncle to Grinnaer.

Drôshiin of Sêchral, Lord – High Councillor; lesser kinsman of Drômagh and Grinnaer.

Dwarves, The – *see Noghru, The*.

Eädhan, House – Median House Noble with lands north of Ellanguan and on the coast south of Sentai; kinsmen to Torkhaal on his mother's side.

Easterners – name given to the peoples of the ancient domains lying east and north of the Blue Mountains.

Ekraan of Eädhan, Lord – High Councillor; Trialmaster for the Council of Magi.

Elissa Dârghûn of Dârghûn, Lady – daughter of Herusen and younger sister of Gravhan.

Ellaïn Dortrean of Arrand, Lady – daughter of Erkal and Karlena; wife to Jared of Arrand.

Ellen of Raudhar, Lady – Archmage; most senior female member of the Council of Magi in terms of magical rank.

Elmirra Vanbruch of Ercusí, Lady – Countess of Ercusí; sister of Farad Vanbruch.

Elvenfolk, The – *see* **Fay, The**.

Eminence, His – honorific title for an imperial counsellor; also used as a derogatory epithet for the Archmage Merrech.

Eonnaï of Gadhrai, Lady – priestess of Brörigr and bursar of the *Vashta* School in Ellanguan.

Eörendin – *Vashta* Lady of Creativity and Earthly Love; consort of Brörigr.

Eralaan, Mage Councillor – Senior Lecturer at the College of Magi in Ellanguan.

Erkal Dortrean, Lord – Earl of Dortrean; husband to Karlena and father of Ellaïn, Solban and Kellarn; Imperial Counsellor.

Faëlla Sentai of Logray, Lady – daughter of Forval Sentai and wife to Hollin of Logray; first cousin to Kellarn.

Faerbran Tollund, Lord – young borderlord; Head of House Tollund.

Faerbran of Tollund, Lord – infant son and namesake of Faerbran Tollund.

Falladan – founder and first King of the ancient kingdom of Ellanguan; son of Furghollan and younger brother of Ferrughôr.

Farad Vanbruch, Lord – Head of House Vanbruch and father of Melissa; a merchant noble of considerable wealth and power.

Farási, House – Median House Noble of Lautun.

Father of All Dragons – *see* **Ilunâtor**.

Fauns, The – magical forest creatures, half human and half beast. *See also* **Forest Folk, The.**

Fay, The – immortal elemental beings, in mystic harmony with one or more aspects or qualities of the elemental nature of the created world (hence sea fay, moon fay etc.); also known collectively as the Elvenfolk.

Ferghaal of Braedun, Lord – High Councillor; Principal of the Braedun Order in Farran.

Ferlund, House – Median House Noble of the eastern borders, rumoured to have giants' blood in their heritage.

Ferrughôr – founder and first King of the ancient kingdom of Hauchan; son of Furghollan and elder brother of Falladan.

Ferunel – one of the moon fay; sister of Losithlîn and kinswoman to Heruvor.

Flower of the Staff – magical name of Herusen Dârghûn.

Foghlaar, High Councillor – Trialmaster for the Council of Magi; expert in the magical arts of glamour and beguilement.

Forest Folk, The – collective name for the magical creatures inhabiting the forests of the Middle Lands, in particular the fauns, centaurs, and wilder spirits of trees, water and stone; rarely used to refer to the Fay.

Forval Sentai, Lord – Head of House Sentai; widowed brother-in-law of Erkal Dortrean; father of Faëlla.

Fraërigr – *Vashta* Lord of War; Head of the House of War; rival brother of Brörigr.

Furghollan – human lord of the Bright Alliance; father of Ferrughôr and Falladan.

Galden – one of the golden fay; friend of Corollin and Kellarn.

Galsin, House – Ancient House Noble from the borders of the Endless Plains.

Garthran of Tollund, Sir – treacherous lesser kinsman of Faerbran Tollund; killed during the retaking of the Tollund manor.

God-King, The – ruler of the Souther empire beyond the sea.

Golden Age of the Magi – historical period associated with the greatest flourishing of the Magi's art, reckoned from the founding of the First Council until about the year 1000.

Goshaún of Sêchral, Lord – youngest brother and personal guard of Grinnaer.

Gradhellan Ellanguan, Lord Steward – former ruler of Ellanguan.

Gravhan Dârghûn of Môshári, Lord – holy knight and commander of the Môshári Order; Herusen's oldest surviving son; husband to Imarra.

Grinnaer Sêchral of Lautun, Lady – Empress Consort to Rhydden; niece to Drômagh.

Guard, Household – personal liveried military force retained by a House Noble. *See also* **Guard, Imperial Household**.

Guard, Imperial Household – personal household guard of the Lautun Emperors, comprising mounted and foot soldiers; only those of Blood Noble admitted to its ranks. *See also* **Cavalry, Imperial Household** *and* **Household, Imperial**.

Guardians, The – ancient wardens of *Aeshta* lore and power; hunted down and eradicated by the rulers of the Lautun Empire in the second half of the fifteenth century, in an attempt to break the tenacious hold of the elder faith of the Six Kingdoms.

Gwydion – a warrior from the borderland earldom of Vansa; friend of Tinûkenil.

Haësella of Braedun, Lady – holy knight of the Braedun Order; former handmaiden to the late Empress Consort Lissaïn.

Haëstren – *Aeshta* Lady of the Moon; daughter of Maësta, and bride of Torollen; depicted variously as maiden, queen, withered crone or guardian panthress.

Hakhutt – Envoy to the Emperor Rhydden from the Northern Lands.

Haldrin of Dârghûn, Lord – eldest grandson and heir designate of Herusen Dârghûn; son of Rogheïn Aartaús of Dârghûn.

Halgan – founder of the ancient kingdom of Khêltan.

Halvar of Mairdun, Lord – holy knight of the Hyrsenite Order of Mairdun; kinsman of Carstan.

Hardhen of Levrin, Lord – knight of the Arrand household;

brother of the late Arisâ Levrin of Arrand and husband to Lienna of Môshári.

Hendraal of Tarágin, Sir – Mage Councillor; a lecturer at the College of Magi in Ellanguan.

Hershôr, House – Median House Merchant Noble of Ellanguan.

Herusen Dârghûn, Lord – former Head of House Dârghûn and Prime Councillor of all Magi; late father of Gravhan.

Heruvor – one of the moon fay; lord of Starmere.

High Clan Chieftain, The – greatest of the Easterner chieftains; ruler of the city of Kara Ko-Daighru.

High Council, The – elite inner circle of the Council of Magi, comprising all High Councillors and Archmagi.

Hirulin – one of the moon fay; daughter of Heruvor; estranged from her father after her marriage to Ferrughôr.

Hollin of Logray, Lord – husband to Faëlla of Sentai.

Household – collective term for the body of servants belonging to a House Noble. *See also* **Household, Imperial**.

Household, Imperial – all non-military servants and attendants of the Imperial House Lautun.

Hrudhli – a greater clan of the Eastern Domains.

Hrugaar, Mage Councillor – unrecognised son of the late Sîraelin of Ellanguan and one of the sea fay; close friend of Rhysana and Torkhaal.

Hýriel – *Aeshta* Lady of Fire; divine mother of Torollen, Lord of the Sun; patron goddess of Dortrean.

Hýriel, Order of – military religious Order of the *Aeshtar*, devoted to Hýriel and Torollen.

Hyrsenites – priests, knights and lay brothers of the military religious Order of Mairdun, devoted to the goddess Hýrsien; principal *commanderie* at Mairdun.

Hýrsien – *Vashta* Lady of Peace and Motherhood; consort of Fraërigr and divine mother of Serbramel.

Idesîn Mairdun of Telbray, Lady – Hyrsenite priestess; wife to Patall Telbray and cousin to Carstan.

Illana – legendary mage of the early sixth century; author of the *Mazes and Psychic Constructs* and disputed author of the

Argument of Command; renowned for technical brilliance and an irredeemably evil disposition.

Ilumarin of Aranara, Lady – Chosen Priestess of Haëstren, released from the contemplative vows of her Order.

Ilunâtor – Father of All Dragons; held to be the first and greatest of all dragonkind.

Imarra of Môshári, Lady – Chosen Priestess of Temrbrin; wife to Gravhan.

Imperial Council, The – formal advisory council to the Emperor, by custom having representatives from at least four Houses Ancient among its eight seats.

Imperial Counsellor, The – frequently used epithet for the Archmage Merrech; formal title for any member of the Imperial Council.

Interregnum, The – name given to the period of political and civil chaos during the regency and early years of Rhydden Lautun's reign.

Iorlaas, High Councillor – retired lecturer from the College of Magi in Farran; most senior mage of Serbramel on the Council of Magi.

Jared of Arrand, Lord – second son of The Arrand; husband to Ellaïn.

Kaïra, Reverend Mother – High Priestess of Serbramel in the city of Telbray.

Karlena Serra of Dortrean, Lady – Countess of Dortrean and wife to Erkal; mother of Ellaïn, Solban and Kellarn; foster mother to Mellin Carfinn.

Keeper Gods, The – ancient deities of the clans of the Eastern Domains, governing aspects of life within the world and in the worlds beyond; among them the Keeper of Life (or of the Living Fire), the Keeper of Secrets, and the Keeper of Souls.

Kellarn of Dortrean, Lord – younger son of Erkal and Karlena.

Kelmaar, House – Greater House Noble; principals of the military religious Order of Kelmaar, devoted to the *Aeshta* Lords of Water.

Kerraïs of Renza, Lady – young daughter of the late Torreghal

Renza and Lauraï; heir to House Renza; accorded deferred right of challenge for the Lord Stewardship of Ellanguan when she comes of age.

Khadhrôgh Scaulun, Lord – Earl of Scaulun; Imperial Councillor.

Kharfaal of Vaulun, Lord – Mage Councillor; younger brother of the Earl of Vaulun and first cousin to the Emperor Rhydden; held to be the mage of highest noble precedence by right of blood.

Khôraillan of Môshári, Lord – Mage Councillor; nephew to Imarra.

Kierran of Arrand, Lord – youngest son of The Arrand.

King of the Elves of the North – ruler of the moon fay in the far north, beyond the Blue Mountains; brother of Heruvor.

Kîrnal, House – Lesser House Noble of Ellanguan.

Kôril – one of the fay; friend of Corollin and Kellarn.

Korren of Arrand, Lord – younger son of Jared of Arrand and Ellaïn; nephew to Kellarn.

Korzhai – a lesser clan of the Eastern Domains, under the sway of the Mughuzhti.

Lanaë – bay mare from the Hyrsenite stables.

Lauraï Raudhar of Renza, Lady – Regent of Renza; widow of Torreghal, and mother of Kerraïs; niece to Ellen of Raudhar.

Lavan Telún, Lord – Head of House Telún and elder brother of Rhysana.

Lienna Môshári of Levrin, Lady – priestess of the Môshári Order; wife to Hardhen of Levrin.

Lirinal of Dregharis, Lord – High Councillor; a lecturer at the College of Magi in Ellanguan.

Lisella – a woman of the Ercusí household in Ellanguan.

Lissaïn Môshári Levrin of Lautun, Lady – former Empress Consort to Rhydden; late cousin of Brodhaur Levrin.

Llaruntôr – founder and first King of the ancient kingdom of Lautun; kinsman to Furghollan.

Lo-Khuma – Easterner name for the great demon captain overthrown by the armies of the Bright Alliance; known as *Atallakûr* among the elvenfolk of the Fay.

459

Lôghur Lautun – forty-fifth High King of the Six Kingdoms, killed during an Easterner siege of Arrandin; reigned 1221–43.

Lorellin Herghin of Arrand, Lady – daughter of Selghan Herghin and wife to Thalden of Arrand.

Losithlîn – one of the moon fay; sister of Ferunel and kinswoman to Heruvor.

Maachel – *Aeshta* Lord of Earth.

Maëghlar of Kelmaar, Lord – elderly High Councillor, now living in permanent retreat.

Maëra of Kelmaar, Lady – priestess and scholar of the Kelmaar Order.

Maësta – *Aeshta* Lord of Waters; divine father of Sherunar and Haëstren.

Mairdun, House – Lesser House Noble; principals of the Hyrsenite Order of Mairdun, the only *Vashta* Order to hold a bloodline of Noble precedence. *See also* **Hyrsenites**.

Markhûl – a *noghr*; Steward of the White Manor of Dortrean.

Marusâ – a woman of Ellaïn's household in Arrandin.

Mataún of Fâghsul, Lord – knight of the Imperial Household Cavalry; nephew to Môrghran.

Melissa of Vanbruch, Lady – pretty daughter of Lord Farad Vanbruch and heir to the Greater House Merchant Noble of Vanbruch.

Melissaë Renza of Carbray, Lady – Regent of Renza; mother of Torreghal and Broneïs.

Mellin Carfinn, Lady – Head of House Carfinn; lesser kinsman and favoured retainer of Erkal Dortrean; fostered by Karlena after her mother's death.

Merrech, Archmage – Imperial Counsellor; boyhood tutor and principal adviser to the Emperor Rhydden.

Minnaíra Aartaús of Arrand, Lady – wife to The Arrand; mother of Bradhor, Jared and Kierran.

Miranda of Kelmaar, Lady – holy knight of the Kelmaar Order.

Mistwise – gray mare from the Hyrsenite stables.

Môrghran of Fâghsul, Lord Priest – Imperial Counsellor;

zealous priest of Fraërigr and one of Rhydden's personal favourites.

Morraï of Môshári, Lady – second daughter of Imarra and Gravhan.

Morrinu – a lesser clan of the Eastern Domains, under the overlordship of the Vengru.

Morvaan of Braedun, Lord – Archmage of the Sun; adoptive father and tutor of Corollin; renowned for his prodigious appetite.

Môshári, House – Greater House Noble; principals of the religious Order of Môshári, devoted to the *Aeshta* Lords of Earth.

Mughuzhti, The – a greater clan chief of the Eastern Domains; slain by Kellarn in Arrandin.

Naëra Kilgar of Tollund, Lady – wife to Faerbran Tollund.

Nerentor – one of the moon fay; former ruler of the lost fay kingdom west of the Black Mountains; father of Ferunel and Losithlîn, and brother of Neriel.

Neriel – ruler of the moon fay west of the Black Mountains; kinswoman to Heruvor, and mother of Tinûkenil.

Nets, The – a vast web of enchantment spread through the northern part of the Whispering Forest, devised by the moon fay to guard the hidden vale of Starmere.

Neutral Theatre, The – a theoretical condition free from all influence of place or circumstance, used as the basis for the determination of the primary gradations of noble precedence according to Blood Law.

Noghru, The – fabled dwarvensmiths of the Black Mountains; also used as a collective term for all the dwarvenfolk. [*s.* **noghr**.]

Northern Envoy – *see* **Hakhutt**.

Northerners – name given to the folk inhabiting the coastal regions north of the Highland Mountains; believed to have shared a common ancestry with the founders of the Six Kingdoms.

Odhragh – a *noghr* from the Black Mountains; friend of Tinûkenil.

Ogh – *Aeshta* Lord of Mountains, chiefly revered by the *noghru*.

Oghraan, Mage Councillor – Secretary to the Council of Magi, and bursar of the College of Magi in Lautun.

Orders Noble, The – religious Orders conferring noble precedence to their members by virtue of hierarchical rank and achievement, even where those members had no prior claim to precedence by right of birth; Braedun, Kelmaar, Môshári and Mairdun hold family bloodlines of noble birth in addition to this conferred precedence, while Aranara and the Order of Hýriel do not.

Osîr – *Aeshta* Lord of the Stars; First Father, from whom all other Lords of the *Aeshtar* are held to have sprung.

Panthress of the Heavens – animal guise of Haëstren.

Patall Telbray, Lord – Head of House Telbray and ruler of the city of Telbray; holy knight of Serbramel; husband to Idesîn.

Perdhan Tormal, Lord – borderlord; Head of House Tormal; kinsman by marriage to Valhaes and Dortrean.

Ranzhaar of Stanva, Lord – Mage Councillor; a lecturer at the College of Magi in Arrandin.

Raunazhrai, The – a lesser clan chief of the Eastern Domains.

Redbeards, The – ancient dwarven clan; formerly dwelt in the Blue Mountains, north of the Hauchan Valley.

Reïkjan of Kôan, Sir – arrogant lesser nobleman of Lautun now dead; former favourite of the Emperor.

Rhydden Lautun, Emperor – supreme ruler of the Lautun Empire; earned the epithet of *Peacemaker* for ending the factious rivalry of the Houses Noble that had ravaged the empire during the Interregnum under the regency of his mother, the late dowager empress; rumoured to have divine or inhuman blood.

Rhysana Telún of Carbray, Lady – High Councillor; honorary lecturer at the College of Magi in Lautun; wife to Torkhaal.

Rikkarn, High Councillor – itinerant mage, working mostly with the craftsmen of the city of Telbray.

Rin – the Emperor's name for Rinnekh.

Rinnekh Solaní Ellanguan, Lord Steward – upstart ruler of the city and lands of Ellanguan; nephew of Drômagh of Sêchral and first cousin to the Empress Consort Grinnaer; one of the Emperor's personal favourites; Imperial Counsellor.

Rinnir – a musician and storyteller from the city port of Farran.

Rogheïn Aartaús of Dârghûn, Lady – widow of Herusen's firstborn son and chatelaine of the Dârghûn manor; mother of Haldrin; niece to Minnaíra Aartaús of Arrand.

Röstren – the fifth month of the year according to Six Kingdoms reckoning.

Ru – shortened name for Hrugaar.

Rúnfyr – bay gelding from the Hyrsenite stables.

Sakhîrlan – one of the fay; a loremaster of Starmere.

Salbaar, Mage Councillor – a lecturer at the College of Magi in Farran.

Sarin, Brother – a lay brother at the Vashta School in Ellanguan.

Sarnîl – one of the stone fay.

Scardhan of Herghin, Lord – treacherous son of Selghan Herghin, and brother of Lorellin; killed during the siege of Arrandin.

Scaulun, Earl of – see *Khadhrôgh Scaulun, Lord*.

Selghan Herghin, Lord – treacherous borderlord; Head of House Herghin; father of Lorellin.

Serbramel – *Vashta* Lady of Justice; divine daughter of Hýrsien and Fraërigr; patron goddess of the holy city of Telbray.

Serengaïa, Sister – a priestess of Serbramel in the city of Arrandin.

Serinta of Dârghûn, Lady – priestess of the Order of Aranara, released from her contemplative vows; daughter-in-law to Herusen, and mother of Aidhan.

Serra, House – Lesser House Noble of the border hills northwest of Farran; paternal kinsmen to Karlena of Dortrean.

Sherunar – *Aeshta* Lord of Oceans; divine son of Maësta; patron god of Ellanguan city; name means *the Dancer*.

Sherunuresh – ancient board game with sophisticated protocols;

used widely in the Six Kingdoms as a vehicle for teaching both mystic and political principals, and as a tool for diplomatic negotiation and philosophical debate; name means *the dances of the gods.*

Sholerghti, The – a lesser clan chief of the Eastern Domains.

Sîlgon – one of the moon fay; a border warden of Starmere.

Skaramak – a mercenary warrior from Farran; friend of Tinûkenil.

Solaní, House – Greater House Noble of Ellanguan.

Solban of Dortrean, Lord – elder son and heir designate to Erkal Dortrean; a lieutenant general of the Imperial Household Guard.

Sollonaal, High Councillor – Prime Councillor of the Ellanguan Magi and Principal of the College of Magi in Ellanguan.

Sóryontel – *Vashta* Lord of Trickery and Material Wealth; divine son of Eörendin and Brörigr.

Southers – name given to the peoples of the southern lands beyond the sea, under the rule of the God-King.

Stellaas, Mage Councillor – appointed Mage in Residence in the city of Telbray.

Syldhar, The – secretive magical race, little known even among the Fay; linked in folklore with dragonkind and shape-shifters; believed capable of assuming human form. [*s.* **syldha.**]

T'Loi – Souther Ambassador; first cousin to the God-King.

Taillan of Carbray, Lord – young son of Rhysana and Torkhaal.

Takshar of Dregharis, Lord – younger son of Soltran Dregharis; former member of the Arrandin City Guard.

Talbren – the fourth month of the year according to Six Kingdoms reckoning, following the Summer Festival.

Tamas – a guard of the Dortrean household.

Tannaïa, Sister – a priestess of Hýrsien in the imperial city of Lautun.

Telghraan, Mage Councillor – mage of Earth; honorary lecturer at the College of Magi in Ellanguan.

Telúmachel – *Aeshta* Lord of Air.

Temrbrin – *Aeshta* Lady of Earth and Fruitfulness.

Terrel of Arrand, Lord – elder son of Jared of Arrand and Ellaïn; nephew to Kellarn.

Thalden of Arrand, Lord – youngest nephew of The Arrand and husband to Lorellin of Herghin.

Tiennaï, Mage Councillor – Moon mage of Souther descent; Librarian of the College of Magi in Arrandin.

Tinûkenil – one of the moon fay; Chosen Priest of Haëstren; son of Neriel, and kinsman to Heruvor.

Tirilanna of Braedun, Lady – holy knight of the Braedun Order.

Toad, The – Hrugaar's epithet for the Archmage Merrech.

Torkhaal of Carbray, Lord – Mage Councillor; a lecturer at the College of Magi in Lautun; husband to Rhysana.

Torollen – *Aeshta* Lord of the Sun; divine son of Hýriel and husband to Haëstren.

Torreghal Renza, Lord – former Head of House Renza; late husband of Lauraï.

Torren of Mairdun, Lord – priest of the Hyrsenite Order; son of Carstan.

Torriearn of the Order of Hýriel, Lord – Chosen Priest of Torollen; instigator and co-ordinator of the rebuilding of the Sun Temple on the Tungit Isle.

Trigharran of Kelmaar, Master – elderly priest of the Kelmaar Order; Principal of the Kelmaar School in Ellanguan.

Tumbrachin, The – *Aeshta* Ladies of Lightning; the daughters of Telúmachel.

Turill of Solaní, Lord – a guard captain of Rinnekh's household; lesser kinsman to Rinnekh.

Twin Gods, The – divine twins Aranel and Arredin; numbered among the *Vashtar*, but not specifically aligned either to the House of Arts or to the House of War.

Ulhennar, The – demonic creatures spawned during the Wars of the Gods.

Valhaes, House – Greater House Noble of the earldom of Dortrean; renowned for military prowess.

Vashtar, The – the imperial gods, first introduced to the Six Kingdoms around the middle of the thirteenth century; divided into two rival factions of War and Arts, with Fraërigr and the related *Vashtar* of War in the ascendancy during Rhydden's reign. [*gen. pl.* **Vashta**.]

Vengru, The – a greater clan chief of the Eastern Domains.

Virkhaîl 'Fastbind' Lautun – third Emperor of the Third Dynasty; succeeded as a minor, and dominated throughout his life by the *Vashta* priests; reigned 1479–99; father of Rhydden.

Vortaar, Archmage – former Senior Lecturer at the College of Magi in Arrandin; killed during the siege of Arrandin.

Warden, The – enigmatic custodian of the libraries in the College of Magi in Lautun.

Wars of Power, The – name given to the chaotic wars between the Six Kingdoms during the fourth and fifth centuries, before the Council of Magi was established to curb the excesses of uncontrolled and abused magical power.

Wars of the Gods, The – name given to the initial age of strife between the Lords of the *Aeshtar*, in which the created world was forged; also used to include the extended period of warfare thereafter, until the ways between the waking world of humankind and other mystical Realms were effectively closed.

Zedron – legendary mage of the sixth century.

Zhaughrai, The – a lesser clan chief of the Eastern Domains.

Zhertan Khôrland, Lord – borderlord; Head of House Khôrland.

Zhiraún of Dortrean, Lord – squire to the Emperor Rhydden; distant kinsman to Kellarn, from a lesser branch of House Dortrean; kinsman by marriage to Drômagh of Sêchral.

Index of Places

467

Blue Mountains – highest mountain range adjoining the Lautun Empire, forming its eastern border; also called the *Diadem of Ogh* by the *noghru*.

Blue River – Blue Mountain river flowing down through the vale of Starmere and the Whispering Forest, and then west across Ellanguan lands to the Blue Sea.

Blue Sea – name given to the eastern reaches of the ocean of Igaerwa along the coast of Ellanguan.

Book Halls of Ellanguan – arguably the most extensive libraries of the Six Kingdoms, and among the most ancient; established in Ellanguan city in the year 106.

Border Road – old paved road running east from Arrandin to the fords of the Blue Mountain River.

Braedun, Commanderie of – principal monastery and fortress of the Braedun Order; located on the northern bank of the Galloppi River.

Cardhási – greater manor on the northwest border of the Lautun plains, beside the Rolling River; hereditary seat and principal residence of House Cardhási.

Carfinn – lesser manor occupying the western part of the earldom of Dortrean; hereditary seat and principal residence of House Carfinn.

Cerrodhí – the great forest in the northeast reaches of the Lautun Empire; formerly the Fifth Kingdom.

College of Magi in Arrandin – smallest of the colleges, following an eclectic tradition and with no formal building complex of its own; founded in 784 after the raising of the Easterner siege upon the city.

College of Magi in Ellanguan – greater of the two ancient schools restored by the First Council; originally founded in 106 with the Book Halls of Ellanguan; claims a more ancient tradition than that followed in Lautun, and reserves the right to elect its own Prime Councillor in addition to the Prime Councillor of all Magi.

College of Magi in Farran – youngest of the four colleges; founded in 1064, after the end of the Golden Age of the

Magi; essentially a junior branch of the Lautun college.

College of Magi in Lautun – oldest of all colleges in the Six Kingdoms, and the most orthodox and prestigious; originally founded in the year 56; governing centre of the Council of Magi.

Dârghûn – rich farmland manor lying northwest of the Lautun plains, on the east bank of the Rolling River; principal residence and hereditary seat of House Dârghûn.

Deadmen's Green – wide mountain vale at the southern end of the Whispering Forest; a site of dreadful battle between the humans of the Six Kingdoms and the inhabitants of the Blue Mountains, and still held to be a place of horror in Ellanguan folklore.

Dhûlann – lesser manor in the southwest part of the earldom of Dortrean; hereditary seat and principal residence of House Dhûlann.

Domains – *see Eastern Domains.*

Dortrean – earldom in the northwest region of the Lautun Empire, between the arms of the Black Mountains; formerly the Fourth Kingdom.

Dortrean Forest – old forest occupying a sizeable part of the earldom of Dortrean.

Dortrean Manor – hereditary ancestral seat and fortress of the earls of Dortrean, built on the cliffs of the Black Mountains near the upper reaches of the Grey River; principal residence of Erkal; also called the **White Manor** because of the peculiar semi-translucent white stone from which it is built, which defies the arts of the Magi.

Dortrean Valley – deep mountain valley in the northwest corner of the earldom of Dortrean, where the Grey River flows down from the Black Mountains; location of the Dortrean Manor and the Temple of Fire.

Dortrean Way – ancient grass track running through the earldom of Dortrean, from the ford of the Rolling River to the stone bridge in the Dortrean valley.

Eastern Domains – name given to the lands inhabited by

the Easterner clans, lying east and north beyond the Blue Mountains.

Eastern Way – ancient paved road running east from the imperial city of Lautun, and all the way south to Arrandin. *See also* **Old North Road**.

Ellanguan – southeastern coastal region of the Lautun Empire; formerly the Second Kingdom.

Ellanguan, City of – traditionally independent city port at the mouth of the Great River; former ruling centre of the Second Kingdom; seat of the Lords Steward of Ellanguan.

Endless Plains – wide region south of the Blue Mountains, stretching west from the Low Mountains to the shores of Igaerwa; beloved for its wild horses and magnificent skies.

Farodh – formerly the Sixth Kingdom, west of Farran and south of the Black Mountains; now uninhabited marshland.

Farran, City of – imperial city port on the southwest coast of the Lautun Empire; effective successor to the lost Sixth Kingdom of Farodh; seat of the Lords Steward of Farran.

Ferlund – borderland manor in the foothills of the Low Mountains; hereditary seat of House Ferlund.

Fersí – borderland village on the road east of Arrandin, under the care of the Lords of Tollund.

Footstool Hills – hill range at the southern end of the Blue Mountains, partly covered by the Holleth Woods.

Fystenur – name given by the Fay to the great forest of Cerrodhí.

Galloppi River – long river which flows southwest from the Blue Mountains to the sea; name more usually applied only to the lower stretch of the river, after it resurfaces from the hills southwest of the Glymn Pool. *See also* **Galloppi Stream**.

Galloppi Stream – name given to the upper part of the Galloppi River, as it flows through the Holleth Woods from its source down to the Glymn Pool.

Gorrendan – small imperial city port built at the point where the old West Road crosses the White River; once notorious for slave trading.

Great Forest – *see **Cerrodhí**.*

Great River – turbulent Blue Mountain river descending through the Hauchan Valley and flowing east to Ellanguan.

Grey Moors – largely uninhabitable moorland region stretching north from the cliffs of The Steeps.

Grey Mountains – ancient mountain range to the south of the Eastern Domains, close to the Stormrider Sea.

Grey River – central river of the earldom of Dortrean; joins the Black River and flows into the Rolling River, to become the White River of Lautun.

Harperschool – oldest and most prestigious music school in the Lautun Empire; located next to the College of Magi in Ellanguan.

Hauchan – the lost First Kingdom, founded by Ferrughôr; name also used for the ruined remains of Ferrughôr's city, on the shores of the Great River in the upper part of the Hauchan Valley.

Hauchan Valley – broad vale reaching into the Blue Mountains, where the Great River makes its descent; traditionally part of the First Kingdom, but now part of the Stewardship of Ellanguan.

Hellenur – the golden forest, stretching along the coast to the west of the White River estuary; principal location of golden birch trees within the Six Kingdoms, and traditionally a hiding place for many strange and magical creatures.

Herghin – lesser borderland manor in the far eastern reaches of the Footstool Hills; hereditary seat and principal residence of House Herghin.

Highland Mountains – lower mountain range forming the northern border of the Lautun Empire beyond the great forest of Cerrodhí.

Hocks, The – a southern spur of the Highland Mountains, dividing the great forest of Cerrodhí from the Wasted Hills.

Holleth – lesser manor centred in a village clearing in the Holleth Woods, where the Old North Road crosses the Galloppi Stream; principal residence of House Holleth.

Holleth Woods – remnants of an ancient forest stretching to the north and west of Arrandin; notionally under the care of the Lords of House Holleth.

Igaerwa – ocean lying to the south and west of the Six Kingdoms; name means *the Wide*.

Imperial Palace – principal citadel and hereditary ruling seat of the Emperors of Lautun; built up around the original summer palace of the horselords of Lautun, on the western shore of the White River estuary; access restricted to those of Blood Noble and their immediate households.

Imperial Plains – *see* **Lautun Plains**.

Kara Ko-Daighru – ancient citadel of the High Clan Chiefs of the Eastern Domains; located some two hundred leagues to the east of the Blue Mountains.

Kelmaar School – oldest and most important academic school of the Kelmaar Order, located in the western part of the city of Ellanguan.

Khêltan – the original Fourth Kingdom, founded by Halgan; destroyed in the first century, but later reclaimed and renamed as Dortrean; name also used for the lost ruins of Halgan's city, by tradition buried deep beneath the Dortrean Valley.

Khôrland – easternmost borderland manor, in a broad vale beneath the cliffs of the Blue Mountains; hereditary seat and principal residence of House Khôrland.

Knees of the Mountains – name given to the sheer cliffs forming the southern end of the Blue Mountains.

Koritalla – mountain forming the northern side of the entrance to the Hauchan Valley.

Lachaïta – name given by the Fay to the stream marking the border between the Whispering Forest and the great forest of Fystenur.

Lautun, City of – imperial capital; largest city and port within the Lautun Empire, built on the eastern shore of the White River estuary.

Lautun Empire – name now given to the combined lands and peoples more traditionally referred to as the Six Kingdoms; under the supreme rule of the Emperors of Lautun.

Lautun Plains – central grassland plains of the Empire, still used primarily for the Emperor's horse herds; formerly the main part of the Third Kingdom, and the ancestral domain of the horselords of Lautun.

Lôghur's Gate – principal outer gate of the Lower City of Arrandin, located on the southwest side of the city; begun in the first half of the thirteenth century at the command of the High King Lôghur, though completed after his death; built with the help of the dwarvensmiths of the *noghru*.

Low Mountains – ancient mountain range forming the eastern border of the Endless Plains, and reaching to the coast of the Stormrider Sea.

Lower City – the larger part of the city of Arrandin, extending south and west from the hill of the Old City on to the more level ground of the plains, within its own encircling wall; noted for the beauty of its large formal parks and many elegant buildings. *See also* **Old City**.

Mairdun, Commanderie of – principal monastery and school of the Hyrsenite Order of Mairdun; located near the upper reaches of the Rolling River, at the eastern end of the Black Mountains.

Middle Lands – name given to the continental area stretching west from the Blue Mountains and south to the far edge of the Endless Plains, of which the Six Kingdoms form but a part; sometimes used in error as a synonym for the lands of the Six Kingdoms or the Lautun Empire.

Monastery of Maësta – monastery temple of the *Aeshta* Lords of Water, built high on the cliffs of the northern side of the Hauchan Valley; under the care of the Kelmaar Order.

Monastery of Telúmachel – ancient holy citadel on an island off the coast west of the imperial city of Lautun; principal temple of Telúmachel within the Empire, under the care of the Braedun Order; also called the Monastery Isle of Telúmachel, or the Telúmachel Isle.

Môshári House – city house belonging to the Môshári Order, in the northwest part of the Old City of Arrandin.

Nobles' Quarter – restricted and guarded area within a city, reserved primarily for the city houses of the Lords of the Court Noble.

Northern Lands – name given to the coastal regions north of the Highland Mountains.

Old City – the original walled city of Arrandin, founded in the year 672 on the site of an earlier hilltop fortress. *See also* *Lower City*.

Old Kingdoms – another name for the Six Kingdoms.

Old North Road – Arrandin name for the southern part of the ancient paved road of the Eastern Way, from the Old City to the cliffs of The Steeps.

Palace of the Arrands – *see* *Arrand Palace*.

Rebraal – fortified ferry town and lesser port on the Strong River; principal residence of House Rebraal.

Renza – *see* *Watchful Isle*.

Ringstream – tributary stream of the Grey River in the Dortrean Valley.

Rolling River – eastern border river of the earldom of Dortrean; joins the Grey River to become the White River of Lautun.

Sâchra – outlying farming village of the border manor of Tollund.

Samsar – easternmost village and trading post of the Lautun Empire, under the care of the lords of Khôrland.

Sentai – greater manor on the southeast coast, governed by House Sentai from the castle of Arveil; fertile hill region, renowned for its vineyards and fine wines.

Six Kingdoms – traditional name for that part of the Middle Lands claimed by the victorious human leaders of the Bright Alliance and their descendants; now also referred to as the **Lautun Empire**; in practice, the original political division of six distinct kingdoms under one High King did not survive beyond the end of the first century.

Souther Empire – vast conglomeration of kingdoms lying to the south, beyond the ocean of Igaerwa; under the suzerainty of the God-King of the South.

Starmere – name given to the hidden dwelling place of Heruvor and the moon fay, in a mountain valley east of the Whispering Forest; more properly the name of the lake within that valley.

Steeps, The – sheer cliffs stretching west from the southern end of the Blue Mountains; traditionally the site of the final battle and victory of the Bright Alliance, and still holding a sinister reputation in folklore.

Steward's Palace – principal residence of the Lords Steward of Ellanguan, in the eastern part of Ellanguan city.

Stormrider Sea – wild ocean far to the southeast, beyond the Low Mountains.

Strong River – forest river flowing in a deep gorge from Cerrodhí; eastern boundary of the old Third Kingdom of Lautun.

Sun Temple – ancient temple on the Tungit Isle in the midst of the Grey River of Dortrean; in ruins for centuries, but recently rebuilt at the instigation of the Sun priest Torriearn.

Telbray, City of – fortress citadel near the southern end of the Black Mountains; holy city of the *Vashta* goddess Serbramel; ancestral seat of House Telbray, under the overlordship of Farran; renowned for its artesans.

Telbray Woods – wild and ancient forest to the east of the city of Telbray.

Telún – greater manor lying east of Ellanguan and south of the Great River, among the steep foothills of the Blue Mountains; ancestral seat and principal residence of House Telún.

Temple of Fire in Arrandin – monastery temple of Hýriel and Torollen, located on the south side of the great parks in the Lower City.

475

Temple of Sherunar – largest temple to the *Aeshtar* in Ellanguan city, and principal temple of Sherunar within the Empire; renowned for its huge silver-blue dome and ancient peal of bells.

Temple of Telúmachel – oldest and largest monastery temple of the *Aeshtar* in Arrandin, dedicated to Telúmachel and the Tumbrachin; located in the western part of the Old City.

Tollund – lesser borderland manor in the hills northeast of Arrandin; hereditary seat and principal residence of House Tollund.

Tormal – border manor in the hills east of Arrandin, between the road and the Twisting Downs; hereditary seat and principal residence of House Tormal.

Tumbling Hills – rich farmland hills stretching north and east of Ellanguan city.

Tungit Isle – holy island in the midst of the Grey River, east of Carfinn; location of the newly rebuilt Sun Temple.

Twin Watchers – great double-peaked mountain, extending from the main body of the Black Mountains between Carfinn and the Dortrean Valley.

Twisting Downs – wild and treacherous area of hills and scrub lying to the northeast of the Endless Plains, between the Footstool Hills and the Low Mountains.

Upper Square – open precinct before the western front of the Steward's Palace in Ellanguan city.

Valemur – citadel and haven of the elvenfolk of the Fay, on the coast of the Stormrider Sea.

Valhaes – greater manor occupying the southeastern spur of the earldom of Dortrean; ancestral seat and principal residence of House Valhaes.

Valley of Two Waters – hidden valley in the Blue Mountains, northeast of Koritalla; dwelling place of Galden.

Vansa – earldom to the southwest of the Black Mountains, bordering the marshlands of the lost Sixth Kingdom of Farodh.

Wasted Hills – hill region to the north of the Lautun plains;

ravaged beyond recovery by the magical conflicts of the Wars of Power.

Watchful Isle – the island of Renza, a day's sail west from Ellanguan; guarded by magical defences little understood even among the senior members of the Council of Magi; hereditary seat and principal residence of House Renza.

Whispering Forest – southeastern spur of the great forest of Cerrodhí; under the sway of the moon fay of Starmere.

White Manor – *see **Dortrean Manor**.*

White River – wide river forming the southwest boundary of the old Third Kingdom of Lautun, from the confluence of the Rolling River and the Grey River of Dortrean.

Whitespear Head – magical fortress of Illana at the confluence of the Rolling River and the Grey River; sealed and guarded by the Council of Magi.

Wizard's Steep – a sheer hillside cliff on the northern bank of the Great River, some four leagues east of Ellanguan city.

Partial Index of Houses Noble

HOUSE ANCIENT

Lautun, Imperial – Rhydden, [Grinnaer]; *Lôghur, Virkhaîl,*
   [*Lissaïn*].
Dortrean – Erkal, Solban, Kellarn, Ellaïn, Zhiraún, [Karlena].
Levrin – Brodhaur, Boldrin, Hardhen, [Lienna]; *Arisâ,* [*Lissaïn*].
Vaulun – Kharfaal.
Ercusí – [Elmirra].
Ellanguan, Stewards of – Rinnekh; *Gradhellan, Sîraelin.*
Scaulun – Khadhrôgh.

HOUSE ELDER (GREATER)

Arrand – The Arrand, Bradhor, Jared, Kierran, Terrel, Korren,
   Thalden, [Minnaíra, Ellaïn, Lorellin]; [*Arisâ*].
Braedun – Ferghaal, Haësella, Morvaan, Aerlan, Tirilanna,
   [Asharka].
Solaní – Rinnekh, Turill.
Sentai – Forval, Faëlla.
Telún – Lavan, Rhysana; *Dergrin.*
Renza – Kerraïs, Broneïs, Melissaë, [Lauraï]; *Torreghal.*
Kelmaar – Maëghlar, Miranda, Camarra, Trigharran, Maëra.
Sêchral – Drômagh, Drôshiin, Goshaún, Grinnaer.
Môshári – Khôraillan, Imarra, Lienna, Morraï, [Gravhan];
   Lissaïn.
Vanbruch – Farad, Melissa, Elmirra.

HOUSE MEDIAN

Eädhan – Ekraan.
Hýriel, Order of – *Torriearn*.
Aartaús – Minnaíra, Rogheïn.
Raudhar – Ellen, Lauraï.
Carbray – Torkhaal, Taillan, [Rhysana, Melissaë].
Fâghsul – Môrghran, Mataún.
Gadhrai – Eonnaï.
Dârghûn – Haldrin, Gravhan, Aidhan, Elissa, [Rogheïn, Imarra, Serinta, Camarra]; *Herusen*.
Tarágin – Hendraal.
Tormal – Perdhan.
Dregharis – Soltran, Takshar, Lirinal.

HOUSE YOUNGER (LESSER)

Mairdun – Carstan, Torren, Halvar, Idesîn.
Serra – Karlena.
Telbray – Patall, [Idesîn].
Kilgar – Naëra.
Româdhrí – Drengriis.
Logray – Hollin, [Faëlla].
Carfinn – Mellin.
Lanvar – Breghun.
Aranara, Order of – Ilumarin, Serinta.
Rebraal – Dernam.
Tollund – Faerbran, Faerbran, [Naëra]; *Garthran*.
Stanva – Ranzhaar.
Kôan – *Reïkjan*.
Khôrland – Zhertan.
Moraan – Dhûghaúr.
Herghin – Selghan, Lorellin; *Scardhan*.

Acknowledgements

No man is an island, but a writer may function as one. The visitors come and go, bringing news and ideas (and supplies!). Some come for a holiday, some come to take over; and some, sadly, can visit no more. When they have all gone home again, their memory remains.

The following people deserve special thanks here for their contribution to my work; for inspiration, support, and patience above and beyond the call of duty: Jane Bennett, Mark Black, Maureen Bourniquel, James Cameron, David Curry, Andrea and Debbie D'Ulivo Rogers, Cosette Desvergez, Dhoot, Carroll Fry, Vickie Henderson, Marie and Marshall Herniman, John Jarrold, Katherine Kurtz, Roger Ladd, Alan Le Couteur, Harald Mahrer, John Richard Parker, Linda Pletz, Jean and Jim Porter, Evelyn Price, Jonathan Schatz, Renée Stern, Diann Thornley, Iain Watson.

Thank you too to those people who read my first published book and made the effort to track me down and speak to me about it. Your comments and encouragement helped greatly in the completion of this book.

Marcus.
Jersey, June 2000

EARTHLIGHT

A SELECTED LIST OF FANTASY TITLES
AVAILABLE FROM EARTHLIGHT

THE PRICES SHOWN BELOW WERE CORRECT AT THE TIME OF GOING TO PRESS. HOWEVER EARTHLIGHT RESERVE THE RIGHT TO SHOW NEW RETAIL PRICES ON COVERS WHICH MAY DIFFER FROM THOSE PREVIOUSLY ADVERTISED IN THE TEXT OR ELSEWHERE.

☐ 0 7434 0893 4	Talisker		Miller Lau	£6.99
☐ 0 6848 6036 8	Celtika		Robert Holdstock	£16.99
☐ 0 6710 2261 X	The Sum Of All Men		David Farland	£6.99
☐ 0 7434 0827 6	Brotherhood of the Wolf		David Farland	£6.99
☐ 0 6848 6061 9	Wizardborn		David Farland	£10.00
☐ 0 6710 1785 3	The Royal Changeling		John Whitbourn	£5.99
☐ 0 6710 3300 X	Downs-Lord Dawn		John Whitbourn	£5.99
☐ 0 6710 2193 1	Sailing to Sarantium		Guy Gavriel Kay	£6.99
☐ 0 7434 0825 X	Lord of Emperors		Guy Gavriel Kay	£6.99
☐ 0 6848 6131 3	The Dreamthief's Daughter		Michael Moorcock	£16.99
☐ 0 6848 6670 6	Silverheart		Michael Moorcock &	£16.99
			Storm Constantine	
☐ 0 6710 2190 7	The Amber Citadel		Freda Warrington	£5.99
☐ 0 7484 0826 8	The Sapphire Throne		Harry Turtledove	£5.99
☐ 0 6710 2282 2	Into The Darkness		Harry Turtledove	£5.99
☐ 0 6710 3305 0	Darkness Descending		Harry Turtledove	£6.99
☐ 0 6848 6007 4	Through the Darkness		Harry Turtledove	£10.00
☐ 0 6710 2189 3	The Siege of Arrandin		Marcus Herniman	£5.99

All Earthlight titles are available by post from:

Book Service By Post, P.O. Box 29, Douglas, Isle of Man IM99 1BQ

Credit cards accepted. Please telephone 01624 675137,
fax 01624 670923, Internet http://www.bookpost.co.uk or
e-mail: bookshop@enterprise.net for details.

Free postage and packing in the UK. Overseas customers allow
£1 per book (paperbacks) and £3 per book (hardbacks).